THINGS TOO TERRIBLE TO LIVE WITH

"Stay where you are or I'll jump."

"Shane, climb back down." Hayden didn't ask. He instructed. "We'll go home and deal with this. I'll get you help—anything you need, but you get down from there."

"It's too late for help."

Hayden's mouth went dry to the point where he couldn't swallow. *How could Shane be this far gone?* he thought. A week ago they'd been laughing and joking. Reconnecting after years lost. Now Shane wasn't just threatening suicide, he intended to carry it out.

Hayden was frightened, truly petrified. Not for himself, but for Shane. Shane was calling the shots, reducing Hayden to a spectator. Pressure built in Hayden's chest, cutting off his breath. He let out a sob. He hoped Shane wouldn't hear, but he did.

"I'm sorry, Hayden, but you don't understand what they've done. What I've done. It's terrible...."

Other *Leisure* books by Simon Wood:

PAYING THE PIPER
ACCIDENTS WAITING TO HAPPEN

We All Fall Down

SIMON WOOD

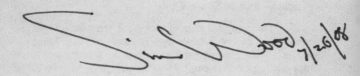

LEISURE BOOKS   NEW YORK CITY

For my friends

A LEISURE BOOK®

July 2008

Published by

Dorchester Publishing Co., Inc.
200 Madison Avenue
New York, NY 10016

ISBN 10: 0-8439-6053-1
ISBN 13: 978-0-8439-6053-2

Printed in the United States of America.

10 9 8 7 6 5 4 3 2 1

Visit us on the web at www.dorchesterpub.com.

We All Fall Down

Ring around the rosie,
A pocket full of posies.
Ashes, ashes
We all fall down!

—A nursery rhyme

PROLOGUE

The BMW 530i's engine screamed, but it was unclear whether it was in agony or ecstasy. Vee8 squashed the gas pedal deeper into the carpet and tipped the balance into the pain barrier. The vehicle accelerated through the narrow car-lined street, occasionally clipping side mirrors as it sped by.

"Spank it, Vee8. Spank it," Donkey shrieked hysterically and thumped the passenger-side dash with his fist. In chorus, D.J. and Trey seconded Donkey's request from the backseat.

Donkey might have been hung like one, but he was also sure as shit as dumb as one. Vee8 didn't need Donkey telling him what to do. He'd been jacking cars since he was fourteen and in four years, he'd thrashed, crashed and cremated more than three hundred of them without ever being caught. The cops had chased him across the San Francisco-Oakland Bay Area, but they'd never come close to netting him. Many had tried, and all had failed. Several had woken up in the hospital to discover that sorry fact. Like that old-school gangster Dillinger, Vee8 would be an old man before they ever got their hands on him. He threw the powerful sedan through the left-handed kink.

He'd learned his trade among the sideshow kings of

Oakland. He'd been taught by the best, until he was the best. Most of them were now in prison, but in their heyday, they'd shown Vee8 how to make a car dance.

Infineon Raceway was only a thirty-mile burn across the Bay. He could have been a legitimate race driver, but why? He didn't have the money or the connections to race. Anyway, they were pussies. Where was the fun in driving on a road where the traffic went in one direction? Oncoming traffic, now that was a challenge.

Even though he was eighteen and old enough to possess a driver's license, he hadn't bothered. What did he need a license for? He didn't own a car, and why should he? There were too many people like him who would have a set of wheels out from under you before you'd locked the doors. No, if he wanted a car, then he had Donkey snatch one. They were more frequent than buses, and nicer.

Donkey started up again. "Vee, get off these pissy little streets. If the po-po catches our scent, we're fucked."

Vee8 hated the way Donkey spoke. Donkey came from the Deep South somewhere. Alabama. Louisiana. One of those fuck-your-sister, marry-your-cousin states. His southern drawl intensified when he whined, and it grated on Vee8.

"Who's fuckin' driving, Donk?"

"You."

"That's right. Me. When you're driving, you can make the decisions."

Although Donkey whined, he was a necessary part of the operation. He was a magician with locks and alarm systems. Cars just opened themselves up to him. In a matter of seconds and with the aid of a few tools that appeared from his pockets, his work was done. Despite Donkey's talents, Vee8 was the star. Essentially, Donkey got them in and Vee8 got them out.

Donkey was right. Tearing strips off the residential

streets was asking for trouble. They'd jacked the BMW from the El Cerrito Del Norte BART station around noon, before the suit returned home from a hard day of stroking his secretary's thigh. Now that it was after eight, the car would be on the hot list and the cops would be looking for it. But like Cinderella's coach at midnight, it would be a rotting husk by the time they found it.

Vee8 threaded his way through the Sausalito streets, avoiding downtown. He didn't fancy a run-in with the cops. He headed for Highway 1. The narrow, coastal road snaked and heaved, and it would put him and the BMW to the test. It contained more than enough thrills for a Wednesday night.

He got clear of the town. The full moon lit the road ahead well beyond his headlight beams. He brought his speed up to eighty-five. The turnoff to the two-lane highway was coming up on his left.

As he approached the four-way, Vee8 eased the BMW hard over to the curb to get a faster turn-in for the left turn. A Honda Civic sedan approached the intersection from Vee8's right, but it didn't bother him. He was on the through road and had the right of way. The Civic would have to stop. Even if he didn't have the right of way, so what? No one in their right mind was going to argue the point when a car was driving at breakneck speed.

Vee8 stepped off the gas and jumped onto the brake. Everyone in the car was thrown forward against the seat belts as the BMW dived on its suspension. He watched the speedometer dial sag as the speed was sloughed off and ignored the whoops of his boys.

Vee8's smiled slipped. The Civic wasn't slowing. It wasn't traveling as fast as he was; no more than fifty, but it wasn't going to stop.

"I don't think he's stopping," Donkey said flatly, seeing what Vee8 had seen.

Donkey's words silenced everyone.

Vee8 pressed down on the brake harder and thumped the horn twice with his fist.

The Civic showed no sign of stopping for the BMW. It leaped across the intersection and into Vee8's path. Everyone in the BMW swore and braced themselves for the impact. Vee8 stamped on the brakes and the anti-lock system went into action. He didn't bother to turn onto Highway 1 as he'd planned. It would have just made the collision worse. The best he could hope for was to T-bone the bastard and do as much damage to him and as little to himself as he could.

For a moment, Vee8 thought he was going to get away with it. The Civic was passing out of his field of vision faster than expected, but not quite fast enough. The BMW clipped the Civic's rear panel and wraparound light cluster. A deafening bang echoed through the car as sheet steel collided with sheet steel. The Civic wiggled after its glancing blow and carried on its merry way unhindered. The BMW was less fortunate. The car plowed on, veering right, and struck the curb hard. The front wheels jackhammered into the wheel arches and relayed their agony through the steering wheel. Vee8's hands and arms tingled in sympathy. The car leaped the curb and came to a halt in the field beyond the pavement.

"Christ, my head," Donkey moaned. He put a hand to his nose, checking for blood. There wasn't any. He touched the dashboard where he'd smashed his face.

Vee8 checked the rearview mirror and found D.J. and Trey were bleeding from where they'd banged heads. Both were looking dumbly at each other and moaning about whose head hurt more. *Christ, what a clusterfuck*, Vee8 thought.

"Am I bleeding?" Donkey asked and jabbed his face in Vee8's direction.

"No, you're not, you dumb shit," Vee8 said.

The BMW had stalled, and Vee8 tried to start the car.

He was greeted by an overlong electronic tone before the engine caught and fired. He jammed the gear shift into reverse and stamped on the gas. The wheels spun on the soft earth, and the car went nowhere. The tires and the engine whined.

"Come on, you bastard," Vee8 hissed.

As if by command, the tires bit into the earth, found traction and the car lurched back.

"Where are we going?" Donkey asked.

"We're going to get that son of a bitch."

The BMW bumped down off the curb, raced away from the scene of the collision and joined the coast road as planned. The engine sounded off-key and the steering sucked. Only one headlight cut through the darkness; the passenger-side light was obviously lost. But none of this bothered Vee8. The coast road went on for miles with no intersections to any other major roads. He had no doubt that he would catch the Civic driver. It was just a matter of when.

Vee8's passengers were still bleating about their injuries and the accident.

"Shut the fuck up!" Vee8 shouted. "Keep your eyes open. Yell when you see that bastard Civic."

Vee8 scanned the fields to his right and the beach to his left. Deep thoughts of what he would do to the Civic driver when he got ahold of him clogged his mind. It wasn't the first time he'd used a vehicle as a weapon, and it wouldn't be the last.

Vee8 caught sight of his quarry in a twisting section descending toward the ocean, then lost him when he hit a series of switchbacks. He drove miles without seeing him again. He turned to faith that the Civic remained ahead, and his faith was rewarded on the descent into the town of Stinson Beach.

"There it is. Down there." Donkey pointed at the beach falling away from the roadside to their left.

The Civic, with its passenger-side taillight snuffed out, sat untidily on the beach.

Vee8 swung the BMW left onto the private road the Civic had taken. He didn't stop at the road's edge. He followed the Civic driver's lead and drove onto the beach. He bumped the BMW over the curb, and the car slithered on the sand, the tires failing to grip the shifting surface. The car tore down the sloping beach before crashing into a sand dune, where it leveled out.

Vee8 and his crew flung the doors open, leaped from the stricken BMW and charged down the beach. The Civic sat cocked at an angle to the rolling waves, with the driver's door open and the engine running. Beyond the car, the headlights picked out its driver, an East Indian, standing at the water's edge.

The broad-shouldered man stood some six inches taller than Vee8. He might have the strength advantage, but Vee8 doubted the guy possessed the fighting skills. Not that Vee8 cared. His blood was up. The prick was going down.

"Hey, bitch," Vee8 shouted. "We need to talk."

The man didn't react. He stared out across the darkened ocean with the moon reflected on its surface. Vee8 heard the man mumbling something but couldn't make out what he was saying.

"What's that? I can't hear you," he barked in a mocking tone.

The man took a step forward into the waves. That stopped Vee8 in his tracks.

Vee8 glanced back at his boys and found they'd already given up the chase. They'd picked up the strange vibe early. Vee8 had been too pissed off to see it.

He gestured to his crew for answers. Donkey shrugged with a what-the-fuck expression plastered across his face.

The man strode out farther. The water lapped over his knees.

There was something very wrong here. It looked pretty obvious what it was. Vee8 wasn't sure he wanted to be part of this, but he already was. Slowly, he followed the man to the water's edge, but no farther. This guy might get lonely and want to take someone with him.

"Hey, Gandhi," Vee8 said. "What are you doing?"

Vee8 had hoped the slur would provoke a reaction, but the Indian didn't respond. The man continued to wade out, chanting his incantation.

"Hey, guy. It don't have to be this way," Vee8 offered. He looked down at his feet. A wave licked at his Lugz, chilling his toes, and he edged back.

"I think we should get the hell out of here," Donkey suggested.

Vee8 turned to face him.

"He's right, Vee," D.J. echoed.

"I don't think we should get mixed up in this," Trey added.

"But we can't just let him kill himself," Vee8 said.

"Can't we? Just watch me," Donkey said and started to back away. D.J. and Trey followed suit.

Vee8 swore under his breath and ran out into the waves after the guy. He caught his breath the moment the ice-cold water hit him. Its chill climbed up into his core, but it didn't stop him from reaching the Indian. Vee8 reached out and placed a gentle hand on the man's shoulder, which stopped him in his tracks. The strong surf thrust against them, urging them back to shore. Vee8 hoped the guy would take the hint. He took the man's hesitation as a positive sign.

"You don't have to do this," Vee8 said. "Nothing can be that bad."

The Indian turned to Vee8. "I have done a terrible thing, and I can't be forgiven. I must pay for it. This is the only way."

Vee8 could have argued with man to get him to see

sense, but he knew there was no point. He'd seen a lot of broken people. Fathers and mothers beaten down by mistakes. Friends lost to booze or drugs. No matter how far gone they were, they still clung to hope. While they hung on, they could be saved. But not the Indian. He'd let go. Vee8 had never witnessed total hopelessness before, but he saw it in the Indian's eyes. He'd surrendered to whatever haunted him. There was nothing Vee8 could do for him.

"I have to do this," the man said.

Vee8 nodded and removed his hand from the man's shoulder.

The Indian smiled and resumed walking out to sea. Vee8 watched him go. The man's final gesture was hypnotic in its incomprehensibility. But by the time the Indian was waist deep, Vee8 had managed to wrench his gaze away and was heading back to shore.

When he reached dry land, Vee8 glanced back at the suicidal man just in time to see a wave wash over his head.

It was obvious the Civic driver wasn't turning back.

CHAPTER ONE

The Saturday morning traffic was behaving itself, so Hayden would make good time from Fairfield to San Rafael. He hoped this weekend would be the start of something big. Marin Design Engineering only wanted someone on short contract, but if he impressed them, the contract might go from short to long. It wasn't an unusual occurrence for him. He'd built a solid reputation as a design engineering contractor over the last three years. He'd been twenty-five when he started contracting, which was a pretty bold move. But his rep hadn't gotten him the high-paying gig at Marin Design Engineering; his old college roommate had.

This gig would be a nice boost to his income. He'd been on contract at Macpherson Water since the beginning of the year and the plan was he'd work for Marin Design Engineering from home in the evening. It wasn't the first time he'd reaped the rewards of working double duty.

Hayden reached the limit of the radio station broadcasting out of Sacramento, and he switched to a San Francisco station. He caught the tail end of a song before the station went to the news. The discovery of Sundip Chaudhary's body was the lead story.

"The body of missing scientist Sundip Chaudhary was found late last night by a jogger on Muir Beach," the newsreader said.

At least they found him, Hayden thought. He shuddered at the thought of the condition of the guy's corpse.

The story had made a stir in the Bay Area. Chaudhary had walked into the ocean three days ago in an apparent suicide attempt. He hadn't left a note, but his car had been found on Stinson Beach with the keys in the ignition and the engine running.

Family and friends cited no problems in his professional and personal life that would warrant a suicide attempt. If it weren't for an anonymous eyewitness account of Chaudhary walking into the sea, foul play or an accident might have been suspected. Speculation centered on the possibility that the eyewitness had been involved in a fender bender with Chaudhary. Chaudhary's car exhibited fresh damage, and debris from a second vehicle was found on the beach. Speculation ended when it came to what had led Chaudhary to walk into the Pacific.

"The Marin County Sheriff's Department urges the eyewitness to come forward," the newsreader said.

Yeah, right, Hayden thought. No one would come forward if they feared any backlash.

Hayden pictured Chaudhary's body on the beach he knew well. Drowning. There were less painful ways of killing yourself. Hayden wondered if that had been Chaudhary's aim. The eyewitness had stated in the 911 call that Chaudhary had insinuated he'd committed an act so severe that he couldn't live with the guilt. The cops had yet to turn up anything to support the claim—or just weren't saying.

The whole subject left Hayden feeling queasy. His cell phone bursting into song provided the perfect reason to forget about Chaudhary's suicide.

"Where are you?" Shane Fallon asked.

"I just got on Highway 37, so I'm about half an hour out."

"I'm so glad you're coming aboard."

"Me too."

"It's going to be great catching up, man." Although college roommates, they'd lost touch over recent years. Work had taken them in different directions. Now it was bringing them back together. "This is going to be a great weekend. See you in thirty."

"In thirty," Hayden said and hung up.

Hayden found the upscale gated community where Shane lived easily enough. He'd known his friend had done well for himself, but not this well. Shane lived in a modest house compared to the monster mansions at the higher end of the price scale, but even so, this was high living and it put Hayden's '50s-built ranch-style home to shame. If Shane's firm treated him this well, they could definitely afford to pay Hayden two hundred bucks an hour for grunt work. He pulled into Shane's driveway.

Hayden was removing his overnight bag from the passenger seat when Shane came out to greet him. Hayden put out his hand, and Shane gripped it before crushing him in a bear hug. Shane didn't have much in the way of brawn, but he was tall and possessed a lot of inherent strength.

"Damn, it's good to see you. I can't believe we've let three years pass without getting together."

"Neither can I."

Shane relieved Hayden of his bag and dropped it by the stairs in the hall. "We don't have to be at the Giants game until midday, so we've got a couple of hours until we leave. Do you want coffee or something?"

"Yeah, coffee would be good."

"C'mon through into the kitchen then."

Hayden followed Shane into a custom kitchen clad in marble and stainless steel. It was all very upwardly mobile. Hayden took a seat at the kitchen table, while Shane poured fresh grounds into the coffeemaker.

"You've done really well for yourself. I'm impressed," Hayden said, surveying his surroundings.

"What can I tell you? Nice things happen to nice people." Shane looked about him. "It's a long way from the dorms at Cal-State and that AMC Gremlin, God rest its soul."

"Amen," Hayden said and wondered whatever had become of that car—it had probably long since been consigned to the crusher.

"Marin Design Engineering treats you well, then?" Hayden said.

"They do." The coffeemaker stopped wheezing, and Shane grabbed the coffees and joined Hayden at the table. "And they'll treat you well too."

Hayden thought of the premium rate they were going to pay him for this short-term contract. "Any chance this'll turn into something longer term?"

"I wouldn't be surprised. MDE takes on specialist design-build projects. No one else can do what they do, so the margins are always high. And because every project is different, they hire a lot of folks on contract. You do okay on this one and I'm sure you'll get a recall."

"So who do I have to impress for future work?"

"Me," Shane answered. "I'm the project manager."

Who said cronyism was such a bad thing? Hayden thought. He raised his coffee mug for a toast, and they clinked mugs.

They spent the next couple of hours catching up and reminiscing before Shane drove them to AT&T Park. San Francisco traffic was thick, and parking was impossible, but MDE had splashed out on a corporate box that came with reserved parking. They entered the stadium through a private entrance. Hayden could get used to this kind of treatment.

They met with Shane's colleagues from MDE for a pre-game lunch in the hospitality suite. A gaunt-looking man wearing a blazer over dress slacks spotted Shane and Hayden approaching and got up from his seat.

"Shane, you made it," he said. "Is this Hayden?"

"Yes, Trevor. Meet Hayden Duke. Hayden, this is Trevor Bellis, Marin Design Engineering's CEO."

Hayden shook hands with Bellis. His grip was surprisingly strong for someone who looked half starved.

"A pleasure to meet you, Hayden. Please call me Trevor. I've heard a lot about you. You're a welcome addition to our team. We'll discuss business after the game. For now, enjoy yourself," Bellis said.

Shane introduced Hayden to the assembled group. They were a mix of MDE employees and contract staff. Most possessed either engineering or scientific backgrounds. They welcomed Hayden in a genuine manner, and he slipped easily into conversation with them. He could see himself working very well with these people.

Hayden noticed an unoccupied place at the table. "Who are we missing?" he asked Shane.

"Our guest of honor, James Lockhart. He's a consultant employed by the client to oversee the project. He's very well-regarded and has done a lot of work for the government and the private sector. If things need moving and shaking, he's the guy to do it."

"Who's the client?"

"I can't discuss that until you've signed up for the job."

Lockhart arrived shortly before the meal ended. His coming brought a subtle change in the mood at the table, but Hayden felt it as strongly as a weather shift. Lockhart introduced an air of formality. He was obviously the big man on campus, and Bellis looked distinctly nervous in the man's presence. Hayden guessed MDE had a lot riding on this project.

Hayden understood the change at the table. Lockhart didn't look as if he'd come out for a ball game. He'd chosen to power dress in a tailored suit and tie instead of something more casual. He looked like he expected to be called upon to give a press conference at any moment. During the small talk over lunch, he weighed and measured each answer before giving it. It was very disconcerting.

Game time arrived, and everyone went to their seats. Bellis kept Lockhart segregated from everyone else, which lightened the mood. While the others got wrapped up in the game, Bellis and Lockhart talked. Hayden cast glances their way. Bellis remained tense around the man. Hayden guessed things weren't as rosy at MDE as everyone liked to make out. Maybe it was good he was working a short contract with these people. The last thing he needed was to sign on for something longer term if they were having problems on the business front. In situations like that, the first people to go were the contract staff. He'd think long and hard on any future offers.

After the game, everyone said their good-byes. Bellis put a hand on Hayden's shoulder. "Let's get you on our team now." Bellis's smile had returned once Lockhart had left. "I've got some paperwork at our offices for you to sign."

Hayden and Shane followed Bellis's Audi A6 back to the MDE offices in Corte Madera. The building was set into the hills and was clearly visible from US-101, making it its own billboard. It was a squat, two-story structure with the second story being octagonal in shape. It smacked of '70s architecture, but that didn't make it any less desirable as a working environment.

Bellis beat them at a stop light and by the time Shane and Hayden arrived, he had the building unlocked and stood waiting for them in the foyer.

"Welcome to MDE," Bellis said.

Hayden failed to acknowledge the welcome. His focus was on an easel, which held a poster-size headshot of an East Indian man in his thirties. At the base of the image was the caption, *Sundip Chaudhary, a friend lost but not forgotten.*

"That's the guy they found this morning."

"Yes," Bellis said. "Very sad."

"Am I his replacement?" The thought of filling a dead man's shoes took the excitement out of the position.

"No," Shane said. "He worked here as an instrument engineer."

"Let's talk about this in the boardroom," Bellis said.

Bellis took Hayden and Shane up to the second floor. At the end of the conference table sat a roll of drawings, a flash drive and a file folder. Shane and Bellis took seats next to each other, and Hayden took one opposite.

"Sundip Chaudhary was a valued member of this company," Bellis said. "Sadly, he let the stress of his work get to him and he took his own life. None of us saw the signs. If we had, then . . ." Bellis let the remainder of his sentence go unfinished.

"That's not what I heard on the news," Hayden said.

"Out of privacy and respect for Sundip's family, we kept the truth from the press," Bellis said.

There'd been no mention of who Chaudhary had worked for in any of the news reports. Hayden wondered who'd pulled those strings—Bellis or Lockhart?

"Is Sundip's death a problem for you?" Bellis asked.

"No," Hayden replied. "It was a just surprise. No one mentioned him at the ballpark today."

"The project that Sundip was a part of is highly confidential," Shane said. "Our client is on the verge of a major technological breakthrough. So much so, they haven't even filled us in on the full purpose of the design."

"Hence the need for privacy," Bellis said.

"And James Lockhart?" Hayden said.

"The client has invested a lot of capital, and James Lockhart is here to ensure they get what they want," Bellis said.

No wonder Bellis was so jumpy around Lockhart. There was probably a lot of ass covering going on. Chaudhary's death may have prompted the client to consider switching firms. Bellis wouldn't want to lose such a high-profile job.

"Obviously, none of what I've told you leaves this room," Bellis said.

It sounded like overkill to Hayden, but it wasn't his problem. "Of course," he said.

"We'd better deal with the red tape," Shane said.

Bellis opened the file folder and removed a sheaf of papers and put them before Hayden. "This is a nondisclosure agreement. Should you divulge any project details to anyone outside of Marin Design Engineering, the firm will take severe legal action against you. The financial penalties we would seek are significant. In addition, our client would be entitled to take separate action."

Bellis's tone sounded like a threat, albeit dressed up in legalese. Hayden didn't like being pushed around, regardless of how politely it was done.

"We've all had to sign it," Shane said. "It's standard practice in this kind of situation."

"I would recommend you read the document before

signing it," Bellis said. "You're welcome to run it by your attorney, but we are short on time."

Hayden had the urge to walk away. He liked to keep business informal and friendly. This was beginning to get a little too serious for his liking. But it was easy work for excellent money. In a couple of weeks, it wouldn't matter. Hayden scanned the twelve-page document. It was pretty much as Bellis had described. If he disclosed any part of his work, MDE would sue—and sue big. The document claimed MDE would seek ten million in damages. Hayden wasn't sure how much was legal bluffing, but it was enough to ensure he kept his mouth shut. He finished reading the document and decided the job was still worth doing despite the overlitigious contract. Bellis held out a pen, and Hayden signed.

With that out of the way, Bellis and Shane spent a half hour going through the marked-up plans with him before handing them to him along with the flash drive containing the drawings he was to correct. It was all straightforward enough, and the meeting broke up. Everyone shook hands and smiled, but the hard sell with the nondisclosure agreement had soured Hayden's mood. The enthusiasm he'd brought with him this morning wouldn't be making the return drive.

Bellis made small talk as he saw Shane and Hayden out. Lockhart's presence in the foyer ended the small talk. He stood before Chaudhary's image on the easel in deep contemplation. He seemingly failed to register anyone's presence in the room with him for a moment.

"A great shame. Sundip was a very talented young man. We should have done more for him," he reflected. "What's going on here?"

"James, this is Hayden Duke. He's joining the team," Bellis said.

Lockhart shook Hayden's hand. "Good to have you

aboard. I look forward to working with you. Enjoy the rest of your weekend."

Lockhart couldn't have made his point any clearer. It was time for them to leave.

"Thanks for making the trip, Hayden. We'll talk next week," Bellis said, before ushering Shane and him out the door.

"Lock the door, Trevor," Lockhart said. "I don't want to be disturbed."

Bellis did as he was told, and Lockhart led the way to Bellis's office. He let Bellis sit while he perched himself on the window ledge. He took in the panoramic view and watched Shane reverse out from his parking spot and drive away.

"Do you know anything about this Hayden Duke?" Lockhart asked.

"Not much. He's a friend of Shane's. Why?"

"I noticed him eyeballing us at the game."

"What do you want?" Bellis asked.

"Watch your tone, Trevor. Just remember who you're speaking to."

Bellis said nothing. Instead he fidgeted in his seat.

"I came here to make sure we're all on the same page about Chaudhary."

"I got the message."

"Did you? I wasn't sure."

"I got it."

Lockhart glanced out the window. Beckerman was out there somewhere watching his back, visible yet invisible. He'd chosen to keep Beckerman out of sight today. He had a habit of agitating situations. Lockhart didn't want things agitated. Today, he wanted calm. More specifically, he wanted Bellis calm.

"You say that, Trevor, but I feel you have questions. If you have them, ask them."

"Sundip's death."

"Yes."

"It's convenient."

"Convenient, how?"

"He'd expressed doubts about the project."

"Did he mention his doubts to you?"

"Only that we'd been lied to. He said the products we're designing weren't for the purpose we were told. He wanted to speak to you, and now he's dead. Did he speak to you?"

Lockhart came away from the window and settled into a chair opposite Bellis. Bellis stiffened and looked cornered. "I met with him. I thought I had set his mind at rest."

"Obviously you hadn't."

Lockhart sighed. "I believe Sundip was overwrought and he cracked. He was delusional. When I think about it now, my answers didn't help him. I thought the truth would bring him around. Instead, it looks to have pushed him over the edge."

"So you believe it was a suicide?"

"Opposed to what, Trevor?" Lockhart could feel Bellis psyching himself up to ask the big question. He wanted the question out in the open so he could put the subject to rest. *Ask me, Trevor. You know you want to.* As if he'd made a psychic link, Bellis asked the question.

"James, did you have anything to do with Sundip's death?"

"How can you ask that?"

He fixed Bellis with his gaze. He left him no room for escape. Bellis would need courage if he were to follow this line of questioning.

Bellis sat up in his seat. "I don't think Chaudhary was delusional. I know he had doubts about the project and was becoming a little difficult to control, but I don't think he was suicidal."

"A little difficult?" Lockhart said. "He was becoming

a grade-A pain in the ass. He suddenly got it into his head that what we were doing was wrong."

"I think that's a little harsh."

"More harsh than you accusing me of murder, Trevor?"

Bellis wiped a hand across his face. Finally, the man saw the ridiculousness of what he was saying. Lockhart saw Bellis's courage leave him in that moment and return to the fold. Bellis might have suspicions and doubts, but he wouldn't take them any further. The project remained intact, and his clients didn't need to hear of this setback.

"I'm sorry, James."

"That's okay. The last few days have taken their toll on everyone. We've lost someone close, and it's shaken us all. Suicide is hard to accept. It's a betrayal to everyone left behind. We'd prefer to have someone else to blame, but in this case, we don't have that luxury. Chaudhary killed himself. There's even a witness who saw him do it."

"You're right. I'm sorry."

Lockhart stood and rounded the desk. Bellis stood to meet him, and they shook hands. Bellis's hand was slick with sweat. It had taken a lot for the man to confront him. Lockhart placed a comforting hand on Bellis's shoulder. "Look, Trevor. Next week, come over to San Francisco and we'll have dinner. I'll explain the facts of life regarding this project. It's time I let you in on a few details. How does that sound?"

"Sounds good," Bellis said, squeezing out a strained smile.

Lockhart saw himself out and drove away. He didn't pick up his phone until he was back on the freeway. He dialed Beckerman's number.

"How'd it go?" Beckerman asked.

"It could have gone better. There are doubts, but the

situation is contained for now. Did you find anything at Chaudhary's?"

"Negative. Anything he claimed to have known, he kept to himself."

"Okay. I want you to keep a close eye on MDE. Any more problems, I want to know about them."

CHAPTER TWO

Hayden fired up his computer in the office he operated out of a converted bedroom. This was only his third night on the MDE job, and he was making good progress. Shane hadn't been wrong. It was grunt work, and he was breezing through it. MDE had placed a sixty-hour estimate on the contract. He'd have it wrapped up in fifty. He'd be robbing himself of a couple of thousand bucks, but it would put him in good stead for a callback. Since he was balancing this contract with his daytime gig, the sooner he had MDE out of his hair the better.

The only difficulty came from MDE's security precautions. Code numbers replaced titles on the drawings, and all notes referred to data sheets MDE hadn't provided. It made Hayden's job difficult, but not impossible. Engineering was its own language. If you could speak it, you could understand it. He realized several key components were missing from the complete design, but he had enough of the jigsaw pieces to fill in the gaps.

He pulled out the marked-up plans and spread them across his planning table. He couldn't see what the fuss was about. MDE claimed their client was on the verge of a breakthrough, but it didn't look like one to him.

Admittedly, he wasn't in possession of the complete design, but he could read between the lines, and he didn't see anything earth shattering. The sum total of the designs consisted of manifold systems and simple pressure vessels. Effectively, he was looking at something like a fire-suppression system. He guessed the magic wasn't in the hardware, but what went inside.

He fell into a work groove and soon forgot about MDE and their client. He worked until 11:30 before calling it a night. He saved his work, then checked his e-mail. He had seven new messages. Among them was an untitled e-mail from Shane with a twenty-meg attachment. He double clicked the e-mail to open it.

Hayden,
    Store this file. Don't open it. Don't read it. Just keep it somewhere safe. I'll explain later.

Shane

The message threw him. The attachment's name, *document1*, didn't help either. He felt as if he'd walked into the middle of a conversation. Why would Shane send him a file, then tell him not to open it? He was tempted to open it, but he held off. Shane had entrusted him with this file and he wouldn't betray that trust, so he saved *document1* to his hard drive.

In this world of dependency on electronic documentation, nothing could be taken for granted. Hard drives crashed. CDs degraded. Human error wiped files. One source of storage was never enough. He launched his Internet browser and logged on to an online storage account where he backed up all his electronic files, private and business. He saved *document1* there too, deleted the e-mail and shut down the machine.

Hayden flopped onto the living room sofa. Despite the long work day, he couldn't just go to bed. He needed to unwind in front of the TV. He hadn't even made it to the end of a sitcom before his curiosity got the better of him. Shane's message worried him. It was weird. Shane wasn't the type of person to send cryptic messages in the middle of the night. Something was wrong. Even though it was close to midnight, Hayden picked up the phone and dialed Shane's number.

It rang for a long time. Hayden guessed Shane was asleep, but he didn't care if he woke him. When Shane eventually answered, Hayden heard caution, not sleep, in his voice.

"Who is this?"

"Shane, it's Hayden."

"I can't talk now," Shane said. "I'll call you back."

"Hey, hold on," Hayden said. "I want to talk about this e-mail."

Shane paused for a second. "You shouldn't have called."

"Is everything okay?"

"Hayden, it's late, and I don't have time for this."

"And I don't have time for dumb e-mail attachments."

Shane's tone switched from dismissive to fearful. "Have you opened it?"

"No. I did as you asked."

"I made a mistake. Forget all about it. Delete it. We'll talk later."

"No. Wait," Hayden said, but he was talking to the dial tone.

What was going on? There had been genuine fear in Shane's voice when he answered the phone. Who did Shane have to fear? He was living large. Maybe he had money troubles and had gotten himself a hungry loan shark, but Hayden didn't think so. His troubles had something to do with the e-mail attachment. Hayden reconsidered opening the file, but he decided not to unless

Shane didn't give him any choice. He wouldn't delete it either, not until Shane explained himself.

He redialed Shane's number and got his machine. "C'mon, Shane, pick up. Something's wrong. Let me help. If you don't pick up, I'm coming over."

The threat did nothing to spur Shane to answer, so Hayden hung up.

He cursed to himself. Shane wasn't helping. It was time to make good on his threat. He snatched his keys and got into his car.

The light traffic at midnight cut ten minutes off the journey from Fairfield to San Rafael. Hayden pulled up in front Shane's house after 12:30. What he found unnerved him. Light from every window in the house punched holes in the darkness, and a pounding baseline disturbed the night air. A flash of movement from inside the house interrupted the light shining from a downstairs window. Hayden slipped from the car and crossed the lawn.

"Hey, you," someone called from behind Hayden.

Hayden spun around. A man in a dressing gown came jogging barefoot across the street from the house opposite Shane's.

The neighbor jabbed a finger at Shane's house. "Do you know that prick?" He didn't give Hayden time to answer. "That son of a bitch has been playing his damn music for the last hour. Some of us have jobs to go to in the morning."

No one living in this neighborhood would be without a job, but Hayden kept the thought to himself. He saw no point in antagonizing the guy any further.

"I'm here to take care of it."

"Make sure you do. If you don't, I'll let the cops settle it."

"Has anyone called the cops?"

"No, but I will if that music doesn't stop."

Hayden was banking on the fact that no one would call the police. The housing association wouldn't want to saddle their upscale community with a bad reputation.

Having flexed his muscles, the neighbor turned to leave, but Hayden stopped him. "Has this happened before?"

"No, and it better not continue." He marched off toward his home.

Hayden walked up to the front door and pressed the doorbell. He felt the vibration of the chimes through the button, but the chimes lost their battle against the music.

He looked over his shoulder for the disgruntled neighbor. The man stood at the window watching Hayden and waiting for him to live up to his word. Hayden tried the doorknob. It wasn't locked. He cracked the door open and called Shane's name, but like the doorbell, his voice failed to penetrate the cranked-up sound system. He stepped inside and closed the door.

"Shane, did you know your door was open?" he shouted above the din.

He got no reply.

Hayden ventured farther into Shane's house. He veered into the living room to kill the sound system and hopefully bring Shane running.

He pulled up short when he entered the living room. The place looked as if a tornado had blown through it. Sofas and armchairs were overturned, sliced open and gutted. A television lay on its back, smoke wafting from the shattered screen. Books and papers covered the carpet. A phone, obviously ripped from its jack, topped the shattered remains of a framed print. The only thing in any semblance of order was the sound system blasting out the music at full volume.

Hayden turned down the volume. He didn't want to

scare Shane by killing it altogether. Shane wanted the music on for some reason, so he'd leave it on, but at a reasonable level. The thud of something heavy striking the floor above him cut off his train of thought.

"Shane," Hayden yelled out and tore up the stairs.

Still, he got no response.

As he reached the top of the stairs, a second heavy impact came from Shane's bedroom. A splintering crack followed. Hayden raced across the landing and slammed into the closed bedroom door, sending it flying back.

He found the bedroom in a similar state of devastation as the living room. Carnage from the master bathroom spilled into the bedroom. The door to the walk-in closet hung off its hinges and the clothes were strewn within its confines. In the bedroom, upturned and emptied drawers covered the floor. A nightstand was in pieces along with everything it contained. The king-sized bed had been upended and the box spring thrown against a wall. Shane stood alone at the center of the carnage, a butcher knife in his hand. He raised it and plunged it down into the defenseless mattress. The knife disappeared up to its hilt. He dragged the knife down two-handed to open a twelve-inch-long gash. He jerked the knife out, and the pillowtop exhaled a puff of foam. He never once registered Hayden's presence, let alone the silencing of the music.

Hayden stood frozen in shock. The blaring music had been Shane's savior. If it hadn't masked the destruction, someone would have called the cops.

"Jesus Christ, Shane. What the hell is going on?"

This snapped Shane from his trance. He whirled on Hayden, brandishing the knife. "Get out of here."

Hayden's heart raced, and his gaze went to the knife clutched in Shane's fist. He wasn't about to give his friend any cause to panic. He was panicking enough for both of them.

"Take it easy, Shane." Hayden did his best to sound as calm as possible. "You don't want to do anything stupid."

"I can't take it easy. I've got to find them."

A tremor crept into Shane. It started at his hands, then traveled up into his arms before his entire body began to quiver. Light glinted off the knife blade in his shaky grasp.

Shane was reaching a tipping point, and if he reached it, Hayden didn't want to think about what would happen to his friend—or himself. He stood directly in Shane's path at the point of his mental collapse.

Shane turned away and slammed the knife into the mattress again. Hayden flinched when the blade pierced the tough fabric, but better that the mattress took the brunt of Shane's frenzy. Shane yanked down on the knife and ripped another long gash.

Hayden took an exploratory step forward, but made sure he kept a clear path to the open door. "What have you got to find?"

"The bugs," Shane answered, like Hayden should know. He plunged his free hand inside the hole he'd just made and rooted inside the mattress' guts. "I know they're here. I know they're listening."

What had happened? Shane's e-mail with the attachment had been date stamped shortly after eight. His tone sounded authoritative. *Do this for me and don't ask questions.* That wasn't the person standing before Hayden now. Paranoia and fear now ruled Shane's mental roost. Something had to have happened to warrant such a personality change in five hours. Could Shane be high? Hayden had never known him to use drugs, but what else could explain his behavior?

Hayden took another step forward. "What bugs?"

"The bugs. The bugs. You know about the bugs. Don't pretend you don't." Shane jerked his hand free from the mattress. Foam stuffing coated his hand, glued in place by bloody abrasions from his hand grazing the bed-springs.

"Have you found any bugs?"

"No," Shane spat. "Of course not. But they're here. I know they are."

It hurt Hayden to hear Shane's delirium. He'd connected with so few people in his life. He counted Shane as one. To see his friend so lost filled him with guilt. He'd let his relationship slip, and only now, when it was too late, had he finally arrived to help.

"Let me help you find them," Hayden whispered and rested a hand on Shane's shoulder.

Hayden had hoped the request would calm Shane, but it ignited the opposite reaction. Shane cast aside the mattress and whipped around. He was an imposing figure, but Hayden stood his ground. He couldn't let his fear or panic show. Shane was a rampaging animal. He needed little provocation to attack.

It took Hayden a moment to sense pressure against his stomach. Shane had knotted up. Veins bulged in his arms and neck and his muscles were guitar-string tight. Hayden looked down. The butcher knife was pressed against him. Its tip had pierced his shirt and pricked his flesh. Another step forward and the blade would be buried in his intestines. His mouth went dry at the thought. He had to be so careful now. This was the tipping point. A simple nudge would get Hayden killed.

Shane followed Hayden's gaze. He looked at the knife tip against Hayden's flesh. Hayden saw a flicker of recognition in Shane's eyes, but he didn't draw the knife back.

"You can't help," Shane growled. "You have no idea what's going on."

"Shane, put the knife down. Please."

Shane jabbed the knife like an accusing finger. Hayden felt the blade's tip prick him again and again. Blood trickled down his stomach into the waistband of his pants.

"You don't have a clue, do you?" Shane demanded.

"No, Shane, I don't." The words caught in Hayden's dry throat.

Shane jerked the knife, snagging Hayden's shirt on the way up. He brandished it under Hayden's chin. "Then tell me, what good are you to me?"

Hayden looked for a hint of sanity in Shane and saw none. That scared the hell out of him. He was now tied to this runaway train, and only he could stop it.

When Hayden didn't answer, Shane jabbed the knife into the soft flesh under his chin until it drew blood.

"Shane, you're really scaring me with that knife. Please put it down."

Hayden saw Shane boil up inside, and he expected the knife to skewer his skull, but Shane emitted a disgusted huffing noise and turned away. He hurled the mattress aside and turned on the box spring.

"You're no good to me. Go."

Relief swept over Hayden now that the knife wasn't pointed at him. Shane had given him a renewed chance to talk him down from the ledge his paranoid brain was on.

"Shane, stop," he commanded. "Stop and tell me what is going on. I'm your friend, and I want to help. I can help, but not if you won't talk to me."

Shane impaled the box spring with the knife and held on to it, trapped in contemplation. Hayden's plea seemed to have gotten through. Shane released his grasp on the knife.

Hayden felt the tension leave the room, so he approached his friend. He made his movements deliberate and nonthreatening. Shane's muscles remained tight, but he didn't strike out or shrink back. Hayden came up behind him and placed a comforting hand on his arm.

"Come on, Shane," Hayden whispered and leaned in to take the knife. "Let's see what we can work out."

Hayden's hand was within an inch of the knife when

Shane finally tipped the balance. He yelled out as if Hayden had stabbed him and snapped his arm back. Shane's elbow smashed Hayden in the face, connecting with his eyebrow. His head snapped back, and dots of light that burned with thousand-watt intensity burst across his vision. A wave of nausea hit him hard, leaving him lightheaded. He staggered back, clipped the mattress and went down hard on his back, cracking his head against a wall.

Shane yanked the knife out of the box spring and fled the bedroom.

Hayden jerked himself up, triggering an explosion inside his skull that ensured he remained prone. He needed a moment for the pain to pass.

A crash came from somewhere in the house. The noise cleaved Hayden's injured brain in two. He heard Shane curse, which was followed by the whine of the garage door opening.

"Shit," Hayden murmured.

He rolled over and climbed to his feet, using the wall for support. The nausea returned, and he steadied himself before staggering through the bedroom doorway. He clambered down the stairs and felt every jarring footfall inside his skull.

A car engine roared into life. Hayden yanked the front door open in time to see Shane's Infiniti sedan reverse out of his garage and come to a messy halt in the middle of the street. He called out to Shane, but his friend stamped on the gas and sped away.

"Jesus Christ, Shane."

Shane was no longer just a danger to himself or Hayden. He was a now a high-speed weapon.

Hayden bottled his pain and charged across the lawn to his car. He threw himself behind the wheel.

Shane's complaining neighbor emerged from his home and stood in his driveway. The security light lit up his angry expression.

Hayden gunned the engine to his Mitsubishi Eclipse and pulled a fast U-turn using the angry neighbor's driveway. The neighbor jumped back when Hayden drove straight toward him. He called something out, but Hayden didn't care. He hoped this prompted him to call the cops. He needed the cops now.

Shane had a four-block jump on Hayden and extended it. Recklessness was his advantage. He didn't care for his or anyone else's welfare. There weren't many people on the road, but he elbowed other vehicles aside, drove in the oncoming lane and failed to stop for lights or signs. Only self-preservation on the part of the other drivers and pedestrians prevented carnage.

Hayden didn't possess Shane's recklessness, and he had no option but to watch Shane's lead stretch and stretch. As long as he kept visual contact with Shane's car, he didn't care about his lead. He might not be able to prevent him from getting to where he wanted, but he could stop him from doing whatever he planned when he got there.

Shane took the surface roads and picked up Sir Francis Drake Boulevard. He went west toward San Anselmo. The road was narrow and slow through town. Hayden cut into Shane's lead, but that advantage disappeared once Shane passed through neighboring Fairfax. The road opened up, and Shane disappeared into the distance.

Hayden couldn't lose him now. He got his cell out and called Shane's number. "Please have your cell," he murmured as the phone rang.

Hayden didn't have a clue where Shane was going. It had to be important, but not much existed beyond Fairfax—just some unincorporated townships and parklands. Of course, in Shane's current state of mind, he could be chasing after anything. Hayden didn't care what Shane was chasing, as long as he stopped.

Hayden had just about given up hope when Shane answered the phone. "Stop following me."

"I can't. I want to help."

"It's too late for that."

Hayden eyed his speedometer. His speed had dropped since Shane answered the phone. Multitasking at break-neck speeds wasn't possible. Something had to give. He just hoped talking was slowing Shane down too.

"Shane, where are you going?"

"Far away."

"You can't outrun your problems."

"Who says I'm running?"

Hayden didn't like Shane's tone. The craziness he'd witnessed at his friend's house was gone, replaced by a robotic cool. The calm did nothing to settle Hayden's nerves. The quantum personality shifts didn't bode well.

"Okay, if you're not running, can I come with you?"

"No."

"Goddamn it, Shane. Where are you going?"

"Somewhere good."

Hayden raced past a sign for the Samuel P. Taylor State Park. Forest closed in around the road, shrouding it from the night's sky. A creek snaked alongside the road, occasionally crossing under then back across. The road coiled up in a series of twists and turns. Shane had been out of sight for some time, but he hadn't left this road. There was nowhere to turn off.

"Tell me about the attachment. What is it?"

"Delete it. Forget it. It can't help anyone."

"Then tell me about it."

"I should hang up now."

"No. Don't. I'm your friend and you're treating me like an outsider. Is that fair—to either of us?"

That gave Shane pause. Hayden listened to Shane's engine slow then rev up as it worked the curves in the road. He couldn't be that far ahead. Hayden powered down his window and listened. Nothing but wind noise poured through Hayden's open window.

"Yes, you are my friend," Shane answered. "You deserve answers, but it's too late for that."

"It's not. While I care, it's never too late."

"I'm sorry, it is."

The sound of Shane's car coming to a fast stop on dirt followed by the *ping-ping* of the open-door sensor came down the line. Hayden cursed. Shane had beaten him to his destination. Hayden floored the gas pedal.

"This is where I say good-bye."

"No, it isn't."

"It is," Shane said and hung up.

Hayden tossed his phone down and put everything into his driving. He threw his Mitsubishi into the switchbacks. The coupe slewed across the road but maintained its speed. He tried to imagine how far Shane would be getting on foot. Not far compared to the frightening speed registered on Hayden's speedometer. There was still a chance he'd catch up with him.

He threw his car into a blind right bend and his heart stopped.

The road stretched ahead before it disappeared around another bend. Before the bend, a wooden truss bridge built for pedestrians crossed low over the road and high over the creek. Shane had climbed to the top of the bridge. A rope trailed from his neck to the wooden beam.

Hayden stamped on the brakes. His front wheel slid off the roadway and onto the dirt. The Mitsubishi threatened to send him off the road and into the creek, but the other three wheels averted tragedy. He came to a messy stop in the middle of the road as his cell rang. He recovered it from the passenger foot well. Shane's name lit up the small screen.

"Stay where you are or I'll jump."

"Shane, climb back down." Hayden didn't ask; he instructed. The time for pandering was over. "We'll go home and deal with this. I'll get you help—anything you need, but you get down from there."

"It's too late for help."

Hayden's mouth went dry to the point where he couldn't swallow.

"Why did you bring me here?"

"I didn't. You followed. I'm doing this for me."

How could Shane be this far gone? Hayden thought. A week ago they'd been laughing and joking. Reconnecting after years lost. Now Shane wasn't just threatening suicide, he intended to carry it out. Hayden tried to shut it all out by listening to the rumble of his car engine.

"You are right about one thing," Shane said. "You are my friend."

"Then you know if you do anything stupid here, you'll hurt me."

"Yes." There was a finality to his answer.

"A friend wouldn't do this to another friend."

Shane didn't answer for a long time. "Then I'm a shitty friend."

Hayden was frightened, truly petrified. Not for himself, but for Shane. Shane was calling the shots, reducing Hayden to a spectator. Pressure built in Hayden's chest, cutting off his breath. He let out a sob. He hoped Shane wouldn't hear, but he did.

"I'm sorry, Hayden, but you don't understand what they've done. What I've done. It's terrible. I'm going to hurt you and so many others, but I have to do it."

"Shane, I don't get this. Explain it to me."

Hayden stalled for time. He hoped and feared for another motorist to change the dynamic.

"Maybe another time."

There was a smile in Shane's reply. It felt like punch in

the heart to Hayden. Shane sounded human again. His insanity had been pushed aside to let a moment of clarity shine through, but the clarity was flawed. No sane man has a conversation with a rope around his neck.

"Please, Shane. Don't." Hayden was spent. It was everything he could muster.

From across the distance, picked out in the moonlight penetrating the trees and Hayden's headlights, Shane shook his head and tossed the phone away.

Hayden lifted his foot off the clutch and stamped on the gas. The car leaped forward, accelerating hard. A hundred yards wasn't a large distance to travel. Sprinters covered it in less than ten seconds. If he could position his car under the bridge, Shane wouldn't have anywhere to jump.

But a hundred yards didn't measure up to the speed of gravity and the length of rope around Shane's neck. He jumped, coming to the end of the tough drop in the blink of an eye. Hayden was nowhere near saving Shane when his neck snapped.

Hayden didn't rush from the car. There was no point. He just sat in stunned silence, watching Shane's limp body rock slowly back and forth in the night.

CHAPTER THREE

Detective Ruben Santiago was dressed and waiting when Deputy Mark Rice called him on his cell. The call from the Marin Sheriff's Department watch commander had woken his wife, then him, when she drove an elbow into his ribs. Santiago let himself out of his house without reawakening his family. Rice sat parked on the street in an unmarked car.

Under normal circumstances, he would have worked the call alone, but Rice was on trial with the detective's unit and had been paired with a senior detective. Rice was an okay guy in Santiago's book. He was ex-navy and keen to get ahead in law enforcement. If he wanted to get ahead, then there was no reason he shouldn't get woken up in the middle of the night too.

Santiago jogged across his front lawn to Rice's vehicle. The moment his butt connected with the seat, Rice stepped on the gas.

Santiago glanced over his shoulder at his home, dark and quiet. It had gotten quieter since his son, Alex, had joined the Marines and quieter still since he'd been deployed. Not a moment slipped by without his thoughts turning to Alex's safety. Rice gave him hope. He'd survived his time on active duty. Alex would too. He returned his gaze to the road ahead.

"So, what do we know?" he asked.

"Nothing that makes a whole lot of sense. A little over an hour ago, Shane Fallon, twenty-eight, left his home in San Rafael, drove out to the Sam Taylor Park and hanged himself from a bridge."

Another suicide, Santiago thought. He hoped it wasn't the beginning of a hot new trend in Marin. He hadn't even finished with the paperwork on Sundip Chaudhary's death yet.

"Witnesses?"

"One," Rice answered. "Hayden Duke, a friend of Fallon's."

"A friend? What were these guys doing there at one A.M.—sightseeing?"

"Duke claims Fallon was tweaking and he took off. Duke followed, and when he caught up, Fallon was standing on top of the bridge with a rope around his neck. Before Duke could stop him, the guy jumped."

"Tweaking," Santiago echoed with disdain. Suddenly, this simple suicide had gotten complicated. "Are we sure Fallon wasn't pushed?"

"It sounds solid, but those are the limitations of a single witness account."

Rice cut through residential streets to pick up Sir Francis Drake Boulevard. He wound up the speed and swept through the sleeping towns with his lights on but siren off. Santiago gripped the sides of his seat. He hated fast driving. Rice's breakneck speeds didn't last long. The road coiled up when they entered the state park, forcing him to slow.

Red and blue lights spilling from between the trees told Santiago they'd reached their destination. Rice slowed for a sharp bend, and organized chaos came into view. Deputies had closed the road down to one lane. Two

Marin Sheriff's units hemmed in an ambulance, an Infiniti sedan and a Mitsubishi coupe. Rice stopped the car, joining the end of the daisy chain of vehicles.

A rope dangled from the bridge, but no body hung from its end. Santiago counted his blessings at not being faced with a corpse, and he and Rice slipped from the car.

The canopy of trees retained all remnants of the previous day's heat. That and the pleasant scent of pine took the unpleasant edge off the night's duties.

The deputy minding the store jogged over and officially unloaded the case onto Santiago. He wouldn't have minded so much if the guy hadn't looked so damn happy about it. The deputy ran through the facts, which didn't go any further than the history Rice had given him already. Santiago thanked the deputy by giving him the traffic-control duties.

"I want statements from you and your partner by the end of your shift."

The deputy nodded. "You'll have them."

Santiago didn't have to ask for the body's location. He spotted the yellow shock blanket covering a corpse at the edge of the road. One of the deputies had been smart enough to park his cruiser in front of the body to block it from prying eyes.

"Coroner's investigator?" Santiago asked.

"In route."

"How'd you get him down?" Rice asked.

"We didn't. The witness did."

Interesting, Santiago thought. Maybe there was more to the story after all. "Really? Where is he? I'd like to ask him why he did that."

"With the paramedics. Fallon worked him over before his swan dive."

Santiago and Rice went over to the ambulance where a female paramedic crouched in front of Hayden. She applied the finishing touches to him while he sat on the ambulance's bumper. It was impossible to tell whether she had an attractive figure under the clumsy and unflattering overalls. She placed a Band-Aid on Hayden's forehead.

Despite the signs of assault, Hayden Duke was a cleancut guy. A Dockers catalog was out there somewhere with his name on it. He wasn't quite the person Santiago had pictured under the circumstances.

Santiago got introductions out of the way, then asked the paramedic, "How is he?"

"Nothing too serious. Abrasions." She pointed to where Shane had caught him with the blade. "A nasty contusion on the back of the head. Maybe a slight concussion."

"And a killer headache," Hayden added.

The paramedic smiled. "And a killer headache, apparently."

Without being told, the paramedic left them to their business.

"Can we talk, Mr. Duke?" Santiago asked.

"Sure."

"Let's get out of these bright lights," Rice said.

They walked Hayden over to the turnout overlooking the creek. Santiago positioned himself facing the bridge, forcing Hayden to keep his back to where Shane had jumped. There was a time when the sight of the severed rope dangling from the bridge would help to open the witness up.

"I've been apprised of events, but I have some questions for you," Santiago said. "You're okay answering them?"

"Sure."

"Did you know Shane well?"

"We were college friends."

"Is there any next of kin we should contact?"

"He has a sister, Rebecca. She lives in L.A."

"You live in Fairfield. Is that correct?"

"Yes."

"You're a long way from home on a school night," Santiago said.

"I work with Shane at Marin Design Engineering. I'm on contract with them."

"So you commute?" Santiago asked.

"No. I work from home."

"Okay. I think I understand. Why the late-night call to Mr. Fallon? Eleven thirty is a little late for a business call."

"MDE is under a tight deadline, and they're working around the clock on this one. Shane's my contact for questions, and I had a question, so I contacted him."

"What was the question?"

Hayden reeled off some technobabble Santiago didn't understand. His response sounded solid enough, but Santiago saw the lie. Hayden looked up and away—a classic liar's reflex. Santiago sighed inside. He didn't like it when witnesses lied. It never worked out well.

"Okay," Santiago said. "It says here you drove from Fairfield to San Rafael, some fifty miles, just because Shane didn't sound like himself."

"Yes."

Santiago cocked his head. "Excuse me, but that sounds a little overzealous."

Hayden glanced over in the direction of the body. "Considering my friend is dead, I wouldn't say that."

Santiago tapped the report. "You told the deputy that Shane claimed to have done something terrible. Any idea what that terrible thing could be?"

"No."

Hayden didn't look up and away this time.

"But you're good friends. You must have some idea."

"We are, but we'd lost touch until last week."

"How long were you out of touch?"

"Three years."

"You said Shane seemed high."

"It seemed that way. He was delusional. He trashed his home looking for bugs that weren't there. I don't think he really knew who I was."

"Is that why he tried to stab you?"

"He didn't stab me."

Santiago pointed at the bloodstained holes in Hayden's shirt. "Didn't he? Whether you like it or not, your friend assaulted you."

Hayden riled up to say something but bit it back. Santiago wished he hadn't. Hayden might let something slip if he lost his temper. Santiago decided to push a little harder.

"Do you know what drugs Shane used?"

"He didn't use drugs," Hayden snapped.

"But you hadn't seen him in three years," Santiago said. "You don't know what he was into."

The remark took the fight out of Hayden. "I know my friend. He wasn't an addict. He wasn't the type."

"Do you think we'll find drugs in his system?"

"Yes," Hayden conceded.

"Do you have an explanation for tonight?"

Hayden shook his head. "He seemed fine during the weekend."

Santiago nodded. "We'll be looking into Shane's life to see if we can unearth anything. Do you take drugs, Mr. Duke?"

"What kind of bullshit question is that?"

"Steady, Mr. Duke," Rice said.

"Steady, my ass," Hayden spat. "I just saw my friend hang himself and now you're looking to bust me for drugs?"

"Mr. Duke," Santiago said. "Everyone has a skeleton or two in their closets, and understandably, they don't want them aired to the world. Now, I'm not looking to bust you on a drug charge or even trash Shane Fallon's

name. I just want to get to the heart of the matter. Mr.
Fallon was disturbed. If drugs pushed him over the edge,
I want to know. It'll save a lot of time and embarrass-
ment if I can get answers now." He paused for Hayden
to absorb the speech. "Now, did you provide Shane with
drugs, or do you know what drugs he took tonight?"

"No."

"Thank you," Santiago said. "Why did you cut the
body down?"

Hayden looked back at the bridge. "Shane was hanging
over the road. Any passing vehicle would have clipped
him. Cutting him down was the humane thing to do."

Santiago stared at the low bridge. He doubted an
eighteen-wheeler would make it underneath. "How'd
you get him down?"

"I drove my car underneath him to support his body,
climbed on the roof, cut the rope and lowered him onto
the ground."

"That couldn't have been pleasant. Especially since
he was a friend."

"It wasn't."

"What did you cut Shane down with—the knife he
used on you?"

"I have a box cutter in the car."

"You're very practical."

Realization lit up Hayden's eyes. Santiago had lost his
element of surprise. Hayden knew he was being tested.
He'd be wary now. It didn't bother Santiago. Liars gave
themselves away in other ways.

"Put it down to my engineering background."

"I need to get this on the record," Santiago said. "I'd
like you to return to my office and make an official
statement. Please follow us, Mr. Duke."

Santiago and Rice walked Hayden back to his car
before getting into their own. Rice led the two-car procession back to their home base at the Civic Center.

"You think he's lying," Rice said.

"He's definitely holding something back," Santiago said. "That's for sure."

"Do you think he pushed Fallon?"

"Don't know. It may have been a drug party gone bad. I won't know until I've squeezed Mr. Duke a little harder."

It was still dark, but it no longer felt like night by the time Hayden left the sheriff's office in San Rafael. The dashboard clock said it was 4:16. He'd be lucky if he got an hour's sleep before he had to leave for work. That was, if he could get to sleep at all.

The roads were clear, and he tried pushing the speed, but found he didn't have the energy for it. Santiago and Rice had taken all he had to give. The interview had been harsh, but not brutal. Santiago pressed the possible drug element. Did Hayden know what drugs Shane used? Where did Shane get his drugs from? How long had he been a user? The guy lived in a great neighborhood. Did he deal too? These were all questions Hayden couldn't answer.

Eventually, Santiago backed off, let him sign his statement and go. Hayden took no comfort in the move. It felt like a trap. Santiago was giving him all the opportunity he needed to incriminate himself. It was a wasted tactic. He had no involvement in tonight's carnage other than being a witness. The only question that needed answering was why Shane killed himself, and there was no crime attached to that tragedy.

Hayden blamed himself for his treatment at Santiago's hands. It was a self-inflicted wound. They'd picked up on his reticence. They misread his unwillingness to tell them about the file Shane had sent him as a drug issue. Hiding the file had been a stupid move on his part, but he was just trying to protect Shane's name.

Shane deserved privacy. If something embarrassing lay at the heart of his suicide, the world didn't have to know about it. Hayden would open the file when he got home. If the contents were relevant to Santiago's investigation, then he'd hand it over. If they weren't, then it wasn't any of their business.

He tried to blot it all out and focus on not falling asleep at the wheel, but he found himself on autopilot, replaying the interview. He couldn't shake Santiago's point. He hadn't seen Shane in three years. What made him think he knew Shane the way he knew him in college? They were close back then. Best buds. He'd been there at the lowest point in Shane's life—when his parents had been killed. But that was then. Their lives had taken them in different directions, and their relationship had drifted. If they'd really been close, that wouldn't have happened. The truth of the matter was that he knew the Shane of old, not the current Shane. The admission left him feeling sick to his stomach.

He pulled over onto the shoulder and broke down. He cried for a friend he couldn't save. He cried for how frightened he'd been when Shane pressed the butcher knife against his stomach. He cried because he was tired, confused and grieving and he couldn't think straight anymore. He cried himself out. He didn't feel better for it. He still felt nauseated and his head was pounding, but he was good enough to drive.

It was just after five when he pulled off I-80 and pointed his car in the direction of his home. His skin crawled against his soiled clothes, and his brain felt stuffed with cotton balls. He just wanted to go to bed to blot out the last six hours. He'd call the office and tell them he'd be in late.

Hayden hit the remote and parked in the garage. He was dead on his feet as he slipped from the car, but a preternatural sense snapped him out his daze. As soon as he pushed open the connecting door from the garage to the house, he pulled up short. He detected a disturbance in his home. He didn't hear or smell anything. It was much subtler than that. Someone had been inside his home. He knew that as surely as he knew Shane was dead.

He inched inside, not bothering to close the door behind him. He stood very still and listened. He heard nothing but the hum of the refrigerator. Whoever had been inside wasn't there anymore. He went to the front door and found the lock intact. The same couldn't be said of the sliding door in the kitchen. Its lock had been drilled out. Not surprising. The front door with its deadbolt would have taken time, but not the patio door. It shared the same security technology as a desk drawer.

He switched on the hallway lights and waited. No shuffling of startled burglars greeted him, so he went into the living room, turning on lights as he went. The room was a mess—furniture overturned, breakables broken, and his TV and DVD player missing. Just what he expected. His house looked as if Shane had dropped by.

The bedrooms were a similar story. Finally, he checked his office. Drawings, papers and CDs carpeted the floor. His computer and laptop were gone. So too, was any chance of reading Shane's file.

CHAPTER FOUR

A Fairfield police officer woke Hayden up. When he hadn't answered the door, the officer had entered the house the same way the thieves had, through the kitchen slider. The officer found him stretched out on the living room floor. Hayden would have crashed on his bed or sofa, but seeing as both of those were overturned and the dispatcher had told him not to disturb the crime scene, the floor made for the next best thing. He hadn't expected to fall asleep since he had to use his crossed arms for a pillow, but exhaustion proved him wrong. It took a brisk shove from the officer to rouse him. Hayden checked his watch. It was six.

"Hayden Duke?" the officer asked.

Hayden nodded.

"Can we see some ID?"

Hayden dug out his driver's license and handed it over. The officer examined it and handed it back. "I'm Officer Rick White."

White surveyed the carnage. "You came home to this?"

"Yeah." Hayden ran a hand through his hair.

White sighed. "At least you weren't home. One thing homeowner's insurance can't replace is you."

Hayden didn't respond to the homegrown philosophy. It was too early for that.

White looked Hayden over, then went on an unguided tour of the house. He looked over the kitchen slider's damaged lock before walking through the house, tiptoeing around the mess. Hayden had no option but to follow.

"I'll be honest with you. I doubt we'll recover any of your possessions unless something specific or rare was taken," White said while standing in Hayden's hardest hit room, his office. "Do you know what's been taken?"

"Pretty much, but it's all replaceable stuff. Nothing you'd find on *Antiques Roadshow*."

"Could you make a list for me?"

"Yeah. Sure." Hayden picked up a legal pad from the floor, and White handed him a pen. He looked at the gaps where his possessions used to sit and outlined the stolen items.

"I'm going to call this one in," White said. "Like I say, I doubt we'll find any prints that'll track back to anyone, but you never know your luck. I'll get some more people to work the scene and canvas the area."

"Thanks. I appreciate the effort. I realize this is pretty much a lost cause."

White smiled and left the room while talking into his radio.

Hayden completed cataloging the missing items in his office and extended his search back into the living room. White stood perfectly positioned between the front door and the open slider in the kitchen.

"Okay if I get your statement?" White asked.

Hayden nodded and walked White through events while White wrote it up. Unlike his statement to Santiago and Rice, this one was short. He had come home and found the house ransacked and called the police.

"Why home so late?"

Hayden didn't want to get tangled up in explaining Shane's death. "I was visiting friends."

"The stamina of youth. You can't beat it." White smiled, but it quickly turned into an accusing grimace. "Were you and your friends fighting?"

Hayden followed White's gaze to his torn and bloody shirt. He couldn't believe his stupidity. He hadn't changed out of his clothes. He cursed under his breath.

"Do you want to tell me about it?"

Hayden now understood White's interest in calling backup and forensic people for a burglary with no chance of an arrest. White was bringing in reinforcements for something much larger. Hayden saw any chance of keeping Shane's death and Santiago out of the conversation disappear. If he didn't want to end up spending the day explaining himself, he had to come clean.

"My friend committed suicide. I've been with the Marin County Sheriff's Office all night." He removed Santiago's business card from his wallet and gave it to White. "He can tell you all about it."

White wrote down Santiago's details. Hayden hoped White wouldn't pursue Santiago beyond confirmation purposes. He could do without being squeezed between two sets of cops.

White handed the business card back. "And the blood?"

"My friend assaulted me before killing himself. I'd prefer not to talk about it. I haven't slept all night, and it has nothing to do with what happened here."

"I'll make that determination, Mr. Duke." White's tone turned abrasive. No one was going to tell him who ran this investigation. Hayden nodded his apology. Antagonizing White was only going to complicate things. He might talk the case up with Santiago and get him riled. Hayden didn't need the detective seeing things that weren't there. Santiago already viewed him as a suspect.

White got a brief statement out of Hayden about Shane's suicide just as a second officer and a crime tech arrived. White left the house to check Hayden's account while the second cop watched over him and the crime tech went over the house for prints.

The shift in mood was palpable. No one viewed Hayden as a victim anymore. He was a person of interest now, which was a polite way of saying he was a suspect until proven different. There was a strong sense of glee from White's fellow officer when they fingerprinted him "for elimination purposes." He didn't get upset. Despite what anyone thought, he wasn't the bad guy here. The best thing to do was let them come to that conclusion on their own.

White returned after a few minutes. Whoever he'd talked to had confirmed Hayden's account. His affable nature didn't return along with him, but neither did any itchiness to reach for his cuffs. The cops wrapped up things and filed out while White stayed behind.

"We'll be interviewing your neighbors to see if they heard anything," the officer said, "but at a more reasonable hour."

A more reasonable hour wasn't far away. It was fully morning. His neighbors with longer commutes were already leaving for work.

White saw himself out. Hayden followed him to the threshold.

"I'll be in touch very soon."

About what? Hayden wondered. *The theft or your conversation with Santiago?* He'd ruffled the cop's feathers enough, so he just thanked him and closed the door.

His ravaged home was his again to do with as he pleased. He reattached the wall phone in the kitchen and dialed his dad's cell. From the background noise, he figured he'd caught his father on his way to work.

Hayden said, "My house was broken into."

"I'll be right over, buddy."

"But don't tell Mom."

He didn't want to worry her. She'd fuss and he loved her for it, but fuss and worry wasn't what he needed right now. The last thing he needed was to be told how it would have been different if he'd just . . .

John Duke arrived fifteen minutes later. He let himself in as Hayden came out from his bedroom. Hayden had removed the Band-Aids covering the stab wounds.

John Duke stopped short when he saw the wounds. "Jesus. You didn't say they worked you over."

"No, that's from something else." Hayden pulled on a T-shirt. "When's Tommy coming?"

Tommy had been one of the reasons Hayden had called his father. Tommy was John Duke's friend and a twenty-four-hour locksmith. Hayden couldn't leave his home until he had a new lock on the door, unless he wanted to see the rest of his belongings disappear.

"Should be here within the hour. He's on another job. You're not the only one suffering from a nasty case of thieves."

John Duke ignored the carnage, went over to his son and lifted his shirt. "You want to tell me about this?"

Hayden didn't. It was another reason he hadn't wanted his mom around. Shane's death would send her fussing and worrying into overdrive. His father was different. John Duke would worry and he would fuss—a parental prerogative—but he'd keep it hidden from Hayden. Still, he didn't want to talk about Shane. He hadn't processed it himself. But his father stood waiting for an answer to his question.

They flipped the sofa the right way and sat. Hayden told his father about Shane. When he was finished, John Duke said, "I'm sorry, son. Your mom is going to want to hear about this."

"I know."

"Then you'd better call her, or better still, visit." John Duke smiled. "You'd be making your old dad's life easier."

Before Hayden could agree or disagree, a middle-aged man with dirty-blond, curly hair and an equally curly mustache pushed the door open. "By the looks of this fustercluck, I would say that you need new locks. I might have one or three."

Hayden let his dad and Tommy replace the locks and called Dave O'Brien, his boss at Macpherson Water. He explained he wouldn't be coming in because of the burglary. O'Brien was sympathetic, but made it clear Hayden was expected in the next day. Hayden couldn't afford to lose a second day's pay and promised he would be there.

Then he put in the more difficult call to Trevor Bellis. Bellis got twitchy at the possibility of his precious plans falling into the wrong hands, but Shane's death made his agitation fleeting. Bellis cut the call short to inform the staff about Shane and promised to be in touch soon.

It didn't take Tommy long to replace the locks throughout the house. Even though the slider lock was the only one broken, Hayden wasn't taking any chances. Tommy handed Hayden a new set of keys.

Hayden tried to give Tommy some cash, but he refused.

"You can pay me when you've got your life in order."

Hayden had heard this line from Tommy before. No bill would be forthcoming. Hayden would have to give his dad the cash to take Tommy out for a drink sometime. At least one nice thing had happened in the last twenty-four hours.

Lockhart watched Beckerman pick through the contents of Hayden's computers. Beckerman was a skilled technician on a number of levels. Computers were one such level. Lockhart didn't need to observe Beckerman's every move, but fear compelled him to remain rooted at his side. He had to know the extent of the breach and whether he'd caught it in time. Beckerman closed a program and pushed his chair back from the laptop.

"Done?"

Beckerman nodded.

"What's the verdict?"

Lockhart kept the agitation from his voice. He could be anxious as he liked, but he couldn't show it, especially to Beckerman. The moment someone like Beckerman recognized that his boss was a liability, he'd take action to protect his own interests.

"I think we're in pretty good shape. I found the e-mail attachment Fallon sent Duke."

The moment things turned shaky at Marin Design Engineering, Lockhart had instructed Beckerman to monitor Chaudhary's phone lines. When the calls kicked up a relationship with Shane Fallon, Beckerman bugged Fallon's line. That decision proved to be worth its weight in gold when it caught the call between Fallon and Duke. Fallon's suicide provided the perfect opportunity to reclaim anything sent to Duke.

"What about Fallon's computer?"

"He destroyed it in his frenzy. I did take the precaution of removing the hard drive, even though it's toast."

"You should have taken the computer."

"It would have been missed, but no one will notice the missing hard drive among all the carnage."

"Do you think Duke opened the file Fallon sent him?"

"No. There's nothing in the temporary files or memory cache to support that. Besides, the file is password protected, and I don't see any evidence that he gave Duke the password."

"Fallon just saved his friend's life."

"I'd like to monitor Duke's phone line for a few days. I don't think he knows anything, but Fallon could have sent him something else."

Lockhart nodded his approval.

Beckerman rose from his seat. He gestured to the computer, laptop and storage media. "What do you want me to do with all this?"

"Dispose of it," Lockhart said. "I think our leaks are plugged."

Beckerman frowned. The frown dulled Lockhart's mood.

"Something else on your mind?"

"We have one other loose end."

"Do we?"

Beckerman nodded. "The 911 caller."

Beckerman was a security specialist. It was his job to see conspiracies everywhere. It was what made him good, but the 911 caller had been on Lockhart's mind too. He had been an unexpected bonus. Chaudhary hadn't left a suicide note behind, but the caller substituted for a suicide note. His anonymous call to the 911 operator gave Chaudhary's death the validation Lockhart needed. A man commits suicide, and an onlooker witnesses it. The cops wouldn't look beyond the supporting facts.

"I can't see this person being much of problem for us."

"He could be. We both know as we press forward, Chaudhary's death will increase in significance, as will the 911 caller's significance. At some point, he'll turn himself in. That makes him a liability. Who knows what Chaudhary told him before he died?"

"So what do you want to do about it?"

"I want to find this guy before anyone else does."

"You have no leads. You'll be stretched too thin, and I don't want any hired help at this point."

"Do you really want to leave this guy out there?"

Lockhart weighed his decision. "No. You're right. Find the caller."

Lockhart's cell rang. Bellis's name came up on the caller ID. An idea came to Lockhart, and he smiled.

"I may have your solution," he said, then answered the phone. "Good morning, Trevor."

"Shane Fallon hanged himself last night," Bellis said.

Beckerman got to his feet to leave, but Lockhart put a hand up to stop him.

Lockhart wandered over to his window. He stared down at the San Francisco streets below. He kept this office in the city. It was nothing showy and had no view of the bay or the Golden Gate. His view looked into the darkened windows of similar, unimpressive buildings. But it didn't matter. The office wasn't supposed to showcase his business. It was where he and Beckerman could work without interference or scrutiny.

"I know. It made the morning news."

"That's the second of my people to die."

"I know. It's tragic when someone so young dies like that. Maybe the pressure of this project is too much. No matter, we must focus on the task at hand."

"Jesus Christ. Listen to yourself. These are people's lives we're talking about."

"Trevor, calm down. Please." Lockhart gave the CEO a moment to compose himself before speaking again. "I'm not oblivious to the tragedy of these men's suicides."

"I'm not so sure that they were."

"What do you mean?" Lockhart's tone was sharp. He wanted it to be. Bellis wouldn't bully him.

Bellis went silent. Nothing but nervous breathing came down the line at Lockhart.

"Come on, Trevor. What do you mean?"

"Fallon and Chaudhary's deaths seem wrong. They weren't suicidal. Everyone says the pressure of work caused them to snap, but that's the problem. The work isn't that difficult. There's a lot to do, but it's not taxing."

"So what are you saying? If the suicides aren't suicides, what are they?" Lockhart cut the sentence short, leaving the obvious conclusion for Bellis to complete.

"You said the work we do is highly sensitive and risky."

"Yes, I did. The technology is highly prized. It's why I haven't been able to divulge the complete purpose of it. You're not the only one who's signed a confidentiality agreement."

Beckerman studied Lockhart, absorbing the one-sided conversation.

"Would someone kill for this technology?"

It sounded like Bellis was trying to take two and two and make an equation of it. Lockhart guessed two deaths would do that to a person.

"It's possible, Trevor, but I doubt very much someone would kill your people."

Beckerman's expression tightened. Lockhart shook his head in a don't-worry-about-it fashion.

"Trevor, the news said someone witnessed Shane's death. Is that right?"

"Yes, Hayden Duke was there. You met him last weekend."

"Yes, I remember Hayden. He seemed like a smart young man. What's his take?"

"Suicide."

"Well, there you have it."

"Yes, but . . ." Bellis trailed off.

"But what? Shane committed suicide. Sundip committed suicide. There were witnesses."

Lockhart made a dramatic pause to allow the information to sink into Bellis's brain. He was a salesman and knew exactly how to close a sale. He used the moment to look out his window and watch a senior citizen look over his shoulder at a hot little number walking the other way. He smiled. The old guy still had a little tiger in his tank.

"We only have the 911 caller's account of Chaudhary's suicide," Bellis said.

Lockhart stared down at his well-manicured fingernails. The index finger on the left hand had dirt underneath and spoiled an otherwise perfect set. He picked up the letter-opener off his desk and cleaned his nail. Bellis made this so easy. Shepherds and sheep populated the world. Naturally, he came from shepherd stock, whereas Bellis's obvious place was amongst the flock. It had hardly been a challenge to guide him down the path he'd wanted him to go. It was a thing of beauty. It truly was.

"Trevor, don't you think that's a little fanciful?"

"No more fanciful than two of my people dying in a week."

"There's an easy way to resolve this."

"Is there? How?"

"Obviously, the person who called in Sundip's death isn't going to come forward no matter how nicely the police ask. Go to the media. Put out an appeal. Ask the person who made the 911 call to come forward. There'll be no police involvement. I'll put up a reward as an incentive. It'll give some closure to Sundip's family."

"Yeah. Sure. Sounds like a good idea."

"Great. You get it underway. I'll have one of my people handle the reward."

"I'll do that. Thank you, James. I'm sorry if I came off a little rough."

"No need to apologize. Death is never easy to accept, especially under these circumstances. I want answers as much as you do," Lockhart said. "I know this is going to sound callous, but our work still lives on. So I have to ask, when I can expect project completion?"

"We're pretty much finished. We're just getting

everything ready for the handover. I would say by the end of the month, to allow for final corrections to be made."

Lockhart could feel his excitement rising. Once he had the designs, manufacturing could start and theory could be put into practice. "Do you think if you made a push I could have the design package by a week from Saturday?"

"It's doable."

"Then tell your people to burn the midnight oil and I'll send a man to get everything then."

Bellis hesitated. "Okay, then I'll make sure that everything is ready for you."

Lockhart smiled. Bellis would be only too willing to wash his hands of their association. The quicker Lockhart had the designs the better. This project had run on long enough. It was about time he brought this stage to an end.

"You're still okay for dinner on Friday, Trevor?"

"Yes."

"Good. Hopefully, we'll have contact from the 911 caller by then and all your problems will be forgotten."

Lockhart hung up and put his cell away.

Beckerman clapped. "Nicely done."

Lockhart took a small bow. "I think our loose end has been taken care of."

CHAPTER FIVE

Rebecca Fallon drove from L.A. to the Bay Area. A flight would have taken no time at all, but she would have had to pretend to be a normal person in front of her fellow passengers and she wasn't up for that. There was privacy in her car. She could cry and scream and curse Shane for killing himself and leaving her alone in this world. It didn't matter if other drivers saw her emotions get the better of her. No one would stop to ask what was wrong or offer help. She drove because it let her mourn.

The call had come in just as she was leaving for work. A Marin Sheriff's detective had broken the news and broken her heart at the same time. Shane had betrayed her. How could he have left her? He was all that was left of their family. In less than a hundred miles, she would drive over the section of I-5 that had claimed both of their parents. No one knew the exact circumstances of the accident. All the witnesses had burned. Evidence suggested that a gasoline tanker had jackknifed after being cut off by an impatient driver. A pickup truck hit the tanker in just the right spot to flip it on its side. The inevitable fireball followed when vehicle after vehicle struck the vulnerable tanker trailer.

Rebecca's parents weren't one of the vehicles to hit

the tanker. They were just one of the nineteen vehicles caught in the subsequent pileup, trapped inside their car as the flames ripped through them.

Jerry and Dee Fallon represented two of the twenty-seven people to die that day. Every child expects to bury their parents, but not as a teenager. Shane, as her big brother, ensured it didn't affect her as much as it could have. He took over as father and mother as well as brother. At that point, the future only existed because Shane made it exist. The sun rose and set because Shane said it would.

"You and me, right?" he'd said after the funeral. "We need each other. This family is as small as it gets, but it's strong. Nothing can break it. Not you. Not me."

"But it can be broken," she said to the memory. "You broke it, Shane."

The section of freeway before Los Banos came up more quickly than she expected. She'd always avoided driving over the spot where her parents had died, and now it was upon her. Time and new asphalt hid the exact spot, but she knew when she'd driven over it. A chill scurried through her and unleashed fresh tears.

She realized how tenuous the sequence of events had been. Her parents had only been on the road that day to spring a surprise visit on Shane at college. If they hadn't been such spontaneous people, they'd still be alive.

Now she was making the same trip her parents had, but for totally different reasons.

Why hadn't she recognized any signs in her brother? In some respects, it was her fault. She had her own life, and she didn't call him as regularly as she used to. Did it matter if they only got together for birthdays or holidays and not "just because"? Maybe. Maybe not. She knew she shouldn't blame herself. She hadn't tied the rope around Shane's neck or given him the nudge he needed to jump. But she hadn't been there to untie it and help him down from the edge either. Right now, she couldn't forgive him for what he had done, but she couldn't forgive herself for what she hadn't done either.

She drove the rest of the journey on autopilot. Neither San Francisco's elegant skyline nor its famous Golden Gate Bridge managed to shake her from thoughts surrounding her brother. She threaded her way through San Rafael to Shane's house and pulled into the driveway.

She had her own key, but she remained behind the wheel with the engine running. She didn't have to go inside. She didn't have to see how her brother lived out his last day. Somebody else could take care of it. But that was a coward's way out. Shane had taken that route. She wouldn't. She switched off the engine, grabbed her luggage from the trunk and let herself in.

She'd failed to prepare for the carnage inside. The detective had told her that Shane had trashed his home, but she hadn't expected this level of devastation. She dropped her bag at the door and rushed into the living room. She scoured the wreckage for the picture frame. She found it, in pieces, the photograph inside punctured but intact. It was a picture of the Fallons taken the Christmas before Jerry and Dee had died. Creased but smiling faces looked up at her. This was the last time she remembered smiling and meaning it. She couldn't see herself smiling again. She dropped the shattered frame on the floor. It was instantly lost among the debris. Just like her family.

The broken picture frame galvanized Rebecca into action. She began restoring order to Shane's chaos. She called the local trash service to make a special pickup for the following day. She bagged up what had been destroyed, then righted furniture that still could be used and rehung clothes in closets. Order would never be restored, but it would be respected.

The plane tickets stopped her. She found a receipt outlining a vacation to the Caribbean between Christmas and New Year. The names on the tickets were hers and his. She'd found her Christmas gift. The realization set her crashing to the floor. She'd been cursing Shane's existence from the moment the call came, but he'd been planning to take her on vacation for Christmas. She looked for a purchase date. Shane had made the reservations two weeks before. Could someone lose his love for life in two weeks? She remembered her parents' deaths and knew someone could. But surely nothing that horrible had happened to Shane.

She pulled out her cell and dialed the detective's number.

"Santiago."

"It's Rebecca Fallon."

The detective's tone softened at the mention her name. "Yes, Ms. Fallon. How can I help you?"

"I'm at Shane's house. I'm going through his things, and I found something strange."

"What is that?"

"Shane booked a vacation two weeks ago."

Santiago didn't respond to her revelation the way she had expected.

"What kind of person books their Christmas vacation then kills himself two weeks later?"

Santiago sighed. "I wish I knew. I've encountered a number of suicides over the years, and I've never managed to find an explanation. All I know is that your brother killed himself."

"Are you sure it wasn't murder?"

"Yes. I have an eyewitness."

Rebecca appreciated Santiago's directness. He could have sugarcoated his answers, but it was the last thing she needed. She needed answers, not coddling.

"Rebecca, I need to be upfront for a moment. As I mentioned in my call this morning, it appears Shane was under the influence of narcotics."

"My brother wasn't a junkie."

"I didn't say he was. It could be a one-time thing. Maybe he had a bad reaction to the drug. Some drugs act as depressants. That might explain Shane's behavior. Look, at the moment, drugs are only a suspicion. We won't know one way or the other until the tox screen is complete."

"Hayden Duke is your eyewitness, right?"

"Yes. You know him?"

She remembered how kind and supportive he'd been when her parents died. He'd been the glue that kept Shane together when he needed to be strong. She took comfort from the knowledge that Hayden had been there when Shane had died. No one deserved to die alone.

"Yes, I know him. Hayden is my brother's friend from college. Did he say Shane was high?"

"Yes, he did."

The answer felt like betrayal. "Did he see him take drugs?"

"No, I don't believe so."

"Did you find any at his house?"

"No."

"Then all you have is Hayden's account of the truth."

Santiago pounced on her remark. "Is there some reason to doubt Hayden's account?"

Was there? She hadn't realized what she'd said until she'd said it. It wasn't a conscious remark. She'd just been in a hurry to dispel the taint of drugs. But was she on to something? Could Hayden have been involved? Could he have even supplied Shane with the drugs that night?

What was she thinking? Hayden was a good guy. She tried to dislodge her disparaging remarks, but couldn't. She didn't know what to think. Santiago was trying to prepare her for the possibility that Shane had taken drugs. Shane never touched drugs, but if the tox screen proved otherwise, then everything she believed was a lie. It just seemed wrong.

"Ms. Fallon?" Santiago prompted.

"I don't think there's any reason to doubt Hayden's account."

"If you don't mind me saying, that doesn't sound like an emphatic no."

No, it doesn't, she thought. "All I'm saying is that I wasn't there. You weren't there. All we have is Hayden's account."

"I know."

She had questions that Santiago couldn't answer. She needed to talk to someone who could.

"Do you have a phone number for Hayden?"

"Yes, I do," Santiago said.

Rebecca wrote the number he gave her on the palm of her hand.

"He doesn't have to talk to you if he chooses not to."

"I know that, Detective Santiago, but he'll talk to me."

Hayden returned home after punishing his credit card on a shopping trip to replace everything that had been stolen or broken. He carried a replacement PC from his garage into the kitchen and stepped into a show home. Someone had gone through his recently burgled house and turned it into a home again. The good Samaritan's identity was pinned to the fridge door by a Hello Kitty fridge magnet.

> Hayden,
>   I tidied up. I've put the spare key in the kitchen drawer. Don't worry, I've made a copy for myself. I'm sorry about Shane. Call me.
>
>   Love,
>   Mom

Hayden put the box down and inspected his home. Everything was in apple-pie order and had been "mom" cleaned. She'd done this in a couple of hours. He couldn't have gotten his place in this good of shape if he'd taken all day.

The act of kindness didn't come without its drawback. No matter his age and what he did with his life, his mom still viewed him as her little boy. And this little boy just proved he couldn't keep burglars out of his world. No doubt there'd be a maternal probation period during which he'd have to endure impromptu visits to discuss real-estate opportunities elsewhere or home security systems. Hayden picked up the phone in the kitchen and pressed the speed dial.

"Hey, Dad."

"I'll get her for you," John Duke said. He knew his father was smiling.

Hayden's mom came to the phone.

"Yes, Mom. I'm looking at it now. It's wonderful. Thanks."

After five minutes of thanking his mom and making her feel good, he found that he'd agreed to go over for dinner. It was just as easy to cook for three as it was for two was the crux of her reasoning. She nailed the deal with her closing argument: no one wants to eat alone after such a traumatic event.

"Okay, Mom. I'll be over later. Now about that spare key . . ."

After his call, he unloaded the rest of his purchases, opened boxes, then set up his new computers. He needed to get back to work. People had expectations. MDE still needed the drawings revised. It was all good, practical thought, and it prevented him from thinking about Shane. He wouldn't be able to distract himself forever, but tonight he could. He switched off his new laptop and headed for the garage.

The phone rang when he reached the kitchen. He expected it was his mom wanting to know when he was coming.

"Hayden, it's Rebecca Fallon. Shane's sister. We met a long time ago."

She'd substituted a long time ago for her parents' funeral. Hayden couldn't blame her. It seemed that a death in her family kept bringing them together. It looked as if he wouldn't be blocking Shane out tonight.

"I wondered if I could talk to you about Shane?"

"Sure. No problem."

"I hope you don't mind me calling you. The Marin Sheriff's Office gave me your number."

"Of course not."

"What can you tell me about what happened?"

This wouldn't be a short call. Hayden dragged a stool over from the kitchen counter and sat. What could he tell her? He'd been there, but he didn't understand any of it. And what should he tell her? Hit her with it all or just the "edited-for-TV" version? Neither appealed.

"Maybe you should talk to the sheriffs," he said.

"I have, but you were there. You were his friend. I'd rather hear it from someone who knew him."

There was no dodging her. She wanted the truth and deserved it.

"You probably won't like what I have to say."

"I know."

He led her through events from his call to Shane to Shane's suicide. She was silent for a long time after he'd finished explaining. He thought he heard crying from her end of the line. He just gave her time to take in the information.

"You told the detectives that Shane was high," Rebecca said.

"That was how he seemed."

"Where'd he get the drugs? From you?"

The question stung with the intensity of a slap. How could Rebecca even think that? But he didn't have to look far for an answer. She'd talked to Santiago. He'd planted the idea in her head. At least it revealed exactly where Santiago placed him in this puzzle.

"No, Rebecca. He didn't get the drugs from me, and you know better than to even think it. You know me."

"Really? Shane never took drugs. The cops didn't find any in his possession or back at the house."

"This is ridiculous. You don't know what you're talking about."

"Don't I? There's something seriously wrong with Shane's death. He'd just booked a trip to the Caribbean. He had no history of drugs. And suddenly, after you come back into his life, he kills himself in a drug-intoxicated stupor. I find that extremely strange, and I want to know what you're hiding."

That was it. He'd been doing his best to be compassionate to Rebecca. She had just lost her remaining relative. He tried to be cognizant of that, but he'd had enough. He jumped to his feet, sending the stool tumbling on its side.

"I've been trying to protect Shane's reputation. That's what I've been hiding."

His remark extinguished the flames on both ends of the phone line. Stunned silence came from Rebecca's end. Finally, he'd gotten it off his chest. He'd admitted to the deception that was getting him into trouble.

"What are you talking about?" Rebecca had lost her accusing tone.

"The reason I called Shane that night wasn't about the job I was working on for him, but an e-mail he'd sent me."

"An e-mail?"

"Yes. He sent this weird e-mail with an attachment, telling me to keep it safe, but not to open it. I called him to ask about it. He tried to brush me off and told me to delete the file and forget all about it, but I couldn't."

"Did you think he was suicidal?"

"No. He sounded cagey, but not suicidal. He was high by the time I reached his house."

"Oh, God," Rebecca said exhaling. "Have you opened the file?"

"Not yet. My house was robbed this morning. My computers were stolen."

"So, the file is gone."

"No, I backed it up. I just haven't opened it yet."

"Can you open it now?"

His mom would be pacing by now, but it couldn't be helped. She'd have to wait. "Sure. I can call you back when I've got the computer up."

"No, I'll wait."

He detected impatience, not mistrust in her voice. He hoped he'd won her over. With Santiago circling him, he'd need a friend.

He picked up the phone extension in his office and booted up his new computer. As he accessed his online storage account, it occurred to him that Shane's *document1* file may be nothing more than a suicide note. It would explain his instructions not to open it. But as much as a simple suicide note would box up Shane's death with a nice, neat bow, he guessed *document1* was something else. Why send him a suicide note? Surely he'd send the suicide note to Rebecca, not him.

"Okay, I've got the file. Do you want me to open it?"

"Why wouldn't I?"

"Shane asked me not to. Neither of us may like what it says."

Rebecca was silent for a second. "No, I want to see it."

Hayden double clicked on the file name before he could change his mind.

The file didn't open. Instead, a dialog box asked for a password.

"Shit."

"What is it?"

"Shane password protected the file. Got any ideas on what it could be?"

She sighed. "No."

"Let's start with the obvious then."

Between the two of them, they came up with family names, nicknames, pet's names, places, stupid phrases Shane said all the time and significant dates, which included the date Rebecca's parents died. What made the process difficult was the length of the password. They had no way of knowing whether it was four characters or forty. Hayden jotted down every harebrained idea they had. He punched in password after password and every one came back with the same response—incorrect.

"Why send you a password-protected file without the password?" Rebecca said.

"Because I wasn't supposed to be the one to open it."

"What do we do now?"

We. She thought of them as we. It looked as if she'd stopped seeing him as an enemy.

"I can see if I can get someone to hack it."

"I'm here at Shane's," Rebecca said. "Do you think the password could be among his things here?"

"I don't see why not."

"If I find something, I'll call back."

They made arrangements to meet up. She had Shane's funeral to plan and she asked for his help. With no family left, she needed someone to lean on. He didn't hesitate to agree. It was the least he could do.

He went to hang up, but she stopped him.

"I need to ask you something. Do you think Shane killed himself?"

"Yes. There's no doubt, but something drove him to it. Something sudden."

Rebecca didn't say anything. She just hung up.

Hayden stared at the screen. It still displayed the incorrect password box. The answer to Shane's death was wrapped up in this file. He knew it.

CHAPTER SIX

Santiago parked in the parking lot of the Mountain Vista funeral home and went inside. Marin County didn't have an official coroner's office with a morgue. It ran a virtual office. A chief coroner worked out of the county office, while his coroner investigators worked out of a number of funeral homes around the county. A funeral director appeared, saw it was Santiago, waved and returned to his office. Santiago was a familiar face to everyone at Mountain Vista. It was something that didn't bring him a lot of comfort in the middle of the night.

He found Richard Dysart in the small office outside the autopsy theater. Dysart looked up from his computer and smiled.

"Hey, Santi, you got my message."

His wife called him Santi. Dysart overheard her call him that at a restaurant once and the *culero* called him it every time they met. "Don't call me Santi."

Dysart stifled a grin, trying to look contrite, and flashed a Boy Scout salute. "It won't happen again."

It was a lie, but Santiago let it go. Dysart didn't take anything seriously, except for his job. Santiago put the tomfoolery down to his unpleasant career choice. The jokes kept Dysart from slashing his wrists with a bone saw. Although, Santiago wasn't entirely convinced Dysart wouldn't be a wiseass regardless of his occupation.

"I assume your summons has to do with Shane Fallon."

"Not so fast, muchacho."

"Leave the Spanish for Cancun, Dick."

Dysart raised his hands in surrender. "Whatever you say, Santi."

"I have a gun." Santiago slid back his sport jacket for Dysart to see. "You know that, don't you?"

"Okay, okay," Dysart said. He failed to contain a smile and held out two files to Santiago. "Ruben, you're getting far too uptight for a Mexican."

Santiago ignored the comment and took the files. He read the names on the files—Shane Fallon and Sundip Chaudhary. The names failed to inspire any excitement.

"My suicides, what about them?"

Dysart frowned. "I can see I'm going to be the one to do all the heavy lifting here."

The coroner snatched the files back from Santiago and flicked through the contents. "You wouldn't think it to look at them, but your two suicides are related. If it wasn't for my supreme talent and keen eye, I would have missed it. Chaudhary was remarkably well-preserved for someone who'd bobbed around in the Pacific for as long as he had, but even so, he made it a challenge."

Santiago wrinkled his nose. Dysart's assessment of well-preserved usually differed wildly from the rest of the world's. He'd seen bodies come out of the ocean before and tried to blot out the image forming in his mind.

"Are you going to impress me anytime soon?" Santiago asked, trying to ignore the odor of embalming fluid in the air.

Dysart jerked a photograph from each of the files and handed them to Santiago. "I thought these would be of interest to you."

The first shot was of Shane Fallon's inside left fore-arm. His skin almost shone white in the overexposed shot. What didn't shine was an untidy, rectangular-shaped bruise located two inches from his wrist. The bruise measured around an inch by half an inch. The second shot was of the right side of Chaudhary's neck. The shot captured Chaudhary's ear, hairline and partial profile. Santiago focused on the bruise and not the damage the sea had done to the Indian's face. Decomposition and Chaudhary's darker skin tone disguised a rectangular bruise on the side of his neck. It was identical in shape and size to the one on Fallon. The discovery stilled Santiago, and he no longer smelled the stench of formaldehyde in the air.

"What is it?" he asked.

"Besides a bruise?"

"Yeah."

"Don't know."

"*Pendejo.*"

"Don't get pissy. I found something interesting. It's not my job to investigate. It's yours."

"Any ideas? You're supposed to be superior to us lesser mortals."

"The bruises are recent. No discoloration. I'd say they picked them up hours before their deaths. Obviously, these guys connected with the same object to get these bruises. There may be something in that for you."

"Are you suggesting something wrongful about their deaths?"

Dysart shook his head. "I'm just offering it up for its weird factor. There's a possible connection. The bruises tie these guys together, but they didn't kill them. Besides, as you know, they're suicides."

Santiago didn't say anything. Gears were turning.

"They are, aren't they? You have witnesses."

"So it seems." Santiago needed time to think this development through. "Fallon was supposed to have been doped up. Find anything to support that?"

"Tough to say. He didn't shoot it, snort it or swallow it. There aren't any puncture marks. I checked all the junkie's usual locations, even between the toes—nothing. Nose linings are clean. So is the throat. If he got high, I don't know how he did it."

"How long before I can get the tox report?"

"A couple of days. I got a rush put on them. You need to know it cost me a couple of Giants tickets."

"Your sacrifice has been noted."

"It better be. I don't know why you're going the extra mile on these suicides."

Dysart was getting ready to blow hard and long about the shortcomings of his position. Santiago wasn't in the mood to hear it, and he didn't have to, thanks to the incoming call on his cell. Rice's name appeared on the display.

"What have you got for me?" he asked.

"A big surprise. You ready for it?"

Santiago let his silence warn the deputy not to waste time.

"Have you checked in with Marin Design Engineering yet?"

"On my way there next."

"You may want to ask them about Sundip Chaudhary, seeing as he and Shane Fallon were coworkers."

The world had just gotten decidedly more complicated. Santiago didn't see that as a problem. People who complicated matters made mistakes. Two suicides were one such mistake. Sure, two people from the same firm could kill themselves days apart from each other. Both men had claimed to be guilty of something unforgivable. A suicide pact seemed logical. The problem with suicide pacts was someone always backed out. He just needed to find out who'd backed out of this one for everything to make sense.

Santiago gave Rice his orders and hung up on him.

"You're grinning, Santi, and you don't grin. Well, not here you don't."

"You asked me about a tie between these two guys. How does the idea of coworkers strike you?"

Dysart grinned, but it only lasted a second. Santiago enjoyed removing it.

"Say good-bye to another pair of Giants tickets. I want a tox report on Chaudhary, stat. It would be nice to have it at the same time as Fallon's."

Santiago left Dysart to his bitching and drove over to Marin Design Engineering. He'd contacted MDE's CEO, Trevor Bellis, and warned him that he'd be dropping by, but he hadn't made an appointment. He didn't want to give Bellis the opportunity to be "out on business" when he arrived. On the drive over, Santiago called to see if Bellis was in and got the answer that he was. He hung up without leaving his name. He pulled up outside MDE's offices fifteen minutes later.

He entered MDE's reception area. Framed photographs of Sundip Chaudhary and Shane Fallon hung on a wall. Above the photos hung a plaque with the inscription, *In memoriam*. MDE knew about the connection. It was a shame no one had seen fit to inform him.

He checked in with the receptionist. His badge surprised her, and he tried a smile to allay her concern. She called Bellis and after a five-minute wait, Trevor Bellis introduced himself, looking suitably solemn. He showed Santiago to his office on the second floor. It was well-appointed with the latest office furniture picked out of the Office World catalog.

Bellis gestured to a chair. "Take a seat, Detective."

"Thank you, sir," Santiago said, and sat down.

"I suppose you're here about Sundip and Shane."

"Yes. I am."

Bellis shook his head. "I can't believe they both committed suicide."

"It's tragic. People rarely see the warning signs until it's too late."

Santiago itched to hit Bellis with the tougher questions, but he needed to settle him down first and win his trust. He didn't need the guy being defensive, so he warmed Bellis up with a few background questions.

"Work can drive people to suicide. Is it particularly stressful here?"

"There's pressure. MDE is in demand. We work long hours, nights and weekends, but I would hate to think the work pushed them over the edge."

"As you probably know, Shane Fallon is believed to have taken his life under the influence of drugs."

"But you don't know for sure."

Bellis appeared to be gearing up to unleash a holier-than-thou speech about the drug-free culture among his employees. Santiago decided to cut it off at the ankles with a little lie. "We don't know the drug he took, but we have evidence to back up the claim."

From Bellis's expression, Santiago had just popped his balloon. Good. With the barrier removed, he could dig deep.

"I was wondering if you ever suspected Shane of drug use."

"No, of course not. We have zero tolerance here for that sort of thing."

"Do you do random drug screening?"

"We screen before employment, but not afterward. Not without foundation, that is."

"And you had no foundation?"

"No."

Santiago nodded. "I see. Would anyone else know if Shane used drugs?"

"Possibly. You would have to ask them."

"Could I?"

"Of course. I've warned my staff of your arrival, and you will have their full cooperation."

Warned. Santiago chewed the word over in his head. It was an odd choice of word. Inform, yes, but warn? You warned people against trouble. So was he trouble? He let the Freudian slip go, but kept it warm for use at a later time.

"I'm guessing you pay very well."

The question threw Bellis for a second. "What makes you say that?"

"Your parking lot has some very nice vehicles in it."

Bellis colored slightly. "Well, yes, we do pay very well. But I pay for the best. What's your point?"

"Only that Mr. Fallon had the disposable income to support a habit."

Bellis snorted. "So does Bill Gates—does that mean he's a crackhead?"

"Well, no."

"Just because I pay good salaries doesn't mean it's to support thousand-dollar-a-week drug habits," Bellis continued angrily.

Bellis seemed genuinely inflamed by any suggestion that his employees were embroiled in a drug scandal. It was understandable, Santiago supposed. Scandal wasn't good for anyone's business.

"I'm sorry, sir. I didn't mean to offend," Santiago said insincerely. He decided to shift the questioning. Now that Chaudhary and Fallon's deaths were connected, it opened up a whole new line of questioning. "Did Sundip and Shane work together?"

"Yes. We're all working on the same project."

"Were they close? More than just colleagues, I mean."

"Not especially so."

"They didn't hang out or anything?"

"No, why?"

"Both men died professing guilt over something they'd done. They knew each other. Worked together. Whatever they did, I'm guessing it originated here. Wouldn't you agree?"

Bellis paled. "Not really. They knew each other through MDE, but any wrongdoings would have occurred somewhere else."

Santiago had kept the photographs Dysart had shown him of the rectangular bruises. He removed them from an envelope and slid them across Bellis's desk. Bellis stared at the images, but made no attempt to touch them. The sight of autopsy shots of people you knew did that to a person. Santiago inched them closer to him.

"You see these rectangular bruises? I was wondering if there's any object here that could have caused them."

Bellis shook his head without taking his gaze from the photos.

"You wouldn't have any problem with me looking around?"

Bellis shook his head again.

Santiago had shocked Bellis enough, and he reclaimed the photos. He slipped them back into the envelope.

"What do you do here? I've never been clear on what it is."

The question refocused Bellis. "We're a design house. Clients come to us with a problem that needs solving. We provide the solution."

"You must have a diverse group of employees."

"Yes and no. I have a core team backed up by contract staff to cover specialties. Although Sundip had worked for us for years, he was a contractor."

That explained why Chaudhary's employment record didn't list MDE as his employer.

"And Hayden Duke?"

"He's a recent contract hire. Shane recommended him."

"How recent?"

"A week or so."

"Before or after Sundip's death?"

Bellis fidgeted in his seat. "After."

"I wonder if I could talk to Shane and Sundip's colleagues now and maybe see the building?" Santiago flashed the envelope to remind Bellis about the search for the source of the unusual bruise.

"Yes, I'll take you to them." Bellis got to his feet and came around his desk to show Santiago the way.

Santiago got up to join Bellis, but Bellis surprised him by blocking his path.

"Detective Santiago, you worry me. I get the feeling that you suspect my company of having some connection to Shane and Sundip's deaths. It doesn't. Is that clear?"

Santiago had ruffled Bellis's feathers. Good. He liked ruffling feathers. It usually meant something.

"Are you withdrawing your cooperation, Mr. Bellis?"

"No. Just the opposite. As of today, I've made a public appeal offering a reward to get the person who called in Sundip's suicide to come forward. That is something your department has failed to achieve."

Yes, he'd definitely ruffled the CEO's feathers.

CHAPTER SEVEN

The motherfucker was late. The situation stank. *Reward, my ass,* Vee8 thought.

He'd been keeping up with the news since Chaudhary had offed himself to see if the cops had linked him and his crew to the Indian's death. They hadn't. They hadn't even pieced together that he'd stolen the car. Their prevailing theory was Chaudhary had gotten caught up in a fender bender with Mr. Law-Abiding Citizen, who'd driven off when Chaudhary walked into the ocean. Christ. Cops. No wonder they'd never caught him.

Just as he thought the heat was off, he'd caught the appeal on the radio. Chaudhary's employers were interested in talking to the driver who'd called 911, and they were offering a reward for any information. No questions asked. No police involvement.

He hadn't known what to do at first. This could be a sting op on behalf of the cops, but it didn't read that way. Besides, that was entrapment or some such bullshit that would have the shittiest of lawyers springing him from lockup before he'd have to take his first piss in a stainless-steel john.

So he'd called. He talked to the boss man of Marin Design Engineering. He didn't sound like a cop—far too clueless—so he stayed on the line. By the sounds of it, he wasn't the only one to call in. The leeches out there in Shitville had tried for a slice of the action. He was required to answer a bunch of questions. Obviously, he'd answered right because they wanted him to come in to talk.

Yeah. Like he had loser written on his forehead. Precautions were necessary. And a little sumthin', sumthin' for his trouble.

"Not so fast, Mr. Bellis. We need to discuss a few details."

"Like what?"

"How much green for my assistance?"

"It depends on if the information is valuable."

Bellis was a shitty poker player. He paused for effect, but he answered too fast and without objection. This cow was for the milking. Vee8 guessed there was a grand in it for him. He'd have to split it with Donkey and the boys, but they'd be busting a nut for a hundred.

"My information will be valuable."

"Could you come in at six tonight?"

"Nah, nah, nah. It don't work that way. You meet me. You want something from me, you come to me."

"Okay. Where?"

"Where" was Broadway and Sixteenth in Oakland. He wanted this discussion in the open and somewhere he knew. If the meet went sideways, he wanted escape routes. He also wanted a witness and backup. Donkey had his back. He was a block away on the roof of a shitty apartment building with a camera. Vee8 nodded up at him. He got a black power fist salute in reply.

He'd moved the time back to nine to move Bellis out of his comfort zone. Broadway was a ghost town at that time of night. Bellis would have the jitters. Good. The money would come quicker if his mind was on leaving as soon as possible. But it was Vee8 with the jitters. It was 9:30. He felt the gaze of unseen eyes burning into him. He smelled setup. Cops had the place sealed off. He was screwed. They didn't have shit on him, but that wasn't the point. He wasn't in their system. He would be if they lifted him now. All that went to the wall if he walked. Pick up BART and go home.

A midnight-blue Dodge Charger ground to an elegant halt in front of him. It was one of the new breed, not one of the classics. It was nice enough, but the idea of a Charger with four doors seemed wrong to Vee8.

The passenger window slid down with an electronic burr. The driver leaned across the passenger seat. "Vee8?"

"Yeah," Vee8 answered, but he didn't approach the driver. He hadn't met Bellis, but this guy wasn't him. The prick looked like a cop for a start and one who hit the gym instead of the donuts. Bellis's voice had shaken during their talk on the phone, but not this guy's. He was confident.

"Get in the car."

"You ain't Bellis."

"No. He sent me."

"And who are you?"

"No one to get spooked over."

Like shit, Vee8 thought. "You a cop? If you are and you lie, you've got nothing."

"I'm not a cop. I work for Mr. Bellis. I've got your money. I just need to know what you saw."

A grand sounded good, but not that good. Bellis had crossed him. Fuck him, then. Vee8 walked away from the Dodge, toward Sixteenth and the BART station.

The Dodge man jumped on the gas and rolled down the street with him. "Hey, what's the problem here?"

"You, motherfucker," Vee8 answered without stopping. "I expected Bellis because Bellis told me he was coming. I don't like liars."

"Okay, okay, he should have told you, but it doesn't

change anything. We need your information, and we'll pay for it."

Vee8 kept on walking. He liked making this prick squirm. Muscles didn't equal brains. Work, dumb motherfucker, work.

"Look, I'll give you two hundred bucks now. Even if you don't have anything that helps, that's yours for coming out tonight. Is that enough of an apology for you?"

Vee8 stopped. "No. Two hundred isn't enough. Make it five and you're forgiven."

The Dodge man stopped. He snorted and shook his head before pulling out his wallet. He removed the five one-hundred-dollar bills and held them out to Vee8.

Five hundred for just talking. How much were these bitches going to pay him? Chaudhary had to have been into something. He remembered the Indian's jumble of words as he walked into the water. Something about doing something so terrible he couldn't be forgiven. Vee8 almost smiled thinking about how much he was going to take this son of a bitch for.

He reached through the open window to the take the cash. The Dodge man didn't release his grip on the money.

"So, you do know something then?"

"I know plenty, so lose the attitude."

The Dodge man still didn't release his grip on the money.

"This is beginning to look a little queer."

"Get in."

"Nah, dude. We talk in the open."

"You want this money, you get in the car."

He glanced over at Donkey on the rooftop. He still had his back covered. Donkey had a car stashed on Fifteenth. He'd be all over this prick before he'd gotten two blocks.

"You win, tough guy," Vee8 said and got into the car.

He took the cash, but before he could pocket it, the Dodge man wound the Charger's engine up. "Hey, where we going?"

"Somewhere we can talk without drawing flies."

Vee8 glanced into the door mirror on his side for Donkey. He didn't see him. Fantastic. The douche bag had fallen at the first fence. Well, if the son of a bitch didn't have his back, then he didn't get a cut.

He looked over at the Dodge man. He didn't like him. Didn't trust him. His jitters intensified, but he took comfort from the switchblade in his sock.

"So what's the deal with this Chaudhary guy?" he asked to take the edge off.

"He was very special to the organization. That makes you special to the organization, seeing as you were last to see him alive. So you want to tell me about what happened that night?"

The Dodge man stayed on Broadway and picked up 880 toward Alameda. The guy knew how to drive and he wasn't frightened to show it. Vee8 wondered if this was for his benefit. Either way, the sound of the six-cylinder working hard relaxed him.

"I jacked a 5-series out of El Cerrito, and it was time to ditch it. I was heading somewhere quiet when your man, Chaudhary, came out of nowhere and T-boned us."

"Us?"

Fuck, he cursed himself. "Yeah, I was with my crew, but fuck them, I was driving."

The Dodge man said nothing.

"Okay, I didn't know he was on a mission, and I chased him. He'd fucked up my night, and I was going to teach him some manners."

"And you picked him up on the beach."

"Yeah. By the time we got down to him, he was ankle deep in the sea."

"Ocean."

"What?"

"He walked into the ocean, not the sea."

"Who the fuck cares?"

"I do. I require accuracy."

What a prick, Vee8 thought. He'd better not short him on his money. "Okay, ocean."

"Did you hit him, hurt him in any way?"

Vee8 dropped the bravado. Seeing Chaudhary kill himself like that gave him no pleasure. He hadn't boasted to anyone about it. He and his crew hadn't mentioned it after that night. Seeing someone getting fucked up, even dying on the street was one thing, but Chaudhary was another. There was something creepy in that robotic nature of his when he strode out into the water. Vee8 wouldn't forget it for as long as he lived.

"No, I didn't hurt him. The guy was in his own world of hurt. I tried to talk him out of it, but he was beyond help."

"You let him kill himself."

Vee8 turned to the Dodge man. "Hey, fuck you. You weren't there. That guy wanted to die. If I tried to stop him, he was taking me with him."

"Okay. Take it easy. What did he say? Word for word."

It took no effort to remember Chaudhary's final words. "He said he'd done a terrible thing and he couldn't be forgiven for it. He had to pay and drowning himself was the only way out."

"Did he say what it was or why he couldn't be forgiven?"

Vee8 shook his head. "Whatever it was, I believed him. It broke him, and there was no turning back in his mind."

The Dodge man glanced over at Vee8. "He said nothing else? Gave no explanation?"

"That's it, man. We didn't get into a major dialogue. I ain't a therapist."

The Dodge man nodded, satisfied.

"Can I get my money now?"

"Yeah, sure. Another five hundred okay?"

"Eight would be better."

Vee8 grinned when the Dodge man didn't object.

The Dodge man reached inside his jacket and a black-jack came out instead of his wallet. He smashed it across the bridge of Vee8's nose. Blinding light filled his vision and seared clear though into his brain. He didn't see the second blow behind his left ear coming or the third, which put him out cold.

The *chug-chug-chug* of a diesel engine vibrating against Vee8's skull brought him around. The engine throbbed in time with his skull. The boat's pitch and roll turned his stomach. He sucked in air to clear his head and get his bearings. The Bay Bridge stood off the stern drifting farther away. Headlights glinted from vehicles racing across the double-decker bridge in both directions. He was aboard a small boat, the kind that took tourists out on the bay. He lay on his side on its fiberglass deck, his wrists bound behind him and his ankles shackled together with chains. A length of chain had been looped through his ankle shackles and padlocked in place. The other end of the chain was connected to two steel truck rims sitting on the end of the stern. Realization turned to panic, and he thrashed to get himself free.

"Hey, take it easy," the Dodge man said. "You keep that shit up, you're going to send those wheels over the side and its over for you."

"What's it matter? You're going to drown me anyway, you fuck."

The Dodge man tied the wheel off and came over to Vee8's prone position. He knelt at Vee8's side and smiled. "Don't upset yourself. You're misreading the situation."

"What am I fucking missing?" Vee8 squirmed on the deck.

"Consider this an incentive program. I need answers. You give them to me, and all is well. Tell me the wrong ones . . ." He let the alternative hang in the night air. "And you'll find out how deep the bay really is."

"People know I'm missing."

The Dodge man frowned and pushed himself to his feet. He looked about, taking in the night, before driving his foot into Vee8's kidneys. Vee8 yelled and rolled over in pain.

"Don't try to intimidate me," the Dodge man said coolly. "It wastes my time."

Vee8 nodded, but he'd be fucked if he'd apologize. He hoped Donkey had gotten the Charger's license plate or better still, caught up with them and was standing next to this prick's Dodge.

"What's your name?" the Dodge man asked. "Your real name. The one your parents saw fit to give you and you pissed all over. Vee8. Christ, couldn't you have been original?"

"Tim Devane." He ground the words out.

"And where do you live, Tim Devane?"

Vee8 told him.

The Dodge man followed up with a bunch of other questions that included his Social Security number. None of the questions filled him with hope.

"Why do you need to know all this?"

"Because if you're lying, I'm going to find you. Now, what you told me earlier—Memorex or bullshit?"

"It was the truth, I swear."

The Dodge man smirked. "You swear. For a godless piece of shit like you, that really adds weight."

"Fuck you."

"Yeah, yeah, sticks and stones. You said you and your crew witnessed Chaudhary kill himself."

"Yeah."

"I want their names."

"You don't need their names."

The Dodge man put his heel against the rims and shoved. They shifted an inch toward the water.

"Okay, okay, I'll give you their names."

"I thought you might."

With a bitter taste on his tongue, he gave the Dodge man Donkey's, D.J.'s and Trey's names and addresses. The Dodge man wrote the information on a pad and pocketed the notebook.

"Happy now? Got what you wanted?" Vee8 knew to keep his temper in check, but there was only so much bullshit he was going to swallow.

"Just one more question."

He knelt by Vee8's side. He reached into his jacket pocket and pulled out a digital camera. Vee8 recognized the camera and turned cold from the inside out.

The Dodge man fiddled with the camera and showed Vee8 a digital image on the camera's view screen. Vee8 closed his eyes to block out the image of Donkey, his neck swiveled around at an unnatural angle and his eyes open in a dead stare. He knew it was over for him at that point. Tonight was his last on earth. He wasn't cool with it, but he wasn't pissing his pants either.

"Who's this?" the Dodge man asked. "Donkey? D.J.? Trey?"

"Donkey," he whispered. "You aren't going to let me go, are you?"

The Dodge man erased the images on the camera and tossed it overboard. He sniffed before answering. "No. This is where we part company."

The Dodge man hoisted Vee8 into a sitting position. He was careful to avoid getting within head-butting or kicking range. He sat Vee8 on the edge of the stern next to the rims.

"You ready for this?" the Dodge man asked.

Vee8 didn't answer. It was easy to play the tough guy

when you were on top. He read the Dodge man. He'd pussy out when his time came. He'd go kicking and screaming. Vee8's only regret was he wouldn't be there to see it.

"Don't clam up now."

"Fuck you."

"Look, I have something of yours I'd like to give back." He pulled out Vee8's switchblade, snapped out the blade and rammed in into Vee8's gut.

Vee8 felt an explosion of pain, but didn't actually feel the blade's intrusion until the Dodge man jerked it out and tossed it overboard.

"A little ventilation for bodily gases. I don't want you floating to the surface."

"Don't you want your money back?"

"Nah, you've earned it."

The Dodge man lifted the rims and heaved them over the side. They punched a hole in the water with their steel fist. The chain scurried after them, dragging against the gunnels. It took only a few seconds before Vee8 was jerked overboard. Reflexively, he held his breath as he struck the water. It was a futile gesture. As futile as the question he'd wanted to ask. Why? What made Chaudhary so important that he and his crew deserved this end? It was the question that left his mouth as the water rushed in.

CHAPTER EIGHT

"Gillis?" Hayden asked.

"Yeah," a cautious-sounding voice answered.

"Hayden Duke. Your friend Lee told you about me."

Gillis's tone eased up a couple of clicks. "Yeah, yeah. You've got a nut that needs cracking. Well, I'm your man."

Beckerman pushed his dinner aside to give this call his full attention. He'd been listening in to all Hayden's calls for the last few days just as a precaution. He'd caught some chatter, but nothing significant. A couple of calls between Hayden and his parents, and a couple to Rebecca Fallon. He detected an undercurrent between those two. He'd been a little slow arranging phone taps, and he felt he'd missed a significant call between them. He didn't let it worry him too much. He'd find out eventually. But Hayden and Rebecca weren't as important as Hayden and Gillis right now. He took a seat in front of the bank of surveillance equipment.

"Don't play coy," Beckerman said to his laptop monitoring the call. "Tell me something."

He sat alone in Lockhart's San Francisco office. This was his command center and home for the duration of the operation. He'd been living out of the office since

Chaudhary went rogue on Lockhart. He looked forward to when he could return to the secluded comfort of his Oregon home. There he could hunt and fish without the interference of the human race. He liked his life, not its people and their baggage. Live clean, live happy was his motto. He pushed his thoughts away from his home life. He couldn't do his job with one eye on other things.

"You think you can crack the password protection?" Hayden asked.

"It's what I do."

Beckerman didn't like what he'd just heard. Was Hayden talking about the file Fallon had sent him? How did he still have a copy? Beckerman thought he'd taken care of it. Lockhart would be pissed when he reported this development.

"Can I bring it over now?" Hayden asked.

"I'm in the middle of something. Make it nine."

"Where?"

Gillis recited an address in Davis, and Beckerman wrote it down at the same time Hayden did.

"I'll be there," Hayden said and hung up.

Beckerman pocketed the address and thanked his good luck. With Hayden in Fairfield and him in San Francisco, Hayden had a fifty-mile head start on him to Davis, but Gillis's delay put things in Beckerman's favor. It was 7:10. That gave him less than two hours to put something together. Tough, but doable if he left now.

He picked up his Dodge from the parking garage. He brought nothing with him. Everything he needed was in the trunk. Tools. Weapons. The lot. Batman had his utility belt. He had his trunk.

Lockhart paid well, but Beckerman wasn't in it for the money. He was in it for the work. The military had trained him to be a guardian and an assassin, a saver of lives and a taker of lives. He enjoyed the skills necessary to complete his assignments, but he was at a loss when the military rotated him out with full honors. He knew some who resented the military for doing this to them. They felt it was a betrayal of a soldier's sacrifice. He didn't. It was just procedure. He had reached retirement age, and it was his time to go. He understood that. Respected that. A military machine needed fresh parts to operate at its optimum. He knew he still had a lot to offer, and if the military couldn't use him, someone else could. Of course he could have made the move to law enforcement or private security, but it wasn't for him. It wouldn't give him the opportunities Lockhart gave him. He liked being part of a machine again. He lived for it.

He slipped through the city to pick up the Bay Bridge. He hoped he wouldn't have to kill two nights in a row. Killing was something he did and did well, but not something he derived pleasure from. Killing Vee8 and his crew last night in the manner he did was a means to an end. Lockhart had charged him with an objective. He was only meeting it. The next couple of hours would determine whether he would kill tonight.

He pulled off the freeway at Davis, drove through the downtown area and across the railroad tracks before parking a block over from Gillis's place. Gillis lived in a shabby two-story place on a corner lot. The corner location gave Beckerman a choice of entry points. It was dark, and that made things even easier. Street lighting was poor. The corner streetlight effectively illuminated itself and little else. It wasn't late, but foot traffic was nonexistent.

He left his vehicle with the only two pieces of equipment he needed—his 9mm pistol and himself. He walked down the long side of the lot. Satisfied no one was watching, he cut across the backyard to the rear door. No fences protected the perimeter and no security light alerted anyone to his movements. Considering what Gillis did for a living, he wouldn't want anything drawing attention to himself.

He sneaked up on the back door and peered through the window into the kitchen. The kitchen served as a repository for fast food. From the looks of things, breakfast, lunch and dinner came out of a box. He hadn't expected much of a problem subduing the guy, but a constant diet of this shit would make him a pushover.

Music played at a neighborly level from the room connecting to the kitchen. The house was small in comparison to the lot. He guessed the adjoining room would be the living room and most likely the only other room on the ground floor.

He tried the back door. It wasn't locked. Not a surprise. Gillis probably kept it unlocked for a fast getaway. He twisted the doorknob and eased the door back. The door creaked, but not enough to penetrate the music. He stepped inside the kitchen and eased the door shut. The house smelled musty, which wasn't helped by the odor of old food in the kitchen.

He removed his pistol, screwed on the silencer and crossed to the doorway. A lone male, skinny despite the fast-food diet, sat with his back to Beckerman while he flitted between typing on a PC and a laptop. The living room had been converted into an IT heaven. A bank of peripherals filled the space where a sofa should have been. Some of it looked state of the art and some looked improvised. Manuals and CDs filled a steel cabinet against a wall. Beckerman had found his hacker.

He aimed his pistol at the twenty-something with his back to him. "Gillis?"

Gillis spun around in his chair. His eyes widened at the sight of the gun, and he stuck his hands in the air.

Beckerman loved complicity. It was going to make this very easy.

"You Gillis?"

Gillis nodded.

"Follow my instructions and nothing will happen to you. Understood?"

Gillis nodded again.

"This is very important. I require a verbal contract."

Confusion crept into Gillis's expression. Beckerman snapped off the safety on his pistol to underline the seriousness of his request.

"Yes. Understood. Whatever you want, you've got it."

"That's the right attitude." Beckerman reinforced his intimidation by invading Gillis's personal space, putting the silenced pistol inches from his face. "You're meeting with Hayden Duke in a few minutes, yes?"

"Yes. He wants me to hack a password protected file."

"You're going to tell him that it'll take some time and he'll have to come back. Then you're going to tell him you can't do it. And this is the important part, you're not going to let him leave with the file he brings you."

The color drained from Gillis's face in increments with each successive demand. "How the hell am I going to do that?"

"I don't care how. Try bullshitting." Beckerman waggled his gun. "Let this be a little incentive."

"I'll try."

"You'll do more than try. Fail and you'll die."

Gillis eyed Beckerman's automatic with understandable trepidation.

Beckerman checked his watch. He guessed Hayden would arrive in the next five minutes. He retreated into the kitchen and switched the lights off.

"I can see and hear you from here. You make one wrong move and it'll be your last. Is that understood?"

"Yes."

"Good. Now forget that I'm here. Think about how

you're going to handle Hayden. You're the one in charge now. Success rests with you."

Judging from Gillis's expression, the pep talk failed to inspire him.

Beckerman found himself a blind spot where he maintained a clear view of Gillis and his operations, but couldn't be seen from the living room.

He watched Gillis chew at his fingernails while he pulled a plan out of his ass. He didn't have high hopes, but Gillis surprised him when Hayden knocked at the door a little after nine. Gillis was like a boxer coming out his corner. He had a job and he knew how to do it.

Gillis let Hayden in. He bullshitted with Hayden for a couple of minutes as they played a "who knows who" game before taking seats at a PC.

"You got something for me?" Gillis asked.

"Yeah," Hayden said pulling out a flash drive. "There's a password-protected file on there. I need you to crack it for me."

Gillis took the flash drive and plugged it into the side of the flat screen in front of him. "A hundred?"

Hayden handed Gillis the cash.

Gillis tapped away at the keyboard, launched software and pulled up screens. After a couple of minutes, he sighed and pushed himself away from the keyboard.

"What's wrong?" Hayden asked.

"This is going to take me some time. This file is *beaucoup* protected."

"Shit. But you can do it, can't you?"

Gillis jerked back from Hayden as if he'd been slapped. "Yeah, I can do it. This is what I do."

"Okay, then do it."

"Come back in an hour."

"I can wait."

"Dude, I don't like being watched over. It fucks with my concentration."

Hayden took in his surroundings. "Yeah. Okay."

Beckerman held in a laugh. Gillis was on fire. He couldn't have asked for a better performance.

He emerged from his hiding spot after Hayden had left. "You did very well. I'm impressed."

Gillis frowned and took his seat at the computer.

"Hey, don't pout. Let's not spoil this relationship."

"Yeah. Whatever. Now what?"

"Open the file for me."

"No way, dude." Gillis put his hands up in surrender. "I open this file and see what's on it and it'll be the last thing I see. If you guys want to kill each other over this file, that's cool with me. Me, I don't want to know about it or you. The less I know, the less of a risk I am."

Beckerman grinned. Gillis wasn't wrong. For a geek, he was pretty grounded. "You've got a point. Can you corrupt the drive?"

"Do bruins defecate in national parks?"

Beckerman tossed Gillis a flash drive. "Copy that file onto there and then corrupt Hayden's file."

It took Gillis only a couple of minutes to comply with Beckerman's request. They sat around waiting for Hayden to return. Not much was said. Beckerman watched Gillis while Gillis watched Beckerman's gun. When the time had wound down, Beckerman returned to his hiding spot. He imparted his final instruction from the dark kitchen.

"You're almost home free, but you have to get him to believe that the file was corrupted."

Gillis said nothing and waited for Hayden's return. When Hayden knocked at the door, he didn't bother letting him back in. He kept him on the stoop and handed the flash drive back.

"I'm sorry, dude. I tried my best, but the file's toast."

"What?" Hayden looked as if Gillis had slapped him.

"Someone with some pretty powerful kung fu protected that file. It burned itself the second I cracked its shell. Whatever was on there is gone."

"Shit."

"I know, it sucks man. Here's your money back."

"No, keep it. You did your best. Do you know who would have done this?"

"No, and I'm not sure I want to know."

Hayden thanked him, and Gillis closed the door and leaned against it for a long moment.

Beckerman entered the living room. "Well done."

"Are we done?"

"Just about. The question is, can I trust you?"

Dread filled Gillis's expression. "No, man, you don't have to do it. Haven't I done everything you asked?"

"Sit."

Gillis traipsed over to his chair and fell into it. "I don't know your name. I didn't see the file. I'm not going to talk. Who am I going to tell?"

Beckerman squeezed the trigger. Gillis clamped a hand to his cheek, but no bullet had struck him. The bullet's wake had only brushed his face before punching a hole in the flat screen over his right shoulder. He ignored the monitor's death throes behind him.

"You talk, I'll know," Beckerman said. "Do I have to say more?"

"No, man. Your word is golden."

"Then we have an understanding?"

"Yeah."

Beckerman let himself out with Gillis's promise trailing behind him. He'd have someone watch Gillis, but he knew the hacker wouldn't talk. He smiled on the way back to his vehicle.

CHAPTER NINE

Hayden filed into the church with the rest of the mourners. The church's cool interior made for a welcome relief from the late summer heat outside. Although everyone kept their conversations hushed, the vaulted ceiling caught and amplified their murmurings.

Shane's open casket sat in front of the altar. The mourners formed a line for the viewing. The last thing Hayden needed to see was his friend's face again. The memory of Shane throwing himself off the bridge was far too vivid. He'd relived it too many times already. But he couldn't ignore his friend on this day of all days, so he joined the line.

The line inched forward and his turn came all too quickly. He took a breath and walked up to the casket. He was going to pay his last respects without looking at Shane, but Shane, even in death, drew him in. He looked so peaceful. Any sign of trauma inflicted by the rope had been covered by the mortician's skill. He looked as·Hayden remembered him.

He never should have let Shane reach that bridge. A knot of tension cinched itself tight around his chest. "I didn't do enough, Shane," he murmured. "I'm sorry."

A hand slipped into his. The human contact was

exactly what he needed. It took away the pain. He squeezed the hand holding his, not caring to whom it belonged.

The hand belonged to Rebecca. Even though he hadn't seen her since she was a teenager, he recognized her instantly. She looked so much like her brother. She shared his Nordic looks—tall, slender and blond. It was her eyes that reminded Hayden most of him. Their deep blue color lit up her face. Now twenty-four, she'd lost all traces of adolescence. She'd grown into a striking woman.

"It's good to see you," he said. "I'm just sorry it has to be under these circumstances."

She hugged him. "Will you sit with me?" She indicated the section reserved for family. "You're the nearest thing I've got to family."

It brought home to Hayden how much Rebecca had lost. "Sure. Of course."

As they sat in the front pew, he searched for familiar faces. He recognized Bellis and the others he'd met at the Giants game among the congregation. Lockhart appeared late and took his seat next to Bellis. Hayden looked for college friends, but saw only strangers.

The minister walked over to the pulpit and began the service. Rebecca kept it together during the eulogy. He admired her in that moment. She'd lost her whole family to tragedy, but she remained strong. He reached over and took her hand for the rest of the service.

After the service ended, Hayden rode with Rebecca to the wake, which was being held at Shane's house. As the limo pulled up in Shane's driveway, Hayden felt like a criminal returning to the scene of the crime. He expected to see remains of the earlier devastation, but the house had been made over. Everything damaged or destroyed was gone. A TV from the den replaced the destroyed plasma in the living room. One sofa remained where there'd been two. The coffee table that had separated them was missing.

He went over to a framed print hanging on the wall in the living room that he remembered hanging in the hall previously. He eased the picture to one side and discovered a dent where a chunk of sheetrock and paint had been gouged out during Shane's rampage. Not all traces of that night could be easily erased. He slid the picture back.

He glanced toward the stairs and wondered if the makeover extended to Shane's bedroom. His curiosity didn't need fulfilling, and he touched the healing stomach wound left by Shane's butcher knife.

He filled a plate with finger food and wandered aimlessly around the house. He felt that if he stopped, someone would engage him in conversation.

"Hey, you were there when Shane jumped. How did that happen? How did you let it happen?"

This was a conversation he didn't want to get into. The only person he felt comfortable talking to was Rebecca. He found her in the kitchen with a middle-aged woman who was offering her condolences. Rebecca thanked the woman and slipped away.

"How are you doing?" he asked her.

"About the same since the last person asked me thirty seconds ago."

"Dumb question. I'm sorry."

She laughed and touched his forearm. "It's okay. I just needed to say it, and you're the only one I feel I can say it to."

"I've found out a few things," Hayden said. "Want to talk?"

Rebecca surveyed the mourners. They'd settled into groups. "Sure. I don't think I can handle another person telling me that Shane's death was untimely."

Her remark was said without spite. Hayden guessed every heartfelt condolence must feel like a painful reminder after a while.

She led him into the sunroom and closed the door before sitting next to him on a padded rattan loveseat.

"Did you get anywhere with Shane's file?" she asked.

He shook his head. "My guy came up dry. It's more than just password protected. The file self-destructed when he tried to open it."

"So we've lost the file."

"No. He worked on a copy. I still have a backup. I'm asking around for someone else."

"I'm not sure you should. Shane either protected that file for himself or for someone else. It should stay closed until someone comes to you with the password."

"What if that never happens? Don't you want to know?"

"Right now, I'm not sure I do. Shane is entitled to his secrets."

Hayden didn't feel that way. The answer to Shane's death could be wrapped up in that file. He wanted to open it, but he understood Rebecca's need for privacy. Shane never gave him permission to open it. His last request was to delete it. Rebecca was his heir and it was her call now.

She reached up and examined the yellowish-green bruise smeared across Hayden's eyebrow and spreading into his hairline at the temple. "I can't believe Shane hurt you."

"He wasn't himself."

"I wish I'd been there for him." Her chin trembled and her face cracked. The cracks became ruptures, and she burst into wracking sobs as her fragile façade was smashed to pieces. She fell into Hayden's arms, and he hugged her tightly.

"There wasn't anything you could do. I was here, and I couldn't stop him. I don't think anyone could have helped him."

She seemed so brittle in his arms—her frame so delicate that he could crush her if he wasn't careful. He pushed her from him and lifted her face. Her tears had reddened her eyes and her face was flushed, but she still managed to look pretty.

He smiled. "Hey. Enough with the tears. Forget all about the bad and remember the good. Okay?"

She managed a smile and nodded.

"I must look a sight."

Hayden cocked his head to one side. "For sore eyes maybe."

She half laughed and pulled a fresh Kleenex from her pocket. After she'd made herself presentable, they returned to the living room only to find Santiago blocking their path.

"Detective Ruben Santiago, Marin County Sheriff's Office. We spoke on the phone, Ms. Fallon. My condolences to you and your family."

"I am my family now, Detective."

There hadn't been any barb intended in Rebecca's remark, but it dealt a blow to Santiago's bravado. "I'm sorry to hear that. Hello, Mr. Duke. Paying your respects, I see?"

Santiago's sarcasm was hard to miss, but Hayden ignored the remark.

"I'm sorry I couldn't make it to the funeral," Santiago said, "but a prior engagement got in the way."

"It's nice of you to come."

"As a matter of fact, my delay has to do with your brother, Ms. Fallon. You see, I'm very attached to my work. Many of my cases involve deaths and I never get to meet the victims, but I get to know them through witnesses, family and friends. Already, I feel that I know your brother, and I'm finding it difficult to walk away. I won't do that until I understand why Shane did what he did. Does that make sense?"

"Yes, it does," Rebecca said. "Thank you. That means a lot."

"I'm glad it does," Santiago said. "Do you both have a few minutes to discuss some things? There have been some developments, and I'm hoping you can enlighten me as to their meaning."

"Of course," Rebecca said.

Rebecca and Hayden showed Santiago into the sunroom. Santiago closed the door and stood with his back to it, as if blocking their escape. He pointed to the loveseat and indicated for them to sit. He remained standing.

"I've received the results from the tox screen, and it's not good. You were right, Hayden. Shane was under the influence of narcotics the night he died."

So it was official. Shane had been high when he killed himself. The news brought Hayden some comfort. Drugs he could understand. A sudden psychotic break he couldn't. But this answer gave rise to a new question. What had driven Shane to drugs in the first place?

"What did he take?" Rebecca asked.

"No one's quite sure. All anyone is willing to say is it's new and lethal. To quote the toxicology report, 'it's the equivalent of LSD drenched in rocket fuel.'"

A flash of Shane tearing his bedroom apart with a butcher knife ripped through Hayden's mind. He knew how nasty the drug was. It turned an ordinary person into a lunatic.

"Any ideas where Shane would have obtained something like this?"

Both Hayden and Rebecca shook their heads.

"This drug isn't like anything else on the streets. It's nasty. Obviously, I'd like to get it off the streets before it kills a third person."

"A third?" Rebecca said. "Who was the second person?"

"Sundip Chaudhary. A coworker of Shane's. He drowned himself the week before your brother died. His tox screen came back positive for the same drug."

The bond that tied Shane and Chaudhary's deaths had just become unbreakable. Both men worked together. Both men committed suicide a week apart. Both men swore they'd done something unforgivable. Coincidence didn't work anymore. The drug united them. They killed themselves for the same reason, but what reason?

"Don't you think this situation is odd?" Rebecca asked.

"Very," Santiago answered. "And I want answers."

"I'm sorry, we don't have any for you," Hayden said.

Santiago fixed him with a disapproving glare.

A knock came at the door, and one of the caterers poked her head through. "Rebecca, do you have a minute?"

Rebecca looked to Santiago, and he nodded his approval. She excused herself and left with the caterer. Hayden attempted to follow her out, but Santiago stopped him.

"We still have things to discuss," he said and closed the door.

Hayden retook his seat, and Santiago dragged a chair over to him and sat. When he sat, his jacket splayed out and the gun on his hip showed. It wasn't subtle, but it had its effect.

"You say you were close friends with Shane, yet you know nothing about his drug problem."

"In all the time I've known Shane, he's never taken drugs. Could he have hidden the fact from me? Yes, he could have."

Santiago frowned his disapproval. "How much is Marin Design Engineering paying you?"

"I don't see what business that is of yours."

"Just answer the question."

"Two hundred dollars an hour."

"Is that good?"

"Yes. What has this got to do with anything?" Santiago's cryptic bullshit was pissing him off. Santiago obviously thought something wasn't on the up and up, so why didn't he just say it? "My business with MDE has nothing to do with Shane's death. Shane committed suicide. Tell me what it is you want and let's end this."

"Mr. Duke, I think you're holding out on me, and I wish you would come clean. I don't know what it is you know, but you're obstructing my investigation, and that is a crime."

"There's nothing to tell," Hayden said, but his gut knew otherwise and turned a couple of times in sympathy. He wanted to tell Santiago the truth, but until he knew what the truth was, he would keep it to himself and take his chances.

"Have it your way, Mr. Duke," Santiago said. "Did you know Sundip Chaudhary?"

"No."

"I better not find otherwise."

"You won't. Why would you?"

"There's something else that ties these two men together," Santiago said.

"And what's that?"

"You. You were hired slap bang between their deaths."

Santiago still wanted to hang the title of drug pusher on him. He felt the detective slipping a noose around his neck. The man was so far off target it wasn't even funny.

"True, but I had nothing to do with their deaths."

"I have only your word on that. You can bet I'm going to find the truth."

Santiago stood and went to leave. Hayden jumped to his feet.

"If you're looking at me for a drug connection, you're way off. I have no convictions or history of drugs."

"I know. I've checked you out." Santiago opened the door. "It's not very healthy being a Marin Design Engineering employee these days. You should hope no one else falls prey to the same fate as Mr. Fallon and Mr. Chaudhary. Thank you for your time, Mr. Duke. We'll be talking again."

Santiago said good-bye to Rebecca on his way out. He pointed to his watch, and Rebecca led him through a tangle of people to the front door. Many of the faces were turned toward Hayden in curiosity. One belonged to Trevor Bellis. Hayden crossed the living room toward him. He extracted himself from his colleagues and met Hayden halfway.

"Hayden, I need to talk to you. Circumstances have changed regarding the work you're doing for us. The timeline has been accelerated."

"Tell me when you need the work completed, and I'll do it."

"No, you don't understand. MDE no longer requires your services."

"If this is about the break-in at my home, I told you MDE wasn't comprised. The thieves were interested in my computers, TV and anything they could hock, not the plans. The plans weren't even touched. I take the precaution of backing everything up online. None of the work was lost."

Bellis held up a hand. "The decision has nothing to do with the break-in. As I say, circumstances have changed."

Hayden hadn't seen this coming. His pride kicked in. He never walked away from a job, voluntarily or otherwise.

"I'm nearly finished. It'll only take a couple of days to complete."

Bellis's expression tightened. His professional smile

was stretching into a grimace, and his polite decorum disappeared. "I'm sorry, Hayden. I'm the client here. Your services aren't required. End of subject. Okay?"

"Yes. I'm sorry. I just don't like to disappoint my clients."

Bellis's affability returned. "You haven't disappointed me. You've been professional under difficult circumstances, but those circumstances have resulted in a change of thought. I'm the one who's sorry. I'll be sure to contact you for our next project."

It sounded good, but Hayden wasn't buying it. He knew a Dear John when he heard it. Bellis would never consider him for another job, which was fine with him. MDE meant only bad memories.

"Okay," Hayden conceded.

"Good. We're wrapping the project up this weekend. Come by the office Saturday at ten with everything. Be sure to bring your timesheets and a final invoice."

Bellis turned away and left.

Hayden wondered what the hell had triggered that decision. If the project had been accelerated, then why fire him? Bellis still needed someone to complete the work. The break-in could have been a deciding factor in the decision, but Hayden didn't buy it. Okay, if this design was the technological breakthrough MDE's client claimed, they might fear industrial espionage, but firing him didn't help matters.

Bellis walked over to Rebecca and said his good-byes. This signaled the rest of the MDE contingent that it was time to leave. Lockhart fell in at Bellis's side on the way out. Hayden guessed he had Lockhart to thank for his dismissal. Bellis might have given him the bullet, but Lockhart had pulled the trigger.

Rebecca saw them out and came over to him. "What was that all about?"

"Bellis just fired me."

"Oh, I'm sorry."

"It doesn't matter. It was only a short-term thing. I just didn't see it coming."

Bellis's exit initiated an exodus. Rebecca saw the last of her guests to the door. Hayden remained to help out. He collected plates and loaded them into the dishwasher while Rebecca dealt with the departing caterers. She returned to the kitchen.

"Leave that," she said. "It can wait, but this can't." She held up a bottle of wine.

She handed him the bottle, and he opened it while she rinsed out two oversize glasses. She filled the glasses nearly to the rim.

"Don't you think that's a little too much to drink?"

She admired her handiwork. "No, I don't."

He didn't think so either. He followed her into the living room and they sat on the sofa. Somewhere along the line, he'd lost a handle on the time. It was early afternoon, but it felt much later.

"What are your plans now—back to L.A.?"

"Eventually, but I'm here for another week. I have to tie up all of Shane's affairs and then there's this house. Shane left it to me, but I don't know whether to keep it, rent it or sell it."

"Don't rush anything. If this place sits for a month, so what? Look, I'm back here Saturday morning to settle up with Trevor Bellis. If you'd like to meet to talk things through, I'd be happy to do it."

She fixed him with a gaze he couldn't avoid. "That's really kind. I'd like that very much."

They sat in a comfortable silence for a while. Hayden didn't feel the need to talk. Just sharing some quiet time for a change suited him fine. Rebecca ruined the moment by hurling her empty wineglass into the fireplace. It exploded on impact.

"Goddamn you, Shane." Her body was taut. Tendons

stood out on her arms from balling her hands into tight fists. Her eyes shone with tears. "Goddamn you for getting so high you went and did something stupid. Suicide. What were you thinking? What would Mom and Dad say?"

When her questions went unanswered, she sagged back into her seat.

"Feel better?" Hayden asked.

She palmed away the tears. "Not really. I want to know why he did it."

"And we'll find an answer."

She turned to him. "Why are you doing this?"

"Because Shane was my friend, and he entrusted that file to me. He wanted something done with it. I don't know if you're right and someone is looking for it, or whether he intended to do something with it later, but I want to finish what he started."

She shook her head. "I can't believe you're doing this. Shane has cost you so much already."

"He hasn't cost me anything."

"What about your job at MDE?" she said. "Do you think Trevor Bellis fired you because of Shane?"

"I don't know. Maybe. It's not really important. It's a job. I have another one," he said with a smile. "I think this has more to do with the narcotics floating around MDE."

"Just because two people employed there died after taking a new street drug doesn't mean you're the connection. The connection is MDE."

"That's not what Santiago thinks."

"Detective Santiago doesn't like you very much."

"Did your women's intuition pick up on that?"

"Wasn't necessary," she said with a smile. "It's hard to miss."

He wondered if Santiago really had it out for him. The detective wasn't stupid. Maybe he saw him as the wedge that would open up whatever was going on at MDE. It was easier to go after him than Bellis. Bellis had lawyers on his side. He didn't.

The smile that had looked so good on Rebecca's face suddenly faded. It saddened Hayden to see it.

"What's up?"

"Okay, Shane and Sundip got high, but it doesn't explain why they killed themselves."

It didn't. It couldn't. The drug was only one part of the equation. The confessions were something else all together.

"It all comes back to MDE," Hayden said. "I'll use Saturday to get some answers."

CHAPTER TEN

Early Saturday morning, Hayden parked his Mitsubishi in front his father's business, JD Engineering—Specialist Machinists. Even on a Saturday, his father would be working. He'd grown up seeing his father leaving for work, but John Duke never neglected his only son. He always had time to shoot some hoops or play ball, even when Hayden knew he was dog tired. Their time together during Hayden's formative years may have been short, but John Duke made sure it was quality time. He was one person Hayden could turn to for help.

Hayden grabbed a roll of plans off the passenger seat. He'd copied MDE's plans the morning after Bellis told him to return them. If MDE proved to be at the heart of Shane's death, he wasn't giving up anything that could be evidence.

Hayden stepped inside JD Engineering, and the smell of cutting oil threw him back twenty years. Before his father started the business, he had worked in Sacramento as a maintenance supervisor. The factory shut down for two weeks in the summer for an annual overhaul. The line workers stayed at home while John Duke and his crew fixed what needed fixing, and Hayden went with him. Cal/OSHA would have thrown a fit if something had happened, but Hayden remembered it as good times.

Hayden had enjoyed his childhood jaunts with his father. Where else could he drive a forklift, albeit on his father's lap, open valves that made steam spray out from floor grates and drink nasty coffee from a vending machine? His reminiscence made him smile as he spotted his father operating a lathe. The machine whined as a continuous tangle of aluminum swarf peeled off the bar like silver wool off a spinning machine.

"Hey, Dad," Hayden yelled over the din.

John Duke looked up and waved. "Let me finish this cut, okay?"

His father had started JD Engineering after taking early retirement. Finding life as a retiree didn't sit too well, he took over a bankrupt machine shop. He sunk a sizeable chunk of his 401(k) into the venture, but the gamble had paid off. His reputation as a quality machinist meant he was rarely short of work.

His father wound back the saddle and shut off the lathe. The machine's whine died as it came to slow stop. "Aluminum is a bitch. The damned stuff never breaks off." He checked his watch. "What can I do for you at nine on a Saturday morning?"

Hayden smiled. "I need a favor."

His dad frowned. "Another one?"

Hayden followed his dad into the shop's cramped, corner office. His dad poured himself coffee from the Mr. Coffee on his desk and offered Hayden a cup, but he declined. The last thing he needed was stimulants. He was about to cross a line. If he shredded the plans and wiped the flash drive now, he wasn't breaking MDE's contract, but the moment he handed the copies over to his father, there was no going back.

His dad sat behind his desk. "Okay, what's the favor?"

Hayden put the plans on the table. "Can you hold on to these for a while?"

"Depends. What are they?"

It was just like a parent to ask questions, but only a parent would do what he was asking.

"You know this job I was doing for Shane?"

John Duke nodded.

"There's something not quite right about it."

His father sat up in his seat. "How so?"

Hayden didn't exactly know. It was all feeling, nothing substantial, but he felt its presence like a black cloud.

"I'm not sure. The job's very secretive. I had to sign a nondisclosure agreement. There's a ten million–dollar penalty for breaking it."

John Duke frowned. "Tell me you've got an eleven million–dollar reason for doing this."

"Because two people are dead."

Hayden had spoken the words before he realized what he was going to say, but once he'd said them, the force of them made his decision final. He felt the strength of his convictions.

"Two people?"

"One of Shane's coworkers killed himself the week before Shane did."

His father was silent. The look on his face said he was trying to make sense of the situation and failing. "How do you know their deaths are connected?"

"I don't, but what are the odds that two guys working together would commit suicide a week apart from each other?"

"You must have something more than that to risk a ten million–dollar court date."

He did. He had Shane's password-protected file. He had the super drug both Shane and Chaudhary had taken before killing themselves. He had Santiago breathing down his neck. He had Rebecca's belief in Shane. A belief he shared.

"I do, but I don't want to involve you."

"It's too late for that. You telling me any of this is involving me. If you're expecting me to help you, you'd better start talking." John Duke's irritation radiated off him in waves.

"MDE fired me at Shane's funeral."

"Why?"

"I don't know. After Shane's death and the break-in, they closed ranks and shut me out. Then at the funeral, Bellis fired me."

"Are you getting paid?"

"Yeah."

"Then what are you worried about? If this is sour grapes about getting the axe, let it go. Firms don't show loyalty these days. It's a fact of working life. Get used to it."

"It's not like that. There's something underhanded going on here." He pulled out a flash drive and put it on the desk between them. "On there is a file Shane sent me the night he killed himself. He told me to keep it safe and not to look at it. It's password protected. I think whatever is on there is the reason Shane killed himself."

John Duke picked up the flash drive and examined it. "There's something else, isn't there?"

His father had seen through him. He hadn't wanted to discuss this part, but he wasn't going to get his father's cooperation without telling him.

"Both Shane and his dead coworker took the same drug. It's difficult to say whether it was an overdose or not, but the stuff was potent enough to turn their brains inside out. They committed suicide—there's no doubt about that—but the drug might have shoved them in that direction. The detective investigating the case thinks I'm a dealer or something."

"Where the hell did he get that idea?"

"Timing. The deaths didn't start until I reconnected with Shane. Guilt by association, I guess."

"Jesus, Hayden. What did he say when you told him about this file?"

"Nothing. I didn't tell him."

"Are you stupid? Why not?"

"I didn't want to tell him until I'd seen what was on it. I figured that if it was connected to Shane's death, I'd give it to him, but if it was nothing, then no one needed to know about it."

"That's why he's all over you. He can tell you're holding something back."

"I know," Hayden conceded.

"Then tell the detective. Give him this stuff and let him deal with it."

Hayden said nothing. Despite his father's good sense, he wasn't ready to hand everything over to Santiago. He still hoped to open the file.

"I'll think about it."

"You're a fool. I don't see why you've gone to all this trouble."

"Something isn't right here. My friend and one of his colleagues are dead. What would make them kill themselves? I don't know, and I don't know who to trust. I don't trust Trevor Bellis or anyone at MDE. I don't trust the police to do the right thing until I can give them something to go on. But I do trust you."

John Duke could only frown. The ball was in his court. "What do you want me to do?"

"Put the plans and the flash drive in your safe until I ask for them."

John Duke didn't answer.

"Will you do it?" Hayden asked.

"Of course I will. What kind of dad would I be if I didn't?"

Hayden got to his feet to leave. "Thanks, Dad."

"Where are you going now?" John Duke said, getting up with his son.

"I'm returning the originals to MDE. I hope to come away with some answers."

Hayden saw himself out and hit the road before his dad could change his mind. Despite his dad's concerns, he felt upbeat. He might be in way over his head, but at least he was doing something to swim to the surface.

He arrived at MDE forty minutes late for his appointment. He hadn't counted on the Q&A from his dad. It had held him up long enough to hit the weekend migration into the Bay Area, which slowed him down even more.

Cars lined MDE's parking lot. It looked as if Bellis had called everyone in to finish this project. Hayden wondered if their client was pushing or Bellis just wanted to draw a line under the project. Either way, Bellis was about to draw a line under him. His official part in all this was about to end. He parked on the street and scooped up the original plans Shane had given him, an envelope containing timesheets, his final invoice and the flash drive with an electronic version of the revised plans.

From the street, Hayden could see the main lobby entrance was in darkness, so he tried the side entrance where a dozen vehicles were clustered. The door was protected by a card-key entry system along with a squawk box. Someone had smashed the control box. It trailed from a tangle of wiring extending from the wall.

He picked up the box and examined it. Without even trying the squawk button, he knew it was pointless. The damage looked recent, and he wondered if it had happened before or after Bellis and his crew had arrived this morning.

He tried the doorknob, but it was locked.

He took out his cell phone and dialed Bellis's number. Bellis's phone went to voice mail, and he left a message. He tried MDE's main number, but that also went to voice mail.

He backed up and stared up at the second floor. No doubt Bellis would have them up there. He called out, but no one responded. He couldn't believe this.

He rounded the building to the main entrance. He redialed Bellis's number on the way. Again, he got voice mail. If no one answered in a minute, he going to shove everything through the mail slot and they could mail him his damn check.

Hayden pulled up short when he reached the front of the building. A thick length of steel chain encircled the door handles and was fixed in place with a padlock. He hadn't noticed the chains from the street.

What the hell was going on? He peered inside the foyer. The lights were off and nobody was home. If it weren't for the vehicles parked outside, he would have thought MDE had gone out of business. Chains seemed like an extreme security measure.

He pounded on the glass doors with his fist. The glass panes shuddered, but he didn't alert anyone, despite the noise.

He called Bellis's number one last time. The line rang and rang.

He stood back from the covered entrance and looked up. He saw no movement at the window.

"Come on, come on, pick up the damn phone," Hayden said. Bellis pissed him off. If he'd changed his mind about the meeting, he could have done him the courtesy of informing him. As expected, Bellis's phone line switched to voice mail. "Trevor, it's Hayden. I'm here at the office, but no one is here to let me in. I'm leaving your plans and my invoice. Call me if you have any questions."

He hung up and put the phone away.

The mail slot was big enough to take the plans, but not the protective tube. Hayden slid the plans out, flattened them and poked them through the slot. Smoke leaked from the opening. Its acrid bite assaulted Hayden's nostrils. He yanked the plans free and dropped them.

He leaned in against the glass door and cupped his hands around his eyes to cut out the glare. He stared hard inside. The foyer looked normal, except for the smoke bleeding from behind the door leading to the offices. Smoke also wafted up from behind the receptionist's desk. The trails merged together and crept across the floor.

"Shit," he murmured and yanked out his cell phone.

The moment before Hayden's brain formed the word fire, an explosion erupted from above. The concussion blew out the windows on the second floor, sending a shower of fragmented glass raining down. The intensity shook the glass doors in their frame. The building's awning protected him, but instinctively, he dropped to one knee and covered his head against the flying glass.

Hayden darted out from underneath the awning. He slipped on the layer of glass covering the sidewalk, but kept his footing. His breath jammed in his throat as he caught sight of the carnage. The blast had blown out every window on the second floor. Flames flashed out of the shattered windows, hungry for oxygen, and burning embers rode the thermals before drifting to the ground. Dense, black smoke billowed from every gap. From the crackle and roar of the blaze, it was taking hold of the building's interior. The heat radiating off the building hit Hayden with a physical force, but the sound of faint screams coming from within chilled him.

He tried to shut out his imagination and failed. All he could see were burning people. Burning people he knew. The imagery rooted him to the spot.

"Jesus Christ," was all he could say.

A blackened and raw arm poked from a window, catching on a jagged edge of the glass. It flailed for help that wasn't there.

The sight shocked Hayden into action. He raced over to his Mitsubishi, which was frosted by a layer of glass and debris. He yanked open the trunk lid and snatched up the lug wrench. The wrench was the typical piece of ineffectual crap that car makers supplied with their vehicles. The shank was short, giving him virtually no leverage. It wouldn't make for a great pry bar, but it would break through those glass doors.

He glanced back up at the window for the arm. It still jutted from the window, but it wasn't moving. He refused to read anything into that and raced up to the glass doors.

A second explosion rocked the building, shooting out spearheads of flame. Raw heat nipped at his flesh from above. He dived for cover under the awning again. It was on fire now, but it provided the only protection from the heat and flying debris.

He picked himself up and smashed the wrench against one of the glass doors. If it had been heavier or longer, it would have added some real force, but instead, it bounced off the tempered glass, leaving behind only a dime-sized crack.

He smashed the wrench twice more against the door, each time aiming for the same spot. The blow increased the size of the crack, but the door wasn't about cave in any time soon.

He became chillingly aware of the screams from within the building. They'd stopped. They hadn't been drowned out by the roar of the fire; they'd just stopped.

He dropped to his knees and scooped up his cell. He punched in 911, then resumed smashing at the glass doors. Thick smoke belched into the foyer. Even if he broke into the building, there was no way he could help anyone without any breathing apparatus, but at least he would give those inside an escape route.

He looked to MDE's neighboring businesses for help, but all he saw was empty parking lots and locked doors. MDE was the only business operating this Saturday.

The 911 operator came on the line.

"I'm at Marin Design Engineering off Tamalpais Drive. The place is on fire and people are burning inside." He never stopped working at the glass doors while the operator got the details from him.

"The fire department has been dispatched," the operator said.

Fire now glowed from behind the receptionist's desk and smoke leaked from the doorframe. Hayden tossed his phone aside and threw his whole weight against the doors. The chain rattled from the blow. The doors took the impact and shoved him back.

"Break, you fucker," he shouted.

Every second he took to break in the doors robbed the people inside of their chance of survival. He had to try one of the other doors. Maybe if he jammed the wrench on the side entrance's doorframe, he could break in that way.

Hayden stepped back from the entrance. In the reflection of the doors, he saw a figure charging toward him from the parking lot. That was more like it. Finally, help had arrived.

Hayden had turned halfway toward his Samaritan to speak when the man plowed into him. The impact sent Hayden reeling. He slammed into the building, his head striking the stucco wall hard and leaving him dazed. Half-formed words spilled from his mouth a second before his assailant delivered a crunching blow to the side of his head. Fireworks filled Hayden's vision, then died with his loosening grip on consciousness. His legs buckled, and he slumped against the glass doors. He tried to focus on the man's face, but his view of the world was spinning. It turned black when the madman kicked him in the head and left him to burn with the other poor bastards inside.

CHAPTER ELEVEN

A repellent odor jerked Hayden from unconsciousness. It overwhelmed the stink of smoke trapped in his nose, mouth and throat, which was some relief.

"You're okay, buddy," said the paramedic standing over him.

Hayden blinked until the soot clouding his vision was gone. He was lying on a gurney in the back of an ambulance. The ambulance doors were open and beyond them people shouted instructions over the growl of diesel engines.

"I need to get up," Hayden said and pushed himself onto his elbows. The moment he moved, a spike jabbed his brain.

The paramedic pushed him back down. "You ain't going anywhere, pal."

Hayden shoved him aside. He stumbled when he jumped down from the ambulance, but he kept his footing. His head throbbed and felt the pressure of his injuries where he'd been kicked and punched. He dropped down hard onto the ambulance's bumper.

The ambulance was fifty yards from what remained of Marin Design Engineering. Firefighters were winning the battle, but it looked too late for anyone inside.

Two fire crews directed hoses into the building. They'd smashed in the front doors that he'd failed to penetrate. The fire looked to be out, but smoke rose from the ruined building, and it still looked too hot to enter. He heard the hiss of water striking the building at hundreds of gallons per minute and a fire chief yelling to someone that the roof had caved in at the rear. The place would be a carcass by the time they got control.

All those people, Hayden thought.

The paramedic blocked Hayden's path. He tapped an ambulance service patch stitched to his shirt. "Do you see this?"

Hayden nodded, careful not to set off the fireworks inside his head.

"It means I'm in charge. Have you got that?"

Hayden nodded again and let the paramedic help him back into the ambulance. The paramedic rushed through a brief exam, checking for injuries beyond the superficial.

"What's your name?" he asked.

"Hayden Duke," Santiago's familiar voice answered for him.

The paramedic's expression tightened. "Do you know what day it is, Hayden?"

"Saturday," Hayden said, "and a bad one."

"That's right, Hayden," the paramedic said. "You're going to be okay. You need treatment for smoke inhalation."

"He isn't going anywhere," Santiago interrupted and climbed aboard the ambulance. He eased the paramedic out of the way and peered down at Hayden. "You've got some explaining to do."

"Shit," Hayden sighed.

"Nice to see you again too, Mr. Duke," Santiago said.

The paramedic objected, but Santiago's big dog bark subdued him. The detective grabbed Hayden's bicep and pulled him out of the ambulance. The paramedic followed. Santiago put out a hand to him.

"You can have him, but when I'm finished with him. In the meantime, I'm sure someone else is in need of medical assistance."

The paramedic sighed and shook his head disapprovingly. His colleague came jogging over from another ambulance. The paramedic stopped him with a raised hand. "We're not wanted."

Santiago walked Hayden toward the wreckage. He never released his grip on Hayden's arm. It was a good thing, too. If it weren't for Santiago's grip, Hayden would be flat on his face. The fire's stench left him light-headed.

"Have you seen this?" Santiago asked when they reached the fire department's cordon.

"Yes."

"You want to tell me about it?" Santiago shoved Hayden toward the carnage. "Again I find you at the scene of a tragedy," he growled into Hayden's ear. "But this time, there isn't just one body. We've got multiple victims. How many died? Do you know?"

Hayden knew there had to be at least ten, but he didn't want to think about it and shook his head.

"I don't think I like your talent for disaster," Santiago said.

Hayden shook the detective's arm off and almost puked. "Don't worry, neither do I."

Santiago grunted. "You wouldn't happen to be the anonymous witness who called in Mr. Chaudhary's suicide, would you?"

"No."

Santiago jerked his chin at MDE. "What happened?"

"I had an appointment with Trevor Bellis. My work for MDE was done. I came to hand over the drawings I did for them and return their specifications. When

I got here, I thought there had been a problem with vandals."

"What made you think that?"

"Someone had wrapped a chain around the front door handles and smashed the card-key entry system on the side entrance. This was definitely arson—you're looking for a firebug."

It was obvious from Santiago's face that he didn't like the burden of finding an arsonist rammed down his throat. He was the man in charge, not Hayden.

"You wouldn't know the identity of my firebug, would you? It would be greatly appreciated," Santiago said bitterly.

"No, but we did meet. How the hell do you think I ended up with my head caved in?" Hayden said sharply.

The fire chief shouted an all clear. Firefighters rushed inside through the front entrance. Other firefighters came out from inside the building. Several of them were shaking their heads as they removed their breathing apparatuses. The fire chief conferred with one of the firemen coming out of the wreckage.

Santiago shouted at Rice, who was helping the uniforms with crowd control. "Find out what they know."

Rice nodded, ducked under the barriers and trotted over to the fire chief. Santiago turned his attention back to Hayden. Hayden watched the deputy join the conference with the firemen.

"Tell me more about this attacker."

"While I was at the front doors, I tried to call to someone inside, and then the top floor blew out. I heard screams and I tried to break in, but as I was trying, someone came at me from behind and landed me one. The next thing I knew, I was waking up in an ambulance."

"I suppose you didn't get a look at this guy," Santiago said.

"No."

"Didn't think so."

"Sir," Rice shouted at Santiago and gestured to him.

"I think we should take a closer look, Mr. Duke."

They ducked under the caution tape, and Hayden's wooziness dropped him to his knees. Santiago grabbed Hayden's arm again, this time in a more supportive manner, and helped him to his feet.

Rice stepped away from the firefighters and came toward them. The firefighters returned to their unenviable task.

"It's gruesome, sir. Every one of the poor bastards is burnt to a crisp," Rice said.

"Christ. How many?" Santiago asked.

"Eleven."

"Did you hear that, Mr. Duke? Eleven. If you'd been on time this morning you could have made it an even dozen," Santiago said.

Hayden didn't need the reminder. The thought was as prominent in his mind as the smoke in his lungs. If his dad hadn't kept him and the traffic hadn't slowed him, he would be a charred corpse. He imagined the thought would keep recurring over the coming days—in his dreams and during the boring moments of the day.

"They definitely know it's arson. The accelerants have been found. The down and dirty opinion is gasoline, based on odor and burn patterns," Rice added. "The chief's going to do his inspection, then hand the scene over to us."

Santiago studied the smoldering building. "Why the hell would someone want to burn these people?"

"You're very lucky to have made it out alive, Mr. Duke. I was talking to the firefighters who found you. That awning saved you," Rice said.

"Did you hear that, Mr. Duke?" Santiago asked. "You're a lucky man. Do you feel lucky?"

"No. I feel sick."

"Well, take comfort in that. Only the living can feel sick," Santiago said.

Hayden couldn't keep his temper any longer. Santiago kept poking at him. A jab here. A jab there. It wasn't acceptable. He was a witness. Not a criminal. He grabbed Santiago's forearm. "What the hell is wrong with you?"

"Keep it contained, Mr. Duke," Rice warned.

"Eleven people are dead, burned alive, and you think it's some sort of joke. You should be out there looking for the bastard who did this."

Santiago shook off Hayden's hand. "Maybe I don't have to look too far. Maybe I've found the bastard."

Firefighters, uniforms and rubberneckers stopped what they were doing and gawped at the escalating argument. Rice looked uncomfortable with the ensuing dogfight.

"You're crazy," Hayden said.

"No. Not crazy. First, you're the only witness to a drug-related suicide. Then you're the victim of a burglary. Now you're the sole survivor at an arson scene leaving eleven dead. Yes, let's count them, eleven. Eleven happy homes are in tatters thanks to someone with a gas can and a match. Mr. Duke, it's too much to believe you happen to turn up at these disasters by chance."

"Well, you'd better believe it because that's what happened," Hayden snapped back.

"I don't think we should be airing this conversation in public, sir," Rice said, trying to be the voice of reason.

Santiago grabbed Hayden by the bicep. The detective's fingers bit into his flesh. He dragged him toward MDE's charred entrance. Two firefighters rushed forward to block Santiago's progress, but a single look from him stopped them in their tracks.

"Shall we take a look at the melted faces and see

whether you still know nothing, Mr. Duke?" Santiago
snarled.

Rice pushed his way in between Hayden and Santiago. "Sir, it isn't going to help if you badger a suspect."

Santiago stopped with the disheveled Hayden in his
grip. "What do you suggest? We let this one go, eh? No
way, not until this bastard starts telling me the truth.
Everyone who was anyone at Marin Design Engineering is dead."

"You're wrong." He shook off Santiago's grip. "Not
everyone is dead."

"What?" Santiago said.

Hayden pointed at the parking lot. "Trevor Bellis's
Audi isn't here. My appointment was with him. So, why
isn't he here?" It wasn't until Santiago tried to hang an
arson rap around his neck that he noticed Bellis's missing car.

"He could own other vehicles," Rice said.

Santiago didn't chime in with a dismissive remark. His
mind churned scenarios over. Scenarios that didn't feature Hayden in them.

"Your attacker," Santiago said, his tone respective,
"could he have been Bellis?"

It was nice to have the weight of suspicion off his
shoulders, but he couldn't shift it onto someone else. "I
don't know. I didn't see a face. Just a fist."

Santiago pointed at the burnt-out remains of the vehicles. "Rice, run those plates. I want to know who owns
those vehicles."

"Where are you going?" Rice asked.

"I'm going to tell Bellis his people are dead."

Santiago raced over to Trevor Bellis's Tiburon home,
fearful of what he'd learn. Why the no show? Bellis made
a point of saying how busy his firm was when he'd inter-
viewed the man. His people were working day and night.

If that were true, Bellis, the self-proclaimed workaholic, would be ringside. He wouldn't be two hours late for work. A home overlooking Richardson Bay depended on that type of dedication.

Santiago tried Bellis's home number. No one picked up. It didn't mean he wasn't there.

He would settle on keeping an open mind when it came to Mr. Duke. He'd left Hayden with Rice, who had strict instructions not to let him go. Also, Hayden wasn't to go near his car until someone had checked it out for evidence that linked him to the arson.

Santiago hit redial on his cell. The phone just rang and rang.

"Pick up, damn it."

The answering machine kicked in and went to its message.

Santiago hung up and cursed Bellis, but at least he knew someone was at home. Someone had to have turned the machine on and even money was on Bellis.

Santiago killed the lights and sirens when he reached Bellis's neighborhood. He could do without a car chase. He swung his car into Trevor Bellis's driveway and stamped hard on the brakes. His car skidded to a halt in front of Bellis's Audi, blocking it in.

His heart was pounding and adrenalin pumping. He didn't want to spook the CEO. This guy wasn't the average criminal who ran at the sight of a badge and gun. He needed to be cool. If he was cool, Bellis would be cool, despite having nowhere to run.

He took a deep breath and exhaled. The simple act took ten beats a minute off his heart rate. He switched off the engine, then checked in with Rice.

"I'm at Bellis's. He's here. Call me in ten."

He slipped from his car and approached the house. A combination of mature landscaping and ornate fencing shrouded the custom-designed, two-story house from onlookers. The house wasn't on the water, but high up on the hillside. The front was unimpressive, but the rear would have a dynamite view of the bay.

He pressed the doorbell.

No one answered, but somewhere from inside the house, a TV played and an upstairs window was open.

Santiago pressed a hand to the Audi's hood. It was warm.

"Don't hide," he murmured to himself.

He returned to the door and again tried the doorbell. This time he leaned on the button. Eleven people were dead who shouldn't be. The stench of their barbecued flesh could be smelled for over a block. Hiding from the police wasn't an option. He banged on the lacquered front door.

"Mr. Bellis, please open the door. It's Detective Ruben Santiago from the Marin Sheriff's Office. I need to speak to you. Now."

There wasn't any reply, but someone switched off the TV. *Amateur*, he thought.

He pressed on the doorbell again and didn't take his thumb off the button. The bell chime ran through its tune only to repeat it again and again. After its fifth cycle, the chime sounded like it was in pain.

"Mr. Bellis, please open the door. Don't make me break it in."

Santiago heard shuffling from inside. He stepped to one side of the door. If Bellis had dug himself in with a weapon, he didn't want to be in the line of fire. He unsnapped the clasp on his holster.

Damn it. He should have checked to see if Bellis was a licensed holder. He waited for the door to open.

It opened as far as the security chain allowed. A woman peered at him through the narrow gap.

"Mrs. Bellis?" he asked.

"Yes."

"Mrs. Bellis, could you let me in? I need to speak to your husband."

"Here's not here."

"I know he's here. His car's here, Mrs. Bellis."

"He doesn't want to speak to you."

"Mrs. Bellis, your husband doesn't have a choice. I need to speak to him, and it has to be now. This is official business."

The guy was hiding out. Why? Had Hayden been right about Bellis? Santiago hoped to God that Hayden was wrong. A flutter of nerves crept into him. He couldn't let it show, and he put on his game face for Mrs. Bellis.

"Mrs. Bellis, I need to come in," he said after she made no move to open the door.

She thought long and hard before nodding.

An explosion made Santiago and Mrs. Bellis jump, bringing an end to his speculation. He recognized the noise as a shotgun blast.

"Oh my God, Trevor!" Mrs. Bellis said in a whisper.

"Mrs. Bellis, let me in now."

Cracks appeared in her fragile shell. Tremors set in and the tears flowed.

"Mrs. Bellis."

But she was lost in a nightmare.

"Stand back from the door, ma'am. I'm coming in," Santiago instructed.

The woman disappeared from sight, and he gave her a couple of seconds to get out of the way for good measure. He slammed a well-placed heel on the door, just below the handle. The door went flying inward. He rushed into the entrance hall and found Mrs. Bellis transfixed with her hands to her mouth, staring at the staircase.

"Is he up there?"

Mrs. Bellis said nothing.

Santiago knew it was pointless and left her to her fears. He called for backup with the express instructions that all units were to come in silent and to approach only on his command. He didn't want to escalate the fear level. He would have liked Mrs. Bellis with him to help. A familiar voice might pacify her husband. Sadly, that wasn't going to happen. He'd have to make do until backup arrived.

He bounded up the stairs two at a time and stopped when he reached the landing. The house was deep and a narrow hallway stretched out in front of him. Six closed doors faced him—three to his right, two to his left and one at the end of the narrow corridor. It was Russian roulette with doors, and one room was loaded with an armed and desperate man.

The shotgun blast could mean this confrontation was over, but Santiago knew better than to make any assumptions. Bellis wasn't the first desperate man to lure a cop in with a dummy shot. Santiago put his faith in physical evidence. If he couldn't touch or see it, he didn't believe it. Even if Bellis had shot himself, he might still be alive and want to take someone with him. No, if Santiago expected to take his wife out to dinner tonight, he couldn't believe anything until he saw it with his own two eyes.

He unholstered his weapon and aimed down the corridor. He shifted to a position that took him out of direct line of fire of any door.

"Mr. Bellis, it's Detective Santiago. I need you to come out with your hands up. Can you do that?"

He got no answer beyond Mrs. Bellis's sobs.

He repeated his request and still got no reply.

Life is never easy, he thought and came out from his cover. He went to the closest doorway to his right. He gripped the doorknob and pressed his automatic against the door. He did his best to keep his body flat against the wall, but if Bellis was listening for him to open the door from another room, he could take him out. The sweat on Santiago's palms made the doorknob slippery in his grasp, but it was nothing compared to the sweat trickling down his forehead. He didn't dare wipe it away, not until he cleared the room.

He took a deep breath and released it, then took a second breath and held it. Slowly exhaling, he mumbled under his breath, "One, two, three." In a single fluid action, he twisted the knob and threw the door back, sending it crashing into the wall. He dropped to a shooter's stance, bracing himself for the carnage and ready to return fire.

Nothing happened. The door swung open on a guest bathroom. He ventured inside and cleared the room.

"One down. Five to go," he murmured. If Bellis didn't get him, the stress would.

This business was far too hot for his sport jacket. He slipped it off and the cool of the house chilled the sweat on his back. It almost felt like bliss.

He hung the jacket on the door and edged over to the door opposite the bathroom. As before, he prepared himself and flung the door back.

Nothing.

He knew where this was leading.

Systemically, he worked his way down the corridor, going from door to door. He flung back the doors on the third, fourth and fifth rooms without finding Bellis inside. This should have been comforting. None of the first five rooms contained a crazed gunman. But it was only putting off the inevitable. One of them had to. And it had to be the last.

He should have known the room at the end of the corridor was going to be the one where Bellis was hiding. It was the room overlooking the bay. It would be a favorite room. People liked the familiar. The comfortable.

The last door came with an added problem. The corridor wasn't much wider than the doorway. It didn't give Santiago any cover to hide himself. He couldn't rely on drywall and insulation to protect him. He didn't even have the luxury of an open doorway nearby to dive into for cover. If Bellis opened fire, Santiago was taking it in the face. *Backup would feel real nice about now,* he thought.

He could finesse the situation. His idea wasn't great, but it might be enough.

Santiago repeated his breathing exercise, while gripping the doorknob. He flung the door open and immediately threw himself onto the ground in the vain hope of avoiding a shotgun blast.

Santiago aimed his pistol at Bellis, but he needn't have bothered. The CEO was in the room—in body, but not in spirit.

Bellis sat at his desk, kitty-corner to the picture window that ran the width of the house. What remained of his head lolled back. The shocked look draped across his face made him appear even gaunter than normal. His features screamed that he knew what he was doing, but wasn't prepared for the pain.

Trevor Bellis had placed a double-barreled shotgun under his chin and pulled the trigger. Blood, bone and brain matter covered the study walls. Buckshot had imbedded itself into some of the volumes on the bookshelf. The shotgun lay at his feet.

Santiago stood up. He fought his gag reflex when he got his second view of the dead man. He closed the door for Mrs. Bellis's sake, went to window and swung open the door leading onto the deck. He wanted to wash the stink of cordite and blood out of the air. He stepped onto the deck and surveyed the boats on the bay and tourists lining the streets in Sausalito on a glorious Saturday afternoon. *What would make a guy give up on all this?* Santiago thought.

Santiago returned to the room. He didn't want to go near Bellis's corpse, but he needed to see the blood-speckled handwritten note on the blotter in front of the CEO.

He developed tunnel vision. He saw only the note and not the gaping hole in the top of Bellis's head. With a handkerchief, he picked up the note, then turned his back on the body.

Penny,
    I'm sorry. Please forgive me for what I've done, but I can't live with the consequences of my actions.
    I love you more than I can express.

                                    Love,
                                    Trevor

His cell burst into life. Santiago answered it on the deck. "Rice, get over to Bellis's house, now. Is Duke with you?"

"Yes."

"Get rid of him. Tell him I want to see him tomorrow in my office, at his convenience. I think we've got our arsonist," Santiago said.

CHAPTER TWELVE

Beckerman called before coming up to Lockhart's San Francisco condo. Lockhart left the door open for Beckerman to let himself in. They should have met in their office, but this was a cause for celebration, and Lockhart preferred to celebrate in nicer surroundings.

Lockhart's condo was for entertaining clients. He used the place to put stars in the eyes of people he wanted to use. A few times, he'd used it to trap people when money wasn't enough of a temptation. The bedrooms had caught more than a few people doing things they wouldn't want the world to know about.

His wife, Laura, knew about the condo, but she also knew well enough never to go there. As long as she had the house in Half Moon Bay and the beach house in Hawaii, she forgot the condo existed.

The front door closed with a snap, and Lockhart met Beckerman in the foyer. Beckerman was in disguise, of sorts. Casually dressed in jeans and an expensive sport jacket, he looked like the kind of guy who would visit a person like Lockhart. No one would pay him any mind.

Lockhart didn't have to ask if Beckerman had been successful. He was carrying a plastic drawing tube over his shoulder, and Lockhart had heard about the catastrophic fire on the lunchtime news.

"You did well."

Beckerman's expression showed little satisfaction. Something was clearly eating him. Lockhart waited for his enforcer to get it off his chest.

"The body count is getting high," Beckerman said.

Lockhart tensed. He had seen this coming. Beckerman was a trained killer, but he wasn't a machine. He'd killed eleven people this morning and six more in the previous two weeks. It was bound to have an effect. Still, Lockhart could do without his crisis of faith. "Is that a problem?"

"No. All deaths so far have been necessary kills."

"Then what's your problem?"

"We knew people would die, but not this many."

"That's not true. Your contingency plan included a scorched-earth policy if certain situations arose, and they did. No one's death has been authorized on a whim."

The fire was regrettable but unavoidable. It was Chaudhary's fault. No one was supposed to die at MDE. It wasn't necessary. They didn't know what they were working on, and it was only one corner of the big picture. But Chaudhary had seen more than he should have, and he guessed the rest. Lockhart eliminated Chaudhary, but he'd been too late. Chaudhary had gone viral, infecting Shane Fallon. There was only one remedy for Fallon after that. It wasn't until Fallon's death that it became obvious all of them had to die. A piecemeal approach would have been nice, but it risked too many others finding out. It was better to stamp out the virus. The fire would draw attention. Fingers would be pointed—but at whom? No one was left. After a shaky couple of weeks, everything was back on track.

"Bellis is dead," Beckerman said.

"I know. It just made the news. It's for the best. He was becoming a liability."

Bellis's suicide hadn't surprised him. Not after their dinner meeting the night before. Lockhart had made a real date of it. He'd wined and dined Bellis at an exclusive restaurant in the city, then taken him back to his condo and hit him with the project's true aims. It really was like a date. He'd bought his date dinner and expected him to make good on his side of the arrangement. Except, after Lockhart explained what Bellis's firm was designing, Bellis didn't like his side of the arrangement. As the realization sank in, he broke apart at the seams.

"Don't look so glum, Trevor. Think about the money you'll be getting."

"But it's blood money."

"There's only one way of dealing with blood money and that's to spend it. You buy a second home, a boat, a big car. Splash out on your wife and get her a diamond necklace or finance a mistress. You make it disappear by turning it into something else."

But Bellis showed Lockhart he had been wrong about blood money. There was a second way of dealing with it. You let it taint you. You let every red-stained dollar bill eat you up until there's nothing left and the only way out is by eating a shotgun. That was Bellis's method. It wasn't Lockhart's.

Lockhart wondered if Bellis had thought his suicide would halt the operation. It wouldn't. Bellis had actually helped divert suspicion away from Lockhart. An entire building of people dies as the result of arson. The firm's owner is found dead, killed by his own hand. It was a gift tailor made for the police.

Lockhart watched Beckerman absorb his explanation. He didn't like how this meeting had stalled on the condo's threshold. It was time to bring Beckerman back on track. "Look, Maurice, you've only done what needed to be done. Now, let's see what we've got."

He led Beckerman into the large living room and

climbed the three steps to the marble floor leading out to the balcony. A view of the city's skyline and bay filled the floor-to-ceiling windows.

"Hayden Duke didn't die in the fire," Beckerman said. "He arrived late."

Beckerman didn't have to elucidate any further. Hayden should have died with the others in the fire, but fortune had smiled on him. The question now was whether to make Hayden part of a mop-up exercise.

"How much do he and Fallon's sister know?" Lockhart asked.

"Little to nothing. They have suspicions, but nothing concrete."

Lockhart mused. Hayden wasn't as much of a problem as Fallon's sister. Her death would set off alarm bells. She couldn't die out in the open like her brother. She'd have to disappear. The world would have to believe she had started a new life somewhere. Hayden would make for a fitting partner to join her. While all that could be arranged, it would take time. It was something to have on the backburner.

"You're sure they know nothing?"

Beckerman nodded.

"Then maintain surveillance on them. Let them be a test of our defenses. If they start to break through, then we'll wrap them up."

"We do have one other personnel problem," Beckerman said. "I eliminated eleven people at MDE. Bellis's HR records show the technical team consisted of twelve."

Lockhart felt the fizz of irritation in the pit of his stomach. The operation was progressing well, but there seemed to be a never-ending string of complications. Chaudhary's interference had jinxed affairs. Now he understood some of Beckerman's melancholy. It seemed liked the killing would never end. "Who's missing?"

"Malcolm Fuller."

"Find him. I want a threat analysis."

"Of course."

Beckerman emptied the drawing tube's contents onto the glass dining table. Lockhart smoothed out the drawings with his hands and studied what lay before him. He pointed at the wet bar. "Fix yourself a drink, Maurice."

"I'm good, thanks."

Typical of Beckerman, Lockhart thought. *Never off the clock.*

He returned his focus to the drawings. The design was complete. Production could begin. A flush of success flowed into him, but came to an abrupt halt. He pulled out a chair and dropped into it.

Production signified not only a new phase in the project's completion, but it also marked a point of no return. At this very moment, he had the power to change events. Plans could be burned. Computer files deleted. He could walk away. He'd piss off some powerful clients, but they knew the risk of failure associated with this project. They'd bark, but they wouldn't bite. They needed him too much. If he pushed forward, there would be no going back.

"We don't have to do this," Beckerman said.

Obviously Beckerman had detected the somber mood that had descended over him. *Has he had the same thoughts?* Lockhart wondered. It would have worried him if he hadn't. He didn't want a thoughtless drone working for him.

"No, we started this, and we'll finish it."

Lockhart expected resistance from Beckerman, but he didn't get it. Instead he nodded his understanding.

Lockhart smiled. *Beckerman, ever the loyal solider,* he thought. *The man would follow me through the gates of hell if I ordered it.*

"I think you should go now. They'll be here soon, and I don't want them seeing you. I'll need you to watch my back at some point, and I don't want them recognizing you."

Beckerman noted the brush off but didn't object, and Lockhart saw him out. He dropped the smile as soon as he closed the door.

Loyalty. Beckerman understood it. Lockhart's father had too, but he had been a soldier just like Beckerman. Richard Lockhart had instilled the values of loyalty, honor and sacrifice in his son. It was a shame others didn't hold the same values he did. Lockhart's father stuck to his beliefs even when those he served betrayed him.

Richard Lockhart had been a career soldier, making it to the rank of colonel. Even when he retired, he didn't stop being a soldier. He ensured those who needed the means to defend themselves got what they needed. He never stepped outside government policy. He believed what they believed and played by their playbook. But not all policy is good policy, and when it doesn't work, a scapegoat is needed. In Panama, a scapegoat was required, and Richard Lockhart stepped up. The U.S. labeled him a criminal, and he stood like the loyal solider that he was and said he was guilty of crimes. He never mentioned the State Department had sent him there to make the deal. He died in federal prison eighteen months later, loyal to his last breath.

Lockhart lost his belief in loyalty the day his father died in prison. He went over to the mantel and picked up the framed photo of his father. Richard Lockhart was a good man. A better man than his son. But Lockhart wouldn't go down the way his father had. He placed the photo next to the plans. Yes, he'd reached a turning point. A person with loyalty to his country would turn back. He was loyal to himself and others who were loyal to him, but he wouldn't be turning back. He'd be pressing forward.

His cell phone rang. His visitors had arrived. Lockhart checked his watch. They were right on time.

"I'll be right down." He rode the elevator to the reception and collected his clients. On the ride up, he said, "Good news, gentlemen. We can start manufacturing."

CHAPTER THIRTEEN

Rice had packed Hayden off to the hospital after Santiago called in with instructions to release him. Whatever Santiago had said sucked the remaining affability from Rice. Hayden asked him what happened, but Rice remained tight-lipped. Hayden let it go. He didn't want to know. The stench of smoke clogged his head and turned his stomach.

The release didn't extend to Hayden's car, seeing as it was stuck in the middle of an active crime scene. Considering what had happened, it was hardly an inconvenience, and Hayden rode with the paramedics to the hospital.

The hospital released him after a couple of hours. He'd suffered some minor burns, bruising and had a fresh concussion to add to the one Shane had given him. The doctor who checked him out suggested he not leave the house without a helmet. Doctor humor at no extra charge. A nurse cleaned him up and dressed his wounds. The headache the arsonist had given him was fading, courtesy of the beating, but not the slightly left-of-center sensation that clouded his thoughts. His mental acuity had taken a mauling too. He took a second or two longer answering questions or making decisions. It was like being intoxicated, just without the fun part. An orderly arrived and walked him to the waiting room.

"You can call for a cab or have a friend pick you up," the orderly said.

Hayden searched for his cell phone and came up short. No doubt the phone was so much melted plastic back at MDE. An unfettered memory from the blaze turned his stomach. So many dead. He should have felt elated to have survived, but instead he imagined what it would feel like to burn alive. He felt the sensation of the fire coming at him in all directions at once, without cessation, vaporizing his skin, using him for fuel. He screwed his eyes shut against the images. He staggered, and the orderly caught his arm.

"Still feeling it?" the orderly said, opening the waiting room door. "Here we are."

Rebecca jumped up from her seat. She tossed aside a magazine she'd been wringing in her hands and engulfed him in a crushing embrace.

"I'm so glad you're okay. I've been worried sick. Santiago called me and told me to get down here."

Hayden didn't say anything—couldn't say anything. He saw the concern in her eyes. She cared for him. This wasn't all about Shane. He hadn't realized she'd felt that way about him until now, but he welcomed it. He cared for her too. She was strong, resilient, and he liked that. Despite the circumstances, he was glad he'd found her.

"Let's get you out of here," Rebecca said.

She got him to her car, then scorched the tarmac when she peeled out of the hospital parking lot.

"Take it easy," he said to calm her. He wondered how long she'd been sitting in the waiting room worrying about him.

She eased her foot off the gas. "Sorry. I can't believe how this day turned out."

Hayden imagined a number of families were thinking

the same thing. Today was supposed to be a day in a long series of days with nothing significant occurring. A dinner someplace nice. Taking in a Giants or A's game. Picking the kids up from soccer practice. A whole laundry list of activities was lined up for a bunch of people who weren't coming home to their families.

"I can't believe all those people are dead," Rebecca said. "They were just at Shane's funeral."

"What did Bellis say?"

She flashed him a confused look. "Bellis?"

"Yeah. Bellis wasn't at MDE. Santiago was going to find him."

"He's dead. He started the fire at MDE, then shot himself."

Rebecca's words slammed Hayden hard and left him dazed. The information was the wrong shape to enter his brain. No matter how many times he tried to process it, he couldn't accept it. Bellis might know something about what had happened to Shane and Chaudhary. Hayden believed that. Bellis's behavior had said he was hiding something. But a killer? No, it didn't ring true.

"How? He couldn't. It doesn't make sense."

"It doesn't matter if it makes sense. He shot himself, and he left a note."

"But why did he do it?"

"I'm sure Santiago will find out."

Hayden withdrew into himself for the rest of the short journey back to the house, unable to take his mind off Bellis. Why would Bellis kill his staff, then himself? What possible motive did he have for doing it? Hayden's thoughts brought him back to Shane and Chaudhary's last words. They both blamed themselves for something terrible they'd done. Was Bellis guilty of the same thing? If so, killing himself made sense, but that didn't explain why he would murder eleven people. Unless they were all guilty of the same terrible act Shane and Chaudhary had committed. It was hard to take in. What had these people done?

One thing ruined Hayden's perfect theory. Him. Bellis had left him to die in the fire. He wasn't guilty of any crime. Maybe that was why he'd survived. Maybe he was supposed to be the witness and not the victim.

Another thing didn't work for Hayden. Bellis couldn't have been his assailant. He'd been trying to form an image of his attacker all day. The face was a blur in his memory, but he remembered the silhouette reflected in the glass doors. An athletic man who knew how to fight had attacked him. He'd put Hayden out with a single blow and kick. Bellis was neither an athlete nor a fighter. No, the man who'd left him to die wasn't Bellis.

Fatigue set in the moment he stepped from Rebecca's VW. The mental and physical joined forces and got the better of him. He went to his room and was asleep in minutes.

A scream from someone burning inside MDE and the stench of people roasting in the inferno shook Hayden from his sleep. He sat up in bed and looked out the window. It wasn't even dark outside. Despite the short recuperation, he was feeling himself once more. He still felt his injuries every time he moved, but he no longer felt a separation between his body and brain.

He descended the stairs and found Rebecca watching the news in the living room. The fire at MDE was all over the screen. She heard him enter the room and switched off the TV.

"No, it's okay. I need to see it. I only know part of the story."

"You won't be able to avoid it," she said with a sad smile.

He could only imagine. It would take a pretty big story to knock it off the media map. He joined her on the sofa.

"Want to talk about what happened?"

"Not really."

"I need to hear it, though."

So he told her. She didn't interrupt. She just let him talk until he had nothing left to say.

"It's horrific," she said when he was finished talking, then leaned over and hugged him. Never had a simple embrace felt so right. In her arms, he felt safe, but not invincible.

He pulled away from her. "This doesn't mean it's over."

She looked at him, confused. "Where do we go from here?"

"We know Shane and Chaudhary's deaths aren't isolated incidents. Something happened at MDE to cause this. We've got a lot of questions to ask."

"Who, Hayden? Who do we ask? Everyone's dead."

"Bellis's wife. The families of the dead. Shane might not have left answers, but someone will know what these guys did."

"No." Rebecca's response was emphatic, diamond-hard. She wasn't giving him an answer, but an instruction. "Shane is dead. So are a lot of other people. You nearly died today. It ends now."

"Don't you want to know why Shane killed himself?"

"Yes, I do." She inched closer to him. "I need to know, but not at any cost. If I found out the truth behind Shane's suicide today but you had died, it wouldn't have been worth it."

"So what do you want to do?"

"With so many dead, someone has to know something. Not everyone could have kept what they'd done a secret. But we don't go looking for the answers. Let Santiago do it," she said.

"Santiago?"

"Yes. You have to see him tomorrow. Tell him everything. Tell him about Shane's file and the plans you copied. Let him find out what happened and why Shane killed himself. We'll get our answers through him. The moment we see him stop trying to find answers, we push and we don't stop until he finds out. You okay with that?"

"Sure. Santiago gets full disclosure whether he likes it or not."

"We need to celebrate," Rebecca said.

"We do?"

"Yes. You lived."

"I don't think I'm up for that."

"I wasn't giving you an option." She smiled and kissed him.

The kiss was as big a surprise as a slap, and it must have showed. She smiled again and looked away. There was only one way to break the embarrassing silence building between them. He lifted her face and kissed her back.

Still in their embrace, they guided each other back to the sofa. They crashed onto it, but managed to keep the kiss going. Clothes were mauled by hands not belonging to the wearer.

The phone rang.

They froze.

Rebecca answered it. After a brief exchange, she hung up.

"Wrong number," she said.

It sure was, he thought. The interruption had killed the moment.

She laughed, grabbed him by the hand and pulled him from the sofa. They drove to a creek-side restaurant in Larkspur and ate dinner outside. It was still warm enough to do so without needing a jacket. In a month or so, it wouldn't be. Either cold or rain would limit the number of evenings like this.

As much as the idea of celebrating in the shadow of death brought him no pleasure, he found that he enjoyed himself. The restaurant felt homey. The people at the neighboring tables were happy celebrating birthdays, anniversaries or the fact it was a Saturday night. He could be depressed and angry about what had happened in his day, but he had Rebecca to remind him that tomorrow he could celebrate life all over again.

When the meal was over and they walked out to her car, she stopped him in the parking lot and kissed him again. The kiss had been so fast he hadn't known what hit him until it was over. He couldn't say he didn't like it.

"What was that for?"

"Consider it a thank you for being here."

"You're strange."

"Is that a problem?"

"No. Just the opposite."

The next morning, Rebecca drove Hayden to Santiago's office. She dropped him off in front of the visitors' entrance and drove off in search of parking. He rode the elevator to the second floor.

Hayden smiled as the elevator climbed skyward. Last night with Rebecca had left him feeling buoyed. He couldn't deny his growing feelings for her, but he couldn't take the next step with her until the deaths at MDE were behind them. Coming clean with Santiago was the first big step.

He hadn't informed Santiago that Rebecca would be joining him, but he doubted the detective would mind. He entered the reception area and told the duty officer he had an appointment with Santiago. He signed in and waited for the detective to come for him.

After five minutes, he realized Rebecca should have caught up with him.

The duty officer's phone rang, and he answered it. "Detective Santiago said he'd be with you in a minute," he said after hanging up.

Hayden nodded and looked through the glass doors for Rebecca. She wasn't in sight.

Rice appeared through a door marked PRIVATE and approached. Hayden stood to meet him.

His cell rang. Rebecca's name appeared in the display. "Hey, where are you?"

Rice stood before him.

"Don't tell Santiago about Shane's file," she said,

"What?"

"Don't tell him anything. Everything's changed. I'll wait for you outside."

He didn't want to show Rice that something was wrong. He contorted his face into a smile that hurt and mouthed an apology for being on the phone. Rice smiled back and told him to take his time.

"Are you sure about this?" He wanted to say, "Are you okay?" but he couldn't with Rice in front of him. She sounded agitated, but not frightened. Something significant had happened to change her mind.

"Yes. I was wrong. Don't tell Santiago anything. Not until we've talked."

Rebecca hung up.

What the hell had just happened? He couldn't talk now. Santiago would have to wait. He turned to leave, but Rice called his name. He searched his mind for an excuse that wouldn't raise suspicions and came up short. Rice held the door to the Investigations Department open for him.

Hayden followed Rice to the cramped interview room he'd been in the night of Shane's death. Santiago was already waiting for him, and Hayden guessed the ceiling mounted camera was recording him.

The detective put out his hand to Hayden. "How are you doing today?"

Santiago's concern sounded genuine. Maybe this was a turning point for everyone. "I'm good, under the circumstances. Thanks."

Hayden sat, and the three of them crowded around the small desk pressed up against one wall. Santiago quizzed him on the events leading up to the fire. Hayden kept his answers short and concise. Santiago asked and re-asked the same questions for clarification. The detective was fishing, but not in an attempt to catch Hayden out. He seemed to be hoping Hayden could provide him with some cast-iron facts that centered on Bellis. After thirty minutes of churning over the same ground, Santiago surrendered.

"Is there a problem?" Hayden asked, wondering if it was linked to Rebecca's change of heart.

Santiago switched from frustrated cop to suspicious cop. "What makes you say that?"

If Santiago could fish, so could he. "You. You're chasing me for an answer I don't have. Bellis is dead. You have your killer."

"That may not be the case," Rice said.

Santiago cut the younger detective a sharp glance that halted any further elaboration.

"Things aren't as clear cut as yesterday," Santiago expanded.

"You don't think Bellis started the fire," Hayden said. "Neither do I. I've been thinking it over. Bellis didn't put me down. The guy who hit me and started the fire was bigger and knew how to fight."

"I'm not going to share details of an ongoing investigation," Santiago said.

Hayden wanted to push for clarification, but he didn't need to. He had his answer. The investigation at MDE was far from drawing to a close, and when he thought about it, how could it be? Santiago had a third suicide, eleven murders, a new street drug, an arsonist and more importantly, a horrible event no one at MDE was willing to admit to. With everyone dead at MDE, Santiago was out of leads. Santiago still had a mess to clear up, and Hayden had Rebecca waiting outside with a burning problem.

"Are we done?" Hayden asked.

"Sure," Santiago conceded with a sigh. "Thanks for your time."

"Your car is ready," Rice said and handed Hayden the release paperwork for his Mitsubishi.

Hayden shook hands, signed the forms and hurried out of the sheriff's office. He didn't have to search for Rebecca. She was waiting for him outside. She gunned the engine, and her VW came to an abrupt halt in front of him. He fell into the passenger seat, and she hit the gas.

Her features were tight with nervous excitement. She had a stranglehold on the steering wheel, and her knuckles stretched her skin taut.

"What's going on?" he said.

"Malcolm Fuller phoned me after I let you out."

"Who?"

"He's an engineer at Marin Design Engineering. He was at Shane's funeral."

Hayden didn't remember anyone called Malcolm Fuller, but he didn't care. Someone was alive. "What does he want?"

Rebecca peeled out of the parking lot and pointed her car toward San Rafael. "He didn't go into MDE yesterday because he's got the flu. He's frightened, and he wants to talk."

He has plenty to be frightened about, Hayden thought. "If he's frightened, he should see Santiago."

"But he wants to see us. Maybe we can talk him into seeing Santiago."

Hayden liked the sound of that. "Where does he want to meet?"

"Somewhere public. We're meeting him at the Fourth Street Farmer's Market."

His expression said it all.

"I know, I know," Rebecca said, "but if we want to talk to him, then we have to do it his way."

Hayden didn't like this. He thought his part in the MDE nightmare was over. He'd come too close to dying. He was ready to put Shane's suicide behind him, but it didn't look like that was going to happen. Nothing was solved. Bellis hadn't killed his staff. Someone else was responsible. The reason for the slaughter still existed.

Whatever the motive for the deaths, it had gone to the graves along with the Marin Design employees. All that Hayden could surmise was that MDE had gotten involved with some kind of underhanded business activities. It was the only explanation for why Bellis had done what he had. Death before dishonor might have been the reason Shane, Chaudhary and Bellis had all taken their lives. He was willing to accept that and wanted no more.

"I'm not sure this is a good idea," Hayden said.

"I thought you wanted to know what all this is about," Rebecca said.

"I do, but it's over. Everyone's dead."

"But they aren't. Both you and Malcolm Fuller are still alive." Rebecca reached over and placed a hand on his. He looked down at her hand, then at her face. "Please come with me. This may be something or it may be nothing, but I have to know. Okay?"

Rebecca's face begged support. He couldn't deny her. "Okay. But don't expect too much."

She nodded and smiled. "Thanks."

She drove into central San Rafael and parked on Third Street. They walked up one block and entered the thick of the Fourth Street Farmers' Market. A ten-block section of Fourth Street was shut down for the weekly event. The market had grown over recent years so that now stalls spilled over into the cross streets, and it was no longer limited to produce. A number of cottage industries sold their wares. Hayden followed Rebecca as she threaded her way through stalls and shoppers until she reached City Plaza. The plaza sat in the shadow of Luther Burbank Savings. It was comprised of a water feature and some benches. Rebecca snagged a seat for them, and they sat.

"Where is he?" Hayden asked.

"He said to come here and he would find us," Rebecca answered.

They waited for several minutes. As Hayden scanned the droves of people passing by for a man he'd never met, he wondered what the hell he was doing. After yesterday's fire, it was all too much. Someone had tried to kill him. The smart thing was to give it all up to Santiago. Let him worry about it. He was the cop. It was his job. He pulled out his cell to call the detective.

"What are you doing?"

"Calling Santiago."

"Hayden, no."

"We aren't the cops. Yesterday taught me that."

"I know, but Malcolm reached out to us. If he knows something about Shane's death or any of the deaths at MDE, then we should listen."

Hayden put the phone away. "Okay, but if this guy is blowing smoke, then I'm calling Santiago."

She didn't argue.

Suddenly, a small man cocooned in a fleece over a thick sweater dropped down next to Rebecca. He tugged a Kleenex from a travel packet and blew his nose into it.

"I'm glad you came, Rebecca," he said, putting the handkerchief away in his coat pocket.

"Well, Malcolm, you made it sound like it was in my best interest," Rebecca said.

"It is," Fuller said. "The same goes for you, Hayden."

Hayden didn't recognize Fuller. He hadn't been one of the engineers he'd met at the Giant's game or the funeral. But considering his raw red nose, bloated face, puffy eyes, and the copious layers of clothing, it didn't surprise him that he didn't recognize him.

"Malcolm, you should be in bed," Rebecca remarked.

Fuller ignored the statement and stood. The wind ruffled his greasy hair. "We need to keep moving. We're sitting targets here."

Sitting targets for whom? Hayden thought.

They left the bench behind and lost themselves among the shoppers on Fourth Street. Fuller made the pretense of checking out the produce and putting it down. Rebecca followed Fuller's example. Hayden refrained. He was more interested in keeping his eyes on Fuller. He didn't know what this guy might do. He noticed they were walking in the opposite direction from Rebecca's VW.

Fuller took a haphazard route between the stalls, stopping only to check his surroundings before moving on. Hayden guessed this was so he could spot his pursuer, but it made him very conspicuous. Hayden found the tactic disconcerting, and it left him feeling edgy.

"What are you afraid of, Malcolm?" Hayden said. "Trevor Bellis is dead."

Fuller snorted. "You don't believe that Trevor is responsible for the deaths yesterday, do you?"

Hayden didn't anymore and neither did Santiago and Rice if he read them right, but he decided to play devil's advocate. "That's what the police believe."

"What do they know?" Fuller said scornfully. "They don't know what was going on at MDE."

"But you do?" Rebecca asked.

"I know the end result. Murder. Organized slaughter. None of us are safe," Fuller said and checked over his shoulder again.

"Why aren't we safe, Malcolm?" Rebecca asked.

"Because you're associated with MDE. Everyone connected with MDE is in danger." Fuller dove into his pocket for another Kleenex and sneezed violently into it. "Our work is too dangerous."

Fuller checked over his shoulder. Hayden checked too. If Fuller feared something or someone, he didn't see it. The paranoia reminded him of Shane. Shane had seen bugs that weren't there. Fuller had yet to hit that level of paranoia, but it made Hayden wonder if Fuller had been taking the same drug as Shane and Chaudhary.

"What's dangerous about the work?" Hayden asked. "I was there, and I didn't see anything."

"I wish I knew. Sundip Chaudhary saw something though. He started asking questions, putting something together. I don't know how much he knew, but he knew something."

"Did Sundip tell anyone about his suspicions?"

"Not at first. He was a chatty guy, always had joke, but he went quiet. He started staying late and working long hours. I don't think he was leaving the office until midnight each night. Whatever he worked out, he took it to Bellis. I'd gone back to the office one night to pick up my cell that I'd left on my desk and caught Bellis chewing him out."

"Did you hear anything that was said?" Rebecca asked.

"No," Fuller said shaking his head. "To be honest, I didn't want them knowing I'd seen them. It was heated. Lots of finger pointing going in both directions. After that, Sundip became quite vocal about us being deceived, but Bellis shut him down. He put him on notice for ruining staff morale, if you can believe that. Sundip kept his mouth shut after that, but I know he kept burrowing away for answers."

"When did all this happen?" Hayden asked.

"About two months before Sundip died."

"So Bellis was behind all this?"

Fuller shook his head. "Trevor's hands were dirty. He knew something, but not everything. My guess is that he killed himself when he found out what was going on."

"What's makes you say that?" Rebecca asked.

"Something was weighing on him last week. I thought it was Shane's funeral, but it was more than that. He'd gotten real withdrawn. He spent his days in his office gazing out the window."

Fuller was building a lousy argument. He knew little and was inventing the rest. Hayden saw no point in delivering him to Santiago without something concrete to anchor his skepticism.

"Then who is responsible?" Hayden asked.

"The man who's following me."

The hairs on the back of Hayden's neck prickled. He brushed his hand over them to smooth them down. He didn't want the paranoia surrounding MDE to suck him in. Not yet anyway. A truth lay among the ashes of the building and in between the lines of Bellis's suicide note, but he wasn't ready to believe in shadowy figures stalking their every move. He'd been there at Shane's death. No one had killed his friend. He had done it to himself.

"Who's been following you?" Hayden asked.

"I don't know who he is. I saw him a couple of days ago watching the building when I left to go home. Then I saw him again yesterday afternoon outside my house."

"What did he look like?"

"Tall. Strong. Athletic. Around forty. Dark haired."

Some of the description fit the man who'd jumped Hayden yesterday. He could testify to his assailant's strength and build, but not age or hair color. Since Fuller's stalker could be his arsonist, it was enough to give Fuller the benefit of the doubt. What were the chances that there were two people stalking the staff at MDE? It disturbed him to think in those terms.

"Have you told the police?" Rebecca asked.

"Good God, no." Fuller yanked out another Kleenex and checked for his mystery man. "I can't trust the police. They're probably in on it."

Santiago, dirty? Hayden didn't believe that, but didn't bother pointing this out to Fuller. "Why talk to us?"

"I can trust you because your lives are in as much danger as mine."

Rebecca shot Hayden a glance. Panic filled her expression.

"What makes you think we're in danger?" Hayden asked.

Fuller made way for a large woman coming in the opposite direction. "Because they're cleaning house. Everyone involved is being eliminated. They started with Chaudhary, then Shane and now the rest of us. We've all got to die."

Hayden grabbed Fuller's arm, bringing him to a dead halt. "What are you talking about?" He failed to keep the fear from his voice. "Who's cleaning house? You're not making sense."

"The only way to keep a secret is to make sure that no one is around to talk about it."

"Someone witnessed Chaudhary's suicide," Hayden pointed out.

Fuller snorted. "Yeah, but the 911 caller was probably the killer. Hayden, wake up."

Hayden had woken up. Fuller was full of crap. The

guy added conjecture to some meager facts and called it truth. Fuller couldn't help them find answers, and it was time Hayden proved him to be the deluded fool that he was. Hayden knew something that couldn't be disputed.

"Shane wasn't killed. I was there. No one pushed him— he jumped," Hayden said.

"Trust me, Shane and Chaudhary didn't commit suicide. I don't know how it was done, but they were killed as surely as if someone jammed a shotgun under their chins and pulled the trigger."

"But how? You can't make someone commit suicide," Rebecca said.

"The drugs. It had to be the drugs," Fuller said, clawing for an answer. "The drugs pushed them to suicide."

Hayden shook his head. Fuller was pushing the limits of believability. Santiago had said he hadn't seen a drug of this type before, but a suicide drug? It didn't seem possible.

"How did my brother fit in?" Rebecca asked.

"He and Sundip were close work friends, and they got even closer after Sundip was mugged."

"Mugged?" Rebecca asked.

"Yes. He was attacked outside his home a month ago. I think when Chaudhary died, Shane started to dig deeper," Fuller said.

"Okay, that may explain the suicides, but not the fire," Hayden said.

"You don't get it, do you? The project's finished. Saturday was the project handover," Fuller said excitedly. "Yesterday's contract termination was turned into an extermination."

Fuller's tone and agitated body language were attracting glances from passers-by. It wasn't a good thing for a man who wanted to be inconspicuous.

"Malcolm, let me take you home, and we can discuss this when you're not so upset," Rebecca said.

"I can't go home. I'd be putting my family at risk. The moment I saw him outside my house yesterday, I slipped out."

"You haven't been home since yesterday?" Hayden asked.

"No."

"But what about your family?" Rebecca asked.

"They don't know what's going on. That's the best thing for them." Fuller was looking all around him now, not focusing on Hayden or Rebecca. "I've managed to evade him so far. I suggest you go into hiding as well. Don't go home. Don't go anywhere you would normally go. You're not safe."

Hayden felt his grip on his temper slip. He was tired of Fuller's ramblings. He grabbed Fuller's arm. "From whom?"

Fuller froze, his gaze locked on to something in the distance. He started to tremble. For a moment, Hayden thought Fuller was going to come apart at the seams.

"He's here," Fuller muttered.

"Where?" Hayden demanded.

Hayden spun around in the direction of Fuller's gaze. The market was busy with vendors and customers. No one stuck out among them or made a sudden move. Certainly not anyone matching Fuller's description. Hayden wanted to see Fuller's stalker. He wanted to know whether his stalker and the arsonist were the same person. He'd only glimpsed his assailant for a second, but he hoped his subconscious would kick in and recognize a face. It didn't.

Fuller wrenched his arm free. Hayden lunged for him, but Fuller jerked out of his way. Hayden held his hands up in surrender. He didn't want to spook him any more than he was already.

"Don't go," Rebecca pleaded as Fuller started shrinking away from them. "Malcolm, what's wrong?"

He wavered for a second, then bolted.

"Shit," Hayden said.

He and Rebecca chased after Fuller. He checked over his shoulder. No one made a break with them. No shadowy figures. Nothing. His heart sank. Fuller was just as crazy as Shane and Chaudhary. The guy was seeing ghosts. Part of Hayden wanted to let the crazy son of a bitch go. But a stronger part of him felt that, crazy or not, Fuller knew something. For all his ramblings, some of his story rang true. That something would give him and Rebecca answers. He wasn't going to let this guy get away, and lose those answers.

Despite Fuller's flu, he could move. The guy sliced through human traffic like it wasn't there. He ducked in and out of stalls, disappearing only to reappear twenty feet ahead.

"He really must know this market," Rebecca said.

Hayden started to agree with her, but she slammed into a woman pushing a stroller. Rebecca bounced off the woman without knocking her down. Stunned by the impact, the woman said nothing for a second, then launched into a tirade.

Ignoring the woman shouting at her, Rebecca said, "Go. Don't let him get away. I'll catch up."

He nodded and left Rebecca behind. He spotted the engineer, his lead even longer. Hayden was never going to catch him on foot. He needed some help. "Stop him," Hayden bellowed and pointed at Fuller. "He's got my wallet."

This failed to incite a pack of vigilantes willing to chase Fuller down like a runaway wide receiver, but Hayden did get a little cooperation. People stepped aside and called out words of encouragement. He reeled in Fuller a step at a time, his better health coming to his aid, and a smile broke out across his face.

Fuller burst from the farmer's market and cut through a parking lot toward Fifth Avenue. The parking lot dumped off into an alley. Fuller hit the alley and shot left, disappearing from sight. Hayden feared for a second that Fuller's superior knowledge of the area would give him the edge he needed to escape, but his fear subsided the moment he reached the alley. Fuller was still in sight and slowing. The flu was eating into his stamina. It was a straight footrace now. Hayden would have him in a couple of blocks.

Fuller came to the end of the alley and ducked right. Hayden caught up with him in time to see him tear across Fifth without even pausing to look. One car skidded to a halt to avoid him. Hayden compounded the driver's frustration by running out in front of him.

Fuller made for an apartment complex and disappeared among the warren of buildings. Hayden followed him in and hoped Fuller's stamina would give out soon. He pounded down a walkway with Fuller nowhere in sight. He cursed and dropped his pace in case Fuller had ducked into one of the apartments.

He was jogging past a trash enclosure when a Dumpster slammed into him, knocking him down. Fuller emerged from behind the Dumpster and kicked him twice, first in the stomach, then in the chest. Hayden put up his arms to protect himself, but each kick found its home.

Hayden pushed himself up onto his elbows, but Fuller grabbed a plastic laundry hamper from the Dumpster and smashed it down on Hayden's head. The blow didn't hurt, but it reawakened the concussion still floating about inside his head. Hayden raised his hands in surrender, and Fuller tossed the hamper away.

"Stay away from me. Look after yourself," Fuller said.

"I need answers," Hayden demanded. "I don't understand."

Fuller didn't answer. He'd already run off.

Hayden couldn't let him get away. He rolled onto all
fours and picked up the chase. His pace wasn't what it
had been, and he watched Fuller race over to his car,
throw himself behind the wheel and roar off.

Hayden cursed and leaned against a wall for support.

Rebecca came racing up behind him. "Where is he?"

"He's gone," Hayden answered and pointed in the direction of Fuller's disappearing car.

"No. He couldn't have gotten away."

Her reaction seemed excessive, considering the circumstances. "What's wrong?" Hayden asked.

"I saw him."

"Who?"

"The man following Malcolm. He shadowed you
guys. I tried following him, but I lost him."

"What did he look like?"

"Tall. Athletic. Around forty. Just like Malcolm said. I
couldn't see his face. He was wearing an Angels baseball
cap and sunglasses."

Hayden wanted to believe. He wanted someone to be
caught just so this could end. But the man Rebecca had
seen might not be Fuller's stalker. He could be anyone.
Maybe he was just some guy checking out one man
chasing another. Hayden had to stay grounded. He
didn't want to end up like Shane and Fuller. He'd drive
himself crazy to the point where he couldn't tell up
from down. He had to stick to what he knew for sure.
Shane had killed himself. Someone had burned down
MDE and left him to burn with it. This he believed.
Everything else required proof.

A dark blue Dodge Charger slipped from a side

street. The driver wore an Angels baseball cap and sunglasses. Hayden's stomach tightened.

"Rebecca, the Charger. Is that him?"

"Yes, that's the guy."

The Charger accelerated up the street in Fuller's direction.

CHAPTER FOURTEEN

Rebecca watched Hayden as he slept. The effects of the fire had caught up with him. He was way under, and it would be some time before he surfaced.

She'd put him in her bed and taken the couch. His chivalry protested, but it hadn't lasted against a much needed night's sleep. He'd crashed before nine o'clock. But when it came to her time to hit the sack, she'd slipped into bed alongside him. She hadn't wanted to be alone. She needed the reassurance of being close to someone she cared about—and she cared about Hayden. She'd come so close to losing him in the fire over the weekend. The thought of losing someone else terrified her.

She'd always had someone in her life who looked out for her. There'd been her parents, then Shane after their deaths, and now Hayden. If Hayden died, there'd be no one. She had good friends in L.A., longtime friends, but none of them were like him.

While Hayden had slept through the night, she'd lain awake. Tired beyond sleep, she listened to him breathe, slow and even. She watched the glow from the streetlight outside fade and disappear with the morning light, and as it did, another man dominated her thoughts—Malcolm Fuller. Fuller wasn't some kook. He had a reason to be scared. She'd seen the man stalking him. What frightened her most about Fuller was that if the stalker got to him, whatever secrets were locked up inside his head would die with him. Secrets she needed answers to. She couldn't let Fuller end up like his coworkers.

She slipped from the bed. Hayden stirred but didn't wake. She tried to wash away her sleep deprivation and fears in the shower. The hot water invigorated her, but it failed to dislodge her thoughts about Fuller. Every minute he continued running, his answers got farther away from her. She dressed and retreated to the kitchen.

She made coffee, then sat at the kitchen table with the coffee going cold between her hands. Fuller needed protection. If Santiago believed any of Fuller's story, she knew she could convince the detective to watch over him.

She left the coffee and went upstairs. She wanted to wake Hayden but didn't. He needed the rest. As she thought more about the situation, she realized bringing Hayden with her might not be a good thing. Fuller was jumpy enough already. Hayden's presence could ruin things. Fuller had sought her out, not Hayden. He'd be more likely to open up with no one else around.

The decision to find Fuller was easier than actually finding him. She knew nothing about the man, and there was no one at MDE to ask. The only person she could approach was Fuller's wife.

She dug out a phone book, one of the few things Shane hadn't destroyed in his rampage. She flicked through the pages and found she was in luck. There was one Malcolm Fuller listed. She grabbed the phone and a pen and returned to her tepid coffee in the kitchen. Need overwhelmed her hesitation at invading a broken family's home, and she dialed the number in the book.

"Malcolm?" a panicked woman's voice asked.

"No," Rebecca answered.

"Oh, I'm sorry." Calm returned to the woman's tone. "I was expecting a call from someone else."

"From your husband, Mrs. Fuller?"

"Who are you?"

"I'm Rebecca Fallon. My brother worked with your husband," Rebecca said. Then more sadly, "I met him at my brother's funeral last week."

"Your brother was the young man who committed suicide, wasn't he?"

"Yes, he was."

"I only met your brother once, at a Christmas party. He seemed very nice."

"Thank you. I saw your husband yesterday."

"You've seen Malcolm?" Mrs. Fuller interrupted.

"Yes. He called me and asked me to meet him."

"Do you know where he is?" Mrs. Fuller pleaded.

"No, I don't. That's why I'm calling you. I wanted to see if you knew. He ran off without finishing our conversation. I want to find him, Mrs. Fuller. He seems very frightened."

Rebecca knew she was scaring this woman, but she had no choice. She had to find Fuller.

"I haven't seen him since he ran out of here Saturday. Why did he go to you?" A sob broke from her.

"He thinks he's in danger and that I may be in danger too. He's afraid that if they hurt him, they'll hurt you and the children. He's trying to protect you."

"I don't understand what's going on. Who is he in danger from?"

"I wish I knew. That's why I'm trying to find him."

"I just wish he would come home. He would be safe if he came home."

It wasn't the answer Rebecca wanted. "I know, so let me bring him home, Mrs. Fuller. He'll talk to me. He'll listen. But I need your help."

"You have it."

"Is there any place he would consider a safe hide-away? He's hiding from the world. He'd go somewhere no one knew. Somewhere safe. Where would that place be? Please try to remember, Mrs. Fuller."

"I don't know. There isn't anyone he'd turn to, and there's nowhere he'd . . ." Mrs. Fuller stopped in mid-sentence. "Wait, there is one place, but I can't imagine him going there."

"Where, Mrs. Fuller? Where would Malcolm go?" Rebecca urged.

"My grandfather's farmhouse."

"Where's that?"

"But I don't understand why he would go there."

Hope burned hot in Rebecca's chest. "What's so special about your grandfather's farmhouse?"

"It's where we spent our honeymoon, but it fell into disrepair after my grandfather died. The place is in my sister's name, but she doesn't use it."

"Why do you think he might go there?"

"Because we always said we felt a million miles away from the world and its problems whenever we stayed there."

That was it. It had to be the place Fuller would hide. She felt it. Believed it.

"Mrs. Fuller, where would I find the farmhouse?"

Rebecca scribbled the directions on the page listing Fuller's number, then tore the page from the book.

She grabbed her car keys and cell phone, then scrawled a note for Hayden and hoped he wouldn't be too angry with her for going alone. She drove off with her guilt about ditching Hayden riding alongside her. She piled on the miles. Her guilt didn't subside, but she shelved it. Fuller was all that mattered.

According to Mrs. Fuller's directions, the farmhouse was northwest of Santa Rosa, in the middle of nowhere.

Rebecca pushed her VW hard on US-101. She couldn't reach the farmhouse quickly enough. She could be on the verge of finding out why Shane died.

What drove these people to suicide? she thought. *Guilt? What were Shane and Marin Design Engineering guilty of?*

Rebecca peeled off 101 at Santa Rosa and drove through the town. Once she left the city limits, the landscape turned real rural real fast. The longer she remained on the two-lane road, the less she saw of civilization. Neighborhoods disappeared, and her link to the world came to an end. No wonder Malcolm Fuller thought this was a good place to hide.

Rebecca's palms began to sweat. With nothing solid to refer to, she was worried that she didn't stand a chance of finding the farm. Her only directions were to follow the roads to Fulton, then take River Road west. After four miles, she'd come across a single-track lane on the left that led all the way to Bridgewater Farm, although there would be no sign for the farm now.

Rebecca had zeroed her odometer when she reached River Road. The mile counter had already clicked up 4.2 miles, and she hadn't seen a left turn for over two miles.

"Please don't be wrong about your directions, Mrs. Fuller," she murmured to herself.

There it was. The left turn whizzed past, hidden by overgrown grass. Rebecca screeched to a halt. Luckily, no one was behind to ram her. She jammed the gearshift into reverse and backed up to the turnoff, then found the drive and turned onto the single-track lane.

Unkempt grass battered against the car panels and windows like the brushes in a car wash. Rebecca ignored the incidental damage being done to her car, intent on finding the derelict farmhouse. After a mile on the track, she saw a farmhouse standing off in the middle distance. A surge of excitement swept through her, and she stood on the gas pedal. She'd found the place. But her excitement ebbed away when she reached her destination.

Anything could happen here. The farmhouse and barn to its right were the only things on the landscape. The tall grass all around waved in the wind. She certainly felt a million miles away from the world and it problems—and help.

She drove through the gateway leading to the farmhouse. The gate itself was long since gone. She stopped in front of the farmhouse and walked on the loosely cobbled surface that fought valiantly to keep the weeds from totally overrunning the farmyard. The cobbles stretched from the farmhouse to the barn and cut a path back to the single-track lane. The farmhouse was as derelict as Mrs. Fuller had described—busted windowpanes, decayed stucco and a roof that couldn't be watertight. Rebecca couldn't imagine anyone living here. She pushed open a rotten door that hung on by one hinge and it creaked, as she imagined it would.

"Mr. Fuller? Malcolm, it's Rebecca Fallon. We met yesterday," she called.

Malcolm Fuller didn't answer. She wondered if he was there or whether she was talking to herself.

The kitchen had a black hole's ability to suck in all the light, and it was hard to see anything in the gloom. Dirt on the tile floor squeaked under her boot heels. She tried the old-fashioned Bakelite light switch by the door. It didn't work—the power had long since been disconnected. She began to doubt her assumption about Fuller staying here. The place was in no condition for anyone to live here, except rats maybe.

But someone had been here. She picked up an open can of baked beans from a wooden breakfast table, blackened by damp. The few remaining beans clung to the base of the can in congealed sauce. She sniffed the contents in the can. It smelled relatively fresh, probably no

more than a day old. With no sign of a camp stove, she
assumed the beans had been eaten cold. She wrinkled
her nose at the thought and placed the can back on the
rotten table.

Rebecca wandered through the rest of the farmhouse,
calling Fuller's name. She found no other signs of human occupation. She wondered where he slept, seeing as
she couldn't find a sleeping bag. Finally, she gave up on
the farmhouse and returned outside.

She headed for the barn to see if she'd have better luck
finding Fuller there. She kicked a wooden plank, and it
skittered over the cobbles. Bending to pick up the plank,
she read the carving in the wood. The paint inlay was virtually lost, but was still legible. It read BRIDGEWATER
FARM. At least she was in the right place. She dropped the
sign on the ground and when she straightened, she saw
something move in the barn. Goose bumps immediately
broke out across her body.

Frightened she might not find whom she was expecting to find in the barn, she didn't venture any closer. She
scanned the building, trying to see through gaps in the
doors and holes in the brickwork. She feared finding a
pair of eyes meeting her gaze, even if they were Malcolm's.

"Malcolm, it's me, Rebecca Fallon. Can we talk?" She
called nervously; more and more convinced by the moment that it wasn't Fuller in the barn.

Something clattered against the farmhouse from behind Rebecca. She whirled to find the wind had caught
the farmhouse door, and it swung limply from its single
hinge like a condemned man from a hangman's rope.

Rebecca turned back to the barn and saw a figure dart
back behind the door. She was being watched.

From the single-track lane, hidden in the overgrown
grass, Beckerman watched through his binoculars. He

focused on the lovely Rebecca Fallon talking to the barn. The look on her face was priceless. She was scared out of her wits by whoever was in there. Malcolm Fuller was no one to be scared of. He wasn't violent. But the knowledge that he kept in his head was lethal to Lockhart.

He'd seen Fuller come out from the barn when Rebecca went into the farmhouse. He shot back into the barn when she came out.

Beckerman wished he could thank Rebecca. After losing Fuller on Saturday, then again on Sunday, he had no fresh leads to locate him. He knew Fuller was driving a rental car. His credit card records showed that. Christ, didn't the man have an ounce of common sense to know not to use a credit card?

Credit card records were all well and good, but they didn't tell you where the person was hiding. Luckily, Rebecca found out for him. The phone tap on her brother's phone line kept him abreast of any developments. It was a masterstroke when Rebecca got the distraught Mrs. Fuller to open up. He never would have found out about the farm without her help. *Thank you, Ms. Fallon.*

Suddenly there was action; Rebecca obviously didn't like what she saw. She bolted for her car. She jumped into the VW and roared out of the farmyard. She rejoined the single-track lane and whistled past him at great speed.

"Bye, bye, Becky," he said to the speeding car. "See you later."

Beckerman turned his attention back to the farmyard. Fuller emerged from his barn hideaway and stared back up the road at Rebecca's car. Christ, he looked like shit. He was still in the clothes Beckerman had seen him wearing on Sunday. He'd certainly been sleeping rough. His fleece was covered in dirt and grime, and his hair was plastered to his head. Silently, Fuller sneezed into his handkerchief.

"Hello, Mr. Fuller. It's nice to see you again. I'm so glad we could get reacquainted," Beckerman said and put down his binoculars.

CHAPTER FIFTEEN

Malcolm Fuller swerved off the road and aimed his rented Pontiac G6 at the three-bar wooden fence. The Pontiac slithered on the damp grass, and he sawed at the wheel to keep the car from spinning out. The Pontiac smashed through the fence, reducing it to matchwood, and the driver's side came dangerously close to clipping a post. The sedan bumped and bounced over the park's undulating ground, the suspension crashing into the wheel arches and the tires churning up turf. Fuller loved this park, and he searched for his favorite spot.

He told himself this was the right thing to do. The only thing to do. The stranger who'd visited him at the farm had helped him see the light. What the stranger had to say made total sense now. Fuller didn't understand why they had brawled at the beginning. He gazed at the rectangular bruise with the rounded corners on his wrist and rubbed it with his other hand.

Fuller found the spot he was looking for. He'd first come here with Debbie when they were dating, then once they were married and again with the kids. The kids imagined adventures here, but he felt at peace. That was what made this the perfect place. The Pontiac skidded to a halt among a group of six trees on a rise. The trees, all oaks, were widely dispersed, but their growth was so broad that the branches reached out and touched one another, creating one vast canopy.

"Debbie will understand. She'll know I'm doing the right thing. She'll be able to explain it to Tracey and Kevin."

He got out of the car and surveyed the park for other people. He saw and heard no one. Who would be out here at this time of the morning? It was all working out.

"This is a good place," Fuller said, nodding to himself. "The right place."

He went to the rear of the car and popped the trunk. The morning dew, cold and invasive, seeped into his shoes and soaked his socks. It was a minor discomfort, but it wouldn't do his cold any good.

He snatched up the rope he'd brought from the farm, then sneezed. He wiped his nose on his forearm. As he carried the rope over to the nearest oak, he talked to the trees. Someone needed to hear his confession. It would have been nice if it had been someone he knew. Someone who would understand. But someone like that would get in his way of doing the right thing.

"What we did was wrong," Fuller told the trees.

He held one end of the rope and dropped the remainder on the ground. He tugged a generous length from the loose coil and wrapped his arms around the trunk of one the oaks. The tree's bark smelled musty. It smelled like nature, clean and honest. Nature knew how to keep its charges in check. If something got ahead of itself, Mother Nature was there to slap it down. It was a pity humanity didn't incorporate its own system of check and balances. Sadly, humanity relied too much on a few strong individuals to do the right thing. Strong individuals like himself. He paused for a moment, the rope trailing from one hand. He'd never considered himself a strong-willed person, but he was when it counted. Like now.

"Bellis had the right idea," he said to the silent giants, bristling in the morning breeze. "Killing everyone in one fell swoop was a masterstroke."

He tried to pass the rope from hand to hand, but the oak was too broad and his arms too short. He gave up on the futile attempt and walked around the oak like a child around a maypole instead. When he had traversed the circumference, he tied a knot. He made sure the knot was strong and tight, before he tied another and another and another constructing a braid of even knots running down the tree trunk. He thought of Tracey's ponytail. He couldn't count the times he'd watched his wife braid his daughter's hair. It saddened him that he would never see that ritual between mother and daughter again, but he'd always kept the memory warm in his mind.

"We could never redeem ourselves." He made the statement more to his absent family than to the trees.

He braced a foot against the base of the tree and tugged hard on the rope encircling the oak. The knots tightened, securing their grip. He smiled. It would hold.

Fuller uncoiled the remaining rope, laying it on the ground in a straight line. He looked like a demolition expert unfurling a fuse from an explosive charge. He stopped when he bumped into the car.

Images of the fire at MDE he'd seen on TV filled his head. The scorch marks. The partially collapsed building. The bodies sheathed in plastic. He'd lost a lot of friends in one morning. They'd moved on, and he'd stayed behind. It was wrong, wrong, wrong. "I should have been at work that day. Being sick was no excuse. My place was with you guys, not at home."

He climbed behind the wheel of the Pontiac, closed the door and fed the rope through the open window. He stuck the keys in the car's ignition and twisted it until the radio came on. He scanned through the radio stations until he came upon a tune he loved. He hadn't heard it in years. He had the record somewhere at home. He'd bought it for Debbie. Damn, that had been before the kids were born.

He sung along with the words while he worked. He rested the rope against the steering wheel while he tied a slipknot. He tried the knot's slip action around his wrist. It worked well. He smiled. Always the engineer. He had to test his designs before he tried them out for real. Debbie would be rolling her eyes if she were here now.

"Debbie, I love you," he said.

He removed the rope from around his wrist and slipped the noose over his neck. His elbows connected with the steering wheel and gearshift. He slid the slip-knot close to his neck and tossed the slack out the window, careful it didn't get trapped under the wheels.

Malcolm Fuller buckled his seat belt and started the Pontiac. The car roared to life at the first turn of the key. He selected drive and disengaged the emergency brake. Without hesitating, he took his foot off the brake and stamped on the gas pedal. The tires ripped through the dirt before finding traction. Fuller accelerated away from the tree with the rope chasing after him.

"This is for the best," he said a second before the rope's slack came to an abrupt end.

Santiago's eyes burned from another rude awakening and the drive to Petaluma didn't help. At least he had Rice on hand to take care of the driving duties. The son of a bitch looked to be glowing with youthful exuberance. Where was his? There had been a time when he could roll out of bed ready for anything anyone threw at him, but not anymore. If his sleep routine got disturbed, he spent the rest of the day out of sorts with the world.

A good night's sleep would reset his body clock, but somehow he didn't think he'd be getting regular sleep for some time. Nothing at MDE was resolving itself. It just kept getting bloodier. Today was no different.

Rice slowed for the prowl unit blocking the entrance to the public park, although he could have sidestepped the cop by driving through the hole punched in the fencing. Santiago got out his badge and showed his party invitation to the officer. The officer pointed them in the right direction and backed his unit out of their way.

Rice drove along the narrow two-lane road into the park, following the officer's directions, not that directions were needed. It was hard to miss the fleet of law-enforcement vehicles crowded around a rise encircled by oak trees. Rice drove off the paved road and onto the grass, following the scars left by at least eight different sets of wheels.

Rice parked the car, and he and Santiago approached the crime scene. Detective Trudy Moore spotted them and broke from the group. Moore had previously worked investigations for the Marin Sherriff's Office, but she'd switched jobs eighteen months ago to head up the detectives unit in Petaluma. Off duty, she was an attractive thirty-five-year-old, but on the job, she managed to quash the beauty from her appearance. She drew her shoulder-length, straw-blond hair into a tight ponytail. She wore flat-heeled shoes, comfortable and necessary on this soft ground.

"Morning, Ruben. This is one of yours, I believe?" she said. "Your guy's name popped up on the missing persons when we ran it."

Santiago was pissed. He hadn't discovered that Malcolm Fuller was on the missing persons list until he'd contacted the engineer's home to discuss the aftermath at Marin Design Engineering. Instead, he found Fuller's distraught wife expecting news. Well, she was going to get some news, the worst kind. Santiago had placed a tag on Fuller's case file to be contacted as soon as the engineer was located. He hadn't expected to find Fuller like this.

"This is Mark Rice, Trudy. He's trying to follow in your footsteps."

The colleagues greeted each other.

"Shall we take a look at Fuller?" She didn't wait for an answer and led the way.

"Who found him?" Santiago asked.

"A night-shift worker on his way home."

"Name?" Santiago asked.

"Lou Davis," Moore replied without looking at her notes.

At least it wasn't Hayden Duke.

"He spotted the hole in the fence and the tire tracks, then followed them to the car." Moore indicated at the wreck. "He stopped for a look-see. The poor bastard expected to find someone in the middle of a heart attack. I think this has cured him of his Good Samaritan instinct." She pointed at the wreck. "Have you seen this?"

The nose end of a red Pontiac sedan had struck a tree, and the front end was folded around the tree's trunk. The tree hadn't sustained any substantial damage in comparison to the car—just some gouges in the bark. Thirty feet of rope trailed from the driver's window like a scarf. Following the crazy tire tracks, it was clear that the rope had been part of one knotted around a nearby oak. The tree looked as if it was wearing a necktie. Richard Dysart instructed a photographer on what pictures he wanted taken.

"Where's our night-shift worker now?" Rice asked.

"Back at the station, giving a statement. Understandably, he didn't want to hang around here."

"Don't blame him," Santiago added.

"When did all this occur?" Rice asked.

"Davis found Fuller at five thirty this morning. The car's hood was still warm when we arrived. I'd say he'd been dead less than an hour," she said.

"Hey, Dickie. What's the breaking news?" Santiago shouted at the coroner.

Dysart looked up from his endeavors and frowned. Dickie Dysart without his customary naughty-schoolboy grin was like a hooker without a john—it rarely happened. Santiago took pleasure in being responsible for that frown. He tried not to gloat too much. No doubt he'd pay heavily for this somewhere down the line. Dysart left the photographer to his task and came over.

"Morning, Ruben," Dysart said. "I just wanted to say thanks for calling me out here even though I'm out of my jurisdiction. The county coroner and his staff are more than capable of handling this case."

Oh, yes, Santiago thought, *I'm going to pay for this one, big time.* "Dickie, this one is connected to us, so we should be here to point the locals in the right direction. Now, if you've finished bellyaching, what can you tell me?"

Dysart shrugged off his bad mood for his coroner investigator's hat. "It's quite clear-cut. Another suicide. Quite elaborate. Very gruesome." He jerked his thumb back at the scene. "I wish I knew what your suicides were thinking before they did it."

Santiago shrugged. "Tell me what happened."

Dysart turned to the scene and ran through the course of events, pointing with his hands. "Malcolm Fuller tied one end of the rope to that tree over there and the other end to his neck. He used a slipknot, incidentally. Then he buckled himself into his seat and drove away as fast as he could."

"Click it or ticket," Santiago said, quoting the national advertising campaign slogan for seat belt use.

Moore winced at his humor, and Rice shook his head disapprovingly. Only Dysart wasn't offended.

"Well said, Ruben. An original approach but not a particularly effective one. Seat belts aren't designed to restrain a person from an upward and sideward force, as in this case." Dysart demonstrated with his own head, jerked by an invisible rope. "A modern three-point seat belt restrains you from falling forward in a front impact, and the seat keeps the back and neck straight from a rear impact."

Santiago knew how seat belts worked. He could do without the science class. If he let Dysart have his way, they would be here all morning. "Dickie, just tell me what happened here," he interrupted.

Dysart sighed unhappily. "The upshot is that Fuller didn't hang himself as easily as he thought he would. The rope yanked him from his seat, but he was caught up in the doorframe and the window. He didn't die as quick as a hanging. I doubt the spinal column was snapped right away, although, it snapped eventually with the momentum of the car and Fuller's body having nowhere to go."

"Christ," Rice murmured. "What a hideous way to go."

"Yes," Dysart said. "Very. He was lucky not to lose his head. Mercifully, the rope lost the battle in this deadly game of tug-of-war and snapped before physics showed us what it can do to a human body. The car would have kept on running if it hadn't struck the tree."

"Was it quick?" Moore asked.

"Relatively, in the scheme of things, yes. It probably took no more than a few seconds, but they would have been long seconds for Mr. Fuller. From the damage in the car, there was a lot of thrashing. Would you like to take a look, Ruben?"

"No thanks, Dickie, but I'm sure Rice would love to have a peek," Santiago said.

Rice smiled grimly and followed Dysart to the damaged Pontiac. Santiago stopped them before they got too far. He needed the answer to one question. It was the reason he'd brought Dysart out here. A no answer wouldn't simplify Santiago's world, but a yes answer would definitely complicate it a hell of a whole lot.

"Does he have the bruise?"

Dysart frowned again. "I didn't think you were going to ask."

"Does he?"

"Yes," Dysart answered before returning to his work. "Come along, Deputy."

Moore grabbed Santiago's arm and pulled him away from the scene. The exchange left a confused look on her face. "Malcolm Fuller was a missing person. That's not your department. What was so special about him?"

"I would have liked to have found out," Santiago said.

CHAPTER SIXTEEN

Hayden woke to a hand shoving him. Rebecca stood over him, ashen and close to tears. The sight of her burned the fog of sleep from his brain. He sat up and guided her to the bed.

"What's wrong?"

"Malcolm Fuller is dead. He killed himself."

Hayden understood Rebecca's demeanor. The shock and distress wasn't just for Fuller's death, but for herself. Yesterday, she'd encountered Fuller alone and on his turf. She'd been damn lucky nothing had happened to her. Hayden had underestimated Fuller and come off second best to him on Sunday and had the bruises to show for it. Fuller didn't trust anyone and her tracking him down to his only safe place was potentially lethal. If Fuller had felt cornered, there was no judging what he would have done.

Hayden had drummed this argument into her when he tracked her down after finding her note on the kitchen table. Not that he did much tracking. He'd woken up and found the note saying she'd gone after Fuller. He'd called her cell phone, but she'd been out of reception range. He'd called her every fifteen minutes until he'd finally gotten through. His father-knows-best argument lost its power the moment he got her on the phone. The fear of God that Fuller had put in her did more to underline her error of judgment than he ever could. At the sound of Hayden's voice on the phone, Rebecca broke down and bawled, pouring out her close encounter with Fuller.

"It's okay," he told her. "It's over. You're safe."

"I was so stupid."

"If you want stupid, just take a look at me. I'm a walking first-aid kit thanks to my act-first-think-later approach."

She laughed.

"Look, we need to promise each other something. We don't go anywhere alone. Together we can watch each other's backs. Safety in numbers. Okay?"

She'd agreed and he'd driven halfway to meet her. Still dopey from the concussion, he hadn't lasted too long driving. He stopped at a Denny's and waited for her. They celebrated her safe escape with cherry pie and ice cream.

He liked the smile he put on her face when she slipped into the booth next to him. He missed not seeing it now.

"How did you hear about Fuller's death?" he asked.

"It's on TV."

He slipped into his jeans and pulled on a T-shirt. He followed her downstairs, and they watched the news. The reporter recapped the events before the picture cut away to long shots of a totaled Pontiac embedded in a tree surrounded by cops working the scene. The reporter toned down how Fuller had taken his life, but it still sounded gruesome enough to turn Hayden's stomach.

"I just wish I'd spoken to him instead of running off," Rebecca said. "I might have prevented this if I'd gotten him to come home with me."

Hayden remembered Shane. He hadn't been able to turn Shane around, and they were friends. If Fuller had made his mind up to take his life, there was no talking him out of it.

But why suicide? The question kept going over and over in Hayden's head as he watched the TV footage. Fuller was paranoid. He was hiding out because he thought someone was out to kill him. Suicide seemed like an extreme way of avoiding a murderer, unless spiting the killer was his aim, but Hayden didn't believe that. Maybe Fuller had killed himself to keep the killer from his family. He had gone on the run to protect them from the person following him. The threat against his family would disappear if he wasn't alive to put them in peril. Fuller was a brave man if he'd sacrificed himself for them.

But who said it was suicide? Fuller believed he was being stalked. Rebecca may have spotted his stalker at the farmer's market. Had the stalker gotten to him?

Hayden picked up the remote and rewound the live-action TV, then paused it on a shot of Fuller's crumpled Pontiac.

"What are you doing?" Rebecca asked.

"Just checking something. They're saying Malcolm tied a rope around the tree, then to his neck, got in his car and drove away. Do you think he did it, or do you think someone did it for him?"

Rebecca looked at him.

"We saw someone following him. If you found him, someone else could have as well."

She said nothing and examined the frozen image on the TV. After several minutes, she said, "It's possible. Someone could have put him in the car, slipped the rope around his neck and put a rock on the gas pedal."

It was exactly how he imagined it being done.

"It *sounds* easy," Rebecca said, "but I don't think it would be that easy in reality. If Malcolm was dead or unconscious before the accident, it would show. There's also all the cleanup, removing the rock and all that. What if the car hadn't crashed into the tree? It could have kept on going, making it damn hard for the killer to cover his tracks. It's too elaborate. Too much could have gone wrong. Hanging him from one of those trees would have been a better staged death."

"A staged death?" he said with a smile.

"You did ask."

The analysis had done Rebecca good and her color had returned, but it had done little for Hayden. She'd punched huge holes in his theory.

"I just find it hard to believe that Malcolm killed himself after the big speech he gave us. He wasn't a man on the verge of suicide."

"I know." Rebecca took the remote from him and put the TV on live play. "From here, we can't tell one way or the other. We need to be closer to the facts."

"Santiago isn't going to tell us anything," Hayden said.

"We don't need him. We have someone else. We have Malcolm's wife."

Rebecca called her. Hayden listened in on the extension.

"Mrs. Fuller, it's Rebecca Fallon. Do you remember me? We spoke the other day about Malcolm."

"Malcolm," she managed before bursting into tears.

"I'm sorry, Mrs. Fuller. I didn't mean to upset you."

Hayden felt like a shit listening to this conversation. It was like he was torturing the woman. He and Rebecca were putting their own selfish objectives before Mrs. Fuller's right to mourn her husband. But if they discovered why everyone had died at MDE, then it would be justified.

"I remember you. You said Malcolm was in danger."

"That's what he told me."

"He didn't tell you he was in danger from himself," she said spitefully and started sobbing again.

"Mrs. Fuller, can I come see you?"

"No. I really don't have the time."

"My brother took his own life, so I know what you're going through. It might help to talk to someone who understands."

Mrs. Fuller took a long time before answering. "Okay. Maybe you're right. No one else has any answers. And I don't know what to tell the kids."

"Let me come by and help you."

"Sure. Okay."

"I'll be right over."

The Fullers lived Corte Madera, on a quiet residential street in the shadow of Mount Tamalpais. MDE lay just a mile from the house. Pulling up in front of the address listed in the phone book, Hayden looked across in MDE's direction. Trees and a rise in the topography hid the burnt-out carcass. He was tempted to drive by there after visiting Mrs. Fuller, but decided against it. What was left of MDE couldn't answer any questions.

He and Rebecca walked up to the door, and Rebecca pressed the doorbell. They'd decided in the car that Rebecca would do the talking, and he'd take a backseat. She had a common bond with Mrs. Fuller, and that would work to their advantage. Mrs. Fuller answered the door. Rebecca smiled, but Malcolm Fuller's widow failed to return the gesture. She looked past Rebecca and eyed Hayden with suspicion.

"Mrs. Fuller, this is Hayden Duke. He was my brother's friend and he worked at Marin Design Engineering," Rebecca said.

Mrs. Fuller's expression softened. She stood back and Rebecca and Hayden walked inside. Mrs. Fuller showed them into the living room. A girl, no more than nine, sat reading a Harry Potter book, but appeared not to be getting any enjoyment from it. A boy, a couple of years younger than the girl, lay slouched in an armchair play-

ing a beeping PSP. Like the girl, he lacked any enthusiasm for the game. Both kids were dressed formally in
dark clothes. Neither of them acknowledged the visitors entering the room.

Mrs. Fuller sank into an armchair while Rebecca and
Hayden took the sofa.

"Kids, can you give me a few minutes with these people?" Mrs. Fuller asked.

Wordlessly, the children complied, leaving the room.

"Thanks. I'll come up and see you later," Mrs. Fuller
called after her departing children. "It's a godsend having both of them with me. I don't know what I would do
without them."

Hayden couldn't image what it must be like for the
children to lose a parent. Rebecca could, though. She'd
know what the future held for them.

Mrs. Fuller started crying. Rebecca swooped in with
a comforting arm and guided her to the sofa. Hayden
moved to the armchair the boy had been occupying.

"Come on, Mrs. Fuller. You've got to be strong. Those
children need you. What are their names?"

"Tracey and Kevin. And I'm Debbie."

Debbie was a plain-looking woman—short, carrying a
few extra pounds. She dressed simply and wore her hair in
a low-maintenance style. She looked a million miles away
from the woman in the family photo on the wall. Everybody was happy, smiling and enjoying the moment. Debbie looked vibrant, less dowdy. Her clothes suited her
figure, and her styled hair brought out her cheekbones.
Hayden guessed the photo had been taken in the last
twelve months, judging by Kevin and Tracey's ages. It just
highlighted what death did to a family.

"Debbie, my parents died in a car accident when I
was sixteen," Rebecca said.

"Oh, that's horrible," Debbie said, forgetting her own

troubles for the moment. She placed a comforting hand over Rebecca's.

"Yes, it was horrible. But I can tell you that you'll make it, and so will Tracey and Kevin. I can't tell you what to do and how to do it, but from a person who's been there, I know that you will get through this."

"Thanks. It's nice to hear, but I wish I didn't have to hear it."

"I know. I never thought I'd have to tell someone that."

"And you have to do it all again with your brother." Debbie shook her head. "There can't be a God."

No one challenged Debbie's remark, and a silence fell over the room for minute. Hayden and Rebecca exchanged a glance. It was time to get to their reason for being there. Hayden nodded at Rebecca, and she nodded back.

"Debbie, would it be okay if we asked you a couple of questions about Malcolm?" Rebecca asked.

"We're trying to understand what drove Shane to suicide," Hayden said.

Mentioning the word "suicide" made both women wince, and he regretted using it. Neither had gotten used to the description in conjunction with their loved ones.

"Sure. What can I tell you?"

"Did he ever mention his work at Marin Design Engineering?"

"Sometimes," Debbie said. "He used to talk about it a lot, but less and less over the past year. Why do you want to know?"

"My brother was the same. He went quiet about his work then . . . you know," Rebecca said.

Debbie nodded. She understood the pattern of events.

"We think Malcolm's and Shane's deaths were work related," Hayden added. "Even more so after the fire."

"Shane had no reason to kill himself," Rebecca said. "I want to know if you felt the same about Malcolm."

Debbie stared at the floor in contemplation and shook her head at an unshared thought. "Malcolm hadn't mentioned much about his work until that Indian man drowned himself."

"Sundip Chaudhary," Hayden prompted.

"That's right. When Mr. Chaudhary killed himself, Malcolm said it didn't make sense."

"How so?" Rebecca said.

"Because he had an appointment for the following day. Malcolm thought it was weird. He didn't think suicidal people made future plans."

No, they don't, Hayden thought, remembering Shane's vacation booking that Rebecca had found.

"So, you wouldn't have expected him to have a packed social calendar," Rebecca said, thinking out loud.

"Do you know who Mr. Chaudhary was going to meet with?" Hayden asked.

"Malcolm had the feeling it was the press or someone like that."

"What made him think that?" Rebecca asked.

"Mr. Chaudhary had been questioning the project they were working on, and Malcolm had overheard him fighting with Trevor Bellis. Mr. Chaudhary claimed that he'd been lied to and said he would expose the truth."

"What did Malcolm think when Sundip died not long after?" Hayden asked.

"He thought it was convenient for Trevor Bellis, but I don't think he believed there was anything sinister going on until the fire. I hadn't really thought about it until you asked."

"Do you remember Malcolm mentioning anyone else, Debbie?" Rebecca asked.

"A college professor named Kenneth Eskdale. I only

remember it because that was my maiden name. He was a consultant on MDE's latest project. I know Malcolm said Mr. Chaudhary fought with Eskdale about his involvement."

"Fought?" Hayden asked.

"Yes. Malcolm said it got real nasty."

Rebecca flashed a glance at Hayden. Hayden knew what she was thinking. They had a lead, a place to further their curiosity.

Standing up, Debbie said, "Do you mind if I make coffee? I find it helps if I keep myself busy. It keeps me from thinking about Malcolm and what happened."

"I know what you mean, Debbie. Hayden's been a lifesaver."

Rebecca smiled at him, and he felt his face flush.

"I don't want to take up any more of your time. I would like to say thanks for your help. You've put things back into perspective," Hayden said, getting to his feet.

"Are you sure?"

Hayden nodded.

"Yes, you've been a great help." Rebecca hugged and kissed the widow. "You've got a family to look after."

After the hug, Debbie said, "You're invited to the funeral. I don't know when it is, though, because the police haven't released his body."

"I'll call," Rebecca said.

Debbie Fuller saw Rebecca and Hayden out. She seemed happy, but the veneer looked thin and it wouldn't take much to crack it.

Walking back to his car, Hayden said, "Poor woman. I'm glad she didn't ask about the last time we saw Malcolm."

Rebecca agreed.

Hayden unlocked the car with the remote. "At least we have someone to see now."

"What would a college professor have to do with MDE?"

Hayden smiled. "Let's find out."

Hayden drove Rebecca back to Shane's house. They googled Kenneth Eskdale's name and hit pay dirt. Debbie Fuller had remembered right. Kenneth Eskdale was a college professor. He taught at the University of Northern California in Arcata. Eskdale was the head of the molecular biology department. His credits were impressive, with a lengthy list of published papers not only in molecular biology but also in chemistry.

"Aren't you surprised that with Eskdale's background he would be a professor at a state college? He should be working out of a UC college at the very minimum," Rebecca said.

"Maybe he doesn't like the limelight," Hayden replied. "And how did Marin Design Engineering find him?"

"We'll only know if we ask him." Rebecca checked her watch. "If we leave now, we'll reach Arcata around two. Early enough to catch Eskdale, don't you think?"

"If he's there," Hayden remarked. He picked up the phone and dialed the number off the university's website. He asked if Eskdale was teaching and was told that he was. They got in the car and drove north.

When it came to Eskdale, Hayden didn't know what kind of man they'd encounter, but if he was embroiled in the goings-on at MDE, he wasn't going to talk without some form of arm-twisting. Hayden thought he had just the right wedge to split Eskdale open.

"We need to make a quick detour," Hayden said and drove to JD Engineering. As he parked, he said to Rebecca, "Do you mind staying here while I go inside? I won't be long."

"Don't you want me to meet your dad?"

"It's not that. Family relations are a little strained at

the moment. Last time I saw my father, things were a bit tense."

Rebecca nodded her understanding, although the smile had gone out of her.

Hayden let himself in, and Barry looked up from a sawing machine. Barry was JD Engineering's only employee. John Duke had picked him up out of pity. Barry had been on the job a month at John Duke's old firm when it decided to relocate to Oregon, putting John Duke into retirement and leaving Barry unemployed. Barry didn't want to relocate and found himself without a job. Feeling sorry for the guy, John Duke took him on. He was proving to be a competent machinist.

"What's the good word, Hayden?"

Hayden knew plenty of words, but none of them good. He put on a show for Barry, though. "I'm going to say Albuquerque."

"Good one," Barry said. "Your dad's in his office."

"Thanks, Barry."

"I heard about your buddy. That sucks, man."

"Yeah, it does."

"Amen, brother."

Hayden stopped in the office doorway. John Duke was on the phone placing an order. He gestured at Hayden to close the door, and Hayden did so. John Duke finished his call and hung up.

"You're back. What do you need this time?" His dad's harsh tone said he hadn't mellowed since their last encounter.

"I need those drawings back."

"Wait here."

Hayden leaned against the side of the desk while his dad left the office to open the safe. He returned a few minutes later with the drawings and the flash drive. Hayden went to take them, but his father sidestepped him.

"What are you going to do with these? You can't return them to their rightful owner because everyone's dead. You were damn lucky not to end up dead too. I saw the news. So did your mother. I don't understand why you didn't see fit to tell us. We're your parents, for Christ's sake."

"I meant to tell you."

His dad shook his head in disgust. "Sit down."

"Dad, I don't have time for this."

"I said sit down."

A lecture was coming. It couldn't be avoided, and if he was being honest with himself, he deserved it. Hayden did as he was told and sat down.

His father sat behind his desk and put the drawings between them. He weighted them down with the flash drive. Hayden could have easily snatched the drawings away, but that wasn't an option.

"When I saw the fire on the TV, I almost came here to burn all this crap," John Duke said, nodding at the plans, "but I didn't because that should be your decision."

"I'm sorry. I should have called you and Mom."

"Yes, you should have."

His dad let that hang in the air for longer than was comfortable.

"The last time I saw you, you said you were getting answers. Did you get them?"

"No."

John Duke reached inside a desk drawer and tossed a Zippo lighter at Hayden. He followed up the lighter with a can of lighter fluid and placed it alongside the plans.

Hayden caught the lighter. He ran his hand over its polished surface. It would be so easy to burn the drawings, destroy the evidence and break his ties to the deaths, but he couldn't. He'd been left for dead once. The danger wouldn't go away just because he burned the plans.

Someone out there saw him as a threat. He tossed the lighter back at his dad.

"I can't."

His dad caught the lighter but made no attempt to put it away. "Why?"

"Fifteen people have died at Marin Design Engineering. Every one of them worked on this project." Hayden tapped the drawings with an index finger. "The only surviving engineer contacted me after the fire and warned me that I was in danger. He's dead now. I'm the only one left and I don't understand a damn thing that's going on, but it's wrapped up in these plans. I found a college professor who consulted on this job. He might know something. I want to show him the plans. If he knows anything, then I'm not letting him out of my sight."

"Let it go."

"I can't. I'm not in a position to put my head in the sand and pretend this didn't happen. I have to keep asking questions."

"Even if those questions get you killed? There are a lot of dead people. You're lucky not to be one. Walk away while you still can."

Hayden had squeezed that outcome from his mind and put his faith in denial. He was walking a tightrope. If he looked down, he'd fall.

"You're scaring me, Hayden."

"I know. I'm sorry."

"Don't be sorry. Be safe," John Duke said and tossed Hayden the plans and the flash drive.

CHAPTER SEVENTEEN

Contingencies and problems. Lockhart always planned for both. Nothing in life ran smoothly. Humans were far too random for anything to follow a predictable path. Unpredictability led to the elimination of Chaudhary, Fallon and the others who'd disturbed the delicate nature of his plans. It hadn't been part of his original plan, but he'd made contingencies for interference or wayward events. Problems, like contingencies, came with the territory. It made him a glass-half-empty kind of a guy, but it also made him successful at what he did.

Breakfast presented a fresh problem, which evoked another contingency. He checked his back account in the Cayman Islands and saw the stage payment hadn't been deposited. Twenty-five percent of the agreed sum was to be deposited when manufacturing began. Manufacturing had begun days ago. The clients knew this. Still, no money.

Sadly, he had expected this problem. He didn't like it, but he was ready for it. These clients weren't fools. He'd dealt with many who were. He didn't make a habit of selling substandard merchandise, but those who didn't know an AK-47 from a hole in the ground needed a harsh lesson in the arms trade. He'd once sold three

Russian-made helicopters, not one with solid airworthiness, to an Angolan outfit. He smiled remembering that one. Fools and their money.

But no fools this time. They'd hired Zhou Zeguang to front for them. Zeguang was good. He kept things professional, straightforward and tight. He operated out of his native China, and Lockhart viewed him as his opposite number from the East.

Bringing Zeguang in also kept things clean. He wasn't on any watch lists and could come and go as he pleased. He worked with government approval and protection. He brought a lot of money into Beijing.

Lockhart liked dealing with Zeguang, but one aspect always irritated him. Zeguang took confidentiality to lawyer-like levels. Lockhart didn't know who he was fronting for on this occasion. "Africans," was all he would say. Lockhart knew his industry well. He knew who possessed the finances to pay for what he was selling and who possessed the hate to use it. He'd narrowed Zeguang's clients down to four possible candidates and counted himself satisfied.

Bottom line, he trusted Zeguang. Well, as far as anyone trusted anyone in this line of business. Despite Zeguang's straightforward approach, the missed stage payment smacked of his influence. It didn't worry Lockhart. It was just part of the negotiations.

The question now was should he be the man or the woman in this relationship? Should he call Zeguang or wait for Zeguang to call him? He didn't fancy playing the woman. No doubt if he did, he'd be making a concession today and dropping his panties before he was ready to go all the way. But he wasn't going to call Zeguang and ask why he hadn't been paid. No, if Zeguang wanted to make a point, he could call him. When playing hardball, you couldn't afford to play the pussy.

He didn't have to wait long. He barely had time to finish his breakfast and get through the *Chronicle*. Zeguang called at precisely ten A.M., obviously his deadline on this matter. His eagerness not to prolong the affair told Lockhart something. He wasn't after a discount. Pricing had been determined. But Zeguang and his clients wanted something. Lockhart felt good about this. Providing things was what he did well.

"Morning," Lockhart said.

"My clients haven't paid you as arranged," Zeguang said.

"So I see. Is there a problem?" Lockhart kept his tone unemotional. If he became emotional, everyone became emotional. Emotion led to rashness. Contingencies rarely combated rash behavior.

"We need to meet."

"Okay, let's meet. The usual place?"

"Yes. Shall we say in thirty minutes?"

Oh yes, Zeguang and his clients were after something special. They weren't giving him any time to prepare. They thought they'd get more from him if he was vulnerable and exposed. They wouldn't. They'd get what he saw fit to give them.

He left his condo and took the elevator to the parking structure. He spotted the silver Chrysler 300 with Zeguang's people inside the moment he exited the garage. It slipped into traffic behind him from its parking spot across the street from his building. Zeguang definitely wanted to control the situation. Lockhart would let him think he was calling the shots.

He punched Beckerman's number into the cell. Beckerman answered on the second ring.

"Zeguang's clients are playing hardball. They've balked on this payment, and Zeguang wants to meet now."

"You need me there?"

"No, I want him to think he has the upper hand. Just stay local. I may need you at short notice."

Lockhart hung up and continued with his drive. He kept a keen eye on the Chrysler and watched for a second tail. A second car, another 300, picked him up half a mile later. They made it look very easy, but they knew his origin and destination. It was hard to screw up. Their test would come later, after the meeting.

The meeting was at the Peace Plaza in Japantown. The irony of the location wasn't lost on him considering their business.

All the street parking had been snapped up, so he parked in a lot. The Chryslers didn't follow him in. He spotted the first one parked illegally in front of a fire hydrant. The second one was nowhere to be seen. He imagined it was circling a perimeter to ensure he hadn't invited anyone to the party.

He walked along Post to the Peace Plaza and stopped in front of the commemorative pagoda. It was an interesting structure, spoiled only by a rusting access ladder contained inside.

Zeguang wasn't waiting for him at the pagoda, but he'd be close by. This wasn't a spur-of-the-moment idea. He would have had this spot scoped out long before he called him in, but he'd do his best to make it look improvised. No matter. Lockhart played along and waited diligently.

He liked outdoor meeting spots. They were easy to flee and made spotting watchers easy. No doubt a shooter had him in his sights from a nearby rooftop, but he didn't want to show his concern. Everyone working Zeguang's side of the deal needed to believe he wasn't expecting trouble.

The doors to the Japan Center slid open and Zeguang stepped through, accompanied by a bodyguard. Zeguang had just crossed fifty and sported a build similar to a fire hydrant, whereas his bodyguard was in his late twenties, equine looking and chock-full of steroids. Zeguang called

Lockhart's name. He smiled and waved back. He didn't have a reason to be unpleasant—yet.

"Zhou, good to see you again." Lockhart shook hands and examined Zeguang. He looked for worry, fear, anger, avarice or anything that would clue him in to his mind-set. He saw smugness. An interesting emotion. He really thought he had something on him. "Do we have a problem?"

"There is no problem. Not for a man of your abilities," Zeguang said and smiled. It failed to exuded friendship. Lockhart didn't like this, but he didn't let his concern show.

"I'm glad to hear it," Lockhart said.

"My clients and I have seen the plans, and we are most impressed with your progress. I know you should have received the wire transfer today, and we have every intention of paying." Zeguang kept his smile burning, but his eyes were ice cold. "My clients have invested a considerable amount of money in this venture. Money they have and money they are only too happy to invest, but only as long as what they're buying actually works."

This wasn't some move to back out of the deal. This felt like a delay tactic. The Africans had sunk too much money into this project to walk away. He'd get his money. All the same, he felt they wanted to change things up and get a little something for nothing thrown in. He didn't like it.

"Do you doubt that I can provide what I've said I can?"

"No, no, not at all. Your reputation goes a long way, but your reputation is built on mature technology. This isn't. You claim you have a working product from a previously untried and untested design. That is a cause for a concern."

Lockhart let the "claim" remark slip. He wouldn't be

provoked. He needed to reassure Zeguang, not start a fight.

"Five hundred thousand dollars is a lot of money to pay without any indication that what my clients are buying actually works."

"You want a demonstration," Lockhart suggested.

"Yes, a demonstration." Zeguang beamed. "I knew you would understand. We would like a demonstration before my clients pay you any further funds."

A demonstration had made the list of contingencies he'd planned for as part of this project. He'd hoped it wouldn't be necessary. Zeguang was right about one thing. The project involved technology he'd created, not bought. He'd switched jobs from a dealer to a manufacturer. Manufacturing required much more capital investment. He could afford to complete the project without the stage payments, but he'd be cutting his funds to the bone. The real money would be made when he marketed the product to organizations, factions and governments long after Zeguang and pals were finished.

"I'd be happy to set up a demonstration. Do your clients have a particular target back home that they wish to use it on?"

Zeguang smiled a shark's smile and shook his head. "I think you misunderstand. The demonstration is to take place here."

Lockhart went cold and failed to keep the shock from his expression. A live demonstration on American soil, on American people, wasn't a contingency he'd planned.

"Preferably something public. Something that will capture people's attention," Zeguang said. "Is that going to be a problem?"

"It won't be a problem." The words tasted like ash on Lockhart's tongue.

"Excellent," Zeguang said. "When can we expect the demonstration?"

Lockhart's mind was still reeling, but he slammed on the brakes and thought hard about how he could do this. Options presented themselves to him. He saw a way out.

"In the next few days."

"Good," Zeguang said and walked away with his shadow.

Lockhart headed back to the parking lot. The Chrysler shadowing him remained in place. He still felt the shooter's scope tracking his progress on the street. The Chrysler picked him up the moment he left the parking lot. The second Chrysler picked him up soon after, both cars taking turns at being closest.

It was time to lose them.

He drove toward downtown. The traffic thickened the closer he got, forcing his tails to jockey for position. He needed a break with the traffic and got it. He ran a red. The taxi between him and the Chryslers forced his tails to stop for the light. It wouldn't stop them from regaining position, but he needed only seconds.

He turned on Powell and dumped his car with valets at the Sir Francis Drake Hotel. His tails saw him stop, but he didn't let it worry him and ducked inside the hotel. He strode through the lobby like he was a guest. No one questioned him. He fit in too well with the clientele. He guessed one of his tails would be on foot by now, but it was too late. He emerged from a side entrance on Post, ran against traffic to cross the street and disappeared down the slope into the underground parking lot beneath Union Square. He went straight to the parking stall containing an aging Mercury Sable that Beckerman kept there for such emergencies. It was one of three cars stashed around the city while this operation was in play. He grabbed the key from under the rear passenger wheel arch and let himself in. He emerged from the parking lot, neither of the Chryslers in sight, and drove sedately out of the city.

As he crossed the Bay Bridge, he called Beckerman and told him to meet him. He drove to Piedmont, parked on a residential street in the shadow of Mountain View Cemetery and waited.

He tapped the steering wheel impatiently. He would have killed for a cigarette, but he'd quit nearly three years ago as part of his wife's concerns for his health. Admittedly, his health had improved and, unlike most ex-smokers, his weight hadn't increased. So, all in all, giving up smoking was a win-win situation, except when he needed to do something with his hands.

It began raining. This was as bad as it got in the Bay Area. The rain bounced off the windshield until the clinging raindrops totally obscured his vision. Lockhart pulsed the wipers once to clear the windshield. Nobody walked the street, and who could blame them in this weather? His rapidly disappearing view consisted of parked cars and a row of homes on both sides of the street. At this time of day, he expected most to be uninhabited.

He waited twenty-two minutes before Beckerman appeared. He didn't see a car park on the street or Beckerman walk toward him. The passenger door simply opened and the interior light came on. The noise of the rain was amplified as Beckerman slid into his seat.

He had appeared from nowhere. Lockhart had been looking in his mirrors just moments before Beckerman opened the door and hadn't seen him. Beckerman's stealth pleased him. This was the reason Lockhart employed the man. He couldn't imagine many getting the better of his attack dog. But Beckerman's persona was his weakness as well as his strength. Dogs had a habit of turning on their owners if treated poorly. That left Lockhart vulnerable, which wasn't a good place to be. One day, Beckerman would have to be put down.

Beckerman combed a hand through his hair, squeezing the water out. "Problems?"

"Yes, but first things first. Malcolm Fuller. Did his death have to be so extravagant?"

"I have no control over what people do once I've dosed them. Blame the drug, not me."

"How did you track him down?"

"Rebecca Fallon. I captured a call between her and Fuller's wife. She led me straight to him."

Fuller's death cut Lockhart's stress levels. All of MDE's technical staff had been eliminated. He'd finished what Trevor Bellis had started—as far as the police and public were concerned. For all intents and purposes, the MDE chapter couldn't present any further leaks.

Lockhart pulsed the wipers again. A man with his head down and his hands stuffed in his pockets approached the car. Lockhart stopped talking. Causally, Beckerman removed a small oil-black pistol from an ankle holster and released the safety. He produced a silencer, as long as the automatic, and carefully screwed it onto the barrel of the gun. He performed the task with deft and practiced precision.

The man dashed past the car without giving Lockhart and Beckerman a glance.

"Anyone to worry about?" Lockhart asked.

"No. Just a civilian." Beckerman adjusted the side mirror to follow the man's progress. When he was satisfied, he clicked the safety back on the automatic, but he kept the weapon handy.

"Rebecca Fallon worries me," Beckerman said. "I could have taken her at the same time as Fuller."

"No, I've told you Fallon and Duke are our checks and balances. They tell me if we're too exposed."

"I don't like it. They keep asking questions—finding

things out. She pumped Fuller's wife for information, and they both met with Fuller."

"But do they know enough to harm us?"

"Not yet, but they will. They need to be removed from our equation."

Lockhart knew Beckerman was right, but both Hayden and Rebecca's deaths would create a new problem. They were very much under the watchful gaze of the police. Their deaths would be investigated.

"No, I have something else in store for them. Our clients have requested a demonstration, and Hayden and Rebecca would make the perfect guinea pigs. Can you put something together to make that happen? It has to be public."

Beckerman tensed. "There's a risk of civilian casualties."

"Not if you do it right." Lockhart smiled. "Lighten up. I'm sure you can make it work."

CHAPTER EIGHTEEN

The University of Northern California was hard to miss. It sat right off US-101. Hayden and Rebecca had made good time, arriving in the early afternoon. They parked and approached the reception desk in the main entrance. It was manned by a young woman whose severe hairstyle and dress-sense aged her.

"Can I help you?" she asked, smiling pleasantly.

"Yes, we're looking for Professor Kenneth Eskdale," Rebecca said. "We have an appointment with him."

"Ah, you want the Science Block." She produced a campus map from behind the reception desk and pointed out the area on it. "You'll find Professor Eskdale in room two-two-three."

"Thank you," Rebecca said.

They were turning to leave when the receptionist said, "That's strange, though."

"What's strange?" Hayden asked, turning back.

"Professor Eskdale rarely has visitors." Conspiratorially, she glanced to her left, then right. "He likes to keep to himself. He has too much going on upstairs to be bothered with the rest of the world, if you know what I mean."

"Yeah, I know." Hayden took Rebecca's arm and led her outside before they raised any more suspicions.

Following the directions, Hayden and Rebecca took a series weaving paths between the various campus blocks. Spanish missions influenced the architecture, giving the place character. Landscaped lawns and trees filled the gaps between the buildings. The campus's tranquil feel helped calm Hayden's nerves. He and Rebecca had a plan for dealing with Eskdale, but he had no idea if it would work.

They found the Science Block, located near the campus's center and a long way from where they parked. It didn't bode well for a clean getaway should they need it.

They climbed the steps to the second floor. Hayden knocked on the door with Eskdale's name and room number stenciled on the frosted glass. Opposite Eskdale's room, a class was in full swing and the lecturer was scribbling furiously on the whiteboard.

No one replied.

Hayden tried the door handle, but it was locked.

"Let's try the secretary's office," Rebecca suggested.

Two doors down, they found the secretary in a pigeonhole-shaped office. No leggy blonde for Professor Eskdale; no, he had a petite, silver-haired woman who had to be close to retirement. The office was so small that a single occupant overcrowded it, let alone three. For the sake of not taking all the oxygen in the room, they remained in the doorway.

"Hi, we were looking for Professor Eskdale, but his office is locked," Hayden said.

"You won't find him there. He's teaching," she said with a smile.

"Oh. We have an appointment with him."

"We're just a little bit early," Rebecca explained.

"Oh, yes? What are your names?" The secretary started flicking through a diary.

"Rebecca Fallon and Hayden Duke," Rebecca said.

"Well, he doesn't have your name down for today."

Hayden thought fast, but Rebecca beat him to the punch.

"We spoke to him last night. It was very short notice, I'm afraid."

"What time was he expecting you?" she asked.

"Two," Hayden said.

"I don't think so. He doesn't have a free period until three."

Hayden started backing out into the corridor. "We'll come back at three. Don't worry about telling the professor. I don't want him to know we turned up an hour early. We are supposed to be graduate students, after all. Thanks. We'll be back later."

He caught Rebecca's arm and pulled her away. He turned his back on the secretary before she had the chance to memorize their appearance. They hurried back to the stairs. The secretary stood in the doorway of her office watching them. Thankfully, her suspicion didn't extend to following them.

"What do we do now?"

"Come back at three."

"What if she tells him about us?"

"There's nothing to tell. A couple of students tried to gatecrash a professor's office. Big deal."

Rebecca frowned.

"But, to make sure, we'll come back before three and beat her to it—or just beat her." Hayden smiled and shrugged.

"Come on, let see if we can't find a hideout," Rebecca said, laughing and taking his hand.

They took refuge in a café on the top floor of the

Student Center next to the campus bookstore. The café was about to close, but Hayden talked them into staying open five more minutes. They bought sandwiches and sodas and took their food out to the quad.

Hayden bit into his sandwich. It was a cut above the usual college fare. It took him a couple of bites before he noticed Rebecca's silence. As she ate her sandwich, her gaze never left the ground. There was sadness in her expression. It pained him to see it.

"Penny for your thoughts," Hayden said.

"Sorry, I was just thinking."

"That's good. I would hate for you to be a dumb blonde."

"Ha-ha," she said smiling.

Hayden liked that he'd washed away her melancholy so easily. He grinned. "What were you thinking about?"

"About this. The situation we're in. So far, we have a lot of dead people. What happens when we find out why?"

Hayden thought for a moment. "I don't know. It depends what we find. If it's a matter for the police, we'll take it to Santiago and Rice. If it turns out to be nothing, then we'll do nothing. We'll have to see what turns up."

"And what happens to us?"

"Us?"

The subject of *us* hadn't been mentioned until now. Ever since their interrupted kiss, Hayden had chosen not to broach the topic for fear of rejection. Their clandestine meeting with Fuller had made for a convenient distraction, and he'd placed the subject firmly on the backburner, although thoughts of *us* regularly came to mind.

"I feel we've gotten close over the last couple of weeks. It's weird, but it feels longer. I would like to get to know you better." Rebecca broke her gaze with Hayden and stared at the table. She blushed. "I would hate to lose contact."

"So would I." It was Hayden's turn to be embarrassed. "I feel the same way."

She leaned across the table and touched his face, her hand brushing his cheek. It was cool against his hot skin. He reveled in her touch, but he tried not to show it. She smiled brightly and took her hand away. He felt like the cat that had all the cream, and he wanted to purr. That was until she showed him what she'd wiped from his face.

"Tomato," she said.

Hayden's face got hotter.

Hayden and Rebecca retraced their steps back to Eskdale's office, arriving at five minutes to three. The secretary's office was empty. The lights were out, and the doors were locked when Hayden checked with a jiggle of the doorknob. She was either on a lunch break or a part-time worker. Hayden hoped for the latter.

On Eskdale's door, a yellow Post-it note obscured the professor's name.

> Prof. Eskdale,
> You had two visitors who didn't have an appointment. They seemed odd. Their names were Rebecca Fallon & Hayden Duke. Hope this means something to you?
> See you tomorrow.
>
> Alice

Hayden jerked the Post-it from the door, crumpled it up and stuffed it in his pocket. "We don't need a letter of introduction."

"Can I help you?" a voice said.

Hayden turned to see a man in his fifties approaching

them. The word that sprang to mind was *rat*. The man looked like a rat. He had large ears and an untidy mess of yellowing teeth. Beady eyes were hidden behind wire-rimmed spectacles and his steel-gray, receding hair needed a wash. His pointed face and wispy mustache only accentuated the image.

"We're looking for Professor Eskdale," Rebecca said.

"I'm Professor Eskdale," the rat-man said.

"I'm Hayden Duke, and this is Rebecca Fallon. We were wondering if we could have few minutes of your time, Professor," Hayden said.

"We're graduate students," Rebecca added. "We wanted to pick your brain, if that's okay?"

Eskdale shifted his briefcase from his left hand to his right, checked his watch and frowned. "I can give you ten minutes."

"That's great," Rebecca enthused.

Hayden and Rebecca stepped out of Eskdale's way, and he unlocked the door. He stood back and allowed them in first.

Eskdale's office was larger than Alice's, but it couldn't be called expansive. It had just enough room for his desk, a couple of chairs for visitors, filing cabinets, bookshelves and a small window with a small view of the campus. The office would have seemed larger if it wasn't so cluttered. It didn't look like Eskdale ever put anything away— errant papers littered the room. Rebecca had to move a sheaf of papers to sit, which Eskdale took from her and relocated to another temporary home.

"Take a seat. Well, I know you're not from this establishment. So, where are you from?" he asked.

"Stanford," Rebecca responded, from their pre-arranged script.

"Stanford." Eskdale nodded approvingly. "Good school, good school. Long trip, though."

"Yes." Rebecca smiled and glanced at Hayden.

Eskdale made himself comfortable, putting his briefcase down by his chair and setting aside the paperwork
on his desk.

"So what brings you to me?"

"Molecular biology," Hayden replied.

"Good. The world needs good molecular biologists."

This was where things might start getting sticky.
Hayden knew nothing about molecular biology, and
Rebecca was in the same boat. Some biology had cropped
up during Hayden's college courses, but nothing in
Eskdale's league. The best he could do was to play it by
ear and if he became stuck, hit the professor with the
third degree.

"So you must know McGammon and Jameson?"

Hayden assumed they were lecturers, but he wasn't
going to test his assumption. "Of course," he said.

"Good teachers, don't you think?" Eskdale said.

Hayden felt his pulse accelerate. He felt like he was de-
fusing a bomb. Everything that was said either brought
him one step closer to success or having the whole thing
blow up in his face.

"The best," Hayden said.

"A shame McGammon is retiring."

"Yes. Next summer," Rebecca said.

"The summer you say?"

Hayden's heart skipped a beat.

"I thought it was Easter. But you would know best."

"A shame to see him go," Hayden said.

"Yes, but at least his knowledge and experience is carried over to the next generation." Eskdale indicated Hayden and Rebecca and smiled. "Anyway, I don't have much
time. What can I help you with?"

"Career advice really," Hayden said.

Eskdale cocked his head to one side. "Career advice?"

"Yes. Our career paths"—Hayden pointed to Rebecca

and himself—"are leading us toward a life in academia and we were wondering if that was the right path to take."

"Teaching is a well-respected profession," Eskdale said, his tone took on a defensive note at the possibility he was a lesser mortal for being an educator. This worked in Hayden and Rebecca's favor.

"Yes, but is it a well-paying profession?" Rebecca asked.

Eskdale frowned. "Sadly, the private sector will always pay better. It isn't governed the way the education sector is. There are no limits. That doesn't mean you can't make a good living as a college professor. Grants and expert knowledge can bring supplemental income."

"Expert knowledge," Hayden said. "Does that mean consulting opportunities?"

"Yes, a number of firms have paid for my services and research."

"That's great," Rebecca said. "Which firms have you worked for?"

Eskdale listed half a dozen companies, three of which were Fortune 500 firms, but he didn't name MDE.

"Are you consulting for anyone now?" Rebecca asked.

"No. Not right now."

Hayden caught a flicker of suspicion in Eskdale's dark, beady eyes. He didn't let it worry him. It had to happen at some point. He and Rebecca weren't here to probe, but to get answers. They had to reveal themselves sooner or later. It looked like sooner.

"Have you ever consulted for Marin Design Engineering?" Hayden asked.

Eskdale pressed his lips together so tight, it drained them of all color. "Who are you?"

"That doesn't answer my question."

"What do you know about Marin Design Engineering? Are you reporters?" Eskdale didn't know what to do with his hands. They had been resting neatly on the table, but now they danced nervously across his desk, looking for a purpose they had yet to find.

"How are you involved with MDE?" Hayden demanded. "Did Trevor Bellis hire you?"

"I'm not involved with them."

"Why would you be concerned about reporters if you have no involvement with them?" Rebecca asked.

The question put Eskdale on the ropes. He'd left himself nowhere to go.

"Sundip Chaudhary, Shane Fallon or Malcolm Fuller—do you know any of those men, Professor?" Hayden asked.

"They're dead. Along with many others," Rebecca said. "Why are these people killing themselves?"

Eskdale was alight with panic. His hands trembled, and his body shook. He knew he'd been caught.

"Who are you people?"

"Survivors," Hayden said. "MDE is gone. Everyone is dead, except for us. We want to know why."

"Get out," Eskdale said. It sounded more like a plea than an order. Even he realized how ineffectual he sounded and he repeated himself, this time with more command in his tone.

Hayden produced a folded MDE drawing from his jacket and threw it on Eskdale's desk. With fevered hands, the professor unfolded the drawing and scanned the details. He looked up and his frightened eyes darted from Hayden to Rebecca.

"What are you doing with this?" Eskdale tapped the drawing with a bony finger. "This is a restricted document."

"What are these vessels to be used for?" Hayden tapped the drawing in Eskdale's hands. "What's so special that fifteen people had to die?"

"Why did my brother kill himself? What was so

terrible it made him leap from a bridge to hang himself?" Rebecca said, fighting back the tears.

"You two are committing a crime. You could go to prison for what you've done."

"My conscience is clear. How about yours, Professor?" Hayden demanded.

"Why don't you tell us what you know?" Rebecca's tone was hard and unforgiving.

"I'm going to tell the police, and I'm going to keep this as evidence," Eskdale said holding up the drawing.

It was a cheap intimidation tactic, and Hayden was having none of it. He snatched the drawing from him. Eskdale snatched it back. Hayden was tempted to let him have it just to see who he took it to, but Eskdale would lead them to someone regardless of whether he possessed the drawing or not. Hayden yanked the drawing away, but Eskdale grabbed at a corner, tearing a chunk off.

With the drawing lost, Eskdale seized the phone on his desk and started punching in a number. Rebecca swept her arm across the professor's desk sending the phone and paper-laden filing trays crashing to the floor. The handset went flying from Eskdale's grasp.

The situation was getting away from them. Hayden had hoped they'd intimidate Eskdale into talking, but the professor was panicking. If they didn't do something to regain control, he didn't like to think where this would end up.

Eskdale bolted for the door, sending his chair skidding back into the wall. Hayden rounded Eskdale's desk, blocking his escape. Eskdale ran straight into Hayden, but the diminutive man failed to knock Hayden aside. Hayden shoved Eskdale back into his chair and pinned the professor to the arms of his chair with his hands. He pushed his face in Eskdale's.

"You're not talking to the police or anyone else you

think can help you. You're going to talk to us first and tell us what you know."

Eskdale writhed in his chair. Hayden put a stop to it by pressing his knee into the professor's chest.

"Lock the door," Hayden said to Rebecca. "Start talking, Professor."

Just as Rebecca reached the door to lock it, it opened.

Eskdale's visitor, a tall, angular man, was reading his notes. "Kenneth, I was wondering how you were—"

What he saw rooted him to the spot. Both Rebecca and Hayden stared at him transfixed, awaiting his reaction. Everyone froze in time, waiting for the catalyst to start the world spinning again.

"Bob," Eskdale managed, after a long moment. "Help."

"Christ," the man said. He dropped his notes and backed out of the room on legs that seemed not to have any knee joints.

"Out," Hayden shrieked.

They released Eskdale, who popped up in his tilting chair. Rebecca charged out of the room. Hayden gathered up the drawing and chased after her. Rebecca, first out the door, body-checked the visitor, slamming him into the corridor wall. She made room for Hayden following close behind and they both headed for the stairs, the exit and an escape.

"You all right?" It was the third time Bob Harrison had asked Eskdale the same question.

Harrison's concern wasn't without warrant. Eskdale could only imagine how he looked. He might have only been in his late fifties, but the nearest thing he came to vigorous exercise consisted of writing on whiteboards.

"I'm okay, Bob. Stop fussing," Eskdale barked.

He was being unnecessarily terse with Harrison, but he needed to get rid of him. He had to talk to

Lockhart, and he couldn't do that with Harrison buzzing around him.

"Who were they?" Harrison asked.

Eskdale softened his tone. If he continued to take the harsh line with Harrison, he'd know something was wrong. Everyone knew him as the quiet professor. "I don't know. Thieves pretending to be students. Probably after cash or valuables."

"Jesus, they get bolder by the day." Harrison started arranging scattered papers, but didn't know where to put them. "It seemed surreal when I came in. I couldn't comprehend what I was seeing."

"Well, these things happen."

Harrison shook his head. "I'm not sure I would be so forgiving."

"It's the way of the world these days."

"Do you want me to call the police?"

"No, I'll do it. Bob, will you leave that?"

Harrison looked hurt.

"Bob, I know you mean well, but you don't know where everything goes. I'll put it away."

"Are you sure?"

Eskdale smiled. "Yes, I'm sure. I can take things from here. I'm just glad you turned up when you did."

"So am I," Harrison said. "I wish I had done more instead of just standing there like an idiot."

"You did enough. They're gone." Eskdale wiped a hand over his forehead and widow's peak. It surprised him to find it slick with sweat. "Anyway, what did you need me for?"

"It doesn't matter right now. You get yourself straight, and I'll come back later."

Eskdale smiled again. "Thanks. I appreciate it."

Harrison flashed Eskdale a concerned look and let himself out.

The moment the door closed, Eskdale sank back in his chair. What the hell was going on? First Chaudhary had called him. He'd put two and two together and was going to blow the whistle on him and the work at MDE. Now he'd been roughed up by these two. He hadn't signed on for this. Lockhart had promised him privacy. He was the silent partner. The science. The technology. Not the target of every leak to come out of MDE. MDE was Lockhart's problem. Not his.

He tried to stand and became light-headed. He dropped back down in his seat and leaned forward to put his head between his legs. Pinpricks of blinding light filled his vision followed by a wave of nausea. The sensation passed just as quickly as its onset and he sat up, careful not to reignite the nausea.

He eyed the phone on his desk. He needed to call Lockhart. Lockhart would take care of this. He'd taken care of Chaudhary. He'd used Eskdale's science to do it, but he'd killed Chaudhary without hesitation. It frightened him how easily Lockhart had disposed of Chaudhary and everyone else who stood in his way. He didn't want Lockhart viewing him in the same light.

He wondered if he'd ever get to see the money Lockhart had promised him. He said he'd have it before the month was out. It sounded good, but the money hardly seemed worth it, especially after today.

He eyed the phone again. He couldn't call Lockhart, but he could call Beckerman. He picked up the phone. Lockhart had made him memorize Beckerman's number in case anyone like Chaudhary ever bothered him again. He wasn't to leave a trace of its existence. He tried to remember the number but couldn't. Adrenaline jumbled the numbers and inserted numbers that shouldn't be there.

Relax, he told himself. He closed his eyes, pictured the number and dialed it.

"Yes," Beckerman's emotionless voice answered.

Eskdale wondered what it took to raise the man's blood pressure.

"It's Eskdale. I've just had two people break in here and demand to know my part in the deaths at MDE. They had drawings. They knew I was a consultant."

"Did they give you any names?"

"Yes. Hayden Duke and Rebecca Fallon. Do you know them?"

"I know who they are. I'll get clearance from Mr. Lockhart and have them taken care of."

"How did they know about me?"

"That's not your concern. I have it covered."

"My part was supposed to be secret. Ever since Chaudhary came asking questions, I've been afraid to read the newspapers."

"Forget it. I'll take care of this for you."

"But, Beckerman . . ."

Beckerman had hung up.

Eskdale let his head fall into his hands, and he did something he hadn't done since he was a child—he wept. "How long before it's over?"

CHAPTER NINETEEN

Hayden and Rebecca stopped running and dropped their pace to a fast walk the moment they burst from the building. Hayden hoped they looked like a couple of students late for a class and not two people fleeing an assault on a college professor.

What had they just done? He couldn't lie to himself. If Eskdale pressed charges, it was assault. No two ways about it. He'd been willing to beat the answers from the man. If they hadn't been disturbed, he might have gone too far. What the hell was wrong with him? Was the stress of Shane's death and the deaths of all the people at MDE getting to him? Yes, but it wasn't an excuse.

Hayden shot a glance over his shoulder. No one was pursuing them. It made sense. If Eskdale was tied to anything untoward at MDE, he wasn't about to cry for help. His not calling the alarm just proved he was involved. He and Rebecca were safe for now.

He caught her arm. "It's okay. No one's coming."

She turned to him, panic clear in her expression. She didn't believe him. She whipped her gaze around, looking at every window and exit. When she saw no one, the stiffness went out her body.

He slipped his arm through hers. "We're a couple of

students finished for the day. We're returning to the parking lot to pick up our car and go home."

"Yeah," Rebecca said, nodding.

Hayden relaxed even more when they fell in among other students leaving their classes. Crowds were their friends. They disappeared in a crowd.

"Hayden, Eskdale knows you have copies of MDE's drawings. He's bound to tell someone."

Who would Eskdale tell? Hayden wondered. The arsonist who'd left him to burn? Hayden felt the arsonist possessed other skills beyond starting fires. If Eskdale went to him, he was in no more jeopardy than he was an hour ago. The arsonist knew exactly who he was and probably where to find him. He and Rebecca would have to work fast to avoid another visit from him.

"We can't worry about that now. What's done is done."

They threaded their way through the campus back to the parking lot. A flush of relief swept over him at the sight of his car. His Mitsubishi had never looked so good. He whipped out his car keys and pressed the remote on his keychain.

"Look who we have here," a familiar voice remarked.

Hayden cursed silently. They'd almost made it. They had the car doors open. It was just a matter of getting in and driving away.

Santiago and Rice emerged from their unmarked Crown Victoria parked under the shade of a tree, three rows over from Hayden's Mitsubishi. The detectives approached with the delicacy of a storm. Hayden had been so focused on getting to his car, he'd developed tunnel vision. He hadn't spotted Santiago and Rice standing there.

Hayden felt the heat of Rebecca's stare on him and turned to her. Panic was alive in her eyes. "Eskdale?" she whispered.

Hayden didn't think so and shook his head. Santiago, like them, was a long way from home. He hadn't been called in. He either followed them or had business here.

"Like minds think alike." Santiago stopped behind the Mitsubishi with Rice at his shoulder, ever the shadow. "I have to say that's a nice car, Mr. Duke. I bet it's a lot more fun to drive than what the county issues us. The problem is that I seem to see your car at places where it shouldn't be."

"What can we do for you, Detective?" Rebecca asked, drawing attention away from Hayden.

"I spoke to Mrs. Fuller. She told me that you two visited her this morning and asked her some unusual questions. She also told us that her husband had contacted you two and that you met with him. Why didn't you tell us?"

"I didn't know we had to," Hayden said. "Since when is talking to someone a crime?"

"Mr. Fuller was a missing person," Rice interjected.

"We didn't know that. We're not mind readers," Hayden said.

"No, you're not. Silly of me to think you were. But I would have thought you would have guessed when Ms. Fallon spoke to Mrs. Fuller the first time about two days ago," Santiago said. "Did you find him?"

Santiago's accusation coldcocked Rebecca and surprise escaped with her words. "I . . . I . . . tried, but I . . . did . . . didn't find him," she stammered.

"What is it you want?" Hayden demanded, trying to cut this interview short. Santiago was cutting into their getaway. If Eskdale was sounding the alarm, someone was already on their way.

"Mr. Duke, your interference disturbs me. It doesn't sit right in my gut." Santiago clutched his stomach like it ached. "And now you've got Ms. Fallon involved."

"No one's gotten me involved in anything," Rebecca snapped. "I'm here because I want to be."

Santiago smiled at her politely. "I think we should go somewhere quiet and have a chat. How's that sound?"

Hayden glanced back at the university again. It sounded good. And bad. Going with Santiago and Rice got them off campus, but if Eskdale did decide to call the cops, it was bound to come over the radio. They'd given their names, their real names. Stupid. Stupid. Scaring Eskdale only added to Hayden's tab with the police. Neither of his options had an enviable ring.

"Where do you suggest?" he said.

Santiago smiled. "Follow me."

Hayden followed the detective the short distance into downtown Arcata. The downtown was small and home to mom-and-pop businesses. Big corporations could come in and sweep them away, but there wasn't much point considering the meager business returns available in the area.

Santiago pulled up in front of what had to be the last traditional drugstore in California. The owners had to be aware of their status since the place was aptly named The Drugstore. The drugstore side of the business was gone, replaced by sandwiches and pastries, but a soda jerk manned the soda fountains behind the counter.

Hayden and Rebecca filed inside after Santiago, with Rice bringing up the rear. Hayden wondered if this was to ensure he and Rebecca didn't make a break for freedom.

The floor looked to be the original tiling. It was made up of tiny octagonal tiles no more than an inch across. Santiago went up to the counter and put his foot on the brass rail curling around it.

The soda jerk was an attractive brunette in her twenties. She sported a barbell through her right eyebrow instead of the traditional paper hat and bowtie. She approached Santiago with a smile.

"What's everyone having?" Santiago asked. "It's a hot day, and I'm buying."

The brunette ran through the variety of ice cream concoctions she could conjure up. Hayden felt like he was a child on a daytrip with his grandfather instead of on the verge of a police interrogation. Maybe this was how Santiago operated. He confused his suspects into confessing. Hayden ordered a root beer float, just like everyone else.

Santiago ushered them over to a window table. The four of them crowded around a circular table best suited for two people. They didn't have to worry about being overheard. They were the only customers in the place, and the music insulated them from the brunette behind the counter.

Santiago sucked on the straw in his drink, then wiped ice cream from his mustache with a napkin. "Let's get down to business. I'm getting pretty sick of you two. Tell me, what sent you scurrying all the way up here?"

Hayden and Rebecca exchanged glances with each other.

Santiago pounced on the hesitation. "No conferring, people. This isn't a game show, although today's prize is avoiding a spell in a prison cell."

Hayden knew Santiago was running his mouth about a prison cell to scare them. He didn't have anything on them to make a criminal charge stick, but it wouldn't take much to find something. Santiago only had to check in with Eskdale for an assault-and-battery rap.

His and Rebecca's run-in with Eskdale finally brought it home to him. He'd been incredibly stupid. He was totally out of his depth and had gotten himself embroiled in something he didn't understand. Someone had almost killed him. People were dead. Murdered. Someone out there believed he knew something. Chasing down someone like Eskdale only gave the impression that he did know something. Worse still, he'd dragged Rebecca into this along with him. She should be grieving for Shane, not playing detective. All he had in his defense was he'd done all this for a friend. Shane had confessed his sins to him. The confession meant nothing if he didn't understand the sin. He'd just wanted to honor his friend's memory and provide closure for himself and Rebecca. It had seemed like such a simple task. Somehow, it had gotten complicated.

Santiago eyed him with hunger. Despite everything, Hayden trusted the detective. He would be fair, but fairness wasn't the concern here. Could Santiago protect them? Hayden had seen the inside of the investigations unit for Marin County. It was small. Whatever people were covering up at MDE was big. The person who'd torched MDE was ruthless. If someone feared he and Rebecca knew too much, they wouldn't stop at anything to silence them. Santiago would be swept aside without a second's thought. But with or without Santiago, that threat still loomed over him and Rebecca. Telling Santiago everything at least gave them an ally. It would be nice to have someone watching their backs. It was time to talk, and he felt a weight slide off his shoulders. He looked over at Rebecca and nodded at her. She nodded back and smiled.

"Okay. What do you want to know?"

"It's about time you saw sense. You're an idiot, but at least you're improving."

Hayden smiled. This sounded like a compliment from Santiago.

"Why are you up here visiting Kenneth Eskdale?"

"According to Malcolm Fuller's wife, Eskdale was a consultant for MDE. Malcolm had mentioned to her that Chaudhary and Eskdale had fought over the project's aims."

"Did Eskdale confirm any of this?" Rice asked.

An image of him pinning Eskdale to his chair flashed across his mind. "No."

"Back up," Santiago said. "How did you get to Fuller's wife in the first place?"

Hayden and Rebecca told Santiago and Rice the story in reverse. They began with Eskdale and worked backward to Debbie Fuller, encounters with Malcolm Fuller at the farm and the market, the fire, Hayden's break-in and all the way back to Shane, but stopped short of the e-mail attachment and the assault on Eskdale. Hayden wanted something in reserve.

"Do you have any idea how stupid it was going after Fuller alone, Rebecca? You're lucky he didn't take you with him."

"I know. I'm sorry."

Santiago paused for a moment. "I'm sorry too, Rebecca. You should have brought me in. I could have stopped Fuller before he did what he did."

Rebecca made no attempt to defend their actions, and neither did Hayden. They had made a mistake. If they'd saved Fuller, they would have some answers. But images of Shane popped into his head. There'd been no saving Shane, and Hayden had been right there. There might not have been any way of saving Fuller either, but they'd never know for sure. That would stick with them forever.

"Fuller's suicide doesn't feel right," Hayden said. "He was paranoid and believed he was running for his life from some guy who was following him. That doesn't sound like someone on the verge of suicide. That's someone trying to save their skin."

"Have either of you felt that you were being followed?" Santiago asked.

"Only by you," Hayden said.

Santiago smiled. "I can't make out if you two are blessed or just plain lucky."

"Lucky," Hayden ventured.

"You should have come to me with all this earlier," Santiago said.

"Most of this is hearsay. We would have been wasting your time."

"That's not for you to decide. And fifteen dead people tend not to make any of this seem like a waste of my time."

Guilty as charged, Hayden thought and conceded the point to Santiago.

Santiago leaned back in his seat and his gaze glazed over. The gears were turning. He was putting all he'd been told into context. His expression hardened. He turned his focus to Hayden. "You kept something from me the night Shane died. You're still keeping it from me. What is it?"

"Tell him," Rebecca said. "It's okay."

"If I tell you, you've got to tell us what you know. And I don't want to hear about standard operating procedures, blah, blah. We're at the center of this. Someone tried to kill me. If you want something from me, I want something from you."

"Mr. Duke, this isn't a business transaction. You are involved in a criminal investigation and you are obligated to give us any information that you may have in connection with a crime. If you don't, it's obstruction."

"What criminal investigation? Your investigation into the three suicides is over. You have Bellis on the rack for the fire and murders at MDE. Everything is tied up with a silk ribbon. It's over, but you're still sniffing around. So there's got to be something worrying you to go to all this trouble to follow us up here. We've put up. Now it's your turn."

Hayden watched Santiago squirm under his ultimatum. The detective's expression darkened. Hayden doubted

Santiago normally got placed under these circumstances, but these weren't normal circumstances.

Santiago exchanged a glance with Rice. Hayden used Santiago's words against him. "No conferring, people. This isn't a game show, although today's prize is improving your crime stats."

"Okay," Santiago said. "You've earned a one-time pass. Now tell me what you've been holding back."

For the first time, Hayden didn't feel the weight of suspicion loaded onto his back. Santiago was treating him as a material witness and not a suspect.

"The night Shane died he sent me an e-mail with an attached file. When I asked him about it, he told me to delete it. He acted cagey so I went over there and the rest you know."

"That's it?" Santiago barked. "You lied about a damn e-mail? What's on it?"

"I don't know. It's password protected. I had someone try to crack the password and it self-destructed."

"Do you have a copy?" Rice asked.

Hayden nodded.

"I want one," Santiago demanded.

"Later. You've had your shot. Now it's my turn," Hayden said. "Do you think Trevor Bellis killed those people?"

"No," came Santiago's terse reply. "Gasoline was used as an accelerant. No gasoline traces were found on him or his vehicle. His wife was with him when the fire started."

"Could he have contracted it out?" Rebecca asked.

"It's a possibility. As yet, bank records for him and MDE don't show any major withdrawals. My gut tells me he knew something. He had called everyone there for the meeting but didn't show. His suicide is an admission of guilt, but I don't think it was for the slaughter of his people."

Santiago's admission cast a cold shadow over the group. Hayden lost all appetite for his float and pushed it away.

"I think that's it for now," Santiago said. "Get out of here and keep out of trouble. We've got it covered. Anything happens, you come to us. No excuses."

Hayden smiled. "No police escort?"

"No. I'm going to check in with Eskdale. Maybe I can succeed where you failed."

Hayden's smile faltered. He didn't want to be anywhere close to Santiago when he landed Eskdale. "Yeah, we'd better go."

CHAPTER TWENTY

Hayden picked up the freeway and pointed the car south. He and Rebecca had been damn lucky to escape Eskdale, then Santiago without being charged. Even though Santiago could pick them up at any time, he wanted to pile on the miles between Arcata and them. Taking on Eskdale wasn't a mistake, but it was certainly a mess. They had little to show for their encounter.

He looked to Rebecca to comfort him, but she was silent. Her gaze was fixed on the road ahead, and she was lost in her own thoughts. Maybe silence was the right move. Fear of the future left things unsaid. He had no desire to relive the last couple of hours.

Twenty miles into the drive, Rebecca fell asleep. Hayden felt his own fatigue set in as the day's tension left him. He could have done with Rebecca's company to keep him awake on the monotonous road.

He kept the car stereo switched off to let Rebecca sleep, but checked his cell phone for messages to keep his mind working. He had two messages.

The first was from Dave O'Brien at Macpherson Water to tell Hayden he no longer worked for them. He'd been AWOL from his day job one day too many, and

Dave had canceled his contract. He didn't blame Dave for firing him. He'd given the guy little choice with his absences. The firing should have bothered him, but the job seemed insignificant compared to what was going on. In the scheme of things, it was a bump in the road. He'd pick up a new contract elsewhere later.

The second message cured him of any fatigue. At the sound of the man's desperate voice on the line, Hayden straightened in his seat.

"Hayden, you don't know me, but we need to talk. I don't have to tell you what about. I'm not calling you back on this number. No cells. Land lines only. I tried your home phone, but got no answer. I hope you're still around to call me back. I'll leave word at your home. Be by your phone tonight. I won't call tomorrow. I'll talk to you and you alone. No one else. If I think you've included someone else in this, I'm gone."

The message left him dry-mouthed. Who was this guy? He couldn't be someone from MDE. Everyone was dead. He thought hard. One thing sprang to mind—*document1*. He remembered Rebecca's remark about Shane's password-protected file. The file wasn't for him to read. It was for him to hand off to someone else.

That was a big assumption, though. His skin still felt the effects of the fire. Mr. No Name could be MDE's arsonist out to finish his work. It wouldn't be that hard to track down his home and cell phone numbers. The arsonist was likely to be a man with many skills, considering the body count to his credit.

Either way, he needed to take the call. If this guy knew something about MDE or Shane, then he needed to hear it. If the guy was the arsonist, he could say something to trip him up. He could do this without risk to himself. The phone line separated them.

He looked over at Rebecca, still sleeping. He couldn't

include her in this. He'd been adamant after she'd
run off after Fuller alone that they stick together, but
Mr. No Name had been explicit. He couldn't risk losing
this guy over the demand, and in some ways he was glad.
If the caller was the arsonist, he would want to take Rebecca and him out together. Leaving Rebecca behind
ensured one of them kept the investigation alive.

The Mitsubishi rode over a pothole, waking Rebecca.
She screwed up her eyes at the light. She looked at her
surroundings outside the car then at Hayden.

"Was I asleep long?"

"No."

She latched on to a change in his demeanor and stared
at him quizzically. "What's wrong?"

"I'm in the doghouse with my boss. I have to go in. I
don't want to lose this contract too. I'll drop you off and
stay at my place tonight." He didn't like lying to her. If
the caller panned out, he'd bring her up to speed.

"I can stay with you tonight. I'll go in with you and
explain how you're helping me."

He smiled. "That's a nice idea, but it won't buy me
any favors. It's best if I go in alone and sort it out."

She frowned at his smile. "I thought we were supposed to stick together—never leave each other's sides."

He took her hand, brought it up to his mouth and
kissed it. "Look, I'll be back by noon. I just need to
smooth things over."

"Okay. Just as long as you are back to me by noon,"
she said with a smile.

His corresponding smile felt tight and out of place.
Lying had never felt so hard.

Now awake, Rebecca was up for talking. They fell into
an easy conversation, relegating Mr. No Name to the
back of Hayden's mind. Hayden's lie hit black ice when
Rebecca wanted to stop for food. He couldn't afford the
delay a meal would take. Even without stops, he wasn't

going to arrive home before nine P.M. Mr. No Name could give up on him by then. Rebecca started to suspect something, but he blamed having to go into work for not wanting to stop. He compromised with a stop at a drive-thru and that seemed to allay her suspicions.

He'd dropped Rebecca off in San Rafael just after nine, keeping his speed a few miles per hour over the limit. The moment he dropped her off, he kept the speedometer as high as he could without running foul of the Highway Patrol. He made it home in less than forty minutes.

The moment he stepped inside, the hairs on the back of his neck bristled. For a second, he thought his place had been ransacked again, but he soon realized everything was in its place. The only thing out of place was him. His home felt unfamiliar and strangely uncomfortable. He'd been away only days, but it felt like months. A lot had happened to him. He'd never view the world the same way again, even if Santiago caught the person who'd tried to kill him.

He put his out-of-place feelings aside and went straight to his answering machine. The message light blinked and he hit play. After messages from his mom and Dave O'Brien, he came to those left my Mr. No Name. The same urgent and intense voice spilled from the speaker.

"Hayden Duke, you don't know me, but we need to talk. I can't talk long. It's about Shane. Look, I'll call back at seven, then again every hour on the hour."

The message ended and the answering machine announced the call had come in shortly before six. It was nine fifty. No other messages followed. Either Mr. No Name had hung up at seven, eight and nine or he hadn't called back. If he was calling back, he'd be calling again in ten minutes. Part of Hayden didn't want him to call, but a much larger part needed him to call.

Mr. No Name had said he knew Shane. Hayden wondered how. He couldn't be anyone from MDE, so how did Shane know him? Chaudhary and Shane had shared information. Had they shared contacts too? Was this the person expecting *document1*? The thing that disturbed Hayden most was wondering what had triggered Mr. No Name to call him. There was only one way to find out.

The phone rang at exactly ten. Hayden snatched up the phone. "Hello."

"Hayden Duke?"

"Yes."

"We need to talk."

"About what?"

"Don't play games. You know what."

"Who is this?" Hayden demanded.

"Meet me and I'll tell you."

The silhouette of the arsonist fill Hayden's mind. "Tell me and I'll think about meeting you."

The line went silent. Hayden heard the man's breathing. Good. He wanted this guy under pressure. He wanted answers, but he couldn't be seen as a pushover.

"I'm not taking any chances with my life," Mr. No Name said. "You do things my way or not at all."

"Look, I don't have time for this bullshit. If you know something about Shane's death, start talking."

"Two blocks from your house, there's a pay phone outside a Mexican market. Go there."

The son of a bitch knew where he lived. Was he outside now? Shit, Hayden hadn't thought that luring him to his own house could be a trap. He went to check out front but stopped. If the guy was scoping him out, he would have called the moment he'd stepped inside his home, not waited until the prearranged time. That said, the guy knew where he lived. Mr. No Name had the upper hand on him. It wasn't a good feeling.

"It'll ring for thirty seconds. If you aren't there to an-swer it, it won't ring again. You've got five minutes."

Before Hayden could respond, the man hung up.

He shouldn't do this. The guy probably had nothing that answered his questions about Shane. But what if he did? Hayden couldn't let the questions go unanswered. He snatched his keys off the table and ran out of the house.

He slowed when he reached the street with the mar-ket on it. The pay phone outside wasn't ringing.

He crossed the street. The market was open, and the shop lights illuminated rows of fruit and vegetables on display outside and the lone pay phone. He went up to the phone and felt conspicuous standing in front of it and not using it. He picked up the handset, but rested a finger on the cradle. He glanced into the supermarket to see if he was being watched, but saw no one.

He glanced at his watch. The five minutes had elapsed. Mr. No Name had been specific about the time. Now he was breaking his own rule. Hayden didn't like this.

A silver Lexus pulled into the market's cramped park-ing lot. Black glass hid the identities of its occupants. It pulled alongside him instead of parking in a stall. The passenger window slid down.

Hayden's stomach tightened. It was a setup, and he'd fallen for it. He was looking at a bullet or abduction.

The phone rang and Hayden flinched.

A Hispanic woman hopped from the Lexus and ran into the market.

Hayden exhaled hard in an attempt to untie the knots left by his imagination.

"Hayden?" the voice on the line demanded.

"Yes," Hayden said testily, more angry at his imagina-tion than the caller. "Who are you?"

"I'd prefer not to say."

"Tell me or I'm hanging up."

"Okay. Okay." He mumbled a curse away from the receiver. "I'm Tony Mason."

"So, Tony Mason, what do you want?"

"I know that Shane Fallon was murdered."

"I think you've been misinformed, my friend. I saw Shane die. It was suicide, plain and simple. You should do your homework before you try scamming someone."

"Jesus Christ, Hayden. I know you were there. Trust me, it wasn't suicide."

Hayden flicked his gaze to the market, the street ahead and behind. He felt so exposed at the pay phone—a lamb tethered to a stake in the ground.

The woman darted out of the supermarket with a paper sack in her arms. She jumped into the Lexus, and it sped off.

"Shane didn't know what he was doing. They did that to him. They couldn't be guiltier if they put a gun to his head. They have other ways of pulling the trigger."

This speech was in Malcolm Fuller's territory. The world was populated by *thems* and *theys*. "Who are *they*?"

"I don't want to say on the phone. Meet me?"

Against his better judgment, Hayden said, "Where?"

A loud exhale from Mason's end of the line reduced the line to static. "Thank God. You don't know what it means to me to talk about this to someone who understands."

Hayden still didn't understand anything. He just knew that people kept dying. "Then you know what's going on?"

"Enough to get me killed."

Hayden considered talking Mason into meeting Santiago, but decided against it. He had to earn Mason's trust before he brought up the subject of going to the cops.

"Don't disappoint me."

"I can assure you, I won't."

Mason's meeting point was at the Home Depot in Fairfield. Not in the store itself, but on the service road the delivery trucks used. Hayden knew the place. The Home Depot was located on the south side of the city, twenty minutes from Hayden's house. It was a relatively new development in an extension of the business park that stretched across an ugly section of Highway 12. He cut through Fairfield and turned into the Home Depot's parking lot. The store shared its lots with two other big box stores still under construction but close to completion. The store was closed, so it was a case of the lights were on, but nobody was home. He followed the signs for deliveries and turned onto the service road.

The service road was unlit. He relied on light pollution from the neighboring business park and Suisun City. Rows of deserted loading bays curled around the backside of the store. He saw no sign of any another vehicles or Tony Mason.

The sensation of being a lamb tethered to a stake returned. Hayden pulled up behind a dumpster. "You've been smarter, Hayden," he told himself.

He got out of the car. If Mason was watching, and Hayden had no doubt about that, he wanted the guy to see him. The Mitsubishi's dome light lit the coupe's interior, showing he was alone. He left the door ajar in case this meeting turned sour.

The drone of traffic racing across Highway 12 drowned out his footsteps—and anybody else's.

"Tony?" Hayden called, but the man with all the answers didn't answer back.

Mason had picked smart. There were plenty of places to hide out. Dumpsters dotted the service road. A dense fringe of bushes and shrubs concealed the road from prying eyes—and more importantly, camouflaged Mason from Hayden.

Hayden stepped out into the middle of the road. He kept his hands away from his sides and made each step obvious and deliberate. If Mason were hiding out, Hayden didn't want him getting the wrong idea. No doubt Mason was just as spooked about this meeting as he was. The thought relaxed him. He'd gone through this situation with Fuller. He was an old hand with clandestine meetings. If someone needed to take the lead, it was him.

He continued to walk forward. He checked behind and between a couple of Dumpsters. He called out to Mason twice more without reply. Not a problem. The guy was scared.

"Tony, are you here?" His voice carried on the night air. "C'mon, you called me. You said you wouldn't disappoint me."

The bushes where the service road turned right to curl around the building rustled and a stocky, black man emerged.

Hayden froze. He had an image of Mason, and the person striding toward him wasn't it. He was bigger and stronger than Hayden had expected, possessing a retired football player's build. His blue and black bowling shirt barely contained his barrel chest and Hayden doubted he could button the army jacket he wore loose over the shirt. He was older too. Hayden put him in his midforties.

Some thirty feet away from Hayden, the man pulled up short, as if his enthusiasm had gotten the better of him for a second and prudent thought had taken over. His confident expression retreated to a safe place and Hayden spotted a flicker of nerves in his eyes.

Hayden wished he had a weapon. This guy was nervous enough to bring one. It would be the worst irony if the only person with answers ended up shooting, knifing or bludgeoning him to death.

"Tony Mason?"

The man nodded. "Hayden Duke?"

"Yeah."

Mason smiled and jogged over to Hayden. He offered his hand. Hayden shook it. There was strength in his grasp.

"You don't know what this means, man."

Hayden noticed the crude skull-and-crossbones tattoo on the back of his hand.

"Nice tattoo."

Mason glanced down at his hand. He laughed. "Yeah, I had it done when I went into the army. I thought it would be scary. Half the battle is making the enemy fear you. I have others."

"I'll take your word for it."

Mason nodded. "Sorry for the theatrics. I couldn't take any chances. I wanted to make sure you came alone. Did anyone follow you?"

"Not that I saw. Should I be looking?"

"Yes."

"Who's following me? What's this about?"

Mason stuffed his hands in the pockets of his fatigue jacket. "The project you worked on for MDE. The people who employed MDE are cleaning house."

He knew this already, but hearing someone else say it sent a chill running through him.

"Didn't James Lockhart employ MDE?"

Mason snorted. "He's the middleman. I doubt he even knows what's going on."

"How did you know Shane?"

"Like you, I worked as a contractor for MDE."

"In what capacity?"

"I'm a troubleshooter. I shoot trouble."

Hayden's instincts kicked in a split-second too late. Before he could bolt, Mason slammed a fist into his gut. The pain folded him in two. That moment's immobilization was all Mason needed. He spun Hayden around, put him in a choke hold and jerked a weapon from his jacket pocket.

Mason's arm tightened around Hayden's throat. Hayden's lungs burned with the spent air trying to escape, and his grip on consciousness slipped with every exploding starburst in his vision. If he didn't do something fast, it was over. He was going the way of Shane, Chaudhary, Fuller and all the rest of them. He was going to die, and he didn't know why.

A blinding realization seared all other thoughts away. If this was happening to him, was it happening to Rebecca? Had she received a similar call? Was she fighting for her life this very second or was she next on Mason's to do list? Hayden had two reasons to survive now.

He forced his hand under his assailant's arm. He thrust up, wedging his forearm into the crook of Mason's arm. Hayden didn't have enough strength to break free from Mason's bear-trap grip, but he did have enough strength to take the pressure off his throat. As he sucked air into his lungs, the light-headedness dissolved.

"C'mon, Hayden. Don't fuck around," Mason growled. "Take your medicine like a good boy."

Mason brought his weapon up to Hayden's face. Hayden snatched his wrist with his free hand. He expected to see a knife, but didn't. Mason was clutching what looked like a plastic cigar case, but instead of it being perfectly cylindrical, a rectangular opening flared out at the end from one side. Mason's thumb tightened on a button on the butt end. Hayden thrashed to free himself, but Mason kept him restrained. He was the puppet master and Hayden the puppet. Hayden felt his strength wane. His arm holding the weapon off buckled and Mason brought it closer to his throat as specks of bright light danced in Hayden's vision again.

"Game over. No lives left. Time to die," Mason whispered, his breath brushing against Hayden's neck.

Hayden raised his foot and stamped down on Mason's boot. Feeling bones crack under his heel brought him a smile.

"Fuck," Mason yelled out.

Mason maintained his hold on Hayden, but Hayden felt it waver. Hayden stamped his foot down again, delivering another direct hit on the already damaged area. Mason yelled out again, and this time his grasp on Hayden faded.

Finally, Hayden had room to move. He snapped his head back and butted Mason in the face. He ignored the spike of pain rushing through his brain. Mason's hands shot to his face.

Hayden whirled around on Mason, but Mason put him down with a vicious backhand. It felt like a brick connecting with his cheekbone. He thought he'd weathered the blow well until he realized he was falling. He crashed down on the unforgiving ground on his tailbone. A lightning bolt crackled up his spine, overriding the fire raging in his cheek.

Anger knotted Mason's features. His hands were clenched into tight fists, and the skull-and-crossbows tattoo bulged in the soft flesh between his thumb and forefinger. Hayden remembered Mason's army remark. The guy had been army once, but not now. His discipline was long gone. Rage overwhelmed him, and he charged at Hayden with no thought or plan.

Hayden kicked out with his heel again and connected with Mason's kneecap. He hit the sweet spot and Mason collapsed onto all fours. The weapon in his grasp went skittering across the asphalt. Hayden chased it down and stamped on the plastic case, cracking it open. The splintered weapon hissed in death.

Mason charged and slammed into Hayden's back, snapping his head back and driving him to the ground. Hayden went down with his attacker on top of him. He put out his hands to save his fall, but Mason's weight crushed him. Hayden's hands skidded out on the rough asphalt, shredding the skin from his palms.

"End of the road, Hayden."

Mason snatched fistfuls of Hayden's hair, jerked back his head, and smashed his forehead into the ground. Shockwaves crackled out from the point of impact. Hayden's grip on consciousness wavered. Mason raised Hayden's head for a second attempt. He wouldn't survive a second impact.

"Hey," a voice yelled, halting Mason in his task.

A flashlight beam lit up their faces. The light seared Hayden's vision.

"Don't move a damn muscle."

"Another time, Hayden."

Mason pressed Hayden into the ground as he sprung to his feet and broke into a run.

The security guard behind the flashlight raced toward them.

Hayden had no intention of explaining himself to anyone without Mason cuffed to him. He clambered to his feet and chased after him. He instantly felt the effects of the beating. His first punch-drunk steps sent him stumbling, but his adrenaline kicked in when the security guard yelled at him to stop.

Mason raced back to the spot he'd emerged from earlier. Hayden took pleasure in seeing him run with a limp. At least he'd accomplished something tonight. Still, Mason managed to outpace him. Mason hurled himself headlong into the shrubs and disappeared.

Hayden's head bashing had disabled his brain's ability to absorb shock. He felt every jarring step, but he didn't let it stop him and he burst through the shrubs. The sharp branches raked his face and hands. He ignored the superficial damage they inflicted and emerged on the other side to see Mason charging along the drainage channel that captured the runoff from the business park.

"Stop right there," the security guard yelled.

Hayden ignored the security guard and raced after Mason. The concrete channel was damp and slick with algae. He slipped more often than not, but took comfort in the knowledge that Mason would be suffering the same hindrance.

Although injured, the bulky man moved quickly and efficiently and maintained a healthy lead on Hayden. The drainage channel disappeared under a roadway, and Mason scrambled up onto the road and bolted for the Highway 12. Hayden's heart sank as his attacker disappeared. He was going to lose Mason if he didn't do something. He glanced over his shoulder at his savior chasing him, a security guard in a dark blue uniform, still calling after them.

Hayden reached the end of the drainage channel and climbed onto roadway. He found himself on a dead-end street that serviced a couple of nameless businesses. The street fed directly into Highway 12. Mason had almost reached the busy highway, but his pace had significantly slowed. He lumbered, trying to get his best out of his buckled knee.

Hayden grinned. He had the bastard. Mason's injury spurred him on. He reeled in his attacker a stride at a time.

Mason reached the highway. Hayden didn't see a getaway vehicle waiting for him and thought he had him, but that thought only lasted a second. Mason hesitated then bolted across the highway.

"Shit," Hayden muttered.

A pickup swerved to avoid Mason and roared past with the driver's hand on the horn. Mason clambered over the guardrail and fell flat on his face on the grass median.

Traffic forced Hayden to stop at the roadside. He watched Mason climb over the second guardrail and scurry across the westbound lanes.

The security guard called out again. Hayden ignored him, but couldn't ignore the security guard's boots pounding the road close behind him.

The traffic cleared, and Hayden bolted. Headlights of approaching vehicles lit him up. He plowed on, hurdling the first guardrail. He planted his landing, but slid on the wet grass. He recovered just in time to be struck from behind. The security guard drove him to the ground. The force of his weight crashing on top of him forced the air from his lungs. He looked up to see Mason disappear into a residential street.

"You're not both going to get away," the security guard growled and hoisted Hayden to his feet. "You gonna tell me what you two were up to? What was it? Drug deal or were ya trying to rip off the store?"

"He was mugging me, you moron."

Hayden's frustrated response stopped the guy. "What?"

"He mugged me and you helped him get away."

"How the hell was I supposed to know?" The security guard released his grip on Hayden. "I've seen a lot of shit go down. You could have been up to anything."

Hayden's anger bled out. The guard had a perfect right to suspect the worst. "Okay. You did stop him from finishing what he was doing."

"C'mon, man. Let's get back. I've got a first-aid kit in the trailer. You're welcome to use it."

"No, I'll be fine."

"Suit yourself." The security guard escorted him back across the highway. An eighteen-wheeler honked at them. "Yeah, fuck you and the horse you rode in on," the security guard shouted after the disappearing truck. "Douche bag."

The guard babbled. Hayden gave him scant attention. The significance of Mason's attack dominated his thoughts. He'd been a damn fool and had almost gotten himself killed. He needed to be more careful from now on.

He massaged his head where Mason had driven it into the ground. Blood came away on his hand.

They retraced their steps along the drainage channel and through the landscaping back to the service road. They stopped when they reached the scene of the crime.

"What were you doing back here anyway? The area's prohibited."

Hayden thought fast. "I was lost and I was checking a map."

The security guard seemed to buy the lie, but looked unsure of himself. "I need to call this in."

Hayden had been hoping the security guard wasn't going to go the extra mile. "Look, is that necessary?"

"You were assaulted. Don't you want this asshole busted?"

Doubt crept into the security guard's expression. Hayden couldn't afford the cops gumming up the works. He needed to play this right.

"Look, he didn't get anything and I just want to get home." Hayden wanted to sound weary and didn't have to try too hard.

The security guard considered Hayden's request. Hayden didn't wait for him to answer. He fished in his pocket for his keys and promptly dropped them. He went light-headed when he bent for them and had to close his eyes tight until the fireworks dispersed. When he opened them, his gaze fell on Mason's busted weapon. He picked it up.

"Is that one of those pepper sprays?"

"Yeah."

"Didn't do you much good. Anyway, they're for women. Management offered me one of those, but I said I'd prefer to use a bit of brute force and boxing training to get me through. Know what I mean?"

Hayden examined the weapon. If it was supposed to inflict some harm, he couldn't see how. It didn't look like much. It resembled an asthmatic's inhaler, but not the usual type. From the way Mason had brandished it, Hayden bet it relieved constricted airways permanently. The security guard's pepper spray assessment was way off the mark.

The broken casing exposed a canister. Hayden's heel had burst the delicate container, exposing a fine powder inside. Had Mason let something slip? He'd talked about Shane's suicide not being his will. Was this device the cause?

He suddenly remembered Rebecca. If they were after him, they were after her. He rounded his Mitsubishi and got behind the wheel. He stuffed the weapon in the glove compartment. "Thanks for your help."

Hayden's sudden spurt of speed spooked the security guard. He scurried in front of the car. "You should wait for the cops."

Hayden gunned the engine. "I've gotta go."

"I want you to wait."

Hayden slammed the car into reverse. He powered backward out of the service road and into the parking lot. He put the car into a half spin, then peeled out of the parking lot, leaving the security guard to curse and spit.

Hayden headed toward the highway. He drove one-handed while he punched Rebecca's cell number into his phone. His call went to her voice mail.

"Shit."

He was forty minutes from San Rafael. Someone could get to her in that time. He needed someone to warn and protect her. He punched in Santiago's number.

CHAPTER TWENTY-ONE

The garage door rolled up and Rebecca guided her car inside. She pulled up next to her brother's Infiniti sedan, popped the trunk and hefted out four bulging Trader Joe's paper bags. She was removing the last of her groceries and closing the trunk when he called to her.

"Can I help you with those, Ms. Fallon?"

Rebecca turned. "Detective Santiago. I thought you'd finished with me for today."

There was humor in her tone. Santiago had her trust. He just hoped he could keep it.

He locked his car and crossed the road from his hiding spot. He kept a keen eye as he crossed the street. It seemed like overkill for a private street, but he wasn't watching for a car.

"Could we talk?"

"Sure."

She handed Santiago two of the bags, and he followed her through the garage and into the kitchen, closing the garage door on the way. He placed his bags next to hers on the counter as she opened the fridge and unloaded the first bag of groceries.

"How have you been, Ms. Fallon?"

"Detective Santiago, can we drop the formalities? Call me Rebecca."

"Okay, Rebecca. How have you been?"

Rebecca brought out an armful of apples and dropped them into a fruit basket next to the fridge. "As well as can be expected. Anyway, why the nighttime visit? I'm sure you're not on duty."

"Rebecca, I think you should sit down."

Her face clouded over. "What's wrong? What's happened?"

"Sit down."

When she made no move to sit, he took the lead and sat at the dining table. He patted the chair kitty-corner to him. She relented and sat.

The spark he'd seen in her just moments earlier had been extinguished. Fear burned in her eyes. She expected the worst. With her history, it wasn't surprising. In her experience, people like him always came with bad news.

"What's happened?"

"Hayden's been attacked." He held up a hand to silence her. "He's okay, though. Someone roughed him up, but he gave as good as he got."

She slumped in her seat. "Thank God."

"He's tough, but not as tough as he thinks he is."

"What's that mean?"

"You two are very alike. You both think you can save the world by yourselves. Take it from me, no one's that tough. We all need help."

"What happened? Please."

"I don't have all the details. As far as I can tell, he received an anonymous phone call from someone claiming to have information about Shane's death. He met with this person, and it was a trap. It was pretty obvious he wasn't supposed to walk away from this. He's lucky to be alive."

"How is he?"

"Fine. A little battered and bruised, but fine."

"He called you?"

"Yes, he called me and asked me to look out for you."

"Me?"

"Yes. You. Whatever you two know, or are perceived to know, may be putting your lives in danger."

Santiago paused. He'd said enough to scare her. It was written all over her face. He made no apology for this. He wanted her off kilter. If he had her off balance, she might be more willing to open up.

"Why won't you tell me what's going on?" he asked.

"Where is he? I want to speak to him."

"He's getting patched up. I have a Fairfield officer with him, and Rice is on his way to get a statement. You can talk to him later. Talk to me now. You want some coffee?"

Rebecca didn't object.

Santiago didn't press her while he made the coffee. He wanted her to absorb the severity of Hayden's attack and the threat to her life. She wasn't bulletproof or beyond the attack of others. He'd broken through their defenses at The Drugstore. Now he needed to get them to work with him. He poured the coffee and brought it over to her.

"Have you seen anyone hanging around?"

"No."

"Are you sure? A strange face, an unfamiliar car, hangups, anything?"

"No, I'm sure."

"How about Tony Mason, heard of him?"

Rebecca shook her head.

Santiago sipped his coffee. "Drink up. This is good, if I do say so myself."

Rebecca smiled weakly and sampled the coffee. "You must have a contented wife."

"I don't know about that, seeing as I'm spending more time with you than her."

His remark robbed Rebecca of her smile. It was an unnecessary barb in some ways, but it was a point well made.

"Can you tell me anything else about your visit with Professor Eskdale?"

Rebecca shifted in her seat. She and Hayden were crappy poker players. When he had dropped Eskdale's name at The Drugstore, they'd both looked as if they were passing stones.

"Why, did he say something?"

"That's the problem. He isn't saying anything. He's gone. He seemingly vanished moments after you saw him. He didn't go home, he's not answering his phone, and he hasn't left word with anyone."

Rebecca didn't exactly relax, but some of the tension went out of her body.

"C'mon, Rebecca. It's time to 'fess up. Did something happen?"

She didn't say anything for a long moment. He saw her wrestle with the decision to speak. She wanted to seek counsel with Hayden. It wasn't an option this time. He gave her a little shove in the right direction.

"I thought we had an agreement, Rebecca. Honesty. Openness. I know something happened. I saw it in Hayden's face in Arcata. I can help you if you tell me about it."

She wouldn't make eye contact with him, but finally surrendered. "Things got a little out of hand."

Santiago felt Rebecca's agitation. "What are we talking about here?"

"Eskdale tried to run. Hayden held him down. He wasn't trying to hurt him. We just wanted answers, and we didn't want him running out on us without something."

They'd crossed the assault line and then some. Santiago mumbled a curse and sipped his coffee for comfort.

"You two are like a runaway train. Did anyone witness this?"

"Another lecturer. We ran and then you picked us up outside."

He wondered if he was guilty of aiding and abetting. He shook off the thought. "Forget it. Eskdale hasn't squawked, so it didn't happen. You've got more to worry about than an assault charge."

Santiago's cell burst into song. Dysart's name flashed up on the caller ID. The coroner investigator only called him outside office hours when he had something. He excused himself to Rebecca and took the call. "What have you got for me, Dick?"

"Ruben, can you come see me?" Dysart spoke without his customary laugh track engaged. Something had developed.

"I'm tied up at the moment. What's up?"

"I have your tox results. Malcolm Fuller indulged in the same narcotic as Chaudhary and Fallon."

Bingo! Santiago liked it when he was right.

This was an important development, but not important to warrant Dysart's serious tone. "What else?" Santiago asked.

"The bruise. It's not just a bruise. I found a concentration of the drug under the skin. Not all of it had been absorbed into the bloodstream. There probably wasn't time between application and death."

"How is it applied?"

"I wish I knew, Ruben. I'll drop by in the morning and show you what I've got."

"You do that," Santiago said and hung up.

"What was that about?" Rebecca asked. "Remember, we're in a period of sharing."

He gave her what Dysart had told him.

"The bruise, what does it mean?"

"Don't know, but I'll find out."

She fixed him with a stare that hurt to be under. He finished his coffee quickly and poured himself another cup. When he returned to the kitchen table, her stare hadn't gone away. She was gearing up to ask him a question. He braced himself for it.

"I need to know. Do you think Shane killed himself?"

He was having doubts, and Dysart's call had confirmed them. The bruise had proved to be the source of the drug. What did that mean? It created doubt, but it failed to prompt an answer. "Your brother's death doesn't fit a model scenario."

"You'll get splinters in your butt if you sit on the fence too long."

He grinned, but then turned serious. Her question did deserve a better answer. "I don't want to build up your hopes. We have Hayden's eyewitness account, but something is still wrong with the circumstances. I don't have an explanation, but I'm getting closer to a solution. Just bear with me, okay?"

"For how long?"

"I wish I knew, but while you're a target, I'm going to be watching out for you. I'll start with a security check here."

Santiago walked the house with Rebecca. The doors came with deadbolts. All the windows had locks. The security system would make a lot of noise and send a signal to the cops. It wasn't Fort Knox, but if anyone tried anything, it was going to be noticed.

As he inspected the place, he noticed the reminders of Shane's rampage—gouged drywall and piles of broken possessions consigned to boxes. It brought him back to when he'd first looked the house over after Shane's death.

She walked him back to the kitchen. He told her to

keep the house sealed up tight, and she promised she would.

His cell rang. The patrol unit he'd asked to watch over her had arrived.

"I'm going to go now. Don't leave the house. Don't open the door. I don't care who comes. Not even Hayden. You have good defenses, but only if you keep the door locked."

"Can I call him?"

"Sure. Tell him to do the same."

"I will."

"You like him?"

"Yeah, he's a good guy."

Santiago was leaning in that direction too.

She walked him to the door. He stopped on the threshold and checked the street for something that didn't fit. The right puzzle pieces were in the jigsaw.

"Now promise me you'll lock yourself in for the night. If you need to leave, call me. You've got my number."

She smiled. "Thank you."

"Don't thank me." He smiled. "Just do it."

From the comfort of his car, Beckerman watched Santiago take the grocery bags from Rebecca Fallon and follow her inside. He'd been waiting for her to come home when the detective popped up. The detective ruined his plan, but he could wait. He didn't need to complicate matters by killing a cop. He couldn't even try for a plan B since a sheriff's unit had pulled up out front.

He didn't blame the cop for this development. His arrival was an indicator, like an engine light when the motor ran too hot. Something had gone wrong. Santiago hadn't happened to pop by. He'd been waiting for her, and he hadn't simply followed her in; he'd scanned the street for hostiles. Beckerman recognized the tactic from his bodyguard training. Santiago was expecting an ambush. Now, this could mean the detective was cagey because he had to inform Rebecca of some bad news involving Hayden, but he didn't think so. The timeline was wrong. The cops wouldn't have found Hayden yet. The drug worked fast, but not that fast. But all that was immaterial. Mason should have called in by now. He tried Mason's number, but his call went straight to voice mail. Not good. Not good at all.

The front door opened, and Santiago and Rebecca emerged on the stoop. Their smiles spoke nothing of Hayden's demise. Mason had screwed up. How disappointing.

He powered down his windows to listen. He wasn't a fan of gated communities, but he did like their quiet streets.

"Thank you, Detective."

"You tell Hayden to talk to me. Make him see sense."

"I'll try."

"Try real hard. Good night, Rebecca."

"Good night."

"This car is going to stay here all night. You'll be safe."

The remark underlined Mason's mistake to Beckerman.

Rebecca closed the door, and Santiago checked in with the deputy parked out front before leaving in his own car, parked half a dozen houses from Rebecca's. He'd not only come for Rebecca, he'd come to see who else came for her. Disappointment settled over Beckerman.

The detective gunned the engine and passed Beckerman but didn't see him. Beckerman snorted at the cop's incompetence. That sloppiness might just save the cop's life.

His cell rang. Mason's name appeared on the caller ID. "You're late with your report."

"I had some trouble."

Lockhart should have let him do it his way, but he wanted Rebecca and Duke taken care of at the same time. Beckerman thought Mason's heavy-handed, sledgehammer-to-crack-a-nut approach would be best suited for Duke. Mason lacked the finesse to be effective with Rebecca. She would be his indulgence.

"What went wrong?"

"I got him alone. I was about to shoot him up and some rent-a-cop at the Home Depot fucked everything up."

"You did this in a Home Depot?"

"Hey, it's not as bad as it sounds."

No, it's worse, Beckerman thought. "I assume you were unsuccessful?"

"Yes. I had to abort."

"Jesus Christ. You're supposed to be a professional soldier."

"I am."

"You were."

"I'll try again."

Beckerman didn't reply. He was weighing his options.

"But I'll need another injector. Duke broke it during our fight."

This fiasco wasn't getting better. Lockhart wasn't going to be pleased.

"Is there anything else I should know?"

"He knows my name."

Beckerman cursed silently.

"But don't worry, I'll finish him tomorrow."

"That won't be necessary."

"I am going to get paid, right?"

"You'll get what's owed. Let's meet tomorrow morning, oh-six-hundred. You know where."

CHAPTER TWENTY-TWO

The rising sun spread light over the delta. The chill in the air was enough for Beckerman to pull the zipper up another inch on his jacket. People forgot that California was essentially an irrigated desert. It got cold at night, and it took time for the sun to warm it back up.

He stood atop the levy. At his feet, the river slid by effortlessly. The water looked gray in the dawn light and resembled sheet steel rolling off a mill. He surveyed the levy on both sides. No early morning joggers or dog walkers this morning. Not that he expected many. Urban sprawl had yet to invade out here.

The crunch of dry grass underfoot disturbed the perfect calm.

"Good morning, Tony."

"Christ, you've got good ears."

He didn't. Not really. He just knew how to listen.

"Where's your bike?"

"I stashed it a couple of miles back up the road, but I bet you heard that too."

He had.

He listened to Mason clamber up the levy. The guy labored too hard up the steep incline. Mason was out of shape, but he didn't need to listen to his heavy breathing to know that. He'd heard Mason's bike half an hour ago. Mason should have been able to cover the two-mile distance in well under twenty minutes. Hiring him had been a big mistake.

Mason stopped next to him and stared at the river. He looked like shit. His fatigue jacket and jeans were scuffed with grime, and the right knee of his jeans was ripped. "You and your super power. You always did have ears like a damn dog. What did they call you in the Gulf?"

"Who fucking cares? The Gulf was a long time ago."

"Wake up on the wrong side of the bed this morning?"

"Don't expect me to be pleased to see you after your fiasco yesterday." Beckerman stuffed his hands deeper into his pockets.

"Hey, you can't blame me for that."

"Can't I?"

"Okay, you can." Mason walked to the river's edge and turned around. He blocked Beckerman's view of the idyllic scene. "I fucked up, but I'll put it right."

"Did Duke do that to your face?"

Mason frowned and glanced up toward his own swollen eyebrow. "Yeah. And he busted up my kneecap. I'll have to see a doctor."

"Jesus. Duke is a civilian. You're supposed to be a trained professional."

"What can I say? He knew how to handle himself."

"And you didn't. I'm sorry, Tony. You're off the job."

"I'm being paid what I'm owed, right?"

"You were paid twenty-five hundred up front. That's yours. And under the circumstances, I think I'm being charitable."

Mason stabbed a finger in Beckerman's direction. "That's only half."

"You didn't complete the job."

"Fuck you, Beckerman. I want my money."

Mason made a move for Beckerman. Beckerman didn't hesitate and squeezed the trigger on the Colt hidden in his jacket pocket. The ejected shell brushed the back of his hand.

The bullet struck Mason in the groin. The man doubled up, blood spilling between his clenched fingers. His legs buckled and he dropped to his knees.

"You bastard," Mason croaked and reached behind him for something in his waistband.

"You armed, Tony?"

Mason said nothing and continued to wrestle with whatever was tucked in his waistband. The bullet to the groin had robbed him of coordination. His hand flailed but wasn't going to connect with its prize any time soon.

Beckerman removed the automatic from his pocket and crossed the short distance to Mason. He jammed the Colt's muzzle against Mason's head, slapped his arm away from his back and jerked a Smith and Wesson Chief Special from his waistband.

"Don't you trust me, Tony?"

"What do you think?"

Beckerman pistol-whipped Mason with his own revolver, sending him sprawling. Then he tossed the Smith and Wesson toward his car.

"Don't worry about seeing a doctor for your kneecap." Beckerman fired a round into Mason's knee, and he screamed out, following it with a string of curses. It was a mean move, but it immobilized him, leaving Beckerman to work in relative comfort. Not taking any chances, he picked up the spent shell casing.

"Don't be such a baby." Beckerman returned to his car and retrieved a length of chain and three padlocks from his open trunk.

Mason had crawled down the levy, or rolled to be more exact. He'd gotten only a few feet since then. It was a pointless gesture as it'd taken him thirty minutes

to jog two miles without a couple of bullet wounds.
Beckerman put it down to the indomitable human
spirit. Rousing stuff.

Beckerman snatched a fistful of Mason's collar and
dragged him back to the top of the levy. "You're not going anywhere."

"You piece of shit."

He chained Mason's wrists and ankles behind him
and padlocked it all together. He'd pulled the chain so
tight he was already cutting off Mason's circulation.

"You won't get away with this," Mason growled.

"You'd be surprised what I get away with."

Beckerman kicked Mason in the side, rolling him
over. Mason tipped over the levy's edge and momentum
took over. He rolled over and over into the river. He hit
the water hard, disappearing below the surface in an in-
stant.

Beckerman clambered down the levy into the water,
then waded out to Mason. Air bubbled to the surface
from Mason's nose and mouth. He thrashed as best
he could to get his head above water. Trussed up, he
wasn't going anywhere. If he thought instead of panicking, his natural buoyancy would have brought him
to the surface. But Mason had proved that he wasn't a
thinker. Beckerman grabbed Mason's collar and pulled
his head above the surface. The frantic thrashing ceased,
and Mason sucked in ugly breaths. He panicked again
when Beckerman brought out his Colt. Beckerman
pushed Mason's head below the water to give him something else to think about and waded out until he was
knee deep.

The river looked slow moving, but the current was
strong. Beckerman knew the river well and banked on
its power to do his work for him.

Mason's head popped above the water. "No," he
screamed.

"But yes," Beckerman said and pressed the Colt against the back of Mason's head. Mason stiffened. He knew what was coming. Beckerman fired two rounds into his captive's head. The large-caliber rounds removed half of Mason's face—a helpful but unnecessary fringe benefit. If he were doing a thorough job, he would have removed the head and hands to prevent identification, but thanks to Mason's sloppiness, his identity was known.

The pistol had ejected the two spent shell casings into the water. He liked things tidy and would have preferred to collect them, but in the scheme of things, it didn't matter. He hadn't left any trace or fingerprint evidence, and it was unlikely anyone would find the casings after the river had its way.

Mason was still now. A red cloud blossomed in the steel-gray waters and rapidly lost its cumulous shape in the current, becoming an elongated streak of pink within seconds. Beckerman strode out until the water was chest high before he released the dead man. The river took Mason, and the chains dragged him below the surface.

Santiago felt a flush of excitement when Hayden produced the weapon Mason had tried to use on him. He held it up to the light by the corner of its sealed plastic bag. The device might have been cracked and split, but one part remained intact—the rectangular aperture with the rounded corners. Without a doubt, he knew it would fit perfectly with the bruises on his three "suicides."

He put Hayden and Rebecca in the department's briefing room with coffee and bagels, while he rallied the troops. Rice and Dysart arrived a half hour later, and Santiago closed the door. He slid the bagged contraption across the table to Dysart. The coroner investigator

examined the device through the bag. He brought out a
pair of calipers, measured the opening and nodded. The
results were in. Santiago had his answers.

"Do you know what that thing is?" Hayden asked after watching the back and forth.

"Yes, I do," Dysart said.

"Anything said here doesn't leave this room, okay?"
Santiago said to Hayden and Rebecca.

"You have our word," Rebecca said, answering for
both of them.

Santiago had noticed how they'd become a duo over
the course of this mess. They didn't make independent
decisions. What went for one went for the other. It
made dealing with them somewhat easier. It only got
difficult for him if they disagreed with him. Then they
became an awkward bargaining unit that he had to struggle to break.

Dysart rose and placed the device in front of Rebecca
and Hayden. Santiago and Rice left the comfort of their
seats for a closer look.

"This is a powder injection syringe. They've been
around for a while, but they're still relatively uncommon."

"So, this is the solution for people who don't like nee-
dles?" Rice asked.

"Yes and no. It helps, but it wasn't developed for that
reason. Needleless injections have their advantages. The
likelihood of infection and cross-contamination are eliminated because the skin is never broken. Plus, less drug
is needed."

"How does it work?" Rebecca asked.

Dysart grabbed the pen Santiago was holding. Santiago recognized this as the nearest Dysart could get to
acting out. He kept his playful nature for the cops, but
he was always a professional in front of the public.

Dysart pointed with the pen to what looked like a

super-sized vitamin pill. "The drug is held in this cassette. Behind the cassette is this canister filled with pressurized helium. When the button is pressed on the end here, the helium is released. It busts through the cassette, snatches up the particles of the drug and is fired at a high velocity into the epidermis."

"Does it hurt?" Rebecca asked.

"There's some discomfort. The patient is being jabbed by thousands of minuscule particles shot-blasted into the flesh, but it's nothing major. It's less painful than a conventional hypodermic needle, but it does leave a bruise that fades soon after."

"The bruise has been a common feature of late," Santiago said, returning to his seat. "Shane, Sundip Chaudhary and Malcolm Fuller all had a rectangular bruise on their bodies. It's shaped exactly like this." Santiago tapped the opening on the needleless syringe. "The bruise has bugged me since day one. Although I told you that Shane and Chaudhary had a narcotic in their bloodstream, the autopsy revealed no signs of ingestion or needle tracks."

"After the tox screen came back positive for narcotics, I had the bruised tissue excised and analyzed," Dysart said. "It came back with a high concentration of the drug."

Santiago let Dysart take the glory for this result by not mentioning it was his insistence that the bruised area be tested. He'd keep that tidbit in his back pocket and pull it out when he needed something fast tracked.

"Did you find these syringes on Shane, Chaudhary or Fuller?" Rebecca asked.

"No, we didn't," Rice said.

"So, someone drugged Shane." Rebecca's eyes glistened with welling tears. The tears weren't just of sorrow but of vindication. She now had proof for what she'd always believed. "Someone did this to him."

"What about Trevor Bellis?" Hayden asked.

Bellis was the odd man out. He'd come back clean and sober. No bruise. No drugs. His fingerprints were on the shotgun. He'd pulled the trigger knowing full well the consequences of his last action. Santiago couldn't imagine the courage Bellis had summoned to take his life. People saw victims of suicide as cowards. Yes, they ran away from their problems by jumping off a rooftop or eating a bullet, but a person required guts to follow through on the deed.

"There's no doubt regarding his suicide."

"Why did he kill himself?" Rebecca asked.

"Guilt," Rice ventured. "His suicide after all his people had been killed was no coincidence."

"So he knew what was going on," Hayden said.

"That's our guess," Rice said. He went to say more, but one glance from Santiago told him it wasn't advisable. Santiago had embarked on a sharing exercise with Hayden and Rebecca, but it only went so far. He guided the conversation back to subjects he wanted to cover.

"Getting back to Mason. You gave us a pretty good description and we might even get lucky with some prints off the syringe, but what about the fire at MDE? I know you only saw a reflection of the person who attacked you, but could he have been the man?"

Hayden reflected for a moment before shaking his head. "No. Wrong body type. The guy at MDE was tall and lean. Mason was stocky. Strong but out of shape."

A swing and a miss, Santiago thought. The news didn't disappoint him. While it would have been nice if the arsonist and Mason were the same person, he hadn't expected them to be. There'd been too much collateral damage for it to be one man's work.

Santiago stood. "I'd like to thank you for your time."

Hayden frowned. "You're squeezing us out."

"You've given me a lot to do. I can't do it with you at

my side. What I need you to do is stay out of trouble. Stick together. If any strangers come knocking, you call me."

Hayden's expression said he didn't buy the argument, but he didn't complain. He and Rebecca stood, and Rice saw them out.

"Now that the kids have gone, can we talk using big words?" Dysart said.

"That's why I asked them to leave."

"Whoever concocted this narcotic and decided to use it in needleless syringes screwed up. It acted too fast. If it had worked on a slow release, it would have given the bruise time to dissipate."

"And time for the injected victim to run to a doctor." Dysart shrugged at Santiago's counterargument.

"You know a lot about these syringes, so why didn't you pick up on it at the autopsy?"

"The bruise. The shape was wrong and the bruise too aggressive. These don't normally leave behind such a harsh reminder."

Rice returned to the briefing room and retook his seat. "What are we talking about?"

"These syringes," Santiago said.

"These things have to be pretty specialized. There can't be many manufacturers," Rice said.

"There aren't," Dysart said.

"So, tracking down their customers should be simple," Rice added.

"I think you've just volunteered for your next task, Rice," Santiago said.

"Not so fast, Ruben. It won't be that easy," Dysart said. "This syringe here is a prototype. You can tell from the crude manufacture and the lack of branding. The injectors don't even look like this anymore. I've seen them. They are much more elegant now, and they're totally cylindrical. They look like a plastic cigar and leave a round mark. That's why the bruise didn't click with me. In the scheme of things, this is the Model-T version."

"So you're saying it can't be traced?" Santiago said.

"No, the opposite. I would say whoever has these hasn't bought them and isn't your garden-variety dealer."

"Whoever's using them isn't a dealer, Dickie," Santiago said. "Drug dealers don't hand out force-fed freebies."

Santiago picked up the baggie and examined the injector. They hadn't found a syringe in any of the three victims' possession, but foul play still didn't hang right for Santiago. Hayden had witnessed Shane Fallon's suicide. He was pretty sure if he ever caught up with the 911 caller who'd witnessed Chaudhary's death, he'd tell him that Chaudhary had walked into the ocean alone. There wasn't a witness at Malcolm Fuller's death, but everything pointed to suicide. He didn't like the conclusion he was being led toward. The drug wasn't being used to subdue the victims. It was being used to drive them to suicide.

"This drug," Santiago said. "Someone shot Chaudhary, Fallon and Fuller up with it, but they didn't just curl up and die. They killed themselves. The witnesses and physical evidence prove that. Could this drug have pushed them to suicide?"

Dysart was slow to respond. Santiago slid the baggie across the table to pressure an answer out of him. The baton was his. "The tox report definitely indicates it was a hallucinogen, and there's a certain susceptibility in the subject under the influence, but I'm no expert."

"I know that, but what's your feeling?"

Dysart sighed. "It's possible."

"Then find an expert and find out for sure."

CHAPTER TWENTY-THREE

Rebecca slipped her hand into Hayden's as they crossed the parking lot back to his car. An odd sensation settled over him. He felt squeezed in all directions at once. It took a moment for him to recognize the sensation. He was being watched. He blamed his preternatural instinct on the two attempts on his life. They'd sharpened his fight-or-flight reflex. He had no desire to flee. He was tired of running for his life. It wouldn't save him. Fighting for his life would.

"What's wrong?" Rebecca asked.

He'd tightened his grip on her hand involuntarily. He immediately relaxed his grip.

"Stay calm. I think we're being watched."

Rebecca stutter-stepped, but kept her composure. "Where?"

He didn't know. He scanned the parking lot, tracking with his eyes and keeping his head movements to a minimum. His watcher had stupidly followed them to the sheriff's department. If he didn't alert the dumb son of a bitch, Santiago and friends could nail him. He still felt the weight of someone's gaze, but nobody stuck out among the motionless vehicles and the occasional officer leaving or entering the building.

"I don't see anyone, but we're being watched."

Rebecca didn't tell him he was being crazy. She'd seen too much to question him.

He continued to seek a face among a sea of vehicles and listen for an idling engine that should be silent. Still nothing. His senses said yes, but the evidence said no. They reached his Mitsubishi.

"What do you want to do?" Rebecca asked, pausing outside the car.

Before he could answer, an engine burst into life. He spun around and zeroed in on the engine noise. Vehicles blocked his view of the car, but he saw a flash of dark blue between them. The car emerged at the end of an intersection. A chill grew from within Hayden. It was the dark blue Dodge Charger he'd seen following Fuller. The driver was wearing the same damn Angels cap.

"The blue Charger again," Rebecca said.

"Get in."

"I'll call Santiago," Rebecca said, sliding into the passenger seat.

"No, not yet," Hayden said, gunning the engine. "I don't want Santiago spooking him. This guy is leaving. He won't expect us to follow him." He eased from his parking stall. He didn't want to alert the Angels fan they were on to him.

"Hayden, what are you doing?"

"Nothing that will hurt us. This guy knows where we live. It's about time we found out which rock he hides under."

Hayden turned onto Civic Center Drive and tailed the Dodge onto US-101. The Dodge went south toward San Francisco, but took the Richmond-San Rafael Bridge to the east bay. It zigged and zagged in and out of traffic, forcing Hayden to do likewise. Hayden feared the Angels fan would spot his equally erratic driving in his rearview mirror, or maybe he had already had, considering his aggressive driving. Either way, the Angels fan wasn't doing enough to lose Hayden.

"Is it Mason?" Rebecca asked over the noise of Hayden's Mitsubishi striking a joint in the road.

"No, Mason was a black guy."

"Could he be the arsonist?"

Glimpsing the Angels fan's head and shoulders wasn't enough for a positive ID. He'd know the moment the son of a bitch climbed from the Dodge. But instinct, the same instinct that alerted him to someone watching him, knew the Angels fan was the man who'd left him to burn at MDE. He didn't want to frighten Rebecca and said, "I don't know."

"I hope he is. I don't want someone else out there stalking us."

Neither do I, he thought.

The Angels fan took I-580 into Oakland and beyond. Just as it looked as if he was leading them on a merry dance, he turned off the freeway at San Leandro. They followed him onto the surface streets. If the Angels fan knew he was being tailed, he didn't show it. He didn't make abrupt changes in direction or double back on himself. Hayden got worried when the guy turned into an industrial district. There looked to be plenty of activity, but bystanders were few and far between. If the Angels fan was luring them into a trap, this would be a good place for it.

The Angels fan turned into a parking lot of a firm called South Bay Industries, a gleaming prefab factory unit. He parked, but didn't get out of his car. Like he'd done with Hayden and Rebecca outside the sheriff's office, he just waited.

Hayden stopped his Mitsubishi on the street and they waited to see what the Angels fan would do. If the guy went in, they had him. If the Angels fan was a visitor, he'd have to sign in and there'd be a record. If he worked there, they'd catch the guy with a deception. Hayden would go in and plead stupidity for clipping a Dodge in their parking lot. Either way, they'd have him and they'd see how he fared with Santiago.

"What's he doing?" Rebecca asked.

Hayden didn't have an answer. They'd been sitting there watching the Angels fan watch South Bay Industries. Maybe the guy had picked up their tail and was waiting them out. It wouldn't work. Now that Hayden had him in his sights, he wasn't going anywhere. He would wait as long as it took.

"Hayden, look."

Rebecca pointed to the entrance of South Bay Industries. James Lockhart was leaving the building with two Chinese men. Lockhart was speaking to them, pointing to the building and smiling. He was unaware of the Angels fan parked in his corner of the parking lot. The Angels fan gunned the engine and eased his Dodge out of its slot.

"Shit," Hayden murmured. "He's going after Lockhart."

He saw it fall into place. Now that everyone at MDE had been taken care of, it was time move up the food chain to Lockhart. He'd commissioned the damn job at MDE. If anyone could expose the secret at MDE so many were trying to cover up, it was Lockhart.

Hayden flung his door open and clambered from his car. He bolted across the street, yelling out Lockhart's name. Lockhart and his two associates watched Hayden in stunned surprise.

The Dodge rolled toward Lockhart. It sped up as Hayden closed in, but the Angels fan had parked too far away. Hayden, even on foot, had the drop on the Angels fan, and he knew it. The Dodge screeched to a halt, then shot back into reverse and backed into the street the way it had come. Lockhart gave the Dodge scant interest, reserving his scorn for Hayden. His expression showed little appreciation for Hayden's presence.

With the threat no longer hanging over Lockhart, Hayden slowed his pace. He no longer had to raise the alarm. He hopped a low fence protecting the token landscaping and approached Lockhart and his associates.

"Mr. Lockhart, could I talk to you for a minute?" Hayden asked as Rebecca fell in at his side. "It's very important. You're in danger."

The Chinese men backed up a step at Hayden's approach, but Lockhart calmed them. "It's okay. I know them. What do you want?"

"Marin Design Engineering. Do you have any explanations for the deaths?"

Hayden saw Lockhart gear up for some vehement dismissal, but Rebecca's presence evoked his better manners. "I don't. That's a police matter."

"What's going on here?" the shorter of the Chinese asked.

"Nothing," Lockhart said and ushered the men away.

"Please don't do this," Rebecca said. "We're just looking for answers."

"And I don't have them for you." Lockhart guided his associates toward a black Cadillac STS.

Lockhart cared more about his business with the Chinese than the deaths at MDE. Hayden felt his grip on his temper slip. He wasn't going to let this son of a bitch turn his back on the dead.

"Don't fifteen dead people mean anything to you?" he called across the parking lot.

The question stopped Lockhart and the Chinese in their tracks.

"James?" the squat Chinese man asked.

"Wait there," Lockhart growled at Hayden and Rebecca. He placated the Chinese and put them in his

Cadillac before returning. His jaw muscles flexed from grinding his teeth. "Now, what is it you want?"

Hayden's grip on his temper slipped another inch. "Fifteen people are dead. Our lives have been threatened. I thought you might be interested in that."

Lockhart exhaled as if releasing the pent-up pressure inside his skull. "Yes, I'm sorry. What is it you want to know?"

"None of it makes sense. The police don't seem to know anything, and that's not acceptable considering how many people are dead," Rebecca said. "You must know something they're not telling us."

"Why would I?"

"You're a prominent person in all this," Hayden said. "You work with the government. People are going to talk to you."

Lockhart smiled and shook his head. "You overestimate my importance. I know as much as you do. You should really talk to the sheriff's office." He intensified his smile and backed away. "Now if you'll excuse me, I have some clients that need my attention."

"Do you know that you were followed here?"

Lockhart's smile, the brittle and fragile thing that it was, fell away. Hayden didn't see fear or shock in his eyes, but something else he couldn't nail down.

"What are you talking about?"

"A dark blue Dodge followed you here. That's how we found you. It's the same Dodge that followed us and was seen following Malcolm Fuller before he died."

Hayden gave Lockhart a minute to absorb this news. He wanted to let it sink in, let Lockhart know he wasn't untouchable. He was just as vulnerable as they were.

His expression turned stony. "I don't have time for this crap."

"It isn't crap," Rebecca said.

"Don't waste my time. MDE was an unfortunate affair. I wish the outcome was different, but don't try to drag me into your delusions."

Hayden and Rebecca watched Lockhart return to his car. He exchanged his indignant face for an affable one for his clients before driving off.

"What was that about?" Rebecca asked.

"I don't know, but we're going to find out. Something isn't right here. C'mon."

Hayden followed Lockhart. He'd thrown the Dodge at Lockhart in an attempt to spook him and while it had gotten his attention, it hadn't done it in the way Hayden had expected. He got the distinct feeling Lockhart wanted rid of him and Rebecca.

He trailed farther behind Lockhart than he had with the Angels fan. Now that Lockhart knew a car was following him, he'd be watching his mirrors, and Hayden didn't want Lockhart confusing him with the Angels fan.

Rebecca watched for the Charger. They'd run him off, but for how long? Hayden couldn't see the guy giving up so easily, but so far, the Dodge hadn't made a reappearance.

Lockhart drove the Chinese into San Francisco and dropped them off at the Fairmont Hotel. Hayden double parked with the engine running to watch them. The Chinese tried to the keep their conversation going, but Lockhart cut things short and drove off.

Interesting, Hayden thought. He wasn't the only one Lockhart wanted to ditch.

Lockhart backtracked through the city, and they followed. The traffic bunched them up close to him, but he didn't seem to notice their presence.

Lockhart swung his Cadillac into the underground parking lot at Union Square. With the chronic parking situation in the city, Hayden had little option but to follow him into the lot. Hayden found a spot quickly and parked. He and Rebecca jumped out and walked between the parked vehicles to keep tabs on Lockhart. Lockhart left his Cadillac and exited the lot. He picked up Powell and headed toward Market.

"What's he doing?" Rebecca asked.

"I don't know. He's running scared. I'm sure of that."

"I can't believe what you told him spooked him that much."

Lockhart followed Powell to the cable car terminus at Market. The terminus buzzed with eager tourists waiting to ride the next car. Lockhart ignored them and descended into the BART/MUNI station.

The moment Lockhart disappeared from view, Hayden and Rebecca rushed forward. They couldn't afford to miss whether he took BART or MUNI, and which line. They entered the station. Instead of descending an escalator, Lockhart just stood around in the station. He had his back to them and they hid their presence by buying BART tickets from an automated machine.

Lockhart pulled out his cell phone and called someone. Hayden and Rebecca were too far away to hear what was said, but his body language spoke volumes. He looked as if he'd been stood up, but he didn't leave. He stayed around, wandering in a tight circle. The heavy throng of people entering and leaving the station paid him little attention.

"I feel like I'm sticking out here," Rebecca said and nodded towards the ticket attendant in the booth.

Hayden grabbed Rebecca's hand. "C'mon, let's go."

He pulled her toward Lockhart. He fancied his chances. In the BART station, Lockhart was out of his comfort zone. He wouldn't be able to brush them off and he'd have to behave himself in public.

"Mr. Lockhart," Hayden called out when they got close.

Irritation and disgust marked Lockhart's expression

when he turned to face them. "Did you follow me? That's harassment."

Hayden felt the weight of Lockhart's veiled threat, but pushed it aside. "Why are you here?" Hayden asked. "It isn't for a train."

"Leave me alone, or I'll call police."

"Try it and let's see what happens. I think you have as much interest in having cops nosing into your business as we do."

Hayden didn't have total faith in his bluff, but it worked. Lockhart dropped the hostility.

"Please, leave. You don't know what's going on, so stay out of it."

"What *is* going on?" Rebecca asked. "We're not trying to get in the way. We just want to understand."

"I'm meeting someone who might just be able to help us all understand, but he won't come if you keep hanging around."

Hayden wondered if the Angels fan was Lockhart's mystery man. If so, maybe he'd gotten it all wrong. Maybe the guy had been following him, Fuller and Lockhart not to hurt them, but to talk to them. He cast a glance around him for the familiar baseball cap. It would stick out in this part of the world dominated by Giants and A's fans, but he saw nothing.

Lockhart's cell phone rang. He listened to his caller speak and kept his answers to yeses and nos before hanging up.

"Is that him?" Hayden asked.

"Yes," Lockhart said, "but he's not coming."

"Did he see us?" Rebecca asked.

Lockhart pursed his lips. "No. He says he can't make the meeting, so he's left something for us."

"Where?" Hayden asked.

"You two aren't going to butt out, are you?" Lockhart said.

"Too much has happened," Hayden said.

"It's on the BART platform."

They rode the escalators down to the central platform. A smattering of passengers occupied it. It was well-lit, so anything left for Lockhart had to be in plain sight.

Lockhart led the way to the end of the platform which dead-ended at a wall punctuated by a tunnel on each side. Either out of safety or convenience, no one else ventured to the end of the platform. Their breaking this unsaid taboo drew occasional glances, but Lockhart's professional appearance diffused anyone's concerns.

Hayden felt the heat of the CCTV cameras in the ceiling. Someone had to be watching. Security couldn't be as lackadaisical as the criminal would hope. Whatever had been left had to be found fast and without fuss if they weren't to alert anyone.

"Who is this person you were supposed to be meeting?" Hayden asked

"I don't know. Just someone too frightened to go to the police. He's hoping my involvement will help."

This brought a chill to Hayden. It was all too reminiscent of Mason's trick to lure him. He didn't like the way this felt. He checked behind him for anyone watching them with too much interest.

They reached the end of the platform. There were no trashcans or anything to hide an object. Whatever had been left was either small or the person who'd called Lockhart had lied.

"What are we looking for?" Hayden asked.

"It's down there," Lockhart said and pointed at the eastbound tunnel. "On a ledge."

The package might be on a ledge, but it was still dangerous to go anywhere near the tunnel. Hayden eyed the computer display board. The next train wasn't for seven minutes. Plenty of time to retrieve the package before it came.

"I'll get it. It'll look weird if you do it," Hayden said to Lockhart.

Lockhart and Rebecca provided cover. They stood in front of him and pretended to talk while he dropped to his knees. He gripped the platform wall and reached deep into the tunnel. The tunnel, mercifully dark and silent, stank of grease and trapped air. His hand found the ledge and his fingers slid through the dirt and grime caked to the surface. Just as he came to the end of his reach, his hand slipped through the padded loop belonging to a backpack.

"Got it."

He yanked on the backpack. The pack was far heavier than he expected and slipped off the ledge. Its weight jerked at him, pulling him toward the electrified tracks. He caught himself and swung the pack onto the platform. It hit the tile floor with a metallic clang. He exchanged a confused look with Lockhart. Lockhart hadn't been expecting this gift.

Hayden unzipped the backpack, and his breath caught when he opened it. He knew the item inside, even though he'd only seen it on paper and his computer screen. He peeled the pack away to reveal a pressure vessel the size of fire extinguisher. Just like a fire extinguisher, a liquid slopped about inside. Instead of a hose, a circular manifold with six ports in a rosette formation protruded from the top with an electrical box fixed atop. A single red LED blinked at him.

"Oh, God," Lockhart murmured.

"What's wrong?" Rebecca asked.

"Leave it," Lockhart barked. "Get out."

Just as Hayden put the vessel on the ground, he felt movement from inside. The LED switched from red to green. The actuator inside snapped into place and released the vessel's contents. A colorless and near odorless gas rushed from the rosette ports. Cold and damp, the gas hit the back of his hand.

Lockhart told him again to leave the vessel and get out, but he couldn't. He no longer had the strength to stand. He pushed himself up and fell flat on his face.

Rebecca yelled out. Hayden turned his head, but it took all his muscle control to flop his head in her direction.

Lockhart pulled her away, but she tore herself free and staggered toward him.

He motioned to her to stay, although his control over his arm was pitiful.

But it was too late. Rebecca's legs went out from under her, and she crashed down hard on her butt.

Passengers rushed forward, but stopped short when Lockhart collapsed seconds after Rebecca. When they started dropping, Hayden knew the only person who could save him was himself.

He called Rebecca's name, but she didn't answer. He tried dragging himself across the platform to her, but he had no control over his body. Then he lost control of his eyes. Every time he tried to focus on something, his eyes rolled back. It scared him how little control he had over his body. It was shutting down, betraying him one muscle at a time. It was a mercy that none of it hurt.

A heavy weight pressed upon him. The weight was the inexorable desire to sleep. It took too much effort to lie there on the tile. It was easier to succumb to his longing. He let go and it felt good, as if descending into warm waters, soaking through his body and into his being. He gradually sank to the bottom. The deeper he went the darker it became. He was no longer aware of the panic around him, Lockhart or Rebecca or his impending death. He was aware of nothing.

CHAPTER TWENTY-FOUR

Hayden regained consciousness, and this time it stuck. He'd woken up twice before, but only briefly. His eyes had only fluttered open long enough to take in his surroundings before passing out again. The first time was on the street outside the Powell Street BART station. Then again, in a hospital. Now he was in a windowless holding cell. He tried not to let this fact disturb him.

He didn't know what time it was. His watch had been taken. The absence of windows didn't help. Diffused florescent lighting made it permanent twilight. White-washed walls hemmed him in from three sides, and a Plexiglas wall turned him into a sideshow attraction. He pushed himself to a sitting position and became instantly light-headed. Whatever had been in that canister still had a kick to it.

He had the cell to himself. If he was being held here, where were Rebecca and Lockhart? In neighboring cells? The significance of the holding cell sunk in. He was being viewed as a suspect and not a victim. He didn't dare think about the charges.

He now understood why Shane and fourteen other people had lost their lives. They'd all helped design a weapon—and so had he. They were unwitting dupes, but guilty all the same. No wonder Shane had killed himself. This was his terrible thing. He should have listened to Shane and kept out. Curiosity had killed the cat, but it was going to put him away for life.

He was strangely calm considering his situation. He put it down either to the drug's lingering effects or the fact that he couldn't even fathom how big a hole he was in right now.

He was wondering how he could alert someone when he spotted the camera trained on him from the corner of his cell. He expected someone to come for him now that he was awake, but no one did for an hour. His welcoming committee was a pair of uniformed men.

One man cuffed him while the other watched. They walked out of the holding area and his stomached tightened when he didn't see Rebecca or Lockhart in any of the other cells. They marched him through a number of corridors and an office area. Daylight poured through large windows. He was high up, but didn't recognize the view outside.

"Where am I?"

"The FBI Field Office in San Francisco."

He thought he was in Santiago's custody. He could work with Santiago. Santiago would understand. The FBI wouldn't. His calm demeanor evaporated.

The officers directed him into another corridor that led to a bank of interview rooms, but interview rooms were only interview rooms when you were a witness. They became interrogation rooms when you were the suspect, irrespective of what it said on the door.

The officer who'd cuffed him knocked on an interview room door. A sharp-looking man in a suit answered. He stood back for Hayden and his escorts as they filed inside.

Rebecca was sitting at a table across from a man dressed in a suit. She was pale and looked tired and scared. He smiled at her to lift her spirits. She smiled back, and a sparkle returned to her eyes.

Lockhart was nowhere to be seen. Hayden wondered if he was receiving special treatment elsewhere.

The uniforms uncuffed Hayden and left. He sat alongside Rebecca as directed.

"I'm Special Agent John Bohnert," said the man at the door. "And this is Special Agent Keith Schrader."

Hayden didn't have to ask if he was being considered as a terrorist.

"You want to tell us what happened in the BART station yesterday, Mr. Duke?" Bohnert asked.

Yesterday, Hayden thought. He'd been out for a day.

He walked the agents through their encounter with Lockhart after following the Angels fan from Santiago's office. The agents listened, but they took no notes, even though they had legal pads in front of them. There wasn't any need to write anything down. He guessed everything was being recorded. Not that recording equipment and notepads mattered. The two agents made no effort to hide their disbelief.

"This guy in the Angels cap. Know him?" Bohnert asked.

"No," Hayden answered.

"I'm guessing you didn't get a license plate number either."

Hayden groaned inside. He hadn't. He'd been too wrapped up in the chase. "No."

Schrader leaned back in his seat and let out an over-dramatic sigh. "Another case of some other guy did it. Why can't you people be more original?"

"We're telling you the truth," Rebecca said.

"Of course you are," Schrader said.

Rebecca went to say more, but Hayden put a hand on her forearm to stop her. These guys wouldn't listen to reason. They'd only listen to evidence.

"We've done some checking up on you, Hayden," Bohnert said. "You worked for Marin Design Engineering. They're a very interesting firm considering they're all dead. Even more interesting is that James Lockhart was their last client."

Hayden had his answer as to why Lockhart was nowhere in sight. The FBI saw him as the victim and them as the aggressors. He tried to see it their way. They couldn't know the circumstances. This was a case of mistaken identity.

"Talk to Lockhart," Hayden said. "He'll explain everything."

Bohnert ignored him. "We have witnesses stating you and Rebecca accosted Mr. Lockhart outside South Bay Industries. More witnesses saw you retrieve the device from the tunnel moments before it went off in the station. No one saw a guy in an Angels cap."

"This is insane," Rebecca said. "You've got it wrong."

"Does this have something to do with Shane Fallon's death or MDE firing you?" Schrader asked Hayden.

"No," Hayden said. *Who's giving them their information? Lockhart? Santiago? Both?* He'd been out of the game for a day. They could have gotten to a lot of people in that time.

The case against them kept building and building. It frightened Hayden how quickly Bohnert and Schrader had amassed their information. He guessed it wasn't difficult. His name had made it into the newspapers after the fire, and Santiago had his statements. Okay, he'd had his hands on the device when it went off, but why did Bohnert and Schrader see him and Rebecca as being behind all this? He couldn't believe they hadn't spoken to Lockhart. One word from him would point suspicion in the right direction. So why were they still suspects?

"Is Lockhart okay?"

"Why do you care?" Schrader asked. "Did you wheedle your way into MDE to get to him?"

"What the hell are you talking about?"

"What are your affiliations?" Bohnert asked.

"Affiliations?" Hayden said. "Look, we're victims, not terrorists."

"Do we look like terrorists?" Rebecca pleaded.

"You'd be surprised what a terrorist looks like," Schrader said.

"You used a pretty powerful sedative yesterday. Your stunt not only took out you and Mr. Lockhart, but nine other passengers. It would have been more if the sedative hadn't lost its potency," Bohnert said. "Where did you get it from? If you want to get out of here, give us some names."

"Are you listening to us?" Rebecca demanded. "We don't know anyone because we had nothing to do with this."

"Who manufactured the device for you?" Schrader asked.

"You're not interested in hearing a damn thing we've got to say," Hayden said.

"Your father is a skilled machinist, Mr. Duke," Schrader said. "Did he manufacture it for you?"

Hayden stabbed a finger at Schrader. "Hey, you leave my dad out of this."

"How many more of these devices exist?" Bohnert asked.

Hayden was wasting his time. Bohnert and Schrader had made up their minds. They had their culprits. They had no reason to look any further when they had viable candidates and a nervous public to quell. "I know you're not going to believe me, but I'm going to say this one more time. We didn't have anything to do with yesterday's attack," Hayden said. "What can I do to convince you?"

"Tell me something that doesn't sound like bullshit," Bohnert said.

"Look into Marin Design Engineering," Hayden said. "People started dying long before I started working for them."

"My brother said he'd done something unforgivable before he killed himself," Rebecca said.

"He wasn't the only one to say that," Hayden added.

Neither Bohnert nor Schrader showed any signs of believing them. Hayden didn't give them a chance to launch back into their interrogation. Instead, he detailed recent events including Shane's death, the fire, Malcolm Fuller's beliefs before his death and Tony Mason's attack.

"Y'know," Bohnert said. "It sounds all very convincing, but there isn't one person who can corroborate any of this. Your witnesses are either dead or somewhere in the ether. It doesn't help."

Bohnert sounded sincere, and Hayden couldn't fault his logic. He was right. There was no substance to anything he said. No one other than Rebecca could back him up and not even she could back him up on everything. The only thing he had was the busted needleless syringe, and even that didn't help. Bohnert and Schrader could make a case that it belonged to him. He had never been more scared. Not even when Mason had tried to press the syringe to his neck. With a head-on attack, he could fight for his life. But against the likes of Bohnert and Schrader, he was helpless. He hadn't wanted to play the lawyer card. It smacked of guilt. But he needed protection from a different kind of enemy than the likes of Mason.

"I would like a lawyer."

"You haven't been charged," Bohnert said.

"Then we're leaving."

Hayden stood, taking Rebecca's hand. Schrader moved

quickly to block their path. Rebecca tightened her grip on Hayden's hand.

"Leaving would be a big mistake," Schrader advised. "You leave and you'll kick start a law-enforcement machine that can't be stopped."

Damned if you do, damned if you don't, Hayden thought. If Bohnert and Schrader played their Patriot Act card, he and Rebecca were going to be buried by the power of the law. He backed away from Schrader and retook his seat.

"Smart thinking," Bohnert said.

Schrader remained standing. He retreated to the room's only door and leaned against it.

Rebecca sat alongside Hayden and slipped an arm around his shoulders. "We'll be okay."

He nodded, although he wasn't sure she was right.

"We've searched your homes," Bohnert said.

"I hope you had a warrant."

"Probable cause makes life very easy," Schrader answered.

"We didn't find any more devices or the sedative," Bohnert said. "Tell us where we can find them, and we'll cut you some slack."

"You keep blaming us for this attack, but you're missing one vital point," Hayden said.

"Which is?" Bohnert asked.

"The device was remotely triggered. It went off after I retrieved it. You didn't find a transmitter on us." Hayden didn't wait for a response. "And we didn't have a chance to dispose of it. The sedative took us out."

"Does that make any sense to you?" Rebecca demanded.

Hayden waited for a response that didn't come. He'd punched a hole in their case.

Someone knocked at the door, and Schrader opened it. Santiago stood outside with an FBI escort alongside him. Hayden had never been so happy to see the detective.

"Excuse me, gentlemen. I'm Detective Ruben Santiago, Marin County Sheriff's Office. I was wondering if I can join the circus. These two have some questions to answer for me too."

Bohnert and Schrader glanced at each other and shared an unspoken thought. "All right, Detective," Bohnert said. "I think we've come to a break for now. Maybe you'll be able to get some sense out of them."

Santiago held the door open for the departing agents and closed it behind them. There was an air of privacy that Hayden knew didn't exist. Camera surveillance was on them. With the seriousness of the allegations, there'd be a team of agents glued to everything they said.

"The police grapevine must be working well today," Hayden said.

Santiago seated himself opposite them. "It is, but I find CNN works even better."

Hayden sagged. This mess was getting worse by the minute.

"What the hell are you two up to? I can't leave the pair of you alone for ten minutes."

"You've got to get us out of here," Hayden said.

"Why should I?" Santiago said. "You've been screwing with me for weeks with your own little private investigations. You think you're Nancy Drew and one half of the Hardy boys. Well, I'll give you a shock. You're not. You two are one step from ending up as the next Timothy McVeigh."

"We're sorry," Rebecca said.

"Sorry isn't going to rebuild the bridges you've burned."

"Tell them we didn't have anything to do with this," Hayden said.

"How do I know you didn't?"

"Christ, Santiago, you know we didn't."

"Convince me. Tell me what happened after you left my office."

Hayden and Rebecca gave Santiago the same account they'd given the Feds.

Santiago slammed his fist on the table. "You're idiots. Do you know that? The moment you spotted this guy in my parking lot, you should have called me. If I had stopped him, then we might have prevented yesterday's mess. I thought we had an understanding. You tell me when something happens, and I do something about it."

"There wasn't time," Rebecca said.

"Bullshit. A cell phone call would have changed everything."

"If you'd picked up this guy, we wouldn't have known he was after Lockhart too."

"When are you going to get this through your thick skull? None of this is your decision. It's mine. It's the FBI's. Not yours," Santiago said.

"Okay," Hayden said. "We're idiots. We dug this hole for ourselves. Can you get us out?"

Santiago rose and paced the claustrophobic interview room. "I don't know. I know you didn't have anything to do with this. You aren't smart enough."

The insult was also a compliment. It would be heard by Bohnert and Schrader and their colleagues.

"Let me see what I can do," Santiago said.

The moment Santiago stepped from the room Schrader and Bohnert emerged from the video surveillance room down the corridor. They moved as an offensive line toward him. He imagined there was a lot of pressure on them for results. This would work in his favor.

"Gentlemen, can I have word?" Santiago asked.

Bohnert ushered Santiago into the surveillance room.

Schrader told the four other agents in the room to take a hike and closed the door on them. Hayden and Rebecca appeared on a large flat-screen monitor. The high definition made it easy to see how frightened they were. They'd dug themselves a hell of a hole. He couldn't let them languish.

"Talk," Bohnert said.

"These two weren't behind what happened yesterday."

"So you say." Schrader stood next to the door with his arms crossed.

"Yeah, I do say. Look at them." Santiago pointed at the TV monitor. "Do you really figure these two for this?"

Neither of the agents answered. They were playing "Who has the biggest dick?" with him. He wasn't a Fed, so he wasn't of the same class cop-wise and therefore not entitled to any answers. The tight-lipped act still gave him answers. They weren't talking to him because they had nothing solid on Hayden and Rebecca.

Santiago went over to the monitor and tapped Hayden and Rebecca's images on the screen. "These two are caught up in this, but they're victims. Yesterday provided the perfect smokescreen for the attacker. Whoever was behind the attack will either let them take the fall or take them out if they slip free."

"Why?" Bohnert asked.

"I don't know." Santiago jerked a thumb at Hayden and Rebecca on the monitor. "You heard them. Someone followed them yesterday, and I've got good reason to believe them."

"Give me a break," Schrader said.

"I've been working this longer than you have. I know these two. I know the case. A lot of people have died. Hayden has been attacked, and I've got evidence to back it up."

"So what do you want to do?" Bohnert asked.

"Cut them loose. Tell the media they were unfortunate victims who tried to prevent a disaster but were a moment too late."

"Are you fucking nuts?" Schrader said. "They're our prime suspects."

Santiago ignored Schrader. The man was too interested in proving his tough-guy credentials. People in charge didn't shoot their mouths off. Santiago turned to Bohnert.

"Cut them loose," Santiago repeated. "Someone is interested in them and will come after them if they're released. I want to be there when they do."

"I want our people involved too," Bohnert said.

"No, let me keep it small. If we have too many bodies on the ground, someone is going to spot them. Make it look vulnerable and someone will take their chances. I'll keep you involved, but let me do it my way."

Bohnert was quiet for a long moment as he weighed Santiago's offer. Santiago willed him to take it. He knew they wouldn't want to relinquish control to him, but he was giving them an out by offering himself as a scapegoat. If something went wrong, it was his head on the chopping block, not theirs. The dumb detective had sold them on this line of reasonable doubt and it had gone sideways. It was the stuff plausible deniability was made of. If Bohnert was smart, he'd pick up on this fact and give it the green light. Santiago didn't care about the scapegoat status. He knew he was right.

"You're setting these two up as bait," Bohnert said.

"It's the only way to hook the big fish," Santiago answered.

Bohnert exchanged a glance with Schrader. Schrader shrugged.

"Okay, Detective, do it your way, but don't forget who gave you this opportunity," Bohnert said.

"I won't."

Schrader stood aside for Santiago to let himself out. Bohnert stopped him at the door.

"People think we're the bad guys, but you, Detective Santiago, you're something else."

Chapter Twenty-five

Hayden rode the elevator down with Rebecca and Santiago. Bohnert and Schrader didn't accompany them, but Hayden still felt their presence. Despite Santiago's assurances, he expected the agents to drag them back before they left the building. Until he felt the comfort of the city sidewalk under his feet, he wouldn't relax. The elevator doors opened, and no one blocked their way other than people waiting for the elevator.

"Thanks," Hayden said as they pushed through the doors. "You saved our asses."

"Yes, I did. You two belong to me until this is finished."

It was a nasty reminder that this debacle was far from over.

Santiago walked Hayden and Rebecca to his car. He held the rear door open for them and they slid into the back. It was a less than subtle reminder of where they stood in all this. Bad guys rode in the back.

Santiago gunned the engine, but he didn't pull away. Instead, he turned around in his seat.

"This is the way it's going to work. My job's on the line because of you two, so you're going to do exactly as I tell you. Okay?"

Hayden and Rebecca both nodded.

"Good. This also means we don't let you out of our sight. I'll be with you days and Deputy Rice will cover nights."

"You're going to babysit us?" Hayden said.

"The choice is yours. I can turn around and you're free to sit in a cell on your own."

"So, how long are you and Deputy Rice going to live with us?" Rebecca asked.

"For as long as it takes. We've got the guy in the Angels cap and Tony Mason to find. These guys aren't going to stop at the first try."

It was a sobering thought and one Hayden had already had. The bull's-eye he carried on his back was getting larger and larger, and it was wearing him out. It wouldn't take much to nail him.

Santiago stepped on the gas and his unmarked cop car leaped forward. "You smell like a monkey cage, Hayden. Need a change of clothes?"

Hayden didn't need reminding of his own rankness. "Yeah, but I want to go by my car first."

"Forget the car. I do the driving."

"Trust me. You'll want to see what I've got in there."

Santiago drove Hayden to the lot where he'd parked his Mitsubishi. To his relief, his car was still there. Bohnert and Schrader hadn't gotten to it because they hadn't known where to find it, and Santiago's arrival had short-changed their questioning.

"I need to move it," Hayden said.

Santiago shook his head. "I'll take care of the car. Now, what's inside?"

Hayden removed the plans and flash drive from the trunk. Since putting them in there to show Eskdale, he hadn't had the time to stash them somewhere safe. Now it looked as if his car was the safest place of all.

Santiago took the plans from Hayden and spread them

out on the Mitsubishi's hood. "This is what you worked on at MDE?"

"Yeah," Hayden said and ran through the various design features. "One of the small units was set off in the BART station."

"I can't believe it's so simple," Santiago said.

"It's no more intricate than a can of hairspray. It's what goes into it that's the dangerous stuff."

Santiago rolled up the drawings and locked them in the trunk of his car. Hayden kept the flash drive. If Santiago booked the drawings into evidence, at least Hayden would keep ownership of something.

Santiago took Hayden's car keys, proving their open relationship was still a tenuous one. They returned to Santiago's Crown Vic, and he drove the car across the Bay Bridge toward Fairfield.

"I've got an update for you two," Santiago said. "The needleless syringes tracked back to Kenneth Eskdale. Dysart was right. The syringes were prototypes from PainFree Technologies. PainFree issued samples to academics and doctors. Eskdale's name is on the list."

"Any luck finding Eskdale?" Rebecca asked.

Santiago shook his head. "He's gone."

Hayden guessed they wouldn't hear from Eskdale this side of an ice age. He and Rebecca had exposed him. Eskdale's employer would hide him away so he couldn't compromise them. Santiago would break Eskdale in minutes. Bohnert and Schrader in less time. Hayden wondered if Eskdale would turn up dead.

Santiago pulled up in front of Hayden's house. Hayden opened his door to leave, but Santiago stopped him. "You've got ten minutes, so don't get any ideas."

Santiago meant running. It wasn't an option, let alone an idea. Hayden didn't have the resources or the skills for it. Santiago was his only way out of this mess. Hayden nodded and slid out of the car.

He let himself in and found Bohnert and Schrader's people had visited. They'd made a mess, but hadn't broken anything. It wasn't a lot different than when he'd come home to find his house burgled about a million years ago. It looked as if they hadn't finished. He guessed Santiago's intervention had stopped the search midflow.

His answering machine blinked at him, telling him a stack of messages waited for him. Most, if not all, would be from his mom. He didn't have the stomach to listen to them. He'd call his mom later to smooth things over.

He pulled out an overnight bag and packed it with clothes. He didn't know how much to pack. Enough for a day? A week? The thought of this mess lasting weeks drained him, and he stuffed what he could into the bag.

He left his bedroom for the bathroom to stock up on toiletries. He was leaning across the bathtub for his shampoo when he caught a flash of something reflected in the bathroom mirror. Before he could react, a hand covered his mouth and another arm snaked across his middle to pin his arms against his sides.

"It's okay," the man whispered. "I'm a friend. James Lockhart sent me. Please don't make a noise."

Hayden's heart beat like a jackhammer in his chest, but he stayed silent. After the previous assaults on him, he still hadn't gotten used to being attacked. But, unlike with the arsonist and Tony Mason, he trusted the person restraining him.

"I'm going to let you go, okay?"

Hayden nodded.

The arms released him. Hayden turned around to face a tall man dressed in a polo shirt and jeans who backed away with his hands up. The polo shirt rode up to reveal an automatic pistol pushed into his waistband. Friends with guns. Just what Hayden needed.

"I'm Maurice Beckerman. I'm sorry about breaking

in, but you've created quite a stir. I doubt you've seen the television. You're notorious."

This was something else Hayden didn't need to hear. "What does Mr. Lockhart want? He wasn't too interested in talking to me yesterday."

"Mr. Lockhart wants to speak with you. You're very important to him right now."

"Why hasn't he helped us with the police?" Hayden asked.

"He can't. He's been used. If he goes to the cops, everything leads to him. The attack yesterday was a nasty reminder of what these people are capable of if he doesn't play ball."

"But what can I do? I don't know anything."

"You know more than you realize. Mr. Lockhart wants to apologize to you for not speaking candidly yesterday. You caught him at an awkward time. He also wants to meet you tomorrow."

"We're in police custody and are on our way to San Rafael," Hayden said.

"I know." Beckerman sidled up to the living room window and sneaked a look outside without disturbing the drapes. "Just the one cop?"

"Yeah," Hayden said. "For now."

"Do you know where you're being kept?"

"Yes," Hayden answered and reeled off Shane's address in San Rafael.

Beckerman nodded, absorbing the information without writing it down. "Don't worry about the police. I'll take care of them. There will be a diversion. When it happens, get out. Okay?"

"Hey, wait a minute."

"Do you know where the *USS Hornet* is moored?"

"Yes, but—"

"Just be ready to make a run for it. A car will be waiting for you there tomorrow morning at eight."

This was crazy. People were coming at them from all angles—Santiago, Lockhart, FBI agents, Mason and now Beckerman. God only knew who he was. Lockhart's personal aide? What kind of aide broke into people's homes to deliver a message? Hayden certainly was out of his depth.

"Who are you?" Hayden asked.

Beckerman smiled. "Private security."

That sounded like a polite euphemism for something more mercenary. It made sense for Lockhart to employ someone like Beckerman with all that was going on.

"Look, I'm in enough crap with the cops. The guy outside is a good guy. Let's bring him in on this. It'll give Mr. Lockhart an ally."

Beckerman's expression hardened. "You breathe a word to the cops and you're on your own. We need each other right now, but we can do this without you. You can't afford the same luxury. The FBI has enough on you to jail you into the next century. Do you understand me?"

Hayden did. For all of Bohnert and Schrader's accusations, all they really had was circumstantial evidence and conjecture. Unfortunately, his possession of the plans, survival while others perished, and the fact that he was there at every stage of this mess turned circumstantial evidence and conjecture into something more solid. It wouldn't take much to prove means and opportunity. He had no motive, but others would invent one for him. He didn't like being cornered like this. Beckerman was no different from the FBI agents, except the FBI agents weren't offering him a lifeline.

"I'll be waiting for your diversion tomorrow."

"Smart man," Beckerman said. "If the police are outside, we don't have much time. Do you have the designs?"

With everything moving so fast, Hayden almost missed

the significance of Beckerman's question. "How do you know about the designs?"

"Eskdale. He's part of Lockhart's team. Look, I don't have the time to explain the ins and outs of all this. I just need to know you're on board and that you have the designs."

Hayden wished they had more time. He wanted to choose his options, not have them thrust upon him, but he didn't have that luxury. Not with Santiago's clock ticking. "They're in the car with the detective."

"Bring them. What are you meant to do now?"

"I'm just packing a change of clothes."

"Okay. Do that."

"What about you?" Hayden asked.

"I'll stay here until you've gone, and then I'll slip out."

"Will this be over soon?"

"I hope so. With your help, I can guarantee it."

Hayden emerged from the house with his overnight bag with Beckerman still hiding inside. He did his best not to look ruffled. He slipped into the car alongside Rebecca, leaned in close and whispered, "There's been a change in plans."

Santiago missed the surreptitious remark. Rebecca fixed Hayden with a nervous glance, but she knew better than to ask questions. They'd snatch a private moment later.

Santiago called Rice on his cell and they talked game plans. Santiago made no effort to disguise his call. Hayden guessed he wanted to show him and Rebecca that everything was under control.

Poor bastard, Hayden thought. Arrangements had already been made to destroy the detective's plans. He felt like telling Santiago, since he'd put his neck out for them, but he knew he couldn't. As much as he hated to dance to Lockhart's tune, Lockhart held the answers.

CHAPTER TWENTY-SIX

Beckerman had watched them come and go all day and night from the living room window. He'd beaten Hayden, Rebecca and Santiago back to San Rafael. He even spotted the helpful Deputy Rice sitting in his car waiting for the fight to come to him. Rice had left after Santiago moved in with Hayden and Rebecca, but returned during the night with takeout and to relieve Santiago. Other than that, nothing else had happened. He could have rigged up his listening equipment to monitor what was going on in the house, but there wasn't any point. The trap was set, and no one could do anything to change it.

Before Santiago arrived with Hayden and Rebecca, Beckerman had stashed his Dodge Charger on a neighboring street and walked up to 2337 Oleander. The house wasn't directly across from where Hayden and Rebecca were staying, but it had a clear view of their place. He pressed the doorbell and waited for someone to answer.

He'd selected 2337 not for its location, but its occupant. He needed someone who lived alone and had hermit tendencies. Doreen Morley fit the bill. She was seventy-two and a widow with no children. A search of public records had narrowed his search to Doreen, and a little Q&A with the neighbors filled in the gaps.

Doreen opened the door as wide as the security chain would allow. Her face appeared in the gap.

"Hi, I'm from PG&E," he said. "It's fall and we're helping people check their pilot lights before the cold nights begin. I'd be happy to check yours for you."

Beckerman didn't know if Doreen was the nosy type so he'd used this line on several of her neighbors. Only one person out of the four homes he'd visited had asked him to check their pilot light, which he'd done. He hoped Doreen would follow suit, but if she didn't, he had a backup plan to gain entry.

"Can I see your identification?" Doreen asked.

"Of course." Beckerman produced his PG&E picture ID badge. It was one of many forged IDs in his possession.

Doreen examined his identification through thick glasses. She handed it back and let him in.

Doreen was cautious, but not cautious enough. Although she'd checked his ID, she hadn't noticed he wasn't wearing a PG&E uniform. He smiled and pocketed the ID.

"Come this way," Doreen said and let him in.

He followed her to a closet situated in a hallway between the kitchen and a guest bedroom. Eaten with arthritis, she moved at a snail's pace. It didn't bother him. It gave him time to scope out the house. He listened for a visitor. This wouldn't work if someone else was there. He heard no one other than the voices on NPR spilling from a stereo in the living room. She tugged open the closet door, and he dropped to his knees to examine the furnace.

"You live here alone?" he asked causally.

"Yes."

"A big place for you to rattle around inside," he said with a smile.

"We moved here when my husband retired from Nortel, but he died six months into his retirement."

"That's awful."

Doreen squeezed out a pained smile. "This place was important to him. I didn't want to leave."

"Good for you," Beckerman said and meant it.

He checked the pilot light, saw that it was burning bright and told Doreen she was in good shape. He stood and closed the closet door.

"I was making coffee," Doreen said. "Do you have time?"

"I do. Coffee would be great."

Coffee provided the distraction he needed, and he followed her to the kitchen. He leaned against the countertop while she poured out two cups. He took the mug she held out to him and said, "Thanks, Doreen."

He realized his error before he finished saying her name.

"How do you know my name?"

"Billing," he said covering for his mistake. "I get everyone's name with the address. After you, I move on to the Bertholfs next door."

The suspicion he'd witnessed moments earlier disappeared just as swiftly from Doreen's expression.

"Apologies for spooking you there," he said and put his coffee down.

"No, I'm sorry. It's so obvious." Suddenly, Doreen lost interest in what she was saying. She was staring at his clothes. She had finally noticed his lack of a PG&E uniform.

He pointed behind her. "Doreen, the coffeemaker."

She spun around on reflex. It was a cheap trick, but it worked. With her back to him, he moved in behind her. He clamped one hand over her mouth to keep a scream in and braced her against him with his other arm. She attempted to wriggle free, but he had her too well constrained.

"Please don't struggle," he said in a calming tone.

To his surprise, she complied and relaxed in his grasp.

"Forgive me," he whispered and broke Doreen's neck.

Doreen went slack. Small and slight, she was no weight at all. Beckerman scooped her up in his arms, carried her into the downstairs bathroom and placed her in the tub. He would have liked to have wrapped Doreen in the shower curtain, but since there wasn't one, he worked with what he had and slid the shower door closed.

He returned to the kitchen and loaded his coffee mug into the dishwasher with all the other dishes and switched the machine on. It was a simple piece of housekeeping he could afford to do. He'd sanitize the place and dispose of Doreen after completion of the assignment.

He figured he had at least two days before anyone missed her. It wouldn't take two days to do what he needed to do. It would be all over by this time tomorrow. He'd make sure of it.

With Doreen safely out the way, Beckerman planted himself in front of a window and watched Rebecca's house.

He checked his watch. It was just after seven A.M. now. Doreen had been dead sixteen hours and he'd been up for over twenty-four. He was good for another eighteen. He swallowed the last of his final energy bar before gathering his binoculars and cell phone and replacing the armchair in its original position. He snatched up the keys hanging on a hook by the back door and slipped outside, locking it after him.

It was time.

The shattering of glass and a wailing car alarm woke everybody in the house. Hayden sat bolt upright in his bed in the guest room. Was this the sign Beckerman had told them to look out for? Or was it Tony Mason back to finish his job? Either way, Hayden was prepared. He flew out of bed, fully dressed. After he'd filled Rebecca in on Beckerman's plan, they'd agreed not to undress for bed in case of a rude awakening. She emerged from her room as he reached the upstairs landing.

"Is this it?" Rebecca asked.

"It's something. Let's go."

They pounded down the stairs. Hayden expected a run-in with Rice, but he was nowhere to be seen. He didn't let it worry him, and he cut through the kitchen to snatch up the drawings. Santiago had intended to book them into evidence, but Hayden had talked him out it. Rebecca overtook him and raced into the garage. She hurled herself behind the wheel, gunned the engine and hit the garage door clicker.

The door rolled up to reveal Rice standing in front of his unmarked Crown Victoria parked in the street. The Ford lay slumped on two punctured tires.

"I think that's our sign," Hayden said.

Rebecca jammed the shifter into reverse and peeled out of the garage.

Rice whirled around from his stricken car. Confusion turned into panic as Rebecca's VW launched itself off the driveway and slithered to an untidy halt on the street. The deputy rushed forward. He stopped in the middle of the street with his arms spread to block their path.

Rebecca hesitated for a second.

"Go," Hayden said. "He'll get out of the way."

Rebecca stamped on the gas and pointed the car at the deputy.

Rice stood his ground.

"He'll get out of the way." This time, Hayden didn't sound as confident.

Rebecca jerked the car to one side to avoid hitting the deputy, but Rice lunged to block. Space between the VW's hood and Rice's body shrank. He wasn't going to get out of the way.

Rebecca stamped on the brakes.

Rice, the human roadblock, inched toward them. "Turn off the engine and get out of the vehicle."

Hayden turned to Rebecca. "If we want answers, we've got to go."

"I know," she snapped.

Rice repeated his instruction. His hand went to his pistol on his hip.

"There's no way around him," Rebecca said

"Just try not to hit him too hard."

Rebecca jumped off the brake and onto the gas. The VW lurched forward. A look of pure shock overwhelmed Rice's expression. He jerked his gun out, but he didn't get to aim it. Rebecca swerved to avoid the deputy, but she clipped him. The VW's hood scooped him up and tossed him aside. He struck the asphalt on his back.

"Is he okay?" Rebecca asked, her voice tight with fear.

Hayden looked. Rice tried standing, but fell on his butt. He aimed his weapon, but didn't fire.

"He's okay."

Rebecca released a long held breath.

As she accelerated hard through the narrow streets, Hayden cast another look at Rice. He was on his feet and hobbling toward his car.

"I think Rice has more to fear from Santiago than us."

Rice watched Rebecca VW's reach the end of the street and disappear, along with his career in law enforcement. He couldn't believe he'd fallen for a dumb diversion gag. Worse still, he couldn't believe Rebecca had just run him down.

He stared at the gun in his hand. He could improve department arrest figures by shooting himself.

"You're an idiot, Mark," Rice told himself.

As his pity party ebbed, the pain in his hip increased. He hobbled over to his stricken vehicle and leaned against it to take the weight off his throbbing hip. He jerked his cell phone off his belt to call Santiago with the good news. He could only imagine the chewing out he'd be getting.

A green Toyota Camry screeched to a halt next to him. The passenger door flew open and Santiago leaned across the seat. "Get in the damn car."

Rice jumped into the passenger seat and Santiago stamped on the gas. The force of the car's acceleration slammed Rice's door shut without his help. Santiago threw the car into a one-eighty.

"I'm sorry, sir. I screwed up."

"No, you didn't. I expected this."

"What?"

"I knew someone would come for these two. They're too valuable."

Santiago yanked the wheel hard to the left and the car barreled onto the next street. The tires slithered as they tried to find a grip. Rebecca's VW was small in the distance.

"Hayden mentioned a dark blue Dodge Charger following them. It was parked at the end of Hayden's street. No one was in it, so the driver had to be inside Hayden's place. And Hayden is no Oscar winner. When he left his house yesterday, he couldn't have looked any guiltier if he tried." Santiago thumped his steering wheel with his fist. "Shit. I really thought I'd gotten through to them."

Santiago came up on another turn. Rice held on to the handle above the door. "Where have you been hiding?"

"After I left, I went around the block, came back and parked at the end of the street."

"I wish you'd told me all this."

"What, and rely on you giving the performance of a lifetime? No way." Santiago grinned. "Smile, Deputy Rice. You're part of the chase now."

Santiago got within a safe tailing distance and backed off.

"Are we going to intercept them?" Rice asked.

"No. Someone went to a lot of trouble to spring them. I want to see who that someone is and what they want from them."

Santiago and Rice trailed Hayden and Rebecca onto I-580 and across the Richmond-San Rafael Bridge to join I-80. For a moment, it appeared they were taking a long-winded route back into San Francisco until Rebecca's VW peeled off the freeway in the direction of Alameda. They trailed them into the city through the Webster Tube under the Oakland Inner Harbor onto the island. It was obvious where they were going when Rebecca turned toward the former Alameda Naval Air Station. They followed her to the *USS Hornet*. The World War Two aircraft carrier was now a floating museum.

"What are they going to do at the *Hornet*?" Rice asked.

"We're going to find out."

Santiago pulled up short on the street while Rebecca parked her VW in the museum's vast parking lot close to the ship. She and Hayden jogged across the road toward the *USS Hornet*'s pier. The museum wasn't open, but the carrier wasn't their destination; a black Cadillac parked in front of the pier's entrance was.

James Lockhart emerged from the Cadillac. Lockhart had been named on TV as one of the victims in the

BART station attack and Santiago had seen him with
Bellis at Shane's funeral. Lockhart spoke briefly to Hayden and Rebecca before they all got into his car.

"What the hell is going on?" Santiago murmured.

CHAPTER TWENTY-SEVEN

Lockhart smiled as he pulled away. Finally, he had things under control. He put the recovery down to his contingency plans. Zeguang and his clients had thrown him a curve ball when they wanted a demonstration of the device. He complied, but they weren't happy with him, according to Zeguang. They felt cheated. They'd expected a deadly demonstration, but they hadn't been specific. He knew it was an underhanded move to use a harmless sedative, but there was no way he would let himself be implicated in an attack on U.S. soil. But any hard feelings Zeguang's clients harbored didn't last. The media frenzy following the BART station attack showed them the potential of what they were buying, and the wire transfer hit his account without further delay.

The BART attack wasn't just to satisfy his clients, but also to hook Hayden and Rebecca. They were the only people left who could cause him problems. It had been Beckerman's idea to implicate them in the BART attack. He orchestrated a plan to lure them to the Powell Street BART. It not only disposed of them, it also blunted any investigation. With Hayden and Rebecca as obvious suspects, no one would care about looking any further.

He hadn't expected them to be released so swiftly, even though he knew it was a possibility. No matter, he had contingencies for such an event, and they'd worked perfectly. He had Hayden, Rebecca and the plans. Now it was time to tell them the lies that would keep them docile.

"Thanks for agreeing to this. I realize the chance you've taken by meeting me."

"We're fugitives now," Hayden said.

And they were. Their fugitive status made them easier to control. Who could they run to now? Him and only him.

"I should have taken you into my confidence earlier."

"Why didn't you?" Hayden asked.

"I wasn't sure I could trust you. People were dying at MDE, and I didn't know who was responsible. You were an outsider. You could have been the person threatening me."

"Who was threatening you? What is going on?"

"A hate group. A terror cell. I don't know. I was hoping to find out at the BART station. I was supposedly meeting with someone from the group with a conscience. Instead, we were part of a trap to demonstrate their power."

Lockhart reached the freeway and pointed his Cadillac north toward the installation. He clung to the fast lane, the needle riding above eighty-five.

"Where are we going?" Rebecca asked.

"I'm taking you somewhere safe that will explain all this. I want you to see the work we're doing and understand the situation we're in. Hopefully, you can help shed some light on recent developments."

"We?" Rebecca said. "Who's we?"

"My team. I've put together a group of people to help combat what happened at the BART station."

Lockhart eased off the gas. A quarter mile ahead, a

bridge abutment partially hid a CHP speed trap. He drifted by the Highway Patrol unit at a legal sixty-five. He couldn't afford to get pulled over with Hayden and Rebecca in the back.

"I'm trusting you today. You don't mention anything you see or hear to anyone."

"Of course," Hayden said. "What can you tell us?"

Truth and lies, Lockhart thought. *Truth and lies*. For a deception to work, it needed to be loaded with as much truth as possible. Hayden's question gave him the opportunity to skirt so close to telling the out and out truth that there was no lie.

"That's a fair question. The world lives in fear of terrorist threats. Intelligence sources have assessed that the threat from terrorists and rogue nations isn't going to come from nuclear weapons or complex explosives. Everyone cries dirty bomb, but it's unlikely. Radioactive material is scarce and accessibility is limited. The greater danger comes from chemical and biological weapons. The Soviet Union may have collapsed long ago, but the technology hasn't. There are a lot of unemployed technicians out there for hire. I've been working with Marin Design Engineering and a number of other private firms on countermeasures should a biological attack happen."

"So, what went wrong?" Hayden asked.

"A leak is my guess. These people found out about the work I was doing and eliminated everyone at MDE to obtain the research." Lockhart eyed Hayden and Rebecca from his rearview mirror. His comment had chilled them. He saw the fear in their expressions. "Any thoughts on who could have been working the inside?"

Hayden shook his head. Then a look of puzzlement crossed his face. "I'm confused. They used MDE's design as the weapon in the BART station."

Lockhart laughed bitterly. "MDE designed an excellent system for neutralizing a biological agent. The flipside is that it can be just as easily converted into a weapon for delivering the biological agent."

"Talk about shooting yourself in the foot," Hayden said.

"You're not wrong," Lockhart said.

He eyed Hayden and Rebecca more closely, searching them for cracks. He felt he had them. They were buying what he was selling. Rebecca looked relaxed and docile enough. He hadn't done anything to tip her off. He couldn't say the same of Hayden. He was frowning. Had something clicked? Lockhart replayed everything he'd said for something that could have tipped Hayden off, but came up short. He had to play it careful. He just needed their trust for a few more hours.

"Something wrong, Hayden?"

"Shane's last words. Before he killed himself, he said he'd done something terrible."

Lockhart saw the pain in Rebecca's expression.

"The news reported that Sundip Chaudhary admitted something similar before his death. It implies they were aware of what they'd done, but you're saying the opposite. You're saying someone infiltrated MDE."

Rebecca turned on Hayden. "Shane didn't sell out MDE. He wouldn't help these people develop a weapon."

"I'm not saying that. What Shane said to me doesn't make sense now."

"It does to me," Lockhart said. He liked it when he was forced to think on his feet. "I've been thinking long and hard about Sundip and Shane's last words. At first, I thought Sundip was confessing, but nothing proved he was involved with the people behind the attack. The same goes for Shane. Their last words do make sense if they'd unearthed the truth. I believe they found that they were being used, and the shame was too much for them."

Neither Hayden nor Rebecca said anything.

"Hayden, I have some things that need clearing up," he said. "You've created some very hot water for yourself when it comes to MDE's confidentiality agreement. You could be sued."

"But who would sue me? MDE is finished."

"Not quite. It still exists as a legal entity, but I want to help you. Surrender all documentation to me today, and I'll ensure that no legal action is brought against you."

"Sure. Thanks."

Hayden's gratitude was less than overwhelming. Lockhart didn't let it worry him too much. He put it down to Hayden having to give up some of his power. He should have had the sense to realize it wasn't his power in the first place.

"Thank you, Mr. Lockhart," Rebecca said. "That's great."

"You're welcome. I have to give you credit for guts, Hayden. Not everyone would have copied the designs with that legal threat pending. Kenneth Eskdale unnerved me when he told me you had them."

"What is Eskdale to you?" Rebecca asked.

"A brilliant man—his background in genetics and chemistry is astonishing. He prefers obscurity, but I convinced him to help me. For the last few years he's been advising me on my projects. He has done amazing things." Lockhart hardened. "You two scared the life out of him. He thought you were going to kill him. I want to know why you had copies of MDE's designs."

"Shane sent me a password-protected file the night he died and asked me not to open it. So, I backed up the attachment and all of MDE's drawings to an online storage account and copied the data to a flash drive." Hayden produced the drive from his pocket.

Lockhart feigned shock. He liked how well he took to acting. He put it down to his business dealings over the years. There was a lot of performance in closing a deal. "Have you read this file?" he asked.

"No, I tried, but I couldn't work out the password."

Thanks to Beckerman, Lockhart thought.

"I have a question for you," Hayden said.

"Shoot."

"When the FBI picked us up, why didn't you help us? One word from you would have made a lot of difference. If not for Detective Santiago, we wouldn't have gotten out of there."

"I wish it were that easy. These perpetrators have put me in a tight spot. Not only have they weaponized MDE's work, they've used it to leave a nasty trail of evidence leading to me. The moment I go to the authorities and they investigate, they'll go after me as an accomplice. And that won't do any of us any good."

"You could have done something to help us."

"I did what I could." He injected a sorrowful note for effect. "Just know that I was monitoring the situation. I wouldn't have let it get out of hand."

"This isn't out of hand?" Hayden gestured around him. "We're fugitives. We skipped out on the cops."

"Hayden, Rebecca, I appreciate the position you two are in. It's not a lot different than mine. Give me a couple of hours and I'll have this all cleared up. You'll be free of this. Will you do that?"

Both Hayden and Rebecca nodded after long pause. They lapsed into an uncomfortable silence after that.

Lockhart didn't like the turn in the conversation. He felt his grip on Hayden and Rebecca slipping. He needed to distract them. It didn't matter if they didn't believe him. He only needed to keep their faith until they reached the facility. He asked Hayden about his involvement since receiving Shane's e-mail. Hayden talked him through the fire at MDE, Malcolm Fuller's clandestine meeting, their heavy-handed interrogation of Eskdale and Tony Mason's murder attempt. Lockhart listened as his Cadillac ate up the miles.

Lockhart's cell phone rang. He examined the caller ID and took the call.

"Am I on speaker?" Beckerman asked.

"No."

"Bad news. You're being followed by two Marin Sheriff's detectives in a green Toyota Camry three hundred yards behind you."

Lockhart glanced in his rearview mirror and picked out the Toyota rounding the curve. He kept his gaze in the rearview so short as not to alert Hayden and Rebecca. He didn't want them turning around and spotting the cops.

"Yes, I see. I thought you had taken care of that issue. What happened?"

"I underestimated their resourcefulness."

"Obviously."

"Do I have a green light?"

He'd hoped to keep this final stage of the operation clean, but clean had gone out the window the day Sundip Chaudhary connected the dots. Now it was about how little mess he could leave behind. Sadly, his mess was about to get a little messier. He didn't like killing cops. It always complicated matters, but it couldn't be avoided now.

"Of course. What do you want me to do?"

"Nothing for now. The detectives have had ample opportunity to stop you. They want to see where you're heading. They won't attempt anything until you arrive at the facility. I can't try anything on the freeway, so I want you to get off at Santa Rosa and take Highway 12 toward the coast, then make your move. Put some distance between you and them, and I'll take care of the rest."

"Don't disappoint me," Lockhart said and hung up.

"Problems?" Rebecca asked.

"Oh, no." Lockhart smiled into the rearview mirror at her. "None whatsoever."

A road sign flashed by. He was getting off at the next exit.

CHAPTER TWENTY-EIGHT

Lockhart guided his Cadillac off the freeway and picked up Highway 12, where he led a procession of vehicles. The narrow highway was busier than Santiago would have liked. It forced him to bunch up on Lockhart. If the guy was observant, he'd spot the tail. Santiago slotted himself behind a pickup giving him a two-vehicle gap for cover.

Lockhart barreled along at a steady fifty-five, but it didn't last when he caught up with an RV crawling along in front of him. Santiago cursed the RV. It forced all the vehicles to follow nose to tail. Two car lengths separated him from Lockhart. He took comfort from the fact Lockhart would be more interested in the ponderous RV than the daisy chain following in his wake.

Then it happened. Lockhart looked into his rearview mirror. His gaze cut through the two vehicles between them and focused directly on Santiago. Lockhart only looked at him for a second, but that was long enough. He stamped on the gas and jerked the Cadillac into the oncoming lane.

"Shit. He's seen us," Santiago cursed.

"Are you sure?"

Yeah, I'm sure. Santiago jerked his car out onto the left

side of the road. He didn't want Lockhart getting the drop on him. He wouldn't make it past the RV, but he could make it into the gap left by Lockhart. One thing was working against him. He was in his wife's car, not his unmarked. He didn't have his lights and sirens, and he didn't have the horsepower, which meant he wouldn't get the cooperation from the other motorists. To everyone on the road, he was an impatient dick.

What Santiago lacked in acceleration, he gained in surprise. The two vehicles ahead of him didn't expect him to pull a brain-dead stunt, and he shouldered his way into the gap left by Lockhart behind the RV.

Lockhart didn't have it so easy. He ramped up the Cadillac's speed. Santiago estimated he was pushing sixty miles per hour. A USPS truck lumbered toward the Cadillac in the oncoming lane. The gap for passing the RV shrank as the vehicles closed in on each other on a collision course.

The USPS truck flashed his high beams at Lockhart. Lockhart was committed now. There was no room for backing down. Santiago was in his spot and had no intention of giving it back to him. The son of a bitch fought it out and snuck back onto the right side of the road seconds before the mail truck shot by.

A thick line of vehicles trailed in the USPS truck's wake, killing Santiago's chance to overtake. He cursed, flashed his lights and leaned on his horn to get the RV out of his way. Its driver stuck steadfastly to his speed and course.

"*Culero*," Santiago murmured.

A horn blared from behind. Santiago ignored the driver's sour grapes.

Rice glanced in a side mirror and groaned. "Behind us. We've got company."

Santiago glanced in his rearview and saw the familiar dark blue Dodge Charger had squeezed in behind them.

"Get backup," Santiago said. "I want this son of a bitch off my ass, but no one touches Lockhart. They're to follow, but not to engage. I want to see where he's going."

Rice nodded and punched a number into his cell.

Even in the best case, backup was a good ten minutes away. That was ten minutes too long. Santiago needed to lose the Dodge man and now.

The shoulder wasn't quite wide enough, but it would have to do. He stamped on the gas and lunged around the RV. His door mirror snapped off and disappeared behind him.

"Jesus Christ," Rice said.

"Grow a set, Rice."

He leaned on his horn. A startled face appeared in the RV side mirror and inched over to let him pass. The Toyota bucked on the shoulder's poor surface. Twice it grazed the RV's side. He tried not to think about the damage he was incurring. It wouldn't matter once he shouldered his way past.

A clear road stretched ahead and Santiago ramped up the speed. Lockhart's Cadillac was still in sight. His lead was considerable, but he wouldn't be impossible to catch. Santiago kept the accelerator pressed to the floor.

Horn blasts filled the air from behind. Santiago checked his mirrors in time to see the Dodge driver shove the RV aside. It looked as if the RV driver had attempted to prevent anyone else from passing him, but the driver had turned it into a futile gesture and picked up some serious damage for his trouble.

"Our friend is through," Santiago said. "You watch our rear."

"Okay."

Lockhart's Cadillac crested a rise and disappeared from view. Santiago prayed it would still be there when he cleared the rise.

"He's closing," Rice said.

The Charger filled Santiago's rearview mirror. It was obvious what was coming. The Dodge man was going to take them out. If it got past them, it was over. Santiago moved to the center of the road, straddling both lanes. He weaved left and right to block the Dodge man.

He braced himself for an impact from the rear. He'd taken away the Dodge driver's options.

"He's dropping back," Rice said.

In his mirror, Santiago watched the Charger drop a hundred feet behind then hold position.

They crested the rise. Lockhart was still in view. His Cadillac turned left off Highway 1 toward the coast. Santiago followed, ever fearful of the Charger looming behind, waiting to strike.

"Oh, shit. This is it." Rice sat forward in his seat and checked his seat belt.

It doesn't look like our backup will be arriving in time, Santiago thought as he watched the Dodge build up a head of steam in his mirrors. Santiago had the gas pedal floored, and the Dodge was reeling him in. The car accelerated at a frightening rate. It kept coming until it slammed into the Toyota's rear.

The impact shook the car and Santiago and Rice were thrown against the seat belts. The Toyota slithered on the asphalt, but Santiago kept it on the road.

The Dodge dropped back, and Santiago wrung every drop of speed out of his vehicle to escape the attack. It wasn't enough. The car slammed them again, this time with more force.

The Toyota fishtailed from the impact. Santiago wrestled with the wheel for control, but the roadway took the decision out of his hands. The car danced and struck the undulating road the wrong way. It bucked, ripping the wheel from his grasp, veered right and rode the grass verge. The Dodge went in for the death blow and clipped the Toyota's right rear corner. The Toyota left the road, launched itself off a grassy rise and ripped through a barbed-wire fence.

The car's nose dug into the plowed earth. The hood crumpled, the windshield split and airbags detonated. Momentum grabbed the Toyota and tossed it end over end before it ended up on its roof.

Santiago's neck tingled. The roof had buckled and swiped the back of his head. Although his car had stopped spinning, it took a moment before the world stopped spinning.

The sound of the Dodge skidding to a halt on the road snapped the world back into place for him. He unclasped his seat belt and dropped onto the roof liner.

Rice moaned. Blood dripped from somewhere in his hairline.

"Out my side. C'mon, out."

Santiago's door opened after a kick. He clambered out on all fours, his fingers digging into the dirt. He got to his feet and looked for his assailant.

"Sir, I can't move."

Gasoline trickled from the ruptured gas tank and pitter-pattered on the earth.

The Dodge man jumped down the slope. The sound of him clicking off the safety on his pistol was unmistakable.

Lockhart turned the Cadillac off the road onto a disused airstrip somewhere in the Mendocino County. A cracked service road ran parallel to an inoperable runway. Every window in the air traffic control tower was busted, and graffiti marred the stucco. Lockhart followed the service road to an aircraft hangar large enough to house a medium-sized jetliner. The lack of people and activity added to the desolation.

The sight of it all disappointed Hayden. He hadn't

felt safe for a long time. Lockhart had changed that.
He provided warmth in the form of safety and experience. He had all the bases covered—security, experience,
technology and resources. The decommissioned airfield
robbed Hayden of his faith.

"Are we in the right place?" Rebecca asked, echoing
Hayden's thoughts.

"It's all about camouflage." Lockhart stopped the car
in front of the hangar. "People see a disused airstrip,
they think nothing of it."

Lockhart removed a garage door remote and pressed
the button. The hangar doors slid back, and he drove inside. He pressed the remote again, and Hayden watched
the world disappear from sight.

Lockhart wasn't wrong. The inside of the hangar was
a world apart from its exterior appearance. Arc lamps
illuminated a freestanding building fabricated from
aluminum. The single-story structure was windowless
and somewhere in the region of a thousand square feet.
An overelaborate double-door entrance provided the
only way in. The place looked like a prototype space
station.

Lockhart led the way. Their footfalls, like their words,
echoed throughout the hangar, rebounding off every
surface.

"Impressive, don't you think?" Lockhart said.

"Certainly well camouflaged," Hayden said.

Lockhart pressed a button on the intercom to the left
of the doors. "We're here," he said.

He produced a card key and swiped it through the slot.
The doors drew back with a pneumatic hiss, and they
stepped into an airlock. The inner doors opened when
the outer doors closed. Hayden's ears popped from the
difference in air pressure.

"Please," Lockhart said and pointed inside.

Hayden followed Rebecca into the lab, and the inner

doors closed. Diffused fluorescent lighting rebounded off the polished stainless-steel lab benches and white plastic fixtures. Three small labs ran the width of the main lab with huge Plexiglas viewing windows in the rear. One of the labs held eight caged beagles. The dogs showed no excitement at the sight of visitors.

Kenneth Eskdale emerged from a small office. He scowled at Hayden and Rebecca.

The feeling's mutual, Hayden thought.

"Don't be like that, Kenneth," Lockhart said. "We're all friends now."

"I don't see why they need to be here." Eskdale's rat features twitched.

"I've told you, we need their help."

Eskdale snorted.

"May I have the drawings and the flash drive?" Lockhart requested.

Rebecca handed over the drawings, and Hayden offered up the flash drive after fishing in his jacket. Lockhart placed the items on the lab bench next to him.

"Is that everything?"

"Yes," Hayden replied.

Lockhart raised an eyebrow. "The truth, please. I can't have other copies—paper, electronic or otherwise."

"That's everything," Hayden insisted.

"Good." Lockhart tossed the drawings at Eskdale. The professor caught them clumsily. "Shred them."

"No. Wait," Hayden protested. People had been murdered for producing those designs. To destroy their work was blasphemy.

Lockhart put out his arm, stopping Hayden from reaching Eskdale. "Hayden, it doesn't matter. Manufacturing has begun. Uncontrolled documents such as these can fall into the wrong hands."

It made sense, but it hurt to see Eskdale feeding the drawings into the shredder.

"I can't afford for those plans to become public. Our security has been breached already."

A crunching sound tore Hayden's focus from the shredder. Lockhart had dropped the flash drive onto the floor and had stamped down on it, splitting it in two.

Lockhart came over and slipped an arm around Hayden's shoulders. "Come with me. Let me show you what we do here."

Lockhart unfurled his arm, but kept a comforting hand on Hayden's shoulder. Rebecca came close, and Hayden took her hand. Lockhart guided them to the back of the facility, toward the small labs.

"Our focus here is the bubonic plague. We've cracked its genetic code. That means we can counteract it on a genetic level. Should a biological attack be launched, we'd have a far more efficient vaccine to fight infection. You see the dogs in those cages?"

The beagles shuffled in their cramped cages, scratching themselves or staring at their captors.

"They've been contaminated with the plague and cured. They're quarantined at the moment, but that's a precaution. We just have to follow procedure."

"Unbelievable," Rebecca said.

"But it's fact. These will look familiar to you."

They stood in front of the middle lab, the largest of the three. On the stainless-steel benches sat three canisters identical to the one from the Powell Street BART station. Hayden's mouth went dry.

Lockhart swiped his card key through the electronic lock and opened the door.

"Don't worry," Lockhart said. "These devices aren't harmful. Marin Design Engineering created these aerosol devices for mass dispersal. If people were infected with a disease on a mass scale, like with the Tokyo subway attack, we'd be able to fight back with these."

Lockhart led them into the small anteroom. Environmental suits hung on hooks. There was barely room for all three of them. He closed the outer door and opened the inner one before leading them into the lab.

"Shouldn't we be wearing those suits?" Rebecca asked.

"No. The room is clean."

Hayden picked up one of the aluminum vessels. A liquid slopped around inside.

"That's the vaccine."

"Glad to hear it," Hayden said.

Rebecca took the flask from him and examined it herself.

"You can see how something designed for good can be turned into a weapon," Lockhart said.

"Only too well," Hayden said.

"It's frightening," Rebecca said.

"Rebecca, I want to talk to Hayden for a little while, in private. Feel free to look around."

"Okay," she replied. "Have fun."

Lockhart escorted Hayden out of the lab, back into the anteroom. The door automatically locked after them.

"How's she going to get out?" Hayden asked.

"Don't worry, she can open the door herself. The door has to lock afterwards or the airlock won't work."

When they returned to the main lab, the outer door locked as well, but Lockhart went one step further and swiped his card key through the slot, causing the door to beep.

"Hey, what are you doing?"

Rebecca looked up from inside the lab. She went to the door and tried it. It was locked. She looked confused.

"Let her out."

"After we've finished our business."

"No. Now," Hayden demanded.

"Sorry, it doesn't work that way." Lockhart pressed a button on the intercom. "Don't worry, Rebecca. Sit back and relax, and you'll be out soon."

"Let me out."

Lockhart took his finger off the intercom.

"What do you want?" Hayden asked.

"You're going to show me that password-protected file you've got online, and you're going to erase it for me."

"What if I don't?"

Lockhart produced a remote control similar to a car's keyless remote. He pressed the intercom for Rebecca to hear. "If you don't play ball, I'll activate one of those canisters—and this time, it won't be a sedative. It'll be genetically modified bubonic plague. Now, what do you say?"

CHAPTER TWENTY-NINE

Santiago crawled inside his stricken Toyota to help Rice. The deputy was hanging upside down, held in position by his seat belt.

"I can't reach the release," Rice said.

Santiago pressed the button, the seat belt snapped back and Rice tumbled onto the roof liner, landing hard on his neck.

Two shots tore through the passenger window, spraying them with glass. Rice stiffened, the color draining from his face.

"Rice?"

The deputy just shook his head.

Blood leaked from under Rice and pooled around him.

"Christ," Santiago murmured. "Don't move."

Rage and anger fueled Santiago. He burst from the car with an agility that defied his age and size. He snapped to his feet and jerked his 9mm off his hip in one fluid motion.

The Dodge man darted toward Santiago, dropped to one knee and fired. The shot went wild, but Santiago ducked behind his car for cover.

He looked in at Rice. The bullets he'd taken had taken years off him. He looked like a kid.

Santiago's Toyota might have been his only cover, but he had to draw the gunman away from the vehicle. The chance of a stray bullet hitting either Rice or the spilled gasoline was too high. It sounded like a smart and prudent plan, but he was in the middle of a featureless field with nothing to use for cover. The Dodge man would pick him off before he got ten feet.

"Throw down your weapons and come out where I can see you," the Dodge man yelled.

"Hang in there," Santiago told Rice. "I'll take care of him."

"C'mon, I don't have all day. Or do I have to put another bullet in your partner to get your compliance?"

"Okay," Santiago yelled back, but remained crouched behind the vehicle.

"Throw out your weapons."

Santiago tossed his 9mm away from him. It bounced to a stop ten feet from the front of end of his Toyota.

"All your weapons. I'm not stupid. Hurry it up."

Santiago felt pretty stupid. He didn't have a backup piece.

Rice unholstered his 9mm and slid it over to him.

"I'm just getting the deputy's gun." Santiago leaned in and took Rice's 9mm, but he also grabbed the nightstick resting next to him. "I'm throwing out his weapon."

"Do it."

Santiago tossed the 9mm hard into the air. It climbed, spinning end over end and catching serious air time. He didn't bother to think, calculate or pray. He just acted. He sprang up. The gunman's gaze went to the flying gun just as he'd hoped. He hurled the nightstick at him, tomahawk style. The nightstick flew straight and true.

The Dodge man spotted the flying nightstick too late, but he still fired off a round before the stick smashed him in the face, shattering his nose and sending him to the ground.

Santiago didn't wait to see if his throw connected. The moment the nightstick left his hand, he dived for his 9mm. He snatched it up, aimed and fired two suppressing shots. He needed the son of a bitch alive. He wanted someone involved in this orchestrated slaughter to answer for all that had gone on. The gunman snapped to his feet. Blood cascaded down his face from his busted nose. The pain must have been immense and blinding, but he trained his gun on Santiago. Santiago didn't wait. He aimed and fired. His bullet punched the Dodge man in the right shoulder, knocking him back. Santiago clawed himself to his feet and raced toward the gunman with his 9mm aimed at his chest.

The Dodge man forced himself up into a sitting position and lifted his pistol.

"Don't even think about it," Santiago warned.

The Dodge man ignored him and aimed.

Santiago dived on top of him, his bulk crushing the gunman's pistol between their bodies. The son of a bitch wouldn't risk shooting himself.

Santiago pinned the Dodge man's free hand down with his free hand and jammed his 9mm against the side of the gunman's head with the other. The Dodge man bucked underneath him. He felt his hold on the gunman slip, and he was forced to take the gun away from the Dodge man's head and use his hand to support himself.

The Dodge man was worming his gun hand out from between their bodies. Santiago knew he wouldn't think twice about shooting him and head-butted the gunman across his already broken nose. Bone and cartilage crunched, but the son of a bitch took the blow, just huffing blood and snot clear of his clogged nasal passages. He head-butted the man again and again, ignoring the lights dancing in his own vision. Blood spread across the Dodge man's brow. Santiago wasn't sure whether it was his or the gunman's.

He felt the Dodge man jerk his gun arm from between their bodies. Santiago grabbed his wrist. The man's tendons felt like steel rods as his wrist twisted in Santiago's grasp. The gun's muzzle curled toward Santiago's temple. He tried to force it away, but the Dodge man pressed its hard, unforgiving end against his skull.

The Dodge man grinned through bloody teeth. "Time to die."

"I don't think so." Rice smashed the nightstick across the Dodge man's forearm. The shattering of bone turned Santiago's stomach. The gunman's face blanched, and his gun arm fell away.

Santiago sat up and drove a roundhouse punch into the Dodge man's jaw. The blow was hard enough to send him into the realms of unconsciousness and fracture Santiago's middle finger.

Santiago rolled off the Dodge man and fell on his back next to him. Rice stood over him, hunched over and holding his right side. He was pale and weak, but managed a bright smile.

Santiago smiled back. "You took your damn sweet time."

Rice wrestled the pistol from the Dodge man's grasp while Santiago got to his feet. "Give me that thing before you hurt someone with it."

Rice handed the gun over.

"You look like shit. Get in his car and rest up."

Rice nodded. He hobbled over to the Charger, which still had its engine running.

Santiago hoped Rice was going to be okay. He went back to the Toyota and scrabbled inside to get his cuffs.

Another shot rang out.

Santiago scrambled to his feet. The Dodge man relaxed from a shooter's stance. He'd produced another gun from somewhere and had shot Rice in the back as he reached the edge of the field. Rice fell forward without so much as a grunt. Santiago aimed at the Dodge man and fired. His shot struck the gunman in the shoulder. He swung around and aimed at the detective as Santiago fired again. A hole opened up in the Dodge man's chest and he went down.

Santiago raced over to Rice, dropped to his knees and rolled his deputy over. His eyes were open, but they were unseeing.

"Mark, I'm so sorry." Santiago held his dead colleague in his arms.

Movement by the car distracted Santiago from his mourning. The Dodge man was preparing to take another shot.

"Fuck you."

Santiago fired a shot into the Toyota's bleeding gas tank. The car erupted into flames, spilling burning fuel over the Dodge man. He listened to the gunman scream and watched him burn as he rocked his friend's body.

"What's it to be?" Lockhart asked.

Hayden glanced at Rebecca trapped in the lab. She looked angry instead of scared. Her beautiful eyes burned balefully at Lockhart. Her hatred for him was almost tangible.

"What choice do I have?"

"None whatsoever."

"So, you aren't combating biological weapons. You're creating them," Hayden said.

"Guilty as charged." Lockhart showed Hayden into Eskdale's office.

"That's everything shredded," Eskdale said and stepped from the machine.

"Now, it's your turn, Hayden." Lockhart pointed to the PC on the desk.

Hayden took a seat in front of the computer. Lockhart

rounded the desk and stood behind him. He made sure Hayden saw the transmitter in his hand, his thumb poised over the button.

"Professor Eskdale is a brilliant man. The British cracked the genetic sequence to the bubonic plague. While others saw cracking the code as a defense against a potential outbreak, he saw what else could be done with the code."

"Like what?" He didn't want to hear Lockhart's speech, but if he kept the guy talking, his focus would be off Rebecca.

"You see, Mother Nature is a bitch. She creates some nasty little trap doors for the human race. But whatever she can do, man can top it. Once we had the code, there was nothing stopping us from bending it to create a new and improved plague. The pathogen in those canisters is far more efficient than the original plague, and current vaccines can't combat it. If I were to press this button, it would be too late for Ms. Fallon six hours after she was exposed. All thanks to Kenneth here." Lockhart slapped a hand on Eskdale's shoulder. "Impressive, huh?"

"Spectacular," Hayden said and typed in the URL for his online storage account.

"So, what was your terrorist attack?" Hayden asked.

"A demonstration. My clients wanted to make sure what they were buying worked. What better way than to fake my own terrorist attack? Beckerman set it up. It was his idea. All in all, it worked very well. It got plenty of media attention and drew you out of the woodwork."

"Who were those Chinese guys I saw you with—your customers?"

"In a manner of speaking."

"So, this is all for money?"

"It makes the world go around."

Hayden had hoped for more. If so many people were to die, then they should die for something. Even if it was love or hate, he could understand it. They were passionate emotions that in some twist of nature justified themselves. But all this for money? It was just so shallow.

"Why kill everyone at MDE?"

"Chaudhary didn't like the taste of what he was being fed and challenged poor Kenneth here and stole a file." Lockhart patted the professor like a faithful dog. "Kenneth couldn't subdue his fears, and I knew I couldn't allow Chaudhary to live."

"You used the drug."

"Yes. Like I say, Kenneth is brilliant. He made his name in drug development before he switched to genetics. He's still a skilled technician in that regard. I wanted a weapon that was effective but wouldn't raise too many questions, and Kenneth had something on hand."

"And Shane?"

"Chaudhary showed Shane what he'd found, and people being people, Shane sent you a copy. I saw a trend developing, and I knew no one at MDE could be allowed to make the same discovery."

"Did Bellis know what you were doing?"

"Not until after Fallon's death. His suicide was convenient and saved me the trouble."

Hayden felt numb. He listened to Lockhart recount his atrocities, but the true horror of what he'd done hadn't sunk in yet. He doubted if it ever would.

He glanced at the screen. The website was up. "Here's my account."

Lockhart and Eskdale crowded around Hayden. After a minute, the screen filled with a list of file names.

"Which are Marin Design Engineering's files?" Lockhart asked.

Hayden sorted by date. "These last twenty-five entries are MDE's and this last entry is the file Shane sent me."

"Delete it all," Lockhart instructed. When Hayden hesitated, Lockhart's expression soured. He shoved the remote in Hayden's field of vision and thumbed the button. "Hit your delete button before I hit mine."

Hayden locked gazes with Lockhart. His heart pounded, but he showed him no fear. Lockhart wouldn't respond to a frightened man. "I'll do it. I'll delete it, but I have a request."

"A request," Lockhart repeated, as if trying out the words for the first time.

"I can do it," Eskdale said and leaned into Hayden to shove him aside.

Lockhart stopped him with a raised hand. "What's your request?"

"I want to know what's on the file. Chaudhary and Shane died because of it. I just want to know what was so damn special about it that so many people were killed."

"Don't listen to him," Eskdale said. "Just delete it."

Hayden read Lockhart's expression. He was considering Hayden's request.

"James, you can't be honestly considering this."

"Shut up, Kenneth. Your mistakes created this mess," Lockhart said. "Okay, Hayden, I'll show you. You say this file is password protected. Who do you think password protected it?"

More games. Hayden didn't have time for it, but he had little choice under the circumstances but to play along. "Shane or Chaudhary."

"Chaudhary, really?"

Lockhart really was trying Hayden's patience, but he bit back. "Okay, I thought Shane protected the file."

"Well, you bet on the wrong pony," Lockhart said with smug satisfaction. "It's Kenneth's file. He protected it. Chaudhary was smart enough to know the value of the file, but not smart enough to get the password. It became a hot potato that got tossed around until you caught it. Kenneth, open it for him."

Eskdale frowned but did as he was told. He brushed Hayden aside and typed in the password. The computer accepted it and unlocked the file.

Hayden felt incredibly dumb. It had never occurred to him that Chaudhary had come into possession of the protected file. It made sense. If he'd unearthed the answers, he wouldn't have buried them. He would have gone to the police or the media, but he hadn't because he didn't know what the file contained. Shane had signed his death warrant by believing in the conspiracy and accepting the file.

Lockhart smiled. Hayden recognized a winner's smile when he saw it. He held his gaze before turning to the screen.

The document was untitled. It was a PDF file, the pages scanned from handwritten notes. Eskdale's name marked the upper left hand corner of every page. His handwriting was neat and legible, and although Hayden didn't understand a word of it, he recognized the format. He was looking at the pages from a lab notebook containing experiment histories. This was Eskdale's how-to guide on weaponizing the plague.

"Erase it," Lockhart told Hayden.

Hayden didn't move.

"I said, erase it."

"Do it yourself."

Lockhart thumbed the button on the transmitter again to remind Hayden of what was at stake. He made damned sure Hayden saw what he was doing. "Now, erase it along with everything else."

Hayden erased *document1* along with the backups of MDE's drawings and everything else in his storage account. He watched years of work disappear in seconds. It should have mattered, but it didn't. He had more important things to worry about.

"Thank you, Hayden. You fought a good game, but you lost to the better man. Shall we?" Lockhart indicated to the main lab with his arm.

Hayden headed out into the lab. Rebecca smiled weakly at him from her glass cage. He smiled back just as weakly.

"Open up, Lockhart," Hayden said. "You got what you wanted."

"I don't think I can do that, Hayden."

Hayden turned to face Lockhart. "What do you mean?"

"I can't have any loose ends. You two are liabilities."

Lockhart smiled and pointed the transmitter at the lab holding Rebecca.

"No," Hayden screamed and lunged for Lockhart's hand, but the man jerked his arm out of harm's way, then pressed the trigger.

CHAPTER THIRTY

Rebecca whirled at the hissing sound behind her. The canister fizzed like the one in the BART station. And just like that one, whatever poured out of it had no color, no scent and no taste. She didn't see any point in holding her breath or hiding in a corner—she would breathe in the contagion and absorb it. She knew this gas wasn't an antidote to the bubonic plague. The gooseflesh on her arms told her quite the opposite.

Hayden pounded on the Plexiglas behind her and called out her name, but she ignored him. She couldn't tear her gaze away from the canister discharging its deadly load.

The temperature in the room hadn't changed, but she felt physically cold and mentally numb. It was shock, she supposed. It was obvious what was happening. Lockhart had killed her—shot her with a slow-acting bullet. Still, she couldn't quite believe it all. This was it. She was going to die. It couldn't be happening.

The canister was spent after a minute. It signaled its end with a splutter and a cough. She wondered how long it would be before she felt the effects of the disease. The nursery rhyme invented for children to recognize the symptoms of the Black Death popped into her head and she recited it under her breath.

"Ring around the rosie. A pocket full of posies. Ashes, ashes. We all fall down."

She remembered the meaning behind the rhyme. The ring of roses as the lesions that would cover her skin. The posies were to hide the stench of her decay. The ashes referred to her ultimate end. Her body would have to be burned to prevent her from infecting anyone else. She wondered how long it would be before she fell down—dead.

"Becky, talk to me." Hayden's voice crackled over the intercom.

She turned to face the viewing window. Hayden's face was a mask of despair, and his hands were pressed against the glass. Lockhart sat on a stool looking pleased with himself. Eskdale stood at his office door and it all seemed beyond him.

"I'm okay," she said.

"I'm going to get you out."

Lockhart laughed. "That's not going to happen."

"Hayden, there's nothing you can do." She smiled to diffuse his pain. "It's the plague this time, isn't it?"

He nodded.

She pressed a palm against Hayden's hand with only the glass between them. But no glass was thick enough to prevent her from feeling his warmth.

"There has to be a way," he said.

"There isn't."

She hated watching him struggle with this fact. She watched a thousand ideas race across his face. Finally, futility set in and hope died in his eyes.

"How can you be so calm?" he asked.

Her smile was bleak. "I'm not calm. I just can't waste time on panic when I want to spend that time with you. I just hope it isn't too painful."

"You hope in vain, Ms. Fallon," Lockhart said, his voice hollow over the intercom.

Hayden's expression turned to rage, and his finger slipped off the intercom. She could only watch the silent play unfold.

Hayden whirled on Lockhart. "You son of a bitch."

"Sticks and stones, Mr. Duke," he said. "Sticks and stones."

"Why do it? I gave you what you wanted. You didn't have to do this."

"I can't have witnesses. She's a witness. So she has to die."

Hayden couldn't bear to look at Lockhart. The man disgusted him that much. He looked away, and his gaze turned to Rebecca. She smiled at him again, but her smile faltered. It looked as if the realization that her life was over had started to sink in.

Hayden stormed over to Lockhart. His hands tightened into fists, and he invaded Lockhart's personal space. Lockhart didn't even flinch.

"Get her out."

"I can't. She steps one foot from that lab and we're all dead."

"Bullshit. You cured those dogs. You can cure her. You wouldn't have developed this shit without a get-out-of-jail-free card for yourself."

Lockhart smiled and held up his hands in a "what are you going to do?" gesture. "There's nothing I can do." Lockhart pointed at Rebecca. "She knows she's dead. We know she's dead. It's time for you to accept it."

Hayden didn't accept it. He couldn't stand by and let this happen. He wasn't about to let Lockhart get away with it, irrespective of the cost.

It was so damn unfair. Life had robbed Rebecca of her whole family. Now she was going to die, and she wouldn't even have the luxury of a quick death, like her parents and Shane. The plague would ravage her body, slowly picking her apart until she couldn't hold on any longer.

Hayden knew he couldn't save her, but he couldn't let her die alone. He snatched up a stool close to him. Without a second thought for the consequences, he swung it by the legs. Rebecca saw what he was going to do and jumped back from the glass. She screamed silently for him to stop. He didn't, and the stool connected with the glass.

"No," Eskdale screamed.

The stool bounced off the glass like it was a rubber sheet. He tried again and again, but he didn't even make a scratch.

"That glass is shatterproof, bulletproof, shockproof, Hayden-proof and any other kind of proof you care to mention. You can't get in unless you have one of these." Lockhart waved his card key in the air.

Hayden dropped the stool and approached Lockhart. "You'd better give it to me," he growled.

"I don't think so."

"I'll have to take it then."

Lockhart smirked and started putting the card key away. Hayden drove a fist into Lockhart's face, snapping his head back. The impact knocked him off his stool and sent the card key flying out of his hand. Hayden grabbed it off the floor.

"Bastard," Lockhart said, nursing his split lip.

Hayden returned to the contaminated lab.

"What do you think you're doing?" Eskdale remained rooted to his spot. "You can't free her. The contagion will escape."

Hayden knew this, but he didn't care. The most dangerous man in the world is one who doesn't have anything to lose. Lockhart had underestimated him. He'd said he couldn't have any witnesses. Hayden knew he wasn't leaving here alive. Lockhart would make sure of that. He'd either end up with a bullet to the back of the head or die in agony as one of Eskdale's lab rats. He didn't welcome death, but if it was coming for him, and it surely was, he would go out on his terms with Rebecca at his side. So what if he took Lockhart and Eskdale down with him? At least there was some payback in that.

He swiped the card through the slot. Silently, Rebecca begged him not to open the door. He couldn't look at her while he did it. He wasn't sure his resolve would hold. He opened the outer door.

"Hayden."

He turned to face Lockhart.

"You open that inner door, you'll kill us all. There's enough pathogen in that lab to infect everything in a five-mile radius."

Hayden turned to Lockhart. He liked seeing the panic in the man's face. For once, the bastard got to experience futility. It was something so many people had experienced—from Chaudhary and Shane, who'd killed themselves, to the people who'd burned inside MDE. They'd all seen their futures sheared off, leaving a hard, blunt end. He smiled at Lockhart. "I don't care," he said. "I can't watch her die, unless I die with her."

Eskdale backed away from Hayden, believing in his determination. His action was pointless, since being a few extra feet from the lab wouldn't make any difference to his survival.

"Give me the card key back and I'll make sure she receives the antidote before it's too late."

Hayden stared into Lockhart. Lies fought for space behind his eyes.

"I don't believe you."

"Oh, my God," Eskdale murmured.

Lockhart dropped his head. There was nothing to be said. He swiped the card and opened the inner door.

Immediately, an alarm sounded. Red lights flashed on the walls throughout the lab. A dispassionate man's voice interrupted the alarm as part of a recorded loop, saying, "Contamination breach. Lockdown procedure effective. Contamination breach. Lockdown procedure effective."

Rebecca walked over to him. She slipped into his embrace. "Oh, Hayden, why?"

He didn't reply at first. He just hugged her, enjoying her contact and the warmth of her body. "Because I love you," he said. It was why he'd consigned everyone to a hideous death. He would rather die with her in his arms than live without her. He loved Rebecca Fallon, plain and simple.

"You do?"

"Yes, I do."

She kissed him deeply before he took her hand and led her out of the lab. He couldn't stop smiling.

Lockhart couldn't believe what had happened and shook his head at Hayden. He pulled up another stool and plopped himself down on it. "Congratulations, you've killed us."

"Hayden," Rebecca screamed and tightened her grip on his hand.

She pointed at Eskdale, who had burst from his office brandishing two needleless injectors identical to the one Tony Mason had tried to use on Hayden.

Hayden wasn't about to go out screaming like a loon the way Shane and Fuller had. He charged Eskdale. The professor started to run, but panic took over and he froze like a deer caught in a car's headlights.

"No, you don't understand," Eskdale jabbered.

Hayden smashed into the professor's gut with his shoulder. Both men crashed to the floor with Hayden on top. One of the injectors flew from Eskdale's grasp.

"Becky, break it before he can use it," he shouted. "It's the drug that killed Shane."

Rebecca raced to the strewn syringe. Lockhart chased after the same prize, hoping to beat her to it.

Hayden punched Eskdale in the face, disarming the frail man with a single blow. He took Eskdale's arm with the remaining injector in it and bashed his wrist on the floor until it bounced from his weak grasp.

Lockhart got to the syringe first and bent to retrieve it, but before he could pick it up, Rebecca kicked it from his outstretched fingers. They chased after the spinning injector, fighting each other off with flailing arms. Rebecca beat Lockhart to the injector, the same device that had driven her brother to suicide. With all her might, hate and disgust for its existence, she brought her weight down on it. It split like rotten fruit under her heel.

"What have you done?" Lockhart said.

Hayden jumped to his feet. Eskdale didn't try to stop him. He only groaned and positioned himself better to see Hayden destroy the syringe. Hayden smiled at him as he did it. Eskdale shook his head.

"You've made a big mistake," the professor said.

"No, you made the mistake. I'll be damned if I'll die like Shane and Chaudhary," Hayden said.

"You will be damned. It wasn't the drug, you idiot." Eskdale showed his frustrated anger by shaking with rage. "It was the antidote."

"What?" Immediately, sweat broke out across Hayden's brow. The look in Eskdale's eyes told him he wasn't lying.

"What have we done?" Rebecca said.

"Killed us twice," Eskdale said. "We keep an antidote in case of an accident or a breach."

"Don't you have any more?" Lockhart asked.

"Everybody who works here is issued with one shot

each." Shakily, Eskdale got to his feet. "It never leaves their side. I personally kept two shots for myself."

"Can you make any more?" Rebecca asked.

"Not in time. After six hours, the effects of the mutated bacteria can't be counteracted."

Eskdale brushed past Hayden and went inside his office. Collapsing into his chair, he held his head in his hands and sobbed.

"We're fucked, thanks to you," Lockhart spat.

"Don't get high and mighty with me. You made this shit to kill people," Hayden retaliated. "What's it like to get a taste of your own medicine?"

Lockhart snorted and turned his back on Hayden. He swung an arm and swiped several textbooks and a glass beaker off a lab bench. The beaker smashed on the floor.

"Can't you call someone? Don't you have a cell phone?" Rebecca asked, trying to inject sanity into the situation.

"There is a decontamination crew on alert, but I left my phone in the car," Lockhart said.

"Aren't there any phones in here?"

"For security reasons, no."

Hayden went over to Rebecca and hugged her. "It doesn't matter. They wouldn't have let us go. This way we take them with us."

"I suppose. It just feels like we've lost." She kissed him briefly, then buried her face in his chest.

CHAPTER THIRTY-ONE

Rebecca sneezed. It split the room with the intensity of an assassin's bullet. Everyone stopped what they were doing to look at her. Lockhart stopped pacing and Eskdale emerged from his office. No one spoke. The significance of a simple sneeze was startling and frightening to everyone, including Rebecca.

She had been lying across Hayden's lap, but sat up since she was the center of attention. "It's nothing. Allergies. That's all."

"This is a hermetically sealed room. The air is filtered. There are no allergens in this facility."

Rebecca had her hand on Hayden's thigh. Her fingers bit into his flesh. "Then it's something else, but it's not what you think. It's just a sneeze."

Lockhart shook his head and looked away. Eskdale shut himself back into his office.

"It's a sneeze, okay? Just a damn sneeze." But no one was listening, and she broke into a sob.

Hayden pulled her tight to him and rocked her. He stared hard at Lockhart. He didn't have to be such a prick under the circumstances. "It's okay," he murmured. "You're right. It's just a sneeze."

Thankfully, Lockhart kept any further remarks to himself and resumed pacing.

Hayden rocked Rebecca until her sobs ceased. He welcomed her sneeze. It broke the tension that had formed over the last hour since he'd released the pathogen. Everybody had been waiting for the shoe to drop and in some ways now that it had happened, they could relax. Rebecca could be right. Her sneeze could be just a sneeze, but it didn't matter if it was or it wasn't. They had a glimpse of the future and instead of fighting the inevitable, they could just move on. The end could begin.

Hayden still hadn't felt any of the plague symptoms, but he wasn't in any doubt of his contamination. He had only to look at Lockhart and Eskdale for confirmation. Eskdale had gone off the rails the moment he knew he was infected. He'd torn up half the facility trying to fast track an antidote, but soon came to the realization he didn't have the materials or the time to come up with it and had laid waste to the rest of the lab, then locked himself into his office. Occasionally, weeping broke the silence coming from the office. Lockhart had kept it together somewhat better than Eskdale. With no phone connection, he'd tried to get word out via the lab's Internet connection, but Eskdale had severed the line during his rampage. Screwed again. After that, Lockhart resorted to pacing the lab like a caged animal trying to conjure up an escape plan. Hayden stopped listening after the first five minutes as everything Lockhart came up with was an impossibility.

Rebecca tightened her hold on Hayden and sighed. He liked the feel of her body heat against him, but found himself wondering if it was a sign of elevated temperature. He ignored the thought, leaned in close and whispered, "It's going to be okay."

She looked at him, stared into him. He believed what

he was saying. Death was death. It came to them all. He was okay with it now. When the end came, he knew he'd be scared out of his wits, but he was still okay with it.

Rebecca's face lost all signs of anguish, and she smiled at him and kissed him. He remembered their first kiss back at Shane's house. He knew it wouldn't be their last.

Hayden made eye contact with one of the beagles in its cages, trapped on the right side of the disease. Should anyone find this place and break in, the only survivors they'd find would be the beagles.

"I would have liked to take you somewhere," Rebecca said.

"Where?" Hayden asked smiling.

"The Caribbean. Shane had bought those tickets for me for Christmas. It would have been nice to have taken you with me."

He kissed her forehead. "I would have loved to go."

Lockhart snorted at Hayden's pointless plans.

"For Christ's sake, sit down," Hayden commanded, tired of Lockhart's pacing.

"I can't," Lockhart replied. "I've got to keep moving."

Just like a shark, Hayden thought, *the moment it stopped moving it drowned*.

"It's over," Rebecca said.

Lockhart whirled on Rebecca, pointing a wavering finger. "No, it's not. I've still got options. Beckerman's still out there. He knows I'm here." He checked his watch. "He's got to come soon."

"Give it up," Hayden said, "and answer me a question."

Lockhart grabbed a microscope off a lab bench and hurled it away. The instrument struck the floor with a thud. The violent act took the fight out of him. He drew up a stool and sat. "What do you want to know?"

"Shane. I saw him kill himself, but you killed him, how?"

Lockhart nodded in the direction of Eskdale's office. "He could tell you better than I can."

"I don't care about him," Rebecca said. "He was the weapon. You were the trigger."

Lockhart didn't fight Rebecca's claim. "The drug is a hallucinogen that leaves the user very open to suggestion. After Beckerman injected Shane, he told him a story. He told him he'd done something that was unforgivable, and the best way to atone for his crime was to end it all."

Hayden remembered Shane standing on the bridge with the rope around his neck. He was so convinced of his guilt. The poor bastard died believing he'd committed crimes he never had. The thought left Hayden feeling sick.

"That was a cruel thing to do," Rebecca said.

Lockhart had no answer for her.

"You want to know something else?" Hayden said. "We had no interest in your plans. All we cared about was Shane. We just wanted to know why he died."

Lockhart was silent. Hayden wanted him to say something. He wanted to get into a fight, but there was no point. It wouldn't change anything. They were still all going to die.

Lockhart's silence spread through them. No one talked after that. Rebecca stretched out, putting her head in Hayden's lap.

Hayden didn't know how long he'd been sitting there when a pounding from outside jerked them into action.

"Hey, is anyone in there?" Santiago called through the intercom.

Hayden and Rebecca jumped up and beat Lockhart to the doors. Santiago's face filled the small porthole in the main doors.

"You're late for the party, Detective," Hayden called through the intercom to the right of the airlock.

Santiago frowned and nodded. "How do I get in?"

"You don't. We're contaminated with the bubonic plague."

"Jesus," Santiago managed. "I'll get the CDC or someone."

Lockhart brushed Hayden and Rebecca aside and thumped the intercom. "I'll tell you exactly who to call. None of us have time for red tape." He reeled off a short list of names and numbers, and Santiago yanked out his phone and started dialing.

Hayden embraced Rebecca with a hug that threatened to break her. It looked as if their miracle had arrived.

CHAPTER THIRTY-TWO

The sun beat down on another glorious St. Kitts morning. Through his sunglasses, Hayden had a tinted view of the white-sand beaches, blue skies, crystal clear waters and Rebecca carrying two tall drinks. She sat on the beach chair beside him and handed him the drink. Her skin had bronzed evenly over the length of her body, making it even more pleasing to the eye. She smiled and sucked at the straw as condensation dripped from her glass and soaked into her bikini. She noticed him staring at her.

"What are you looking at?" Rebecca asked.

"Nothing much," he said in mock disapproval.

"Hey." She whipped out her straw and squirted him with the contents. "Now, say something nice."

"Something nice."

She frowned. "I suppose that's the best I can hope for."

Three weeks ago, they couldn't have hoped for anything. They would be dead if Eskdale hadn't given the decontamination team all they needed to treat them. Once they were given the all clear, California seemed too hot to hang around with the incriminations flying, so they left for the Caribbean at the earliest opportunity.

A young black man wearing the hotel's corporate Hawaiian-style shirt and white shorts interrupted. "Mr. Duke, I have a phone call for you."

"Thanks."

"Who can that be?" Rebecca asked, but knew the answer.

It could be only one person. Hayden followed the young man to the beach bar and picked up the phone resting off the hook.

"Hello, Detective. Is this on Marin County's dime?"

"Of course. I wouldn't waste my own money speaking to you."

Santiago had wasted a lot of the county's money on phone calls. He'd called Hayden and Rebecca every few days with regular updates on the situation back home.

"You've been out there two weeks. When are you coming back? You can come home anytime."

"Probably in another two weeks."

"How nice."

It was nice. After his encounters, the thought of going back to the daily grind didn't appeal to Hayden. He'd almost lost his life, so it was time to live it for a while. When he returned home, he had no idea what he was going to do. All he did know was that he was going to have Rebecca in his life. It seemed like a good start.

"How's Rebecca?"

Hayden glanced over at her. She had put down her glass and resumed sunning herself. He smiled, glad to be with her.

"She's good."

"She's a keeper. Don't screw it up."

Hayden smiled. "I won't. Have you made a decision?"

"Yeah. I'm taking the academy instructor's position. If what I teach saves one deputy on the streets, then Mark's death won't have been for nothing."

Losing Rice had hit Santiago hard. An officer under his supervision had died on the job. He'd received a commendation, but he refused the promotion. Instead, he requested an academy instructor's position. Hayden saw the request for what it was—penance. He wished he could offer Santiago some comfort, but he knew the only person who could forgive Santiago was Santiago. Hayden hoped that would happen sooner rather than later.

"You'll be missed on the streets. There are too many people left for you to piss off."

Santiago chuckled. "I might harass you for kicks."

"Thanks. What's the latest on Lockhart?"

"He's finished. Eskdale sold him out. The Feds are tearing through his past dealings. There are a few government and military officials distancing themselves from him, so expect a few resignations in the coming months. The trial should be a gala event when it happens."

"You still involved?"

"Nah. Not once the arrests were made. Since the Feds took over, I've been given the mushroom treatment."

"Kept in the dark and fed on bullshit?"

"Yeah. Although, they did do me the courtesy of giving me updates, but it was nothing I couldn't catch on the nightly news."

"What about the Chinese I saw with Lockhart?"

"Gone. The Feds tore the Fairmont Hotel apart looking for them, but they'd checked out. The prevailing opinion is they fled the country via Mexico."

"At least they didn't leave with the devices."

"I guess we'll call that a tie."

It was over, but the trail of destruction left in its wake was huge. So many people dead, so many lives ruined and for what? Money. He was disgusted, but he couldn't let it get to him.

"So, the world hasn't come to end because I'm not there."

"We can get along nicely without you, believe it or not."

"That's good."

"I've got to go, Hayden. I can feel my ears burning, so the wife must be calling. Give my regards to Rebecca."

"Okay."

Santiago hung up and Hayden returned to Rebecca. She smiled at him when he sat down.

"How is our fairy god detective?" she asked.

"He's okay. Still down over Rice."

Rebecca's smiled slipped. "Only to be expected."

Hayden nodded. He picked up his drink and sipped it. The ice had melted, and it was too warm to drink.

"Hayden, what are we going to do?"

He put his drink down. "Go snorkeling."

"You know what I mean."

He did. The future loomed, but he wasn't thinking that far ahead.

"I meant what I said. Go snorkeling. Anything else gets in the way. Come on, let's go."

He took her hand and helped her up from the beach chair before leading her back to the hotel. The day was beautiful and too good to waste.

"Do you want to stay an extra week?" he asked.

Douglas MacKinnon

President of the United States Shelby Robertson is in the third year of his second term. Four-star general Wayne Mitchell is the man in charge of the nation's land-based nuclear arsenal.

For the past few years, both men have shared a common belief—**the apocalypse in coming.**

And they are determined to hasten the process.

Unless someone can stop them in time, they will set in motion a chain of events that could wipe clean the face of the earth.

The APOCALYPSE DIRECTIVE

ISBN 13: 978-0-8439-6088-4

FIRST TO KILL

Nathan McBride was retired. The former Marine sniper and covert CIA operative had put the violence of his former life behind him.

But not anymore.

A deep-cover FBI agent has disappeared, along with one ton of powerful Semtex explosive, enough to unleash a disaster of international proportions. The U.S. government has no choice but to coax Nathan out of retirement. He's the only man with the skills necessary to get the job done.

On the one side is a ruthless adversary with a blood-chilling plan—and on the other are agents who will stop at nothing to see their own brand of justice done.

ANDREW PETERSON

Coming September 2008   ISBN 13: 978-0-8439-6144-7

PAUL CARSON

BETRAYAL

Frank Ryan knew his position as Chief Medical Officer at high-security Harmon Penitentiary was dangerous. After all, his predecessor had been murdered. But Frank never expected what happened to him the night he got that mysterious emergency call.

As he left his apartment he was
KIDNAPPED,
BEATEN,
DRUGGED,
and interrogated for six days.
Then, just as suddenly, released.

Now he can't find anyone who believes him, and his girlfriend has disappeared without a trace. His desperate search to find her—and some answers—lead Frank deeper and deeper into a sea of conspiracies, lies…and danger.

ISBN 13: 978-0-8439-6145-4

SIMON WOOD

PAYING THE PIPER

He was known as the Piper—a coldhearted kidnapper who terrified the city. Crime reporter Scott Fleetwood built his career on the Piper. The kidnapper even taunted the FBI through Scott's column. But Scott had been duped. The person he'd been speaking to wasn't really the Piper. By the time the FBI exposed the hoaxer, time ran out...and the real Piper killed the child. Then he vanished. But now he's back, with very specific targets in mind—Scott's children.

ISBN 10: 0-8439-5980-0
ISBN 13: 978-0-8439-5980-2

ACCIDENTS WAITING TO HAPPEN
SIMON WOOD

Josh Michaels is worth more dead than alive. He just doesn't know it yet. When an SUV forces his car off the road and into the river, it could be an accident. But when Josh looks up at the road, expecting to see the SUV's driver rushing to help him, all he sees is the driver watching him calmly…then giving him a "thumbs-down" sign. That is the first of many attempts on Josh's life, all of them designed to look like accidents, and all of them very nearly fatal. With his time—and maybe his luck—running out and no one willing to believe him, Josh had better figure out who wants him dead and why…before it's too late.

❑ **YES!**

Sign me up for the Leisure Thriller Book Club and send my
FREE BOOKS! If I choose to stay in the club, I will pay only
$8.50* each month, a savings of $7.48!

NAME: _____

ADDRESS: _____

TELEPHONE: _____

EMAIL: _____

❑ I want to pay by credit card.

❑ **VISA**   ❑ **MasterCard**   ❑ **DISCOVER**

ACCOUNT #: _____

EXPIRATION DATE: _____

SIGNATURE: _____

Mail this page along with $2.00 shipping and handling to:
Leisure Thriller Book Club
PO Box 6640
Wayne, PA 19087
Or fax (must include credit card information) to:
610-995-9274

You can also sign up online at **www.dorchesterpub.com**.
*Plus $2.00 for shipping. Offer open to residents of the U.S. and Canada only. Canadian
residents please call 1-800-481-9191 for pricing information.
If under 18, a parent or guardian must sign. Terms, prices and conditions subject to
change. Subscription subject to acceptance. Dorchester Publishing reserves the right to
reject any order or cancel any subscription.